The Grand Conspiracy

The Grand Conspiracy

William Penn

Writers Club Press
San Jose New York Lincoln Shanghai

The Grand Conspiracy

Writers Club Press
an imprint of iUniverse.com, Inc.

For information address:
iUniverse.com, Inc.
5220 S 16th, Ste. 200
Lincoln, NE 68512
www.iuniverse.com

This book is a work of fiction. Names, characters and some of the places are the product of the imagination or are used fictitiously. Any resemblence to actual events, or persons, living or dead, is coincidental.

ISBN: 0-595-15862-5

Printed in the United States of America

In memory of Commander George "K" Farris, Captain Richard Nash McInerny, and Private First Class Johnny Michael Hairston, each of whom made the ultimate sacrifice during the Vietnam War.

LIST OF ILLUSTRATIONS

(SEE WWW.THEGRANDCONSPIRACY.COM)

ACKNOWLEDGEMENTS

The authors wish to thank Stephen King for giving instant credibility to e-publishing and e-commerce by choosing it as the medium for his novel: *Riding the Bullet.*

We are truly indebted to long-time Grand County residents: Charles W. "Bill" Leach, Marvin Fischer, Joanne Rienhoff, Fran Holzwarth Needham and Bill Needham and to Jack and Patti Applebee and to Jay and Emily Warner for sharing insights, background and folklore about Grand County. Dr. Robert Black's classic history of Grand County, *Island in the Rockies,* provided many interesting leads and should be required reading for anyone who lives in Grand County.

We are especially indebted to our friend, Steve Batty, for coming to the rescue of this novel when it was listing in a sea of ignorance about word processing and the Internet. Without Steve's help, we would still be wondering what to do next. Steve made several helpful suggestions with regard to the structure of the novel and conceived the idea of blending text with the Internet addresses of photographs of the key terrain features mentioned in the text. Scattered through the text, the reader will see the address of the website that is hosting the color photographs that depict some of the key terrain features that play such an important role in this novel. You will find the photographs at: www.thegrandconspiracy.com.

We are grateful to Donna and Scott Ready of Mountain Lake Properties who provided some of the photography the reader may see by going to: *www.thegrandconspiracy.com*. Readers are also invited to go to: *www.MountainLake.com* where hundreds of Scott Ready's wonderful photographs of Grand County are on display.

We are indebted to our friend, Larry Smart, for making it possible for us to have a home that looks out onto much of the terrain described in this novel. Without Larry's help, we would not be where we are.

We want to thank Dr. Ron Greenberg for technical advice and for keeping us healthy through the years this novel has been a work in progress.

Thanks also go to: Mick Wilson, the author of *How to CRASH an Airplane (and survive!)*, and to "Papa Bear" Whitmore, the nation's leading authority on wilderness survival and to Walt Barbo and Mike Baldwin for all-round aviation mentoring. We thank David Morris, Ralph Goulds and Emily Howell Warner for being our flight instructors and friends over the years.

We thank America's leading western song writer and singer, Michael Martin Murphey, for selected passages from his western classic: *Rangeland Rebel*, which can be heard in its entirety on Michael Martin Murphey's compact disk entitled: *Cowboy Songs Four*.

We, and all who live in Grand County, are indebted to our volunteer firefighters, to the volunteers of Grand County Search and Rescue and to the members of the Grand County Sheriff's Department. Their examples were instructive to us and their service is a blessing to us all.

We would like to thank the Northern Colorado Water Conservancy District (NCWCD) for allowing us to take part in their annual tours of the Colorado-Big Thompson Project, for their excellent summer tours of the Lake Granby Pump Plant. We also thank the NCWCD for permission to use some of their maps and photographs and for their fine publications that describe the work of the NCWCD so well.

We thank the Grand County Historical Society and the Grand County Museum for information about the Granby/Grand County Airport (GNB) and its use by the U.S. Secret Service in support of President Dwight D. Eisenhower's fly-fishing trips to St. Louis Creek. See: *www.granbyairport.com* for a view of this fine, and developing, high-country airport. We also thank the Friends of the Granby Airport, Inc. for their unflagging support of the Granby/Grand County Airport (GNB).

We wish to thank the Cozens Ranch Museum for information about President Eisenhower's many visits to eastern Grand County.

We would like to thank Sandra Glantz, Cathy Warner and Bob and Carolyn Doubek for reading the novel and for offering helpful insights and suggestions.

Any errors, either factual or typographical are those of the author.

CHAPTER ONE

The stone-cold silhouette of Abraham Lincoln lying along the crest of the Continental Divide was bathed in a warming alpenglow as the evening sun caressed the outline of our 16th President. For the people of eastern Grand County, Colorado, the reclining Abe Lincoln was a familiar and reassuring sight. As long as Old Abe was up there, gazing up into the Heavens, they felt a sense of order. At the first light of the new day, Abe's silhouette would be illuminated once again. Each morning, and for the rest of the day, President Lincoln would be lying hard-edged and razor sharp against the morning sky. He would be there. They could count on that.

As was their evening custom, Dolly and Buck Madison settled down on their deck to watch the alpenglow play on Old Abe. But, this time, they took their places around the table much more gingerly than normal. Buck was battered and bruised as if he had recently been in a fight, which he had. Dolly's face was scratched from rappelling down an almost vertical rock face just to the north of Old Abe. Both of them were so sore from their recent ordeal that they could barely walk and finding a comfortable way to sit was going to take several more days and many more trips to the hot tub.

Dolly filled their glasses with a nice red wine and, as was also their custom, they drank a toast to President Abraham Lincoln and to the

Union he preserved. But this particular evening was very different and the toast was even more meaningful.

When they looked from their deck across Lake Granby and up into the rugged valley that climbed upward toward Old Abe, the vista brought with it painful memories of the life-and-death struggle that almost cost them their lives.

The struggle took place over three unforgettable days that began when foreign terrorists shot down their private plane. Only their flying skills and the Grace of God landed them safely on top of the St. Vrain Glacier.

On the table in front of them lay an engraved invitation from the White House. It said, in so many flowery words, that Dr. James Buckley "Buck" Madison and Dr. Melissa Rennie "Dolly" Madison were invited to Arlington National Cemetery to attend the funerals of three of their oldest and dearest friends.

"Do you think we should go?" asked Dolly.

"Yes, we should go," said her husband, "but we aren't sitting with the VIPs. We must pay our respects to Chuck, Roberto and Jonathan. But we'll just stand at the back of the crowd; hopefully, unnoticed."

"But what about the RSVP?" asked Dolly.

"I'll take care of it. I'll just call the White House tomorrow and say we cannot accept the invitation."

"Yet we are going, aren't we?"

"Yes, we are going. But we are not accepting the invitation."

"Okay. I see the distinction. It's like when we worked for the Company and they taught us to always try to tell the truth even though something else might actually happen."

"I suppose so," said Buck. "And, I also suppose it was working for the Company that almost got us killed and, at the same time, saved our lives."

"I never thought about it like that, Buck. But I think you are right. Raoul and his terrorists gave us credit for knowing more than we actually knew. That's why Raoul tried to stop us from talking to the Secret Service. Buck, I don't think I'll ever forget these last three days."

"Three days Grand County will never forget. The next time someone asks us to help them locate a presidential fishing retreat, I'll tell them to take a hike."

"Yes, Buck. And, if wishes were horses, you retired infantry types would have been riding instead of walking."

"If only I hadn't answered the phone when the White House switchboard tracked me down."

"If only. That's the story of our lives," said Dolly.

CHAPTER TWO

Early November

The White House
Washington, D.C.
The Oval Office

Given his reduced circumstances, President James Robert Trimmer, was in a surprisingly good mood. Reelected for a second term, impeached by the U.S. House of Representatives, but not convicted by the Senate, Jim Bob Trimmer kept busy. He filled his time with ceremonial duties, by raising money to keep his political allies beholden to him, by taking junkets around the world on Air Force One and by a half-hearted effort to lower his golf score.

The golfing, the fund-raisers, the overseas travel and the ceremonies also helped him keep his mind off his problems. Chief among them was the prospect of being subjected to a series of lawsuits after he left office and being disbarred. But, confident his political friends would pay his legal bills as a form of *quid pro quo* for his fund-raising on their behalf, he turned his thoughts to some other problems. He was almost certain his wife would leave him once he was out of office. But that depended on her political ambitions. If it was politically expedient for them to remain married, then she would put politics first and continue to be, at least in name, his wife.

At least in name. Most of the time he never thought about her in terms of her given name. In Secret Service jargon, she was FLOTUS: First Lady of the United States and he had fallen into the habit of thinking of her as FLOTUS instead of Teresa Trimmer.

Even if she did not formalize the death of a marriage that had long been moribund and if her political career were to take off, he wasn't sure how well he could play the role of a latter-day Dennis Thatcher. But then, his wife might have her own legal problems and, if so, he might be wise to dump her first. The thought crossed his mind that the First Lady didn't look good in orange. Only slightly ashamed of finding some gallows humor in the thought, he resolved to concentrate more deeply upon his putter.

It was almost sundown and even through the thick, bulletproof glass behind his desk President Trimmer could see the golden kiss of sunlight slanting across the south lawn. The President was staying later than normal in the Oval Office awaiting his last appointment of the day.

Just after he stroked the ball and it was rolling smoothly toward its target, the intercom came on. His personal secretary announced the arrival of Mr. Edward T. Briccone, and that, with his permission, she was going home. President Trimmer noted the usual hint of disapproval in her voice. Edward T. Briccone was the President's closest political adviser, political hit man and long-time, skirt-chasing colleague.

Alone, except for Trooper McCoy, the former state policeman and private investigator President Trimmer insisted on keeping as his personal aide and whose almost constant presence annoyed the Secret Service Protective Detail no end, the President ordered: "Send him in. And, yes, you can go."

The Secret Service agent on duty opened the door, motioned for the President's guest to enter the Oval Office and then resumed his post outside the door.

Edward T. Briccone, was a product of the Louisiana swamps. Briccone and Trimmer met during law school where Briccone showed a keen aptitude for Tort Law, Trial Practice and Demonstrative Evidence, clear indicators toward a promising career as an ambulance chaser.

But James Robert Trimmer gave Ed Briccone a new direction in life when Trimmer asked him to manage his first political campaign. They were a winning combination. Trimmer's easy way with people and Briccone's organizational and research skills were made for each other. Early on, Briccone taught Jim Bob Trimmer the secret to political success: Once you learn to fake sincerity, the rest is easy.

For Briccone, politics, and the political fortunes of Jim Bob Trimmer, became all consuming passions. Now, a veteran of innumerable, mostly successful, political campaigns and the master-mind behind some highly-successful campaign management schools, Edward T. Briccone's southern drawl was the nation's hottest ticket on the political operatives' rubber-chicken circuit—at least among political operatives who wouldn't know a scruple even if it bit them on the butt. Briccone's main specialty was what is euphemistically called "opposition research." Those who actually did or thought they had something to hide lived in fear of a "friendly" little call from Ed Briccone. Briccone's other specialty was the fine art of election stealing.

While the late Chicago Mayor, Richard Daley, was famous for his saying: "Vote early, and vote often" and for even getting the dead to vote for his Democrat machine candidates, Briccone was famous for his ability to manipulate the outcome of elections and his ability to even get them overturned once the votes were cast.

With a tug at his signature, yellow polka-dot on blue bow-tie and a futile attempt to button an ancient Harris Tweed jacket over a shirt that still bore evidence of the most recent rubber-chicken dinner, Edward T. Briccone ambled into the Oval Office and planted his 250-pound frame on one of the sofas flanking the fireplace.

Looking up from the next ball in a line of balls to be putted, President Trimmer said: "Talk to me Eddie while I tune up my putting game."

With a nod toward Trooper McCoy, Edward T. Briccone asked, "Mr. President, can we be alone?"

Turning to Trooper McCoy, the President said: "McCoy, step outside please. While you're out, check on the Treasury tunnel. Okay?"

"Now, Eddie, what's on that devious mind of yours?"

"Jim Bob, we need to be doing more about your place in history. We've got some damage control to do.

"What the hell's wrong with my place in history?" asked a President still deep in denial.

"With all due respect, Jim Bob, you must get a grip on reality. You've been impeached by the House, for Christ's sake, and we had to pull out all the stops to keep you from being convicted by the U.S. Senate," said Briccone.

"Wait a minute, Eddie," said Trimmer. "Let's not give ourselves too much credit on the Senate side of things. Granted, you got out your little black book and had certain members of the Congress on both sides of the aisle peeing in their pants. But you know what I think it came down to? It came down to the fact that a lot of Senators, honorable men of both parties, already knew the former Speaker and his heir apparent had been unfaithful to their wives and, to their ever-lasting credit, they just didn't have the heart to convict me for what their colleagues had been doing all along."

"I suppose even hypocrisy has its limits in this town and that came to your aid," said Briccone. "But, on the political side, I don't think the other side wanted to see Vice President Holzhalter run against them as an incumbent President. I take your point that we shouldn't take all the credit for the Senate's failure to convict you. But, like it or not, we took a huge hit in the House and we must take some steps to get the best historical spin out of these last months in office."

"I'll buy that," said the President. "But I do think we have some military and foreign policy successes to build on."

"Jim Bob, I hate to be a nay-sayer. But any of your foreign-policy initiatives could blow up at any moment and come back to haunt you. In fact, your latest attempts to get a peace agreement between the Arabs and Jews ended in failure. They are still blowing each other up and one of our destroyers as well. Face it, Jim Bob, we should never have forced Barak and Arafat to come to Camp David. Barak's coalition government was too shaky to make a deal. Arafat's enemies were just waiting to topple him if he made any meaningful concessions to the Israelis. We tried to force a shotgun wedding that the relatives on both sides weren't ready to accept. It was too little, too soon. Now, we've got a unholy mess on our hands."

"But what about my legacy, Eddie? "I wanted to get out of here with a coonskin, as LBJ used to say, that I could nail up on my memory wall."

"No disrespect intended, Jim Bob, but as I always say: It's the economy stupid. Coming in, we never knew shit about foreign affairs, much less about the military. Anyway, that's why I'm here today. To work on your image, your legacy. In crafting your image, we need to focus on how well we've been doing on the economy," said Briccone.

"Eddie, you can bet your ass I'm going to take credit for a booming economy, but what about those who will say most of the stock market upswing took place after the Republicans took control of Congress?"

"Fortunately, for us, Jim Bob, the Grand Old Party keeps shooting itself in the foot. For some reason, they can't seem to project a coherent message that the gum-chewing public can understand. Again, that's why we need to focus on the economy and we need to soft pedal foreign affairs. As long as Joe Six-Pack has his beer, brats and baseball, he doesn't know Saddam from Siam. But he does seem to like it when we shoot a few missiles at the camel-kissers.

"That sure worked on the eve of that stupid impeachment vote. You've got to give me credit for that," said Trimmer.

"Well, that attack did what I said it would. The polls showed public support for attacking Saddam and I think that kept the impeachment vote closer than we expected."

"Yeah, but we still fucking lost and I still go down in history as being impeached."

"I'm sorry, Jim Bob, but you have to admit we got out of that mess a lot better off than we thought going in. And, just remember this, Jim Bob, I'm always trying to do my best for you. Let's just hope we can get out of here before more things really fall apart.

"Meanwhile, I think we need to try to make sure that history portrays you the way we want you to be portrayed. To do that, we must drive home certain positive themes and we must do what we can to down play certain, uh, less positive aspects of your life."

"Hell, everybody knows about the women. I've confessed to that. It's only a bunch of narrow-minded, pencil-dick Republicans and the radical Christian right who give a shit about sex. Besides, Eddie, there's a lot of Joe Six-Packs out there who admire me as a swordsman."

"Yes, Jim Bob, the polling data give us mixed signals on the sex issue; however, I have another concern where I think the data show more negatives than positives.

"Look, I know we can't fix the entire mess all at one time. We can only fix parts of it. What I'm going to propose won't turn your legacy into FDR's. But I'm hoping to borrow a bit of Ike's."

"President Eisenhower? If you can make a military hero out of me, you *are* a political genius."

"No, Jim Bob, not a military hero. I just have an idea that will give you more of a macho image. More of an outdoorsman."

The mention of President Eisenhower got his attention, so the President put away his putter, sat down behind the desk that had once served John F. Kennedy and lit a contraband Cuban cigar.

"Eddie, would like a cigar?"

"You know I don't smoke. And besides I wish you wouldn't smoke."

"Why? Because you don't like the smell or because they are contraband or because of the public stand I've taken against smoking or because of Jay Leno's stupid cigar jokes?"

"All four. One of these days the big tobacco companies are going to nail you for smoking in private while trying to crucify them in public…"

"They wouldn't dare. I may be a lame duck, but, by God, I can still cut off some of their government subsidies. So, for now, Eddie, you'll just have to endure these Cuban stogies.

"And besides, let's get back to the frigging subject. Just which negatives do you think we can fix?" asked Trimmer.

"Well, let me put all this in the context of the popular vote," said Briccone. "Like it or not, because of Ross Perot, low voter turnouts and other divisive factors, you were able to win with less than 25 percent of the popular vote. That means 75 percent of your countrymen and women either didn't bother to vote or voted for someone else."

"Hell's fire, I know that. Don't you know that's one of the reasons I've had to make so many political compromises with those Republican Neanderthals up on Capitol Hill? I'm taking it in the ass from the liberals in my own party and the right wing of the other party."

"And, up until the time you got involved with that intern, you were doing a wonderful job of finding that fine line between left and right, Jim Bob."

"Damn right I was. So, quit pussyfooting around and tell me which negatives you want to work on first."

"According to our data, and let me stress these are just polling data and not my views at all, your detractors like to say you are less than physically courageous."

"Oh, that's that draft dodger crap coming up again."

"Actually, it's more than that. We think it comes from the fact that you only played in the band."

"Only played in the band! Wasn't that smarter than getting my nuts crushed playing football?"

"Yes, it was a lot smarter. But being perceived as smart is not your problem. I don't know how to put this more gently, Mr. President. But our polls show that a fairly large number of the people polled think you are a wimp."

"Goddamn it, Eddie, I'll tell you who the fucking wimps are around this town. The same generals and admirals who are privately snickering about my ducking the Vietnam War are the real wimps.

"Each time you and I don't like what we're reading on the front page of the *New York Times* or the *Washington Post*, we send those uniformed motherfuckers off to keep some spear-chucking cannibals from eating each other. Or, we order them to launch a few missiles or drop some bombs on some camel-kissers or bohunks. Works every time. My so-called scandals get pushed off to the back pages and below the fold.

"Every time I call all those fucking flag-officers in here and order them to send their troops on some wild-goose chase, I can tell they hate it and I can tell they hate my guts. But, if they had real guts, they'd hand in their retirement papers and head for some Sun City to play golf and drink themselves to death."

"Jim Bob, some of the officers you are talking about risked their lives many times over to defend our country."

"Well, they may have been brave bastards at one time, maybe when they were lieutenants or captains. But, I tell you what buddy, once they get some stars and start hanging around the Pentagon, I think their balls drop off. Back in my radical, anti-Vietnam War days, a hippie slipped me a copy of a study that came out of the Army War College. Some student up at Carlisle Barracks with nothing better to do discovered something called: "promotion-centered dishonesty." He said it was the phenomenon that allowed LBJ and McNamara to get senior officers to carry out the orders that fucked up the Vietnam War.

"So, Eddie, I don't want to hear anymore from you or anyone else about this wimp stuff. The real wimps are those brown-nosing generals and admirals. And, besides, I play a lot of golf."

"Golf, Jim Bob. Even if you didn't ride a golf cart and didn't use a caddy, golf is not considered aerobic exercise and, unless you play with former President Ford, it certainly isn't risk exercise," said Briccone.

"Eddie, have you looked at yourself in the mirror lately? You're a fucking tub of lard and you're talking to me about exercise?"

"Not just any kind of exercise, Jim Bob, I'm talking about risk-exercise. And look, don't get pissed at me. I'm just trying to be loyal. Besides me, the First Lady and the head of your Secret Service Detail, I'm the only one around here with the balls to tell you what's good for you!"

Sensing this was going to be a harder sell than he anticipated Eddie Briccone pulled himself up from the couch and began to amble back and forth in front of the fireplace.

"Jim Bob, I take your point about the wimpy Joint Chiefs, and that just makes my point about my loyalty to you. If those military geniuses had any loyalty to you or to the nation, they would have thrown a hissy fit when you wanted them to attack Yugoslavia using air power alone. True loyalty is having the balls to tell the President of the United States things he doesn't want to hear. The Joint Chiefs have the blood of all those innocent Slavic civilians on their hands just as much as we do and Amnesty International is condemning you and them as war criminals," said Briccone.

"Eddie, don't tell me after all these years you are growing a conscience? Who gives a shit about a bunch of fucking raghead refugees? Look, I thought we could topple a bohunk dictator with a few bombs and missiles and I'd get the Nobel Peace Prize. You even hired a Norwegian PR firm to lobby for the goddam prize. Anyway, so I was wrong. But you're right about the Joint Chiefs. They should have told me and that dumpy Secretary of State that she and I were full of shit."

Sensing he now had his President in the mood to listen, Eddie Briccone pressed his case.

"Jim Bob, I agree we only made things worse in the Balkans. The people we bombed are so mad at us and NATO that some of them kept voting for that sonofabitch Milosevic just to spite us. If we had left things alone, Milosevic would have been long gone much earlier. And besides, his replacement isn't any champion of democracy. But let's forget that and let's get busy doing some more positive things about your image."

"Okay, Eddie. So, why don't you stop pacing up and down and tell me all about this new scheme to save my image for posterity?"

"If you don't mind, I think better on my feet. Look, Jim Bob, we've got to get you out more often into the great outdoors doing guy-type things."

"If it's mountain climbing or skiing or any of those dangerous risk-exercise sports, shove'em up your ass."

"Okay. But picture President Eisenhower fishing in the Colorado high country. Manly, but low risk. When Ike was President, the media ate up those Colorado fishing trips. Even when he was just standing out in the river with nothing on his mind, the public got the idea he was out there thinking great thoughts about how to deal with Khruschev or how to build the interstate highway system."

"You mean fly fishing? I don't know shit about any kind of fishing. I don't even know anything about bass fishing. How the hell am I supposed to look good fly fishing?"

"We'll bring in a coach. Before we leave for Colorado, he'll have you looking like an expert. You can practice fly casting into the White House swimming pool."

"What else do I have to do?"

"You wear waders, step out into the river and make a few casts. You don't even get your feet wet. We'll order somebody to stock the hell out of the local rivers with trout. And, if you don't have any luck on your own, this expert I've hired knows a way to attach a trout to your line without the media catching on. All they'll see is you reeling in some nice fish. We'll even make sure you that you use the Red Quill fly. That was Ike's favorite fishing fly," said Briccone.

"And where am I going to be using this Red Quill fly?"

"I would like to have your permission to send the head of your Secret Service Protective Detail to search for the best location."

"When?"

"I was thinking over the Thanksgiving Holidays. Special Agent Winslow has long-time friends who live in the mountains near where Ike used to fish. People named Madison. Buck Madison, he's a retired Army paratrooper. Spent some time as a spook and still does odd jobs for the Agency. His wife, Dolly Madison, she's a retired CIA analyst, some kind of old China hand. Winslow says they know how to keep their mouths shut. Evidently, Winslow and Dolly Madison were college sweethearts."

"Dolly Madison? Surely that's not her real name?"

"No, Jim Bob. Her real name is Melissa. Dolly is a nickname and so is Buck. It's short for Buckley."

"Probably named for that conservative twit, Bill Buckley. I don't like him already."

"Anyway, Mr. President, this place is up in the Rockies about 65 miles northwest of Denver. Also, I just thought it would be a goodwill gesture toward Winslow to let him go out and ski with his friends. Especially, since the Madisons know all the places where Ike liked to fish."

"I'll be happy to be rid of that holier-than-thou, sonofabitch for a few days."

"I know Mr. Winslow is not your favorite, but he runs your protective detail like a Swiss watch. Besides, he's due for retirement next year and you'll be rid of each other for good."

"But how the hell is Winslow going to hunt for a fishing retreat up in the mountains at Thanksgiving? Aren't the ski resorts up to their window sills in snow by then?"

"Well, not quite that deep, but enough snow for skiing; especially, at the higher elevations. Look, Jim Bob, I've spoken with Winslow and he says searching during Thanksgiving is really an advantage. If it looks good when it's cold, then it will really be nice in the late summer.

"So, we're talking this coming summer?"

"Setting up a presidential fishing retreat takes time. We could probably have it ready, security and all, by next 4th of July. But between Memorial Day and Labor Day the gum-chewing public doesn't pay attention to anything, and certainly not politics. So, I'm thinking we'll shoot for Labor Day of next year. As you know, the State Department is trying to set up a visit by President Popov for about then."

"You mean we're going to entertain Popov out in Colorado instead of here?"

"Yes. This new guy, Popov, doesn't get knee-walking drunk like his predecessor. Popov was KGB and he's in good shape. He's already let our ambassador in Moscow know that he'd like to do some fishing and hiking in the Rockies. Also, a summit with Popov will draw more attention to your being out in the woods. Remember the famous Reagan-Gorbachev walk-in-the-woods that led to the end of the Cold War? We may be able to conjure that image up again, only this time for you and Popov. Anyway, between next fall and the end of your presidency is just enough time to create the outdoor-man image we need," said Briccone.

"Next Labor Day it is, then. That way I'll only have to make one trip to this fish camp of yours."

"It's not a fish camp, Jim Bob. It's a presidential fishing retreat."

"You can call it the Waldorf-fucking-Astoria, but I'm still not gonna like it. But okay. Go ahead. Send Winslow on this 'fishing' expedition. But that's enough of this outdoor sports bullshit for now. I've got an evening of indoor sports planned for us. Remember back when I was Governor and we came to D.C. for a visit? There was that drop-dead, good-looking waitress at that fancy Georgetown restaurant? Menage-a-trois? Yeah, you remember.

"Well, she surfaced again. She's been living with some sugar daddy in Paris. He croaked and she's moved back here."

"Blackmail?"

"Shit no. She just wants to renew our relationship. Like a dummy, I told her one time I might ditch FLOTUS for her. Maybe she figures that's even more likely now. Anyway, with FLOTUS out making speeches and raising money, I thought this would be the perfect time to see her again."

"What if she talks this time?"

"She won't. She wants to be appointed to some high-paying, do-nothing federal commission. I can handle that. Besides, look what happened to the others who talked. You got 'em trashed. Like Nixon and the South, I shall rise again and I'm headed for retirement with full pay and allowances.

"So loosen up, Eddie. When he gets back, Trooper McCoy will escort us through the Treasury tunnel and into the side door of the Willard. If anyone sees us, we'll just say we're attending a political meeting."

"Yeah, I know," grinned Briccone, "and, when the press sees just you and me and that bimbo coming out of a hotel room at 3:00 a.m., we just tell them the political meeting we called was poorly attended. Jim Bob, that's got to be the world's corniest political joke."

"Hey, Eddie, maybe I can get a job as a straight man? Anyway, get that Viagra-eating grin off your face and let's head for the tunnel."

Chapter Three

Mid November

James Buckley "Buck" Madison was wading in the headwaters of the Colorado River just below the Lake Granby High Dam. Just as he was about to maneuver a beautiful Rainbow trout into his net, Buck was startled by the ringing of his cellular telephone.

The satellite cell phone was Company-provided and he was supposed to carry it all times. But it was really at his wife's insistence that Madison, now 60, carried the tiny phone while he waded the sometimes rapid waters of the Colorado River. Despite his felt-bottomed waders, Dolly Madison feared Buck might fall on the mossy rocks and need to call for help.

Buck never bothered to tell her it would be virtually impossible to operate a water-soaked cell phone while trying to swim out of a deep pool. But, if the cell phone gave her comfort, that was reason enough to carry it. Such willingness to accommodate the wishes of the other was why their 30-year marriage was so tranquil. The Company had never used the cell phone to contact him; however, Buck did get calls now and then that brought writing assignments from a well-known newspaper.

At six feet tall and carrying a still firm 190 pounds, Buck figured he was a lot taller than the deepest pool he might find in that particular stretch of the river. Despite his time as a college professor and even more years spent as a writer, Buck Madison was still an outdoorsman at heart. That was why he enjoyed his 20 years of military service. But when advancing rank caused him to spend more time behind a desk than outdoors with troops, Buck and Dolly decided it was time for Buck to do something else.

Unlike many men of his age, Buck still had a full head of hair that was only just now beginning to show a few streaks of gray. He kept it tucked under a battered Akubra purchased many years ago while on R&R in Australia but still worn almost every day as protection against the ultra-violet rays that are so strong in the high Rockies. Despite the hat, in any season, Buck's face was tan from being outdoors so much of the time.

Pulling the brim of his Akubra down a notch to protect his brown eyes from the rays of a setting sun, Buck maneuvered the fish to a spot where his polarized sunglasses could help him see into the water better. The fish was a fighter. It came to the surface flashing a rainbow of colors. With his net at the ready, Buck was about to capture his prize when the phone rang. Startled, he missed with the net. The fish shook its head free of the hook and waved its tail in an insolent goodbye.

"This is the White House Switchboard," said a pleasant, but no-nonsense voice, "please stand by for Special Agent Jonathan Winslow."

Immediately, a mental image of Jonathan Winslow came to mind: Patrician, preppy good looks befitting his eastern establishment elitist heritage and with an accent that was somewhere between Harvard and Yale.

After a brief pause, the man who had once been a platoon leader in Buck's infantry company in Vietnam and was now the head of the Presidential Protection Detail of the United States Secret Service, came on the line.

"Buck, this is Jonathan. Did I catch you at a bad time?"

"Yes. I was about to net a fish."

"Did you do it?"

"No, it got away. But I would have released it anyway."

"Have you become one of those environmental wackos?"

"No, not yet. We eat some of them."

"Listen, Buck. I need to come out your way to do a bit of reconnaissance. Could you and Melissa, I mean Dolly, put me up for a few days?"

"Stay as long as you like, Jonathan. When and how are you coming?"

"I was thinking of coming over Thanksgiving. Would that work for you and Dolly?"

"Yes, it would. We'll be here. Other than by our own plane, you couldn't pay me to travel at Thanksgiving."

"Great. Okay, so much for the when. As to the how, I thought I'd catch a commercial flight out of Ronald Reagan Washington National to the Denver International Airport, rent a car and drive up to your place."

"Negative. I've got a better idea. By the time you clear DIA, hassle with a rental car and drive over Berthoud Pass, you'll spend about three hours. Instead, how's this?"

"Dolly and I will roll our plane out of the hangar, fly down to DIA and pick you up. It's only a 40-minute flight each way. Okay?"

"Sounds great, if it won't be too much trouble," agreed Jonathan.

"But Jonathan there's a couple of things you need to fix for me."

"What's that?"

"Have the White House call the fixed-base operator, the FBO, at DIA and arrange for a car to take you from the Jeppesen Terminal at DIA over to the general aviation hangars. That's where we'll be waiting for you. And, one more thing, see if you can use the Imperial power of the White House to get DIA to waive that exorbitant landing fee they charge to keep us peons in small aircraft from using DIA."

"Consider it done. What if I arrive the day before Thanksgiving and depart a few days later?"

"Sure. No problem. Besides skiing, can you tell me what you're up to?"

"No. It's classified. But you'll probably think it will be a lot of fun."

"Jonathan, we don't need people from the citadel of big government to add excitement to our dreary lives up here."

"Well, if not fun, it'll be interesting. I promise."

"Whatever. When you know your arrival time at DIA, give us a call. Dolly will be delighted to see her old college beau again. But if you make any moves on her, I'll break your knees."

"Does Dolly still let you fly?" said Jonathan, changing the subject.

"We don't fight over the left seat anymore. I fly the first leg, she takes the next. Anyway, you're running up my cell phone bill and I want to find that trout. So, call to reconfirm things the day before you leave D.C. Okay?"

"Affirmative, Sir. 'Till then," said Jonathan hanging up.

The day before Thanksgiving dawned clean, crisp and clear of clouds, the way it often does in November in the high country. With Buck at the controls, the Madisons touched down at Denver International Airport just prior to the arrival of Jonathan's commercial flight from Ronald Reagan Washington National.

Although they really didn't need it, the Madisons bought some fuel from the fixed-base operator. Buying fuel was a thank-you for Jonathan's use of the FBO's courtesy car. While they were waiting for Jonathan and his baggage to reach the general aviation ramp, Dolly busied herself inside getting a weather update and filing an instrument flight plan back to the Granby/Grand County Airport. When Jonathan arrived, Dolly was already in the Cessna, strapped in the left seat and ready to fly.

After hurried greetings, Buck helped Jonathan into the back seat then stowed and secured Jonathan's ski gear in the luggage compartment.

She is even more beautiful than I remembered, thought Jonathan. *Buck is so lucky. Even in a flying jacket and wearing a headset, she looks like she belongs on the cover of Vogue.*

"Sorry if it's a bit crowded back there, Jonathan," said Buck. "Those two rucksacks in the seat next to you are full of survival gear. There's stuff to make fire, shelter and something to eat in there. We never leave home without them."

"Why don't you store them back in the baggage compartment?" asked Jonathan.

"Because we took a course in mountain flying survival. They say if you crash that you need to keep those rucksacks handy where you can pull them out as you exit the plane; otherwise, the aircraft might burn before you can get back for them. We even keep an extra hand-held GPS in there and, of course, my old 30.30 survival rifle," Buck explained.

As Dolly was listening on the radio for her instrument clearance from Denver Center, Buck helped Jonathan fasten his safety belts, adjusted his radio headset and showed him how to wear the nasal cannula from the oxygen system. That done, Buck climbed into the right seat, donned his own headset, safety belts and his nasal cannula.

Jonathan still has that boyish prep-school look, thought Dolly. *But his hair has gone gray. Although ten years younger than Buck, Jonathan's hair is ten years grayer. Vietnam, I suppose. Even so, Jonathan is still as handsome as ever.*

"Welcome to colorful Colorado, Jonathan," said Dolly over the intercom. "Can you hear me okay?"

"Loud and clear," said Jonathan. "Are you sure you know how to fly this thing?"

"Male, chauvinist pig! Still the same old Jonathan," said Dolly.

"Actually, I'm all for women," said Jonathan. "I think every male should own at least two or three."

"Okay, cut the bull feathers while we get out of here," interrupted Buck. "The weather's really good, but Dolly's filed an instrument flight plan, anyway. Makes it easier to get out of DIA's Class B airspace. And, if the weather goes bad, we'll already be in the instrument system."

Cleared for take-off on runway 35 Right and squawking her assigned transponder code, Dolly advanced the throttle and within moments they were airborne. A climbing left turn headed them west toward the Rocky Mountains.

The DIA Air Traffic Control Tower handed Dolly off to the Denver Traffic Control Center (TRACON). Shortly after that, TRACON handed her off to Denver Center. Each time the Cessna crossed into a new control sector, Denver Center asked Dolly to change to the radio frequency for that sector and report in.

Down below to their left was Interstate 70, also known as the skier's highway, beginning to make its climb up into the foothills west of Denver. The once-golden Aspen were bare. For now, the dominant pines, fir and spruce had triumphed over the aspen, leaving the forests all green instead of striped with gold. The early snows covered the mountain peaks and were beginning to work their way downslope. The higher elevation ski areas such as Arapahoe Basin, Berthoud Pass and the almost always snow-reliable Winter Park/Mary Jane complex were already blessed with plenty of early snow.

"We're cleared to intercept the Victor 8 Airway and follow it over Corona Pass," Dolly announced.

"How high's this Corona Pass?" asked Jonathan.

"Only about 11,700 feet above sea level," replied Dolly.

"Only? How about the mountains to each side?"

"Thirteen thousand or so," said Buck. "But we can already see Long's Peak to the north of us. It tops out at 14,255 feet. And, in between Long's Peak and us, I can see the St. Vrain Glacier where we hiked last summer."

"You guys don't think crossing these high mountain passes in a light plane is any big deal, do you?" asked Jonathan.

"Actually, we try to stay far above the mountains," said Buck. "Notice how high we are? Going on an instrument flight plan to the west, we climb up so we can cross the Continental Divide at 16,000 feet. That gives us about a 4,000-foot margin in case there are downdrafts or rotor waves."

As the altimeter showed them reaching 16,000 feet, the snow-capped Continental Divide loomed large in the windshield.

"Are you sure we're high enough to make it over that pass?" asked Jonathan.

"Sure, I can already see down into the upper Fraser Valley and the Winter Park/Mary Jane ski slopes," said Dolly.

"When I'm on this intercom, my voice isn't going out over the radio is it?" asked Jonathan.

"No," said Dolly. "Buck and I are the only ones who can broadcast. The only people you can talk to are us."

"Okay, while we're up here, maybe you can help with my reconnaissance," suggested Jonathan.

"Finally, the mystery is revealed," said Buck.

"Okay, here's the deal," said Jonathan leaning forward between the front seats. "Evidently, President Trimmer, and his main political advisor, have been doing some reading about how President Eisenhower used to come up here to fish for trout. In short, Trimmer wants to be like Ike."

"If Trimmer wants to be like Ike," said Buck, "then he needs to fish St. Louis Creek. That was Ike's favorite."

"Good point. Anyway, you get the picture. A guy who has certainly had his political ups and downs, now wants to reinvent himself in a number of ways. One of those ways is to appear as some kind of macho, outdoor-sports buff. So, they sent me out here to check out Ike's old fishing haunts. Bottom line: I'm supposed to find a suitable, presidential fishing retreat. And, by suitable, I mean a place with all the modern conveniences," said Jonathan.

"If it weren't for the fact this fishing retreat scheme of yours will help our economy," said Buck, "I'd lie and tell you Ike fished on the Roaring Fork next to Aspen and inflict him and his entourage on the Aspenites. But you already know better," said Buck

"Thanks, Buck. And, I appreciate your willingness to help an old war buddy."

"We were not buddies. I was your commanding officer and you were a dumb lieutenant until I made an officer, but not a gentleman, out of you," said Buck.

"Quit that, you two," said Dolly. "Buck, you told me Jonathan was one of the best lieutenants you ever had."

"I must have been drunk. Even so, Dolly and I will help. Mostly because I would hate to see someone I trained lose his job because he couldn't find Ike's old fishing streams. So, we'll begin with a little swing around eastern Grand County beginning right down there with Corona Pass," said Buck.

"It doesn't look like much of a pass, it's pretty open and flat," said Jonathan. "I thought it would be a narrow notch like the Khyber Pass surrounded on all sides by high mountains and thieves eager to fall upon you with curved knives and steal your purse."

"Oh, there are thieves all right," said Buck. "But they live down in Denver and they are in the business of stealing water, not your purse. And, they don't use knives, they use the courts to do their stealing."

"Oh Buck, don't get started on your latest book again," said Dolly. "Just tell Jonathan what he needs to know about the high country geography."

"Sorry, Jonathan," said Buck. "I'll save the water politics for later. Okay. Now, we are over Corona Pass. As you can see, it's just a relatively low place along the Continental Divide. But look up north. There's Devil's Thumb Pass. It's more like the notch you imagined with high ground on each side."

"Yeah, that's more like it. I see the rock chimney that sticks up like a thumb. That must give it its name. Why didn't we cross over the Continental Divide at Devil's Thumb?"

"Because Corona Pass is a bit lower and I like lower," said Dolly.

"Okay, look over to your left and down," said Buck. "See those ski trails? That's the Winter Park-Mary Jane Ski Resort. That's where we'll be skiing tomorrow.

"Now, look to your right. That's the upper Fraser Valley stretching out to the northwest. That river down there is the Fraser River. Ike fished there a time or two.

"Jonathan, you already mentioned St. Louis Creek, but I can't think of a fishing camp on it that would be big enough and modern enough for your needs. But, in a little bit, we'll show you a place on the Colorado River that might serve your purpose.

"Now, we are going to cross that ridgeline just ahead. They call the top of that ridgeline Red Dirt Hill. From there, the road winds down into the lower Fraser Valley to the town of Granby. Just west of Granby the Fraser River runs into the Colorado River and is no more. It's the Colorado River all the way through the Grand Canyon and beyond. Some of the Colorado makes it into the Sea of Cortez and some water even goes to Los Angeles and San Diego."

"You mean it all starts right down there and that tiny, little river went on to carve the Grand Canyon?"

"Yes, it may look tiny from up here but that little river packs a wallop. Now that the engineers have quit moving them around, the 'new' headwaters of the Colorado River begin below the Lake Granby High Dam, not far from where we live," said Buck.

"Look over here, Jonathan," said Dolly. "We're just crossing over the Granby Airport. That's it just north and east of Granby. You see that huge lake up north of Granby? That's the Granby Reservoir or Lake Granby, as people call it. See the ice forming around the edges of the lake? By the end of next month, that lake and the two lakes to the north of it will be frozen over and they'll stay that way until early May or so.

"Lake Granby," said Buck, "is the largest of a chain of three lakes and the key to the Colorado-Big Thompson Water Project which diverts water from the west side of the Continental Divide underneath the Rocky Mountains to the eastern plains."

"Seems sacrilegious. Like playing God," said Jonathan.

"Some folks up here think it is," said Buck. "They think it's an abomination.

"Okay, do you see the long, narrow lake that looks like it's connected to Lake Granby? That's Shadow Mountain Lake. Actually, the two lakes are only connected by a man-made canal. See that big square concrete building on the north shore of Lake Granby? That's the Lake Granby Pump Plant. It pumps water up out of Lake Granby into that 1.8 mile-long canal that flows into Shadow Mountain Lake. After that, the water flows out of Shadow Mountain into Grand Lake. Grand Lake is the smallest of the three lakes and it's just coming into view. From Grand Lake the water enters the Adams Tunnel. The tunnel carries the water about 13 miles underneath the Continental Divide to Estes Park. Once it gets down there, it's used for crop irrigation, drinking water, watering lawns and for making electricity," said Buck.

"I don't mean to take you guys out of your way," said Jonathan.

"Nonsense, we have to lose a lot of altitude before we get down to Granby's pattern altitude of 9,200 feet. Plus, Dolly doesn't want to shock-cool the engine by reducing power too quickly. So, we always take a little tour of the three lakes area while we make slow power reductions and a slow descent."

"Okay, I'm turning back to the south now," said Dolly. "Buck, show Jonathan the possible solution to his assignment."

"Dolly's right," said Buck. "Boy, do we have a deal for you! Okay, we're just over the north shore of Lake Granby. But look over there on the south shore, there's a dam with a spillway. Actually, there are two spillways, but the first one they built broke off and fell about 300 feet into the river. Those other features that look like dams are really only dikes," said Buck.

"I see the concrete dam. It's not very wide."

"No, but it's very high. From the lip of the dam to the catch basin at the bottom of the dam is about 300 feet," said Buck. "Sometimes, if the lake gets too high, they spill some water over the dam. But most of the time the spillway is bone dry. Most of the time they just let the water flow through a big pipe underneath the base of the dam. Anyway, I was right down there when your White House switchboard tracked me down.

"Now, Jonathan, follow the Colorado River as it winds behind that tall hill, called Bussey Hill. Okay, now as Dolly takes us along the gorge of the Colorado, it broadens out so there is a narrow pasture on both sides of the Colorado and some irrigation canals. That place is called: Camp Ouray," said Buck.

"You mean with wild Indians? I mean Native Americans."

"Just a few riding horses," said Buck. "The main thing the camp does is straddle some of the world's best fly fishing waters. It's a combination of condos, private homes and a central lodge set on a rise just above the Colorado River. Most of the private homes are second homes, occupied a few months each year. Only a handful of homes have full-time residents. Some of the residents are good friends of ours.

"Most of the condos, however, are owned by families who work down in Denver or Boulder and come up on weekends. The lodge, that's the really large building you see down there, is the week-end haven for a bunch of yuppie lawyers, CPA's and the like who come up on weekends to fly-fish, drink, eat and tell tall tales," said Buck.

As they circled over the ranch, Jonathan asked, "What are those cabins right down on the banks of the river?"

"Risk-takers, I think," said Dolly. "If the Lake Granby High Dam ever burst, they would be swept 40 miles downstream to the town of Kremmling."

"So, you think the homes and condos and the lodge are high enough up to be safe?"

"Oh, yes," said Buck. "They did a flood study some years ago. Of course, the dwellings sitting right down on the riverbanks would be swept away. But the lodge along with the homes and condos up on the side of the valley would survive.

"The study showed that the flood waters would push on through the reservoir at Windy Gap, to the west, wiping out the town of Hot Sulphur Springs and end up four-feet deep in the streets of Kremmling," said Buck.

"So, if you two were part of the vast, right-wing conspiracy against President Trimmer, you'd blow up the Lake Granby High Dam while the President is there?" asked Jonathan with a grin.

"You mean the vast, right-wing conspiracy invented by Mrs. Trimmer," asked Buck. "Well, we barely have time to attend all their meetings. Seriously, barring sabotage, I would say the chances of the Lake Granby High Dam breaking are somewhere between slim and none. Besides, the luxury home we have in mind for your El Supremo is up by the tennis courts and yet not too far from the main lodge."

"Of course we'll have to look at it on the ground," said Jonathan. "But, from up here, it looks pretty good. We could put the White House staff in the condos and the lodge could be the media center. But what about air and ambulance service?"

"They used to fly one of Ike's twin-engine Aero Commanders up from the old Denver Stapleton Airport into the Granby Airport. So, the old Aero Commander version of Air Force One has already been up here. But, I don't think Ike was at the controls."

"Wait, a minute," said Jonathan. "I didn't know Ike was a pilot."

"Ike got his pilot's license out in the Philippines when he was aide-de-camp to General MacArthur. Ike was MacArthur's eyes and ears and the General had him on the go all the time. With thousands of islands to visit, Ike learned to fly a Piper Cub in order to get around.

"A lot of U.S. Presidents have flown in the 20th Century, but only Ike, George Bush, Sr., and George W. Bush were licensed pilots. George Senior flew a torpedo bomber in World War II and, after the war, owned a V-tailed Bonanza. George W. flew the super-sonic, all-weather, F-102 Delta Dagger interceptor for the U.S. Air Force and the Texas Air Guard."

"Can we get back to the present, please?" asked Dolly.

"Sure. Well, almost. Up until 1979, the Granby Airport used to have DeHavilland Dash Seven or Twin Otter service twice a day. In fact, the airline terminal is still there and in decent shape. You make Camp Ouray a presidential fishing retreat and the FAA will turn the Granby Airport into a mini-Dulles. Be great for the community," said Buck.

"There's a medical clinic in Granby with a great staff," said Dolly. "They relate well to the community they serve. Our physician even won the big fishing contest one year. There used to be another clinic about two miles south of Granby, but it closed. Maybe the White House could get it open again. And, way over in Kremmling, there is a small hospital. But, in winter, it's difficult to get there by road."

As she talked, Dolly dropped twenty degrees of flaps, made her final power reduction and turned onto the final leg of her approach to the Granby/Grand County Airport. With a little chirping sound the main gear touched down on the runway. Dolly pulled back on the control yoke to keep the nose wheel off the runway until the aircraft lost most of its speed and then she gently let the nose wheel settle onto the runway. Even though they had used only a few gallons of fuel, to keep water condensation out of the fuel tanks, they taxied to the fuel pump, topped off the tanks and let Jonathan pay for the fuel with his government credit card. After that, they taxied the Cessna to its hangar, off-loaded Jonathan's gear into Dolly's Expedition, rolled the airplane into the hangar and secured the door.

"What about the people who live full-time at Camp Ouray?" asked Jonathan, as Dolly drove away from the airport. "Will they give us a lot of grief?"

"Not as long as they are not put out of their homes for too long," said Buck. "Besides, I know how the Imperial White House spends money on these presidential retreats. Remember the Johnson Ranch? Remember Nixon's place on Key Biscayne? Offer to pave all the roads, put in low-intensity lamps along all the footpaths, rehab the lodge, and re-surface the tennis court, all that kind of stuff you guys have done ever since LBJ. Charge it off to 'security.' The residents may grumble but, in the end, they'll be happy to go on vacation to some other nice place for awhile courtesy of Uncle Sugar. Also, a donation to help restock their fish ponds would be nice."

"You drive a hard bargain and I haven't even talked with the folks at Camp Ouray," said Jonathan.

"If you think our idea has possibilities," said Dolly, "we'll stop by there on our way home. It's right on our way. Let's get all this business stuff decided so we get up on the slopes and do some serious skiing tomorrow."

Dolly called ahead on her cell phone and made arrangements for them to drop by and see some of their friends at Camp Ouray. They had coffee with one set of friends, drinks with another, made a quick tour of the ranch, said their farewells and left.

"What do you think?" asked Buck.

"I think it's perfect," said Jonathan. "It's got a gate, we can secure both banks of the Colorado River easily and the buildings and their lay-out are just perfect for the staff, media and the political commissars who always tag along. My agents will love living in some of those neat condos."

"Now what?" asked Dolly.

"I go back to Washington, make my recommendation to Mr. Edward T. Briccone who sells it to the President. Following that, a team of engineers and negotiators will come out early next year to cut a deal with the residents. About May, contractors will start making the improvements we will promise the residents plus some security fences and other items I can't discuss."

"So, when's the big date for the presidential visit?" asked Buck.

"If I knew, I couldn't tell you," Jonathan lied. "But I know it's more than just fishing. The State Department has a piece of this pie which makes me think there's some kind of summit meeting involved.

Eventually, they'll get around to telling me whom we have to protect besides President Trimmer."

"I hope it's Benjamin Netanyahu," said Dolly. "Now's there's one head-of-state I'd like to meet."

"Former head-of-state, Dolly," said Buck. "First, it's Jonathan and now it's former heads-of-state I have to worry about."

"Keeps you on your toes." said Jonathan.

"Okay, you two," said Buck. "Let's get home, get you unpacked, have our dinner, make an early bedtime and be ready to hit the slopes first thing tomorrow."

CHAPTER FOUR

Thanksgiving Day

The Timberline Lift that serves Winter Park's Parsenn Bowl only holds two people, so Dolly went first and rode by herself. She waited at the top for Buck and Jonathan to arrive and ski over to where Dolly was taking in the view on a day so picture perfect that it only be described as a "Warren Miller Day."

"Penny for your thoughts, Jonathan," said Dolly.

"At 12,000 feet, it's hard to have any thoughts. I'm too busy soaking up the incredible beauty of these peaks," said Jonathan Winslow.

"Sometimes, we pack a lunch and climb up to the top of North Cone Peak," said Buck Madison. "When there's no wind blowing, like today, North Cone Peak is a magical place. Let's do it."

They left their skis at the top of the Timberline Lift, kept their ski poles to use as hiking sticks, and climbed on up to the 12,060-foot summit of North Cone Peak.

Looking north, they could see across the Fraser Valley and beyond to the Never Summer Range lying inside Rocky Mountain National Park and, beyond that, along the west side of Continental Divide into Wyoming. Looking south, they gazed down onto the Berthoud Pass Ski Area and the highway linking the Winter Park-Mary Jane Ski Resort to Denver. Facing east, James Peak, Perry Peak and Mount Eva along the

Continental Divide seemed close enough to reach out and touch. To the west was Byers Peak and beyond that the Gore Range leading toward Vail Pass and the Vail Valley.

"Buck, when we were in Vietnam, did you ever think we would live to crawl up out of those bug-and snake-infested swamps and be standing here on top of the world?" asked Jonathan.

"Actually, Jonathan, when I wasn't pulling your platoon's chestnuts out of firefights," said Buck. "I was promising myself, if I survived, that I would live somewhere with no heat, no humidity and, most of all, no bugs and snakes."

The majesty of the mountains made talking seem almost sacrilegious, so they sat silently for some time. Finally, Buck broke the stillness.

"Jonathan, we know you don't have much time this trip. How can we be of help?"

"I'm just hoping POTUS won't give me too much grief over picking Camp Ouray as the site for this fishing retreat business."

"POTUS, what's that?" asked Dolly.

"It's not a what, it's a he," said Jonathan. "Just the acronym we use for the President of the United States."

"Well, I can't imagine what objection any POTUS would have to Camp Ouray as the place for himself and all of his camp followers," said Dolly.

"Don't be catty," said Buck. "Jonathan, you said Edward T. Briccone is behind this idea. What's the 'T' for?" asked Buck.

"My agents say it stands for trouble," said Jonathan. "But I've found Briccone much easier to work with than POTUS."

"Do you have a code name for Briccone?" asked Dolly.

"Yeah, it's RASCAL. That's what briccone means in Italian. But it's POTUS who is the real rascal."

"I detect you don't care much for POTUS," said Buck.

"He's a difficult person to understand. But once you figure out his moral relativism and his ability to rationalize whatever he does, he's rather predictable. For example, he almost always needs at least 100 strokes to complete a round of golf. But he'll turn in a scorecard that says 89. His name ought to be Mulligan, not Trimmer. The cheating only bothers me a little. The really scary part is that he actually believes he shot an 89. Anyway, that's enough amateur psychoanalysis of James Robert Trimmer. Maybe I'll tell your more later. But this time and place are too beautiful to spoil with dark thoughts."

"I was just thinking along those same lines," said Dolly. "It must be quite a contrast for you to come up here away from all the sneaky maneuvering and back-stabbing you see going on in the White House and Washington and compare it with the simple, clean beauty of these snow-capped peaks."

The three friends took a lingering look at the surrounding peaks and reluctantly climbed down to their waiting skis. (See: *www.thegrandconspiracy.com*)

"Here's the deal, Jonathan," said Buck stepping into his bindings. "We'll ski Parsenn Bowl until time for lunch. But, before lunch, we'll show you the secret location of the Tyrolian Club."

"What's that?" asked Jonathan.

"It's kinda hidden in the woods, but it's where the old Denver elite meet to eat up here," said Buck. "Actually, they founded this ski area and carved out the first trails—like Mary Jane. Old money didn't mean they were soft. At first, they hiked up and skied down. Finally, they got around to putting in a rope tow. Today, it is said that a seat on the Denver Water Board and membership in the Tyrolian Club carries more weight than being governor of the state. Anyway, Winter Park was their winter playground and Grand Lake was their summer playground."

"Sounds like a nice way to live," said Jonathan.

"Okay, after we take a peek at the Tyrolian Club," said Jonathan, "we'll work our way back over to the top of Winter Park and you can treat us to lunch at the Sunspot Lodge."

Later, as they polished off a delicious lunch in the dining room at Sunspot, Jonathan asked: "How do you two stay in such good shape?"

"You mean you're amazed Buck passed the big Six-O` and is still kicking?" teased Dolly. "Seriously, when you live up here year-round, you tend to stay in shape. Besides, once the snow melts, Buck and I do a lot of hiking in the Indian Peaks Wilderness along the Continental Divide. Last summer, we even hiked the St. Vrain Glacier."

"But, Dolly, you and Buck can't play Mark Trail all the time. You must do something else." said Jonathan.

"I have my own real estate company, but I only work with previous clients or the people they refer to me. I also do a little *pro bono* counseling on the side and I analyze some Chinese documents for the Company now and then. Buck's writing a history of the water wars in this part of Colorado and that takes a lot of his time," said Dolly.

"Water wars? You mean early settlers shooting each other because somebody upstream shut their water off or poisoned the watering hole?" asked Jonathan.

"Nothing that dramatic, yet it's more profound and more recent," said Buck. "The problem is it's tough to make it interesting reading when you're talking about the Front Range cities on the east side of the Continental Divide systematically, and legally, stealing the water out of rivers and lakes on the west side, especially from here in Grand County."

"How much water can you steal out of a single county?" asked Jonathan.

"When your county is almost as large as the State of Delaware, you can steal a lot of water. Basically, they've stolen, 'appropriated,' they call it, almost all the water collected by the Fraser and Colorado River basins."

"So, what's the impact of losing all your water to cities on the Front Range?" asked Jonathan.

"Actually, it's more than losing it to Denver and the other cities along the Front Range. What isn't drained by tunnels and ditches so folks can water their lawns and golf courses along the Front Range is drained down the Colorado River and out to the west."

"Again, what's the impact on Grand County?" asked Jonathan.

"No chance of economic growth. Ironically, the most water-rich county in Colorado isn't allowed to retain enough water to support any kind of light manufacturing. It's tourism and that's it. A kid growing up here grows up in a sportsman's paradise. But once they leave school there's nothing for them to do here except be lift attendants or make beds or wait tables or clean condos. In fact, we have so little water left for our own use, it takes almost an Act of God and a bank loan to get a water tap permit to build a house or condo."

"Boy, that's ironic," said Jonathan, "as I look out the windows here at Sunspot all I see are tons of snow clinging to a ring of magnificent mountains that must almost encompass the entire county."

"Yes. We're about three-quarters surrounded by the Continental Divide. That's why there's so little wind here. We're pretty much protected."

"So, tell me how do they drain all this water out of Grand County?" (See: *www.thegrandconspiracy.com*)

"It's an elaborate system of tunnels, pumps and ditches. They take awhile to explain. But I've got a surprise for you. Tomorrow, we're going on a cross-country ski trip up to The Grand Ditch. That's where the first water theft took place.

"But that's not why we're going up there. It's just a terrific place to cross-county ski and the vistas are magnificent. Besides, I've arranged for you to have a reunion with Chuck Lee, Roberto Chavez and Lou Leclerc."

"I heard those three renegades were up here somewhere. But I didn't realize they lived so close,"

"Oh, yes. Chuck and Roberto more or less grew up in these mountains and came back here after Vietnam," said Buck. "You know, Lou was born in France. Lou was smuggled out right after the Nazis executed his parents.

"He was too young to work for the O.S.S. But after he was old enough to learn to fly, he went to work for the Company—actually, Air America. When we pulled out of southeast Asia, he came here to retire.

"Lou became interested in Grand County when he found out the French trappers were the first people to settle here. That plus, the fact that Chuck, Roberto and I were here, sort of made up his mind."

"Tomorrow sounds like fun," said Jonathan. "So are they working or just raising hell?"

"Some of both. They're all drawing retirement, maybe disability pay as well. Chuck and Roberto from the Army. Lou from Air America. Of course, few can live entirely on military retirement up here, so, like most people, they have several jobs."

"You said Chuck and Roberto have jobs?"

"In the summer, Chuck's an expert fly-fishing guide. In winter, he runs a martial arts school in Granby. Roberto and his wife had a small ranch, but they lost it to the IRS. Now, Roberto works part-time for Chuck in the fishing-guide business and at the martial-arts school."

"What about Lou?"

"Lou, well Lou, I'm not quite sure about Lou. He disappears now and then and I suspect he's off flying some kind of covert missions for the Company. Back when Ollie North was trying to keep the Contras alive until the people of Nicaragua could hold an election and throw out the commies, Lou was flying medical supplies to the Contras off an abandoned dirt strip over by Tabernash.

"Lou lives in the Town of Grand Lake but he has a log cabin near where we're going skiing tomorrow. I think he inherited it from one of the original French trappers. He says it is his private retreat. When he's not in Grand Lake or holed up in his cabin, he's down at Happy Jacques telling tales that sound like 'Terry and the Pirates.' To hear Lou tell it, he was in China with the original Flying Tigers."

"Happy Jacques? What's that?"

"It's the local watering hole for people who actually have to work for a living. Some of them are what you might call the rangeland rebels. They aren't fond of big government, but aren't as far out as the so-called militia movement either," said Buck.

"Anyway, it'll be great to see those guys again," said Jonathan. "Are they okay? I mean, did they make it out of southeast Asia without any serious wounds?"

"Jonathan, as you and I know so well, the overwhelming majority of Vietnam vets came home to lead normal, productive lives. Unfortunately, we've all been given a bad reputation by a small number of so-called Vietnam vets many of whom were either not ever in the service or if in service never went to Vietnam or if they did get to Vietnam never saw combat. You know, only 15 percent of us who went to Vietnam saw actual combat."

"I knew we had a huge logistical tail over there; however, but I didn't realize the actual combat number was so small," said Jonathan.

"Making matters worse is the fact that the liberal media love to interview these wacked-out dirt bags and spread their lies about how they were trained as assassins, sent behind enemy lines and ordered to do such horrible things that they came home hooked on drugs and alcohol. One of these nuts, who was never even in the military one day, got himself elected as head of a state-wide Vietnam vets organization back east. And, even when their lies are exposed, the media will rarely correct the record. All this phoney Vietnam vet stuff got so bad a couple of people wrote a book called: *Stolen Valor: How the Vietnam Generation Was Robbed of its Heroes and its History.* They set the record straight. I'll loan you my copy.

"But you asked about Chuck, Roberto and Lou. Well, they, just as you and I, were in the thick of the fighting and I have to say it took its toll on our friends. Chuck had a couple of flesh wounds. Nothing too serious. And, Chuck's in good shape. Outdoors much of the time. Still holds a black belt in Karate. Even at age 60, I suspect Chuck can whip anyone in the county. Roberto was never wounded, as far as I know."

"Tell me more about Lou," said Jonathan.

"Lou. Well. Although his broken arms didn't heal right, I think Lou's real wounds are more on the inside than the outside. As you know, he was shot down in Laos and then taken to North Vietnam. He spent three years in the Hanoi Hilton where he was tortured. Probably tortured more than most because of Air America's connection with the CIA.

"All four of us get together sometimes and talk about the old days in the 1st Cav. Lou likes to remind us how he flew a Helio Courier full of supplies into us west of Pleiku and then was crazy enough to stay and help us fight off the North Vietnamese."

"Who could forget Lou up inside that abandoned water tower with his .50 caliber machine gun?" asked Jonathan. "I think Lou and his sniper scope really saved our bacon. Once he picked off their leaders, the 66th NVA Regiment headed back into Cambodia."

"That was the one and only time all five us were together in combat," Buck. "In a strange way, it was the best of times."

"Only because you survived," offered Dolly.

"So, here's the point I'm trying to make about our friends," said Buck. "They aren't like the vast majority of us who served over there, came home and got on with life. For example, you can't talk about Vietnam or Cambodia or Laos with Lou. He goes off the deep end. Especially, if you say anything about the anti-war movement or the lack of support from the home front. Torture does funny things to people, and Lou withstood more than his share. Yet, most of the time, old Lou acts like a happy-go-lucky fly-boy. As long as you don't get into the politics of the war, Lou is eager to tell tall tales about hairy take-offs and landings in places most people couldn't parallel park a VW beetle. Oddly enough, most of them are true."

"I'll try to stay with safe subjects tomorrow," said Jonathan. "By the way, I'm taking you two out to dinner tonight so Dolly doesn't have to cook."

"What a minute," said Buck, "I do most of the cooking around here, but we'll accept your gracious offer of dinner out. Dolly, how 'bout giving Jean Claude over at Caroline's Cuisine a call and see if you can make a reservation? I know Jonathan loves five-star French cooking."

CHAPTER FIVE

Now gather 'round cowboys. Saddle up a good horse. And ride for your land, or it'll be a golf course. For they'll tear down the mountains, and cover the trails. You won't find the bean counters, when the banks start to fail. Ride Rangeland Rebels. Ride to beat the devil.

—Michael Martin Murphey

The Day after Thanksgiving

The day dawned cold and clear. Steam was rising from Lake Granby and a few puffs of fog were forming up in Arapaho Bay. The huge lake was in the beginning stages of freezing solid for the winter. But above the steam and fog, the rim of the Continental Divide and the outline of Old Abe loomed sharp as a razor across the eastern horizon.

The silhouette of Abe Lincoln lying on his back contemplating the Heavens is unmistakable. Actually, what appears to be President Lincoln is really the peak of Mt. Toll and the ridgeline stretching southward to Pawnee Peak. The prominent brow, the beard, even his hands folded across his chest in repose, are readily understood by anyone with enough imagination to see people or animals in cloud formations. (See: *www.thegrandconspiracy.com*)

Dolly opted to stay home. She preferred to make the climb up to The Grand Ditch in summer. Truth be known, she really didn't want to go. While she still had a soft spot in her heart for Jonathan, her old college beau, she thought Chuck Lee and, especially, Lou Leclerc, were both several pixels short of a full screen. Only Roberto seemed to have maintained some kind of touch with reality.

But she had to tolerate Chuck Lee because Chuck and Buck had been fellow company commanders in the same battalion in Vietnam. Buck always said it was Chuck's combat savvy that helped him be so successful as a company commander and even saved his life. Anyway, Buck always said the most important things he learned about jungle warfare he learned from Chuck.

Dolly decked Jonathan out in some of Buck's old Nordic cross-country skiwear: an Eveboefoss sweater from Sandane, Norway; a pair of knickers, long stockings, a wool cap and goggles. A pair of rented cross-country boots made Jonathan look like he was ready for the Holmenkollen Games in Norway. Buck wore a turtleneck under a fleece vest topped by an anorak and his, ever present, Akubra with stampede strap. He carried a headband to keep his ears warm. As they were piling their snowshoes and cross-county skis into Buck's Explorer, Dolly brought out two fanny packs containing water, some string cheese and some leftover Turkey. Buck took the two small bottles of wine he had in his anorak and put them in the fanny packs.

Both men gave Dolly a farewell hug and they drove off for U.S. Highway 34, which would take them past Grand Lake, and to the west entrance of Rocky Mountain National Park. Soon, they passed a sign saying Trail Ridge Road was closed.

"Isn't that the road that runs across the top of Rocky Mountain National Park to Estes Park?" asked Jonathan.

"Yes, it's the highest continuous highway in the lower 48," said Buck. "But it's only open in summer. Lucky for us enough of it remains open in winter for cross-country skiers, and unfortunately, snowmobilers as well."

"What's your beef with snowmobiles?"

"They need to convert to four-stroke engines. That would cut down on the noise and the pollution they cause. Also, some of the riders don't understand how they cause the deer and the elk to run themselves to exhaustion. Other than that, they're fine."

Pulling into the parking lot near the Never Summer Ranch, Buck and Jonathan parked beside Chuck Lee's vintage pickup. Jonathan wondered if Chuck Lee and Roberto Chavez still looked like they could play pro-football. The broad-shouldered, but narrow-waisted, Chuck always reminded Jonathan of a powerful halfback while the chunky, low-to-the-ground Roberto would have made the perfect blocking back for Chuck. Lou Leclerc he remembered as tall, thin happy-go-lucky flyboy. He'd soon find out.

Holding steaming cups of coffee in their hands, Chuck Lee, Roberto Chavez and Lou Leclerc stepped out to greet Buck and Jonathan. Chuck and Roberto looked like they were ready to go on jungle patrol in their camo field jackets and camo fatigue pants. Lou was wearing his trademark A-2 leather flying jacket complete with Flying Tiger insignia. All three veterans were wearing cowboy-style boonie hats topped with ski goggles. Obviously, they were being clothed by Cabela's or Pro Bass Shops and not by Land's End. All three had surplus U.S. Army Special Forces rucksacks that they would use to help carry their cross-country skis. Mostly, Jonathan was not disappointed in what he saw. Chuck and Roberto still looked fit. But Lou's blue eyes had a haunted look as if he had endured incredible pain that he wasn't able to put out of his mind.

"Jonathan, you old SOB," cried Lou, "We haven't seen you since about 1966 when you were a shavetail lieutenant who didn't know shit from shinola."

Ignoring the barb, Jonathan took part in the ritual bear hugs and then stepped back.

"Sonofagun," said Jonathan, "it's been too long. I'm just glad I didn't come in summer. In all that camouflage gear, I'd have missed you."

"At least we don't look like Stein Eriksen on a bad hair day," said Chuck. "And, just look at you, Jonathan. You've gained back that baby fat you shed in Vietnam and the hair you have left is almost totally gray. If the safety of our glorious leader depends on you, he's in big trouble."

"Look here, guys, I just manage a bunch of much younger agents. They're the ones who have to be fit enough to protect the President."

"Who wants that dope-smoking, lying, draft-dodging, womanizing sonofabitch protected?" said Lou. "Maybe someone will blow that cocksucker away."

"Okay, Lou," responded Buck, stepping forward to Lou. "Knock it off. Jonathan has taken good care of some other Presidents that you probably liked."

"No, he didn't," said Lou. "He let that wealthy psycho from up by Genesee shoot my man Reagan."

"Now, hold it, Lou," ordered Buck. "Jonathan wasn't in charge back then and he wasn't even on duty that day. Were you, Jonathan?"

"No, I wasn't. But let me get this straight. Lou, are you serious or just pulling my leg? If you're serious, I'll have to arrest your butt for making threats against the President of the United States."

"Shit, Jonathan. I'm just kidding," said Lou. "I just figure, at this point, I'm entitled to say whatever I goddamn well please. You've got a good government job, Jonathan. Don't let my little tirades worry you none."

"With that settled," said Buck, "let's get our snowshoes and skis and head for the Never Summer Ranch."

The plan was to snowshoe up the trail to The Grand Ditch, take a break and then switch to cross-country skis. From that point, they would ski along The Grand Ditch to its upper reaches in Baker Gulch. There they would stop for some wine and some of Roberto's famous Jalapeno deer sausage. The trek was to end by reversing course back to the parking lot.

Many years ago, the Never Summer Ranch was one of the first guest ranches in Grand County. Originally, it was outside the confines of Rocky Mountain National Park. But, like so many pioneer homesteads, it was encapsulated by the growth of the Park. For awhile, it continued to operate under a grandfather provision but was, ultimately, shut down. The chinked-log cabins are now used as living quarters for park rangers.

With Jonathan struggling to keep up, the five men snowshoed across the bridge over the former headwaters of the Colorado River and on through the remains of the Never Summer Ranch. From there, the trail goes steeply upward switching back and forth 13 times until it intercepts The Grand Ditch some 1200 feet above the floor of the Kawuneechee Valley. Fortunately, a park ranger who was up early on a snowmobile to patrol the boundary between the National Park and the National Forest had already broken the trail.

Although the snow wasn't nearly as deep as it would get in the dead of winter, even mountain dwellers like Buck, Chuck, Roberto and Lou were happy to take frequent rest breaks and lean on their ski poles. Jonathan, who was used to living at sea level, wished for even more for breaks but wasn't about to complain.

About the time Jonathan was about to despair of ever seeing anything but the tails of Buck's snowshoes, the trail flattened out onto a shelf about 30 feet wide.

After they caught their breath, Jonathan asked: "So, tell me what I'm seeing up here. It looks like a road cut along the side of this mountain." (See: *www.thegrandconspiracy.com*)

"Actually," Buck began, "it's both a road and a ditch. The outside rim, where we're standing, is a service road. The inside, the side toward the mountain, is a ditch generally about 20 feet wide and six feet deep. The purpose of the ditch is to catch the water draining down the face of the Never Summer Mountain Range and drop it over the Continental Divide over Poudre Pass. From Poudre Pass it falls down into Long

Draw Reservoir and from there the water flows down onto the Great Plains at Ft. Collins where it is used for irrigation and drinking. There's a big brewery at Ft. Collins. So, it's used for beer as well.

"That reminds me," said Lou. "I have to take a piss in The Grand Ditch."

Ignoring Lou, Jonathan asked, "You mean water that would naturally flow toward the Pacific Ocean or the Gulf of Cortez is being tricked into flowing toward the Gulf of Mexico instead?"

"Exactly. Just like when folks up in Vermont put a slash at an angle across a Maple tree to drain the syrup into a bucket, that's what the Ft. Collins Land and Water Company did to this entire mountain range."

"I'll be damned," said Jonathan.

"In the course of a year," said Chuck, "thousands of acre feet of water that should be draining downward to form the headwaters of the Colorado River in the Kawuneechee Valley are diverted to the wrong side of the Continental Divide."

"Well, I have to say it's ingenious," said Jonathan. "Who did this and when?"

"I better let Chuck tell you all that. After all, some of his people helped build it," said Buck.

"Jonathan," began Chuck, "the reason my last name is Lee is because I'm part Chinese. Actually, I'm part Chinese, Swedish and Mexican."

While Chuck was talking, Lou found three small rocks and made a fireplace that would support a GI canteen cup. Under the cup he placed a chunk of C-4 plastique explosive and set fire to it with his cigarette lighter. C-4 burns with an intense heat and, in minutes, the water he put in the canteen cup was boiling briskly.

Virtually every infantry trooper in Vietnam carried a block of C-4 in his rucksack. The official use of C-4 was to blow up NVA or VC bunkers; however, many troopers also used it to heat their C-rations.

Vietnam habits die hard, thought Jonathan. *I wonder just how much C-4 Lou has hidden away somewhere?*

Soon, Lou was passing around the GI canteen cup of instant coffee which, without asking anyone's permission, he slugged with a large ration of brandy. Before they switched to cross-country skis, the five old warriors sat on their packs to pass around their coffee and to hear Chuck's tale.

"The Ft. Collins Land and Water Company started building The Grand Ditch back in 1892 using a combination of Japanese and Chinese labor gangs," said Chuck.

"Wait a minute," said Jonathan. "This ditch was built in 1892?"

"Yes, construction began in 1892. But it wasn't completely finished until the early 20th Century," said Chuck.

"How long is this ditch?" asked Jonathan.

"Today, it's over 15 miles from its upper end where it begins in Bowen Gulch up in the far western reaches of the Never Summer Mountain Range. From there, it runs downhill at a constant two-degree slope to the northeast where its waters drop over Poudre Pass and down, as Buck said, through Long Draw Reservoir and on to Ft. Collins."

"How did they make sure it goes downhill at a constant two-degree slope?" asked Jonathan. "If the ditch flattens out and runs uphill at any point, the water would stop. It would either go over the side or just not flow at all."

"That's right. I can't give my Oriental ancestors credit for the engineering, they only did the stoop labor. The engineering was done by a team of Swedish engineers who supervised the workers. Most of the workers were Japanese; however, some were Chinese. They have some pay records down in Ft. Collins showing wages of just pennies-per hour paid to people with Japanese names. But there are also receipts showing payments being made to 'companies' of workers. Some of the companies may have been Chinese with the payments going to the headman who, in turn, paid his coolies."

"You say you had Chinese and Swedish ancestors up here?" asked Jonathan.

"Actually, my great-grandmother was up here. I used to be embarrassed to tell this, but not now. She worked in a Japanese brothel not far from where we are standing. The Japanese have something of a tradition of forcing young Chinese women to work in their brothels just like they did on Taiwan prior to and during World War II.

"You may have heard of the ancient Chinese Triads. They are secret societies that exist to this day and some are heavily involved in crime in Asia and even here in the U.S."

"What about Tongs?" asked Jonathan, "our anti-counterfeiting division has problems with the Tongs on our West Coast."

"Good question," said Chuck. "The Tongs in San Francisco are the North American off-shoots of the old Triads. Basically, Chinese organized crime syndicates. But Triad or Tong,—same-same—both sold women into what you might call 'yellow' slavery.

"The Tongs had a function somewhat like a union hiring hall. When you needed workers to do tough and dangerous work, you sent to the Tongs in San Francisco and they would dispatch the number of coolies you required along with an amenity for the workers. The amenity was to provide a certain number of women to service the workers."

"God, that must have been terrible for those poor women," said Jonathan.

"From the point of view of the physical labor involved, I guess my great-grandmother was lucky. You see, the Japanese and Chinese men worked up here year-round with picks and shovels cutting this shelf across the face of an entire mountain range. They lived in caves and log huts for protection from the snow. Many simply froze to death. Many dropped from exhaustion or simply got sick and died."

"Weren't there any laws to protect the Orientals?"

"Very few. Colorado did pass several laws back then to encourage Orientals to come here to build works such as The Grand Ditch, to build roads, bridges, and train trestles across high canyons. The Japanese and Chinese were desperate for work and would do things you couldn't get White workers to do."

"Did they all come directly from the Orient?"

"No, some were survivors from the infamous Rock Springs Massacre of 1885."

"What the hell was that?"

"One night, in 1885, a bunch of White miners got roaring drunk and decided to kill all the Oriental miners working near Rock Springs, Wyoming. Dozens of men were slaughtered, the women raped and then slaughtered. But several hundred survived. When they heard Colorado passed some laws giving even a modicum of protection to Orientals, they were willing to come down here. When the Ft. Collins Land and Water Company sent agents to San Francisco to meet with the Japanese War Lords and the Chinese Tongs, the Rock Springs survivors got included somehow in the deal," said Chuck.

"The building of this ditch and the way these workers had to live wasn't in my grade-school history book," said Jonathan.

"No, Jonathan," said Chuck. "But the tale is true. In fact, my great-grandmother, Soo Lee, gave birth to a daughter in a cave somewhere around here. That child was my grandmother."

"Who was the father?" asked Buck.

"The father was a Swede, but I never knew his name," said Chuck. "He was my great-grandfather. I guess he got horny up here and paid the headman to sleep with my great-grandmother.

"But when the child was born, and it obviously was half northern European, my great-grandfather took responsibility for mother and child. He bought my great-grandmother's contract from the Japs and took mother and child down to Denver.

"Once he got to Denver, he placed them with a poor Hispanic family named Reyes. He paid them a monthly stipend to care for them. The Swede came back up here to finish his contract with the Ft. Collins Land and Water Company but one winter there was an avalanche that swept him over the side. He was never found; however, I don't imagine they looked very hard for him either. He lies buried somewhere down below us. So, I've got a lot of family history tied up in this ditch."

"So, what happened to your great-grandmother?" asked Buck.

"She died of TB before she was 30. But when her daughter was old enough, she married a migrant farm worker named Martinez. My great-grandmother was very proud of her Chinese ancestry so, on her deathbed, she requested that her children and her grandchildren all have Lee somewhere in their name. Her request wasn't always honored; however, I was told about it when I was almost grown."

"So, you are really a Martinez?" asked Buck.

"No, my mother was a Martinez. She married a man named Ortiz and that was my original name."

"Then, what happened to the name Ortiz?" asked Jonathan.

"When I was old enough I asked to come up here and see The Grand Ditch. I was so taken with the beauty of this place that I didn't want to leave. So I got a job down on Grand Lake working as a house boy in the mansion of a wealthy Kansas City family that makes greeting cards."

"You still didn't explain what happened to Ortiz," said Jonathan.

"Being around a lot of wealthy Anglos, I figured out that being an Ortiz wasn't going to make me rich and famous. Mind you, I'm proud to be Latino and Spanish was my cradle language. But, given a choice of being Chinese, Swedish or Latino, I decided the name Lee was both Chinese and American. Also, it was a way of honoring my great-grand-mother. So, I decided on: Charles Lee, went to court and had my name changed," said Chuck.

"Sonofabitch," exclaimed Lou, "I always thought you were named after Robert E. Lee—the greatest general who ever lived. Here we been drinking buddies all these years and I never knew all this shit."

"No, Lou. Sorry to disappoint you. I'm just a mix of Chinese, Swedish and Mexican blood who happened to get enough education to go to officer candidate school and make something of himself. So, by an Act of Congress, I became an officer and gentleman in the United States Army. One of the things that kept me in the Army was the notion that I might help others have the same opportunities I had."

"That's the most amazing goddam story I've ever heard," said Lou. "How come you're just now getting around to tell it?"

"Ever since Buck told me something about the book he's writing about the high-country water thefts, I've been intending to tell him this story. You see, Buck's the first one I know who's taken an interest in telling about the theft of the water out of Grand County and I just thought he ought to hear about the original crime right up here where it all began."

"Chuck," said Buck, "this is a terrific story. "For sure, it goes in the book. Maybe, over dinner sometime, you can give Dolly and me more of the details."

"Yeah, great story, Chuck," said Lou, already bored. "Okay, what say we get on our cross-country skis and mosey on up to the upper end of this ditch."

In silence, the five men worked their way up the constant two-degree slope and along the rim of Baker Gulch. Jonathan made sure to stay to the inside of the trail. A slip over the side meant a fall of hundreds of feet almost straight down in places. Bright sunlight forced them to put on their sunglasses, but Jonathan wondered how many men might have fallen to their deaths when blinding snows obliterated the trail?

When they came to the confluence of the two upper valleys where The Grand Ditch begins, they sat on their packs to drink their wine, sample some of Roberto's famous Jalapeno deer sausage and eat whatever else they brought along. For old war buddies who had so much catching up to do, they didn't talk much. It was enough just to be together again, to eat, to drink and look out over the awesome Kawuneechee Valley hundreds of feet below.

The first signs of an approaching storm broke their reverie. They packed away the remains of their meal and began to glide back down the way they came.

Going downhill and in the tracks they had just made for themselves made the trip back a breeze. En route, they were awed by the splendor of the Never Summer Range up above and the snow-capped Continental Divide to their east. Below them the Kawuneechee Valley spread out as it ran toward Shadow Mountain Lake and Lake Granby. Each man kept his own thoughts. But in many ways they were the same thoughts: wonderment that they survived the jungles of southeast Asia and been spared to see this glorious high-mountain scenery and to share these moments together.

But the weather is fickle up on the Never Summer Range. Sunny one minute, a mountain storm can form in moments and turn a pleasant, sun-lit outing into a blinding blizzard.

They still had a couple of miles to go before they reached the trail down to the Never Summer Ranch when a snowstorm hit them with 40-knot winds. They stowed their sunglasses and put on ski goggles. But the snow was in their faces with such power that their goggles became almost instantly caked with snow.

"Buck, I think we should stop and build a shelter," said Chuck. "We can't see three feet in front of us. Our old tracks are covered already. We could go over the edge."

"I think you're right," said Buck, "but at least we're getting a taste of what it must have been like to work up here building this ditch. It makes me understand how much your great-grandmother and grandmother must have suffered."

Shuffling up beside them, Lou said, "Look, I've got an idea. My cabin isn't far from here. I know a trail that leads down from a point just up ahead and it goes along the Park boundary right to my cabin. The trail runs through the trees and they'll help protect us from this fucking snow."

After a brief conference, it was decided to let Lou lead and to follow him down off the ditch. Jonathan, for his part, was curious about Lou's cabin and wondered if that was where he kept his stash of C-4.

Virtually ski tip to ski tail, they followed Lou through tall trees which, as Lou promised, protected them from the winds that were turning the bare places on the mountain into complete white-outs.

After an 800-foot descent, Lou made a sweeping turn to the right. About two hundred yards later, they came to a log cabin set in the depth of the forest. They skied to the lee side of the cabin and took off their skis expecting Lou to open the door of the cabin and invite them into its shelter.

"Stay here," said Lou. "I'll be right out with some blankets."

"Lou, what the hell do you mean 'stay here.'" said Buck. "We're bloody freezing and you say stay here?"

"Buck, my cabin's a mess. I don't want you guys to see it. First, I'll bring out the blankets. Then, I'll bring out some coffee and more brandy. The storm won't last long and we'll all go back down to our cars."

"But, Lou," said Chuck. "This is crazy. You've got a perfectly good cabin and we sure as hell aren't going to sit outside freezing our butts off. Move outta the way, Lou, we're coming in."

"Okay, Okay," said Lou. "But you guys are gonna think I've gone stark-raving mad. Well, maybe I was. Anyway, I'm getting over it."

After they shuffled inside, it took a moment for their eyes to adjust to the darkness. Jonathan was the first to recognize what Lou had been so reluctant for them to see.

"Lou! Have you lost your freaking mind?" exclaimed Jonathan.

Hanging by her neck from one of the cabin rafters was a remarkable likeness of Hanoi Jane. She was dressed in the same tan-colored North Vietnamese uniform she wore when she posed for the cameras astride a North Vietnamese anti-aircraft gun and when she visited the American POWs at the Hanoi Hilton. Even with most of her face covered by a pith helmet, it was obvious who she was supposed to be.

But her left arm was broken above the elbow and it hung at an unnatural angle from her body. Her right arm was broken in a compound fracture below the elbow. The compound fracture was gruesomely realistic.

The bone protruded through the flesh and was surrounded by a gangrenous-looking wound. The creator of the revolting sight, no doubt, Lou LeClerc, had even placed flies and maggots on the puffy, open wound.

"Lou," said Chuck, "that compound fracture is so realistic that it makes me want to puke. "How'd you do that?"

"I went to an Army surplus store and bought one of those moulage kits they use in basic training to teach first-aid," said Lou. "It's pretty good, isn't it?"

Buck felt Lou deserved a chance to explain. "Lou, I think you need to tell us why you felt the need to do all this to Hanoi Jane," said Buck.

"Well, as you know," said Lou. "after I was shot down in Laos, they took me to the Hanoi Hilton where they tried to get me to make tape recordings saying that Air America was nothing but a bunch of drug-running war criminals and baby killers. Of course, I refused and they beat the crap outta me. But they saved their worst treatment for the day when Hanoi Jane came to the Hanoi Hilton.

"You see, I used to be a big fan of hers. Of course, that was before she embraced communism and said that if the American people really understood communism, they'd be down on their knees begging for it. Anyway, I sort of lived the same kind of Bohemian life-style that she did when she was young and I thought she was cool.

"You mean group sex and drugs?" asked Roberto.

"No, I wasn't that far into her kind of life-style, but I sure drank a lot of booze and chased a few women."

"Okay, so why did you hang Hanoi Jane in effigy?" asked Jonathan, growing impatient.

"Well, it was like this," said Lou. "The guards made me look into a little peep hole so I got a look into the next room. There was Hanoi Jane all clean and nice, looking spiffy in her North Vietnamese uniform and making nice-nice with a bunch of North Vietnamese generals and, I suppose, diplomats.

"Anyway, they made sure that I understood that she was just a few feet away on the other side of that wall. Then, they told me that all I had to do was to sign a war-crimes confession and they would not only let me meet her but they would let me go back home with her to the States."

"You had a chance to come home and you didn't take it?" asked Roberto.

"In fluent Vietnamese, I told them to go fuck themselves," said Lou.

"Then, what happened?" asked Chuck Lee.

"Those motherfuckers broke my left arm so it stuck out at a funny angle just like Jane's up there. I still refused to sign their stupid documents, so they broke my right arm so bad the bone stuck out.

"I always told myself that if I survived and got home, I'd track that bitch down and break both of her arms and then kill her."

"But, of course, you didn't do that," said Buck.

"No, I decided the best I could do was break the arms on that mannequin and gussy it up with that moulage kit so it would look real realistic. By the way, don't ever doubt the deterrent effect of capital punishment. If it weren't for capital punishment, I'd be just one of thousands of Vietnam vets standing in a long, long line to kill that bitch," said Lou.

"So how did you survive those two broken arms?" asked Roberto.

"One of my fellow POWs had some emergency medical training. He splinted the simple fracture but you can still see today how I hold my left arm funny. While another POW held me down, he pulled my right arm until the bone slipped back inside and he cleaned the wound as best he could.

"But the wound was infected and my arm puffed up. So, he made a little tent out of mosquito netting and put my arm inside it. Then, he captured some of the flies that were all over the place and trapped them inside the little tent. The flies laid their eggs in the wound and that produced maggots. The maggots, bless their little squirmy hearts, ate the rotten flesh. In other words, the maggots cleaned the wound of the dead and dying flesh. I guess you've sunk pretty low when it takes a bunch of maggots to save your life. So, I thought putting the flies and maggots up there on Jane's arm would be a nice touch," said Lou.

"Lou, have you ever considered getting some counseling, some therapy?" asked Buck.

"Yeah, I knew I was crazier than a bedbug for awhile. But I figured hanging Hanoi Jane in effigy was pretty good therapy. So, sometimes, when I really get to feeling sorry for myself, I come up here to the cabin with a bottle of booze, give that mannequin a little push and just watch Hanoi Jane swinging back and forth from that rafter. When the booze is gone, I head back for town and sleep it off. The next morning, other than a headache, I'm just fine for several months.

"Well, now my secret is out. I suppose you guys are gonna report me?"

"Lou, I gotta ask you this," said Jonathan. "I know you don't like President Trimmer. Would you get this crazy with regard to him?"

"Shit no," said Jonathan. "The last thing the world needs is for some dummy to make a martyr out of that historically insignificant sack of shit. Jonathan, my boy, Trimmer would be safer in my hands than anybody's, even yours."

"Okay," said Buck, looking for closure. "No one is going to ever mention this again. We are still the same Vietnam buddies and we stick together. We stick together because we understand what happened over there. Lou, I can't tell you how sorry we all are that you had to undergo such torture. I suppose we are the only family you have and your family isn't going to let you down."

"Well, I thank you for that, Buck. Except for an ancient Aunt back in France, you guys are my family."

"Okay, guys," said Buck, "what we see here, we leave here. But I have to say, Lou, grotesque though she is, I suspect all of us get some vicarious satisfaction from seeing her hanging from that rafter. So, let's finish up the brandy or whatever that rot gut is you are serving, and head for our vehicles."

After an hour, the storm cleared and they went outside. Donning their skis, they followed Lou to a trail leading them back to the parking lot.

Still upset by what they had seen in Lou's cabin and Lou's tale of horror, they didn't have much to say to each other as they stowed their skis and snowshoes in their vehicles. Lou asked them to join him for a drink at Happy Jacques, but they all made excuses.

"We'll have to do this again on a better day," offered Jonathan.

Yes, they all agreed. They'd do it again on a better day.

Knowing Dolly already thought Lou was nuts, Buck and Jonathan decided to tell Dolly nothing about the hanging of Hanoi Jane. They would just say a fine time was had by all and, although worrisome, the snowstorm just added to the adventure. They enjoyed a fine evening meal with Dolly and, like so many mountain dwellers, turned in early.

The next morning, during breakfast, a black and white cruiser from the Grand County Sheriff's Department pulled up in front of Buck and Dolly's house. Out stepped an old friend, Sheriff Rod Cobble.

"Come in Rod," called Buck from the deck, "you're just in time for breakfast."

Shaking the snow from his boots in the entry foyer, Sheriff Cobble came upstairs to the living room.

"I heard you got a fellow law enforcement type staying with you and I thought I'd drop by and pay my respects," said John.

"If presidential protection is law enforcement, then we've got your man, Rod," said Buck. "Special Agent Jonathan Winslow, meet Sheriff Rod Cobble."

"How do you do," said Jonathan. "At some point, I would be needing to talk with you. So, maybe this is a good time, if you don't mind a few questions."

"Fire away," said the sheriff as he accepted a fresh cup of coffee from Dolly

"There is a possibility, and at this point, I have to stress that it is only a possibility that we've found a place in Grand County to use as a presidential fishing retreat. Specifically, we are looking at Camp Ouray. I'd like your assessment. From a security standpoint, would that give you any heartburn?"

"Actually, I would think it would be pretty easy to secure. Also, I think it would be a big boon for the county."

"How's that?"

"What you are proposing would pump big bucks into our local economy."

"From what I see, it looks like you've got lots of skiers spending those big bucks."

"That's true. But even though we get over a million skiers a year up here, many of those skiers are what we call 'brown-baggers' or 'day-skiers'. They load up their skis on their cars and come out of the Front Range cities bringing their brown-bag lunches, ski for the day and go back home.

"The big bucks in a ski resort business come from the so-called 'destination' skiers who spend five days or a week or more skiing. They have to have lodging, restaurant food, drinks in the bars, rental equipment and that sort of thing.

"You're close to Denver, and your local airport looks pretty good to me." said Jonathan.

"It's okay. In fact, Granby Airport had daily commuter service to Denver until airline deregulation came along and Rocky Mountain Airways couldn't make a go of it anymore. We'll probably see propjet service restored one of these years. Or, maybe small regional-jet service. But, in the meantime, we need to broaden our economic base.

"So, Mr. Winslow, if you look past the lift lines at Winter Park or Mary Jane or Silver Creek or Berthoud Pass during the holidays, our economy isn't all that great. It's almost completely based on tourism. If that goes south, we're hurting. When the economy goes down, crime goes up. To make matters worse Winter Park is owned by the City and County of Denver. We get their skiers, but Denver doesn't help us with law enforcement when their skiers misbehave."

"Please call me, Jonathan. But being owned by Denver, does that help or hurt?"

"It hurts. Denver never does anything to help the ski area yet Denver wants to get an annual royalty of about $2 million. Badly needed ski lifts and other improvements go begging. The ski area claims it doesn't even have enough money to regrade some of the flat terrain that irritates visitors who haven't learned which trails to use in order to avoid the flat spots.

"So, your presidential visit would be a real shot in the arm for our economy. The media alone would fill the motels in Granby and then some." said Cobble.

"Of course, whether or not we establish a presidential fishing retreat isn't decided on the basis of what it will do for the local economy," said Jonathan. "Number one is security. Number two is its recreational value. And, to be candid, number three is a place that makes the press corps happy."

"Buck and Dolly and I were thinking of making another trip over to Camp Ouray to look around some more," said Jonathan. "Would you like to come along?"

"Yes, I'd like that; but I have other work to do. Due to the holidays, we're short-handed so I've got to drive on out to the ranger station at Monarch Lake. That's about ten miles east of here. The phone's out. Probably a marmot chewed through the line. The ranger station isn't staffed in winter; however, there's a monitor on the line. If the line is cut, a red light goes on at my office. Then, a patrol has to go see if someone has broken into the ranger hut and done something to the phone. If that's not it, then it's probably just animal damage to the line and we notify the phone company. Well, it was nice meeting you, Jonathan. I hope we'll be working together on this project."

"Same here. Say, speaking of lights. I notice every time Buck and Dolly drive me across the Lake Granby High Dam there's this light right by the spillway that seems to stay on day and night. It's on that concrete tower building that sticks up out of the dam. What's that?"

"Oh, that light stays on all the time. It shines down on the entrance to the elevator building. They have an elevator they use to go down and adjust the amount of water they let flow through a big pipe under the dam. The light and the elevator are powered and controlled from across the lake at the Lake Granby Pump Plant. You see, by law, they have to let out enough water to keep the fish alive downstream and a certain amount of water that's committed to ranchers. After the water gets through the Grand Canyon and Lake Mead, some of it flows all the way to the Sea of Cortez and even to San Diego and Los Angeles," said Cobble.

"Look, I'll walk you out to your cruiser," said Jonathan. "I'm sure you understand the need not to discuss this presidential fishing retreat business with anyone for the time being."

"No problem. I'll keep this to myself. But do you know what time of year this might take place?"

"Yes, but the White House is not ready to announce that either. Rest assured, we'll let you know in advance of the public announcement."

"Fair enough. Well, enjoy the rest of your stay," said Sheriff Cobble as he drove off toward Monarch Lake.

CHAPTER SIX

Dolly Madison's maiden name was Melissa Rennie. She was descended from a long line of Christian missionaries to China. Her great-grandfather founded Rennie's Mill in the New Territories portion in the British Crown Colony of Hong Kong.

She acquired the nickname, Dolly, in her mid-20s when she married Lieutenant Colonel James Buckley "Buck" Madison, USA. Actually, she thought Melissa Madison sounded rather nice; however, the wives of the other officers decided to call her "Dolly" and it stuck. Although she knew the wife of President James Madison spelled her name Dolley, Melissa felt too junior to correct them and so Dolly it was.

In February of 1948, Melissa was delivered inside a Presbyterian mission with the help of a Chinese mid-wife who then became her Amah. Her Amah, so accustomed to the brown eyes and black hair of Chinese babies, took great delight in Melissa's blue eyes and golden-blond hair. She was even more delighted when Melissa's eye color not only stayed blue but got even bluer as she grew older.

Meanwhile, Melissa's parents lived in constant terror of the Red Chinese. At first, the forces of Chairman Mao left them alone; primarily, because the mission produced a surplus of badly-needed food.

W. Pell Huntington, an old family friend, worked for Colonel William Donovan's Office of Strategic Services during the war and stayed on to work for the just-formed Central Intelligence Agency. His office was in the American consulate in Canton. One hot, dusty August day Mr. Huntington burst into the Rev. Rennie's small manse to announce that all non-Chinese in the area should flee for their lives.

The Reverend James Rennie refused to abandon his flock; however, he entrusted his wife and daughter to the care of Mr. Huntington who offered to deliver them to the safety of the British Crown Colony; specifically, to Rennie's Mill Mission.

Shortly after Melissa and her mother were safely on their way to Hong Kong with the CIA operative, Rev. Rennie stood in the doorway of his tiny church to meet Mao's advance elements. Without ceremony, they dragged the pastor down the steps, herded his congregation in a hollow-square formation, ordered them to watch and then beheaded the Rev. James Rennie. Then, to make whatever point they were trying to make or, perhaps, just for the hell of it, they proceeded to torture, rape and murder the rest of his flock. One of the first to die was Melissa's old Amah who was attending a woman about to give birth and had refused the offer to accompany Melissa and her mother to Hong Kong.

When she was old enough to understand, Melissa's mother described the events surrounding her father's death and the death of her beloved Amah. While Melissa never lost her love for the Chinese people, she grew up with a burning hatred of communism and the Red Chinese regime.

She and her mother lived and worked at Rennie's Mill Mission while Melissa was growing up. She learned to speak several Chinese dialects flawlessly and received excellent training in mathematics and Chinese history from the dozens of the Chinese intellectuals who passed through Rennie's Mill Mission on their way to freedom. At age 17, Melissa won both an academic and an athletic scholarship to Wellesley.

Although intellectually gifted, Melissa was also interested in sports and especially in a dashing, young Royal Cavalry officer who had been posted to the Hong Kong Royal Constabulary. Thanks to the efficiency of the Chinese members of the Royal Constabulary, the British officers had a great deal of time on their hands.

Some drank, some chased women, some did both. But some were keen on sports. A good way to structure time in Hong Kong was to practice for the Military Pentathlon and, if good enough at all of the required five sports, try out for the Royal Olympic Team.

Leftenant Anthony Holmes Hall met Miss Melissa Rennie at one of the many gala balls staged by the ladies of the British Crown Colony. When Melissa learned the military pentathlon included horseback riding, Leftenant Anthony Holmes Hall won an ardent admirer.

Leftenant Hall was also taken with the tall, willowy, blue-eyed blond who kept seeking him out at various diplomatic receptions and telling him about her love for horses.

Soon, Melissa was invited over to the equestrian ring to watch Leftenant Hall put his horse through its paces. In time, Melissa saw Leftenant Hall practice all of skills required for his Olympic event.

In fact, Melissa got to try all five of the military pentathlon sports. While she liked them all and was better than average at all five, shooting became her favorite. In fact, she was a better shot than Tony Hall and any of his messmates who were foolish enough to risk their male egos against her on the marksmanship range. Some of them, but not Leftenant Hall, were happy when Wellesley summoned Melissa to be a member of its marksmanship team.

While at Wellesley, Melissa met Jonathan Winslow at an inter-collegiate marksmanship meet. Jonathan was a member of the Harvard rifle team. Although the two institutions of higher learning are separate, they share some facilities and the rifle range was one of them.

Long before the Boylston Street Bridge became known as the "Love Story" bridge, Melissa and Jonathan would cross it hand-in-hand en route to the rifle range located down in the bowels of the football stadium.

Jonathan, the scion of a wealthy New England family with roots stretching back to the *Mayflower*, yearned to go to sea like some of his

Yankee ancestors. But, ever the dutiful son, Jonathan accepted the family decree that his place was at Harvard and not at the U.S. Naval Academy. Yet Jonathan, his Harvard degree in hand, got his chance for foreign adventure because of the Vietnam War. Unlike so many of the Ivy League college students who found one way or another to avoid service in Vietnam, Jonathan answered an inner call to duty. Because the Army would guarantee him attendance at Officer Candidate School and airborne training at the U.S. Army Infantry School at Ft. Benning, Georgia, Jonathan enlisted in the U.S. Army.

It was a tearful farewell. They promised to write every day. Although the temptation to send Jonathan off with a night of sex to remember her by was strong, the preacher's daughter rejected that notion. If they were to be married someday, the test of time and Vietnam should serve them well. It just didn't work out that way.

Because of her hatred for the Red Chinese and her flawless Chinese language skills, Melissa was an easy recruitment for the Central Intelligence Agency. After initial training at "the farm," followed by an assignment to CIA headquarters in Langley, Virginia, Melissa was posted to the Hong Kong Forward Operating Base or FOB where her language abilities proved invaluable to the station chief and his case officers. With each promotion came another tour of duty at CIA headquarters followed by another posting to the Hong Kong FOB. Each time she returned for another tour at CIA headquarters, Melissa would enroll in night classes. First, came a master's degree from The George Washington University in psychology and, finally, a Ph.D. from Georgetown University in international relations.

Melissa loved the Hong Kong assignments because she could live with her mother at the mission. But then, her mother contracted tuberculosis from one of the refugees and died after a lengthy illness. Heartbroken, Melissa asked to return to Langley where, as chance would have it, she met Buck Madison.

Melissa was in the cafeteria when she noticed a handsome, brown-eyed, black-haired man of about 30 ahead of her in line. He was struggling to separate U.S. coins from a handful of German Marks.

"Here, let me pay," she said, although surprised by her boldness. The man had long, but clean, hair hanging over the collar of what was, obviously, a business suit cut in the pinch-back European style of the time. His shiny, black shoes had that pointed-toed European look so, when he turned to thank her, she expected him to speak German or French. Instead, she heard the flat speech of a mid-westerner with just the slightest hint of a southern drawl.

"Much obliged," said the stranger as he nodded them toward an empty table. "I'm Buck Madison. What's your name?"

"Melissa Rennie. What brings you to the puzzle palace?"

"Oh, I'm just Christmas help. Now and then they bring me back from Europe just so I can experience the dreadful taste of American beer."

"How long do you have to put up with being a second-class citizen," said Melissa as she deposited her spent tea bag in a saucer.

"Like everything around here, Miss Rennie, that's classified; however, if you promise to come to Germany, I'll give you the Cook's tour during which I'll reveal all my secrets." *She didn't say she wasn't a Miss*, he noted.

"I've never been to Europe. China's my specialty. I suppose you speak German?

"Thanks to the Army Language School and a few years of actual practice, I get along."

"I'm that way with Chinese. Born near Canton. Actually, thanks to my Amah, Chinese is my first language."

"Let's both leave the service and open a German-Chinese restaurant," he suggested.

"No one would eat there."

"Why?"

"Because after an hour, you're hungry for power."

"I knew you were going to say that."

"You're a pretty good straight man."

"Speaking of being straight, I have to tell you I'm recently divorced and I've promised myself to avoid entangling alliances until a year has gone by."

"Well, you certainly flatter yourself by implying that I might set my cap for you. But I'll grant that you are certainly up front. Why a year?"

"People do funny things on the rebound. Besides, I'm due for another all-expenses-paid-trip to Vietnam that will keep me off the streets for a year."

"Did the war break up your marriage?" asked Melissa.

"Pretty much. I was for it. She was against it. She used to write me letters telling me the war was stupid and I was stupid for going to Vietnam and for being in the Army."

"Sounds like you didn't get much support at a time when you really needed emotional help from the home front."

"You have a gift for understatement."

"Children?"

"Three. And, yes, I miss them terribly. Misfortunes of war. Except for the youngest, bless his heart, I never hear from them. But I think of them everyday. Pray for them every night."

"So, you're a religious person?"

"My real job requires me to spend a lot of time in foxholes. And, you know what they say. So, I guess that makes me a true believer. Almost as much as a Roman Catholic Marine."

"I'm glad to hear that. My parents were Presbyterian missionaries. I grew up in the church. But now that you've declared yourself off-limits for a year, does that mean you are withdrawing the invitation for a Cook's tour of Germany?"

"The invitation's is still good unless, of course, I find out tomorrow that the Company is done with me for now and is going to let Infantry Branch have its way with me."

"And, when will you know that?"

"Like I said, I'm just Christmas help. The folks upstairs can terminate me at any time."

"Hopefully, not with extreme prejudice."

"You've been reading too much Ian Fleming."

"So, what do you do when you are back in the Army?"

"I'll confess to being a mere paratrooper."

"One of those people who jump out of perfectly good airplanes?"

"Guilty. But I try to remember to always take my parachute along."

"Are you a 007?"

"Ian Fleming again. The 007 myth dies hard. Let's just say those ivy-league types up on the top floor don't like to do their own heavy lifting. They prefer for the armed services do it."

"*Mokkrie dela?*"

"There you go again. Do you speak Russian as well?"

"No, but everyone knows that means 'wet affairs.'"

"Tell you what, Miss Rennie, I'll try to keep my powder and anything else you wish dry until the Company is done with me."

"Are you with FOB Berlin?"

"Actually, I make it a point to never go anywhere near our forward operating bases. They are full of spies."

"A lone eagle?"

"You don't happen to work for James Jesus Angleton do you?" asked Buck. "Trying to see if I'm a security risk?"

"Heavens no. I just find it fascinating that you can walk in and out of here dressed like a German businessman and no one seems to care. And, if you don't mind my asking, did you ever wear a mustache?" asked Melissa.

"You mean a 'beard' in the sense we spooks use that word as a term of art?"

"No, silly. I wasn't asking if you wore a disguise. I was just thinking that a mustache would make you look a lot like a slightly shorter version of the actor, Tom Selleck."

"Never heard of him," said Buck. "But I did have a mustache. I shaved it off during the plane ride back here to the Land of the Round Doorknob."

"Why'd you do that?"

"The Army isn't wild about facial hair. If they reassign me to the Infantry tomorrow, I don't want to look like some hippie."

"Well, I still say it's amazing that you can walk around inside here looking like a Kraut. Not that our security here is that great, anyway."

"I thought Langley was the Mecca of internal security, semi-annual polygraphs and all that."

"Now, you're the one who's been reading too many spy novels. All the guys in the 'club' upstairs, the ones who have first names that sound like last names, they think they are too good to be polygraphed and some of them are out to discredit people like Mr. Angleton who thinks we have a mole and I wouldn't be surprised if we did."

"Last names for first names? Give me an example."

"Aldrich Ames for one."

"Don't know him."

"You haven't missed anything. He's a drunk. He tried to pinch me on the behind and I slapped him. Anyway, let's stop talking shop and talk about you."

"Okay. Like I say, I'm only Christmas-help. The guys in the club, as you call them, they think folks like me are a pain in the rear because we don't check with them before drawing every breath. Actually, they call us: specialized assets. Once we've done whatever it was they wanted done, they send us back to the Army or the Marines wherever we came from."

"What was Vietnam like?"

"During my first tour, I was a company commander with the 1st Air Cavalry Division. Professionally, it was very satisfying."

"Getting to kill people?"

"No, leading some very fine young men into combat and getting none of them killed. That was the reward for years of training. We followed the dictum of General George Patton: 'Don't go out there and die for your country. Instead, help those bastards to die for theirs.' We helped a lot of them."

"I have a close friend from college who was with the 1st Air Cavalry Division. We used to write to each other but then I guess he found someone else."

"What was his name?"

"Jonathan Winslow."

"If you are talking about Jonathan Winslow of the blue-blood, New England Winslow family, Jonathan was one of my platoon leaders. A really fine officer."

"Do you know where he is now?"

"Ft. Benning, Georgia, last I heard."

Shifting a bit in her chair, Melissa asked, "Is he married?"

"Yes. He went on R&R to Hong Kong where his brother was posted as a foreign service officer. Jonathan met a Chinese gal who worked with his brother. Jasmine is her name. Evidently, from a very good family. Anyway, they got married and I think they're still down in Georgia."

"I see."

"Does that hurt?"

"Well, I wouldn't say it feels good. But it explains why he stopped writing to me."

"Did you love him?"

"I guess you could say we were college sweethearts. I know that sounds terribly old-fashioned. I certainly cared a lot for him when we were in college. It's been so long. You forget. I guess I'm just hurt that he didn't tell me what was going on."

"War makes people do strange things. By the time Jonathan was half way through his tour he had seen some pretty rough action. When he got to Hong Kong, I think it was a case of grab for the gusto and Jasmine grabbed back and neither of them would let go. I hope you haven't been sitting on the shelf all this time."

"No. I go out with some guys within the intelligence community here. And there's a cute Swiss banker in Hong Kong. But nothing serious either place."

"I can't imagine a Swiss banker being cute."

"Come to think of it, cute doesn't fit. How about less serious than most Swiss?"

"I'll buy that."

"That's enough about moi. Can we win in Vietnam?" asked Melissa.

"We could have. Between 1966 and right through TET of 1968, we could have won. We had them on the ropes. Especially after we wiped out the Viet Cong as an effective fighting force during TET of 1968. But Johnson and McNamara tied our hands, stopped the bombing and gave Charlie a chance to catch his breath. Now, it's too late. The major media have eroded public support to the point we're just looking for a face-saving way out."

"Even so, you're still going back?"

"I took an oath. I'm Regular Army. It's my profession. Would you have me run to Canada or Sweden or get a student deferment to Oxford or Cambridge?"

"No. I just don't like to think about your being hurt or killed."

"I don't either. But I may be safer back in the 1st Cav."

"Why's that?"

"My partner and I just completed a highly successful operation against the East German Intelligence Service. It made them rather angry. So angry they took some of their senior officers out into a court-yard and, as you call it, terminated them with extreme prejudice. Last week, the East Germans discovered they shot the wrong people. So now, they are after my partner and me. That's why we're back here for reassignment or whatever and another reason why I canned the mustache."

"Pulled back to a safe haven?"

"You could call it that. Anyway, today or maybe tomorrow, those REMFs upstairs will decide what to do with us."

"What's a REMF?"

"My, you have led a sheltered life. RE stands for rear-echelon. I'll let you figure out the rest."

"Oh."

"I'm sorry I made you blush. REMF is just military slang for those who send the rest of us out into harm's way."

"It's crude, but the initialism is apt."

"We, who may be about to die, think so."

"Buck, please don't say that."

"Okay. So, do you know how long you'll be around this puzzle palace?"

"Another 24 months and then back to Hong Kong."

"May I have your permission to come back and look you up after whatever it is they decide I'm going to be doing?"

"I'd like that."

The next day the Company terminated Buck's CIA assignment with a very private medal ceremony in the DCI's office. The Director shook his hand and asked Buck to remain on a roster of "specialized assets" for possible later recall. Buck did not object.

The following day, Buck reported to the Infantry Branch Assignment Office across the Potomac River at Ft. McNair. Because Buck was with U.S. troops during his first Vietnam tour, his assignment officer, AKA "flesh merchant," at Infantry Branch, wanted Buck to be an advisor to the South Vietnamese during his second tour. He said it would enhance Buck's chances of promotion.

Buck asked to take a bathroom break, went to a pay phone and called an old mentor—a major general who had just returned to the States after commanding the 1st Air Cavalry Division during the relief of the Marines at Khe Sanh. The general told him to wait 20 minutes and then return to his assignment officer.

Once the allotted time expired, Buck returned to his "flesh merchant" and was told Infantry Branch had just decided his prior experience in airmobile operations was needed, after all, back in the 1st Air Cavalry Division. His assignment officer explained that Buck's career needs must give way to the greater good of the Army. Doing his best to keep a straight face, Buck said he understood perfectly. He only asked for a two-week leave to visit his parents prior to departure.

Prior to boarding a military transport at Travis Air Force Base near San Francisco, Buck sent Miss Melissa Rennie a post card giving his new A.P.O. address and expressing the hope that she would write to him. She did.

CHAPTER SEVEN

January

Vieques Island east of Puerto Rico

Under the dilapidated thatched roof of a tropical building that had seen far better days, Fidel Castro made a slight bow to his guests and then motioned for them to take their seats around a large, square table covered with a stained, burlap tablecloth. The Cuban president's place was marked with a miniature Cuban flag.

To Fidel's left sat the venerable Son Yat Soo, head of foreign intelligence for the Peoples Republic of China. To Fidel's right sat Muhammar Gobanifar, head of foreign intelligence for Iran. Sitting directly across the table was Tarik Hussein, one of Saddam Hussein's closest relatives and the head of the Iraqi Central Intelligence Service. A portable, simultaneous-translation system—a relic of the time when Cuba received almost $6 billion a year from the USSR and could afford such fine East German electronic devices—connected all the conferees.

Remaining seated, and holding an unlighted cigar in his hand, an aging—and clearly ailing—Fidel Castro began:

"Gentlemen, I wish to thank you for coming to Vieques Island for this meeting. While you know, in general terms, the purpose of our meeting, let me explain why I had you transported from Havana by boat to gather here on Vieques Island which, as you can see, is not the most glamorous small island in the Caribbean.

"I chose Vieques Island for two reasons: First, because we can meet in secrecy in this part of the island; and secondly, because this island is symbolic of the inevitable decline of what you, Comrade Gobanifar, call the Great Satan and what we Cubans call the Yanqui Devil.

"For too many years, Vieques Island has been used by the American armed forces as a gunnery range. Their naval guns, their artillery pieces and their fighter-bombers pounded this island into rubble. But President Jimmy Carter, in one of his naive moves to try to win public approval, placed a number of restrictions on its use by the American military. As a result, the island has been used less and less as the punching bag for the U.S. Navy in the Caribbean. In fact, the Americanos became so unfamiliar with the island that they recently made a map-reading error and dropped a bomb that killed an innocent civilian. Naturally, my agents used this incident to pressure President Trimmer into giving complete control of Vieques back to the Puerto Rican people. As usual, we expect President Trimmer to sacrifice the best interests of the American military on the altar of public opinion.

"This building is one of those abandoned by the Americanos. Vieques is virtually uninhabited right now and this particular portion of the island is totally deserted. Otherwise, we would not be here this morning. But, it gives me great pleasure to meet here on American soil.

"I love this little island because it will represent the first piece of land in this hemisphere to be given back by the Americans to its rightful owners. Like the give-back of the Panama Canal, another Jimmy Carter idea, I see Vieques as just the precursor of much more land to come."

Mention of the Panama Canal drew a smile from Comrade Soo who had just concluded an arrangement with the Government of Panama whereby the locks and lakes of Panama Canal would be operated by a communist Chinese engineering company. If war broke out between the People's Republic of China and the United States, the Panama Canal would be rendered useless by the Chinese operating company and the United States would have to fight the war with whatever naval forces it had in the Pacific. Naval reinforcements from the Atlantic Ocean would be a long time in coming, if at all.

"But, I did not bring you here just so I could talk about Yanqui Imperialism," Fidel continued. "We are gathered here for two purposes:

First, for you to receive a detailed briefing on our next strike against the United States; and second, for us to finalize your financial contributions toward this enterprise.

"As you are aware, the collapse of the Soviet Union has had a substantial, negative impact on my country's balance of trade. For that reason, we are unable to finance this operation entirely by ourselves. Yet, what we bring to the table is worth far more than gold or oil. We bring the leadership, the expertise and the ingenuity needed to strike devastating blows against both the United States and Russia.

"In the briefing you are about to receive, a person very personally close to me and whom I have hand-picked to lead these attacks will tell you how we intend to carry out this mission. But let me give just a brief overview of what we intend to do:

"We will disrupt the major cable and fiber-optic communications links between the eastern and western United States.

"We will destroy a major water-diversion system that takes the rain and snow-melt waters from the western slope of the Rocky Mountains and diverts them to the cities and farms on what the Yanquis call, The Great Plains.

"But, our most important objective is the simultaneous assassination of the American and Russian Presidents," said Fidel stabbing the air with his cigar for emphasis.

Fidel smiled to himself as he saw the mouth of the supposedly inscrutable Chinese representative fall open. From the collective body language of his guests, it was obvious the representatives of Iran, Iraq and Red China were stunned by his last statement.

Son Yat Soo was the first to recover. "With all due respect President Castro," said the Chinese, "my government must have more precise knowledge of just how you plan to accomplish such ambitious projects before I could possibly turn over to you the vast sum of money you have asked us to bring to this meeting. Moreover, at some point, I must ask you to explain your rationale for wanting to assassinate President James Robert Trimmer. We have invested huge sums in the Trimmer apparat and gained considerable missile technology and trade concessions as a result. We would not like to see our investments go to waste."

"Totally understandable, Comrade Soo. That is why I now present to you a man you shall only know as Raoul. But I can tell you this about Raoul, he is an assassin without peer. But if I recounted his long string of successes, you could deduce both his identity and, perhaps, his previous clients. That is neither prudent nor necessary for our purposes.

"Therefore, even at the risk of appearing overly dramatic, I have asked Comrade Raoul to wear a hood while he speaks to you. This is for your protection as well as Raoul's because, in the unlikely event that this operation goes wrong, your governments will need to be able to make the claim of plausible denial," said Fidel.

Fidel signaled to one his bodyguards. With a Latino flare, the guard swept back a black curtain revealing a man, his face hidden by a black hood, standing about six feet tall and weighing a trim two hundred pounds. His age could not be detected, but some small dark spots on the backs of his hands suggested he was of middle age. He was so light-skinned he could pass for White. His posture and the self-assured way he swept into the room suggested the man possessed great physical strength and poise.

Donning a headset over his hood and picking up his microphone, he began:

"Good morning, Comrade Fidel. Good morning, gentlemen. My name is Raoul and here, with your generous support, is what is about to befall the Great Satan:

"Actually, since his impeachment by the U.S. House of Representatives and his resulting diminished capacity to govern, our main interest has been the assassination of President Trimmer; however, his security is so tight in and around the White House that we have been looking at alternative venues.

"For several months, I have been carrying out my third reconnaissance of a remote region of Colorado where I discovered some unprotected targets that are tailor-made for a crippling strike against the United States. Allow me to deal with these targets first and then I'll get back to how we plan to assassinate Presidents Trimmer and Popov.

"Recently, I discovered two major tunnels running underneath the Rocky Mountains. Both of these tunnels lie within a political subdivision called: Grand County. These tunnels are used to divert millions of liters of water from the west side of the Rocky Mountains to the east side of the Rocky Mountains. The farms, factories and the people who live within the giant Denver Metroplex on the east side of the American Continental Divide are almost totally dependent on this water.

"But these tunnels have another function which is relatively unknown. They are also the conduits for the major communications cables between the eastern and western United States.

"Good timing and good fortune always play a part in any enterprise. We have both.

"Recently, the Cuban Intelligence Directorate learned the President of the United States plans to spend time in the late summer at a fishing retreat located along the Colorado River. The location of this retreat facility is only six kilometers downstream from a major, high-mountain dam called the Lake Granby High Dam.

"Luck favors those with a just cause and we think we have encountered another bit of good fortune. Our intelligence directorate has also learned the new Russian President, Sergei Popov, has been invited to join the American President at this fishing retreat for the American Labor Day celebration.

"By bursting what is known as the Lake Granby High Dam, both presidents and all their toadying staff members will be drowned by a tidal wave of water. And, gentlemen, this is the best part, we can assassinate both presidents without blame being attached to you or to us.

"The blame for their deaths will be placed upon some unwitting Americans who are sometimes called the Rangeland Rebels. These people are associated with what is known as the Sagebrush Rebellion or, more recently known as the Militia Movement.

Pausing for dramatic effect, Raoul saw skeptical looks on the faces of the foreign guests.

"Gentlemen, I realize your time with us is short. But, as major investors in this operation, you deserve a detailed description of all of our targets and we want to let you see how their simultaneous destruction provides a cover for the twin assassinations.

"Our first target is called: The Grand Ditch. Physically, it is not the most important of our four targets; however, it is of immense psychological and symbolic importance, which I think Comrade Soo, will readily understand.

"Just west of the small town of Grand Lake and up into what is called the Never Summer Mountain Range at an elevation of 10,200 feet or about 3,100 meters above sea level, is what appears to be a long, thin scar across an entire mountain range.

"That scar is actually a water-diversion ditch some ten meters wide and two meters deep carved into the side of that mountain range. The Grand Ditch is almost 24 kilometers long and is used to drain the snowmelt and rain coming down the slopes of the Never Summer Range so the waters flow down onto the eastern plains of Colorado where they are used for agricultural purposes and for urban expansion.

"The Grand Ditch project was the first theft of water from the citizens of Grand County. It was begun in 1892 and was accomplished with the blood and sweat of, and I apologize for this term, Comrade Soo, Oriental 'coolies.' These oppressed Orientals worked year-round in freezing cold and blazing heat at an elevation over 3,000 meters above sea level with only hand tools to create The Grand Ditch. At any given time, hundreds of Orientals suffered under the harsh hands of Anglo engineers. Actually, the engineers were Swedish. But they were oppressive Whites just the same."

"Comrade, Raoul, a question if I may?" interrupted Comrade Soo.

"Certainly, Comrade."

"You say 'Orientals' as if you are aren't sure if the workers were Chinese or Japanese."

"You are very discerning, Comrade Soo," said Raoul. "To tell the truth, we are not sure. Our research has produced some pay records from the Land and Water Company of Fort Collins showing payments of 22 and one-half cents per hour to persons with names such as: Hyaski, Hokasana, Kamatami and Taito, for example."

"Those are all Japanese names," said Soo.

"Yes, but we feel there must have been some Chinese workers as well because some of the other pay records show dollar payments to groups or 'companies' of 'Orientals.' Regrettably, Caucasians tend to see no distinction between Chinese, Japanese or other peoples indigenous to eastern Asia," said Raoul.

"Yes, such callous disregard for ethnic distinctions reflects the cultural imperialism of the White Race," commented Soo. "The racist Whites say we all look alike."

Sensing he was about to make a sale, Raoul pressed on, "Hundreds of these poor workers died from cold, heat, and exhaustion. All for 22 and one-half cents per hour minus 25 cents for each meal. Much of what they earned had to be paid back for food. So, Comrade Soo, part of our purpose in rendering The Grand Ditch useless is to make manifest our socialist solidarity with the oppressed workers of the world, both past and present."

"Were there any women up on this Grand Ditch?" asked Comrade Soo.

"Yes," replied Raoul. "I'm afraid the ancient Tongs and War Lords who sold these people into virtual slavery to build The Grand Ditch also sent along some women who, shall we say, provided some creature comforts for the workers.

"Yet, these high-altitude brothels were not unique. Just down below The Grand Ditch, at a place called Lulu City, the German, Irish, and Scandinavian gold and silver miners had their own brothels and saloons.

"But the racist Whites could not even get along with each other. After one of their drunken shoot-outs, the Germans were driven out of Lulu City to a place the other Whites, in their usual lack of cultural sophistication, called: Dutch Town. Probably, because they couldn't pronounce *Deutsch*."

"One of the great gifts from Chairman Mao was the destruction of the Tongs," interrupted Son Yat Soo. "And, under our Glorious Revolution, the status of women has improved greatly."

Although Raoul knew Mr. Soo's claim was pure Red Chinese propaganda, he continued smoothly:

"The overall water diversion system we intend to destroy is called the Colorado River-Big Thompson River Project. At the core of the Colorado River portion of the project is a chain of three lakes. The second theft of the water from these simple, mountain people begins when water is collected from some minor reservoirs and pumped up into a huge reservoir known as Lake Granby. From Lake Granby, the water is pumped uphill into another reservoir called: Shadow Mountain Lake. Shadow Mountain Lake is at the same elevation as the third lake in the chain called: Grand Lake. So, the water flows from Shadow Mountain Lake into Grand Lake by gravity.

"It is, however, from Grand Lake that the water is actually stolen when it flows down a tunnel that we will destroy. The tunnel leads from Grand Lake down underneath the Continental Divide to the town of Estes Park. It is called: the Adams Tunnel. It is some 20 kilometers long and took four years to construct. We can render all that time and expense worthless in an instant.

"Down below Estes Park are five hydro-electric plants that depend on these stolen waters to produce electricity. No water, no electricity. Already the metropolitan Front Range area of Colorado suffers from a lack of electrical power. When the temperature gets hot, power outages and what the Americanos call 'brown-outs' are common.

"But now let me turn to the second tunnel under the Continental Divide that is marked for destruction. It is almost 10 kilometers long and it is called the Moffat Tunnel. Its western portal is near the town of Winter Park, Colorado. Actually, there are two tunnels running side-by-side. One tunnel carries a high volume of passenger, coal and freight train traffic and there is even a train just for skiers that runs on weekends during the ski season. The adjacent water-diversion tunnel steals additional water out of Grand County and sends it downhill to Denver where it is used for factories, farms, lawns, golf courses and to promote urban sprawl.

"Some of this water is even wasted by automatic water sprinkler systems which are left running even when it is raining. Although it may seem to be a minor point, such waste angers many of the long-time residents of Grand County. This is especially so during dry periods when the theft of the waters out of Lake Granby can become so great that the lake is drawn down to the point that it becomes much less attractive to tourists, fisherman and boaters.

"Turning now to Lake Granby, we must destroy two targets there. As I explained earlier, the destruction of the Lake Granby High Dam means the deaths of both presidents. But almost as important will be the destruction of the Lake Granby Pump Plant which is the central engine of this entire water-diversion project. (See: *www.thegrandconspiracy.com*)

"The Lake Granby Pump Plant raises the waters which have been collected from the Fraser and lower Colorado Rivers into Lake Granby and then pumps them up into Shadow Mountain Lake and on through

Grand Lake into the Adams Tunnel. Without the Lake Granby Pump Plant, the entire water-diversion system is worthless.

"With the destruction of the Lake Granby Pump Plant, the Adams Tunnel, the Moffat Tunnel, The Grand Ditch and the Lake Granby High Dam, Denver and all the cities along the Front Range of Colorado will lose a major portion of their electrical power and water. To repair damage of this magnitude will take decades. Indeed, some of it may be impossible to repair.

"Urban growth from the town of Ft. Collins in the north to Denver in the south will come to a halt. The currently overheated economy will collapse. The capitalist speculators who have invested large sums of money in anticipation of even more growth will be ruined. Like a shock wave radiating out of the epi-center of an earthquake, fear and panic will sweep outward until it reaches both coasts of the United States.

"Equally devastating, but of a shorter term duration, will be the severing of the communications cable and fiber-optic cables that run through the Adams and Moffat Tunnels. An electric power and communications trunk as thick as your thigh runs through the Adams Tunnel. At the Moffat Tunnel, both MCI and Qwest, two of America's largest telephone service providers, just spent huge sums to run their lines through the railroad side of that tunnel. The severing of the communications between the eastern and western United States is just one example of the havoc we will cause," said Raoul.

"Pardon me, Senor Raoul," interrupted Mr. Gobanifar, "but I fail to see how you will be able to get some of the people living in the Grand County—these rangeland rebels, as you call them—to commit such acts of destruction."

"The rangeland rebels or militia, if you will, will be happy to stop the diversion of their precious waters away from their county," said Raoul. "But you are absolutely correct. They would never be party to the destruction of facilities that help them retain their water.

"And, that is the key distinction which must be understood. The locals love the lakes and dams that retain their precious water. They just hate the tunnels, ditches and pump plants that steal their water away from them," said Raoul.

"Then how," asked Gobanifar," are you going to get the local range-land rebels to destroy the Lake Granby High Dam?"

"The locals we recruit are not going to destroy the Lake Granby High Dam because that would be the last thing they would want to see happen. Thus, the destruction of the Lake Granby High Dam will be carried out entirely by my team and me.

"In fact, the level of participation of local recruits in the destruction of the two tunnels, the pump plant and The Grand Ditch will be rather limited. Their involvement will be just enough for them to be blamed but not enough so my teams and I lose control of the operations.

"Forgive me for another question," asked Gobanifar, "but why will the local militia be blamed for the destruction of the Lake Granby High Dam when, as you say, it is not in their best interest to do so?"

"Amidst all the chaos and destruction, the Americano authorities will conclude anyone crazy enough to destroy the two tunnels, a huge pump plant and The Grand Ditch would also be crazy enough to destroy the Lake Granby High Dam as well. I have only to remind you of the bombing of the Federal Building in Oklahoma City, Oklahoma, to prove my point. Or, just look at the Columbine High School massacre in Littleton, Colorado. Obviously, some Americans are irrational and violent. Combine that with the kind of violent swill being churned out of that sewer they call Hollywood and the world is willing to believe virtually anything about Americans and violence."

"Yes, but would these local rebels participate in the deaths of their fellow citizens?" asked Tarik Hussein.

"No, Mr. Hussein, they would not," replied Raoul. "That is precisely why we will design the attacks in which these local rebels will participate in such a way that they will think there is no possibility of the loss of human life," said Raoul.

"Yes, but what if these local militia are caught and decide to confess their crimes?" asked Comrade Soo.

"Very simple. The local militia will not be caught. They will not be forced to talk. Why? Because they will be dead. My men will kill all of the locals we trick into helping us. The bodies of the rangeland rebels will be found in the rubble of their targets. Dead men don't talk," said Raoul.

"But what makes you so certain you can actually recruit enough local militia to perform all these complicated tasks," asked Tarik Hussein.

"Their dislike for government, in general, and their disgust with the administration of President Trimmer, in particular, are well known. And even those who want no part of the militia movement have no great love for the government. Many of these mountain people are war veterans who have no respect for the incumbent American president. His leadership of anti-American demonstrations on foreign soil during the Vietnam War they see as not just draft-dodging, but as treason.

"And, let me add, they are not only furious about the theft of their water, they are angry about it being used to generate electricity for the Front Range cities," said Raoul.

"But why," asked Gobanifar, "do they care about the electricity? Once the water is stolen, it is stolen. It is of no use to them."

"Because, Comrade Gobanifar, the people of Grand County were duped on the electricity issue as well. They were promised electricity at very low rates forever in return for their water. But, as in every case, they were cheated. Some of the electricity generated by their water does flow back to Grand County through the Adams Tunnel, but that power is used only to operate some of the mechanical features that make up the Colorado-Big Thompson Water Diversion Project. So, instead of getting their promised low-cost electricity, they are forced to buy their electricity from a private power company. They must pay market rates, so they got no benefit from their water that made the electricity. Moreover, the electricity they were supposed to get so cheaply is being used to fuel the exploding population growth along the Front Range which, in turn, creates even greater demands for the waters of Grand County."

"These people of Grand County, they cannot be very intelligent to allow all this to happen," opined Tarik Hussein.

"You are correct to a point, Comrade Hussein," replied Raoul. "But back in the late 19th Century, the few people who lived in Grand County were mostly itinerant and illiterate fur trappers, loggers and miners of gold and silver. They did not remain long in one place. By contrast, the people stealing their water were clever lawyers and merchants living down in the urban areas on the Great Plains. Far-sighted and cunning, these powerful men founded something called: The Denver Water Board, the members of which are said to be more powerful in Colorado than the governor and the legislature combined. By the time people of more education and foresight settled in the high country, it was too late. Their rustic predecessors had already been swindled and the water was taken," said Raoul.

"What will the American media make of all this?" asked Gobanifar.

"Our friends in the American media will be quick to place the blame on these local rebels. The American media will call them 'Freemen,' 'Militia Men,' 'right-wing extremists,' or other names the American media like to attach to any group that they do not consider as liberal.

"For example, when the Unibomber turned out to be a man of the Left, the American media soft-pedaled his political affiliations with the Greens and the Earth First! movement. Among the Unibomber's possessions, the FBI even found a well-thumbed edition of Vice President Holzhalter's book in which Holzhalter claimed the automobile was a greater threat to humankind than the atomic bomb.

"Yes, we can count on our friends in the mainstream American media to blame whatever we do on right-wing extremists, to include the destruction of the Lake Granby High Dam and the assassinations of Presidents Trimmer and Popov," said Raoul.

"And, what of your forces, Comrade Raoul, what will be your cover and how will you escape?" asked Gobanifar.

"Under the provisions of the North American Free Trade Agreement or NAFTA, the Mexican national petroleum company, Petroleos Mexicanos, or PEMEX for short, has been granted the right to perform oil and gas exploration inside the United States. My team will pose as a geo-seismic survey team from PEMEX conducting research in Grand County for natural-gas deposits.

"Prior to our attack, we will spend our days learning the terrain like the backs of our hands. At night, we will be at the local drinking establishments making friends with the locals. They will come to know we have large amounts of high explosives, detonation cord or other explosive elements that we will carry on our trucks as a normal part of our work," said Raoul.

"Forgive me again," said Mr. Soo. "I'm sure Mr. Gobanifar and Mr. Hussein, both from an oil-rich countries, understand geo-seismic survey. But why would you need all those explosives?"

"The way we work is to set an array of seismic sensors, called geo-phones, several hundred meters from a central point. At the central point, we drill a hole in the ground into which we place a certain amount of high explosives. The shock waves from the explosions are recorded by the geo-phones and a computer constructs an image of what the rock formations underneath the ground must look like.

"Ah so," said Mr. Soo. "Then because of NAFTA and the nature of your work, it is perfectly natural for you to have large amounts of high explosives on hand."

"That is correct, Comrade Soo. Nor will the Americanos expect us to stay in Grand County for long. Seismic survey crews such as ours normally only stay in one region for a few months and are transferred somewhere else. We will time the finish of our 'work' so we will have departed just prior to the destruction of these vital facilities," said Raoul.

"And how do you plan to escape?" asked Gobanifar.

"Gentlemen, I beg you to take no offense, but some details we prefer to keep to ourselves. Suffice it to say the helicopter used in our PEMEX work will be available for our exfiltration. President Castro and I just hope you will support this mission because of the damage it will do to the United States and because you feel it is operationally sound and because you believe that my men and I possess the courage and skills necessary to succeed," said Raoul.

Up to this point, Tarik Hussein had little to say.

Finally, he spoke.

"As you know, Gentlemen, my country has suffered terribly at the hands of the United States and its so-called Western-Arab alliance. What you have outlined, Comrade Raoul, is truly a noble undertaking. But I do have some questions, if I may?"

"Certainly," said Raoul.

"First of all, I can understand why Comrade Castro would want to assassinate the Russian president. Even before the collapse of the Soviet Union, Mikhail Gorbachev cut out the almost $6 billion in aid to which Comrade Castro referred in his opening remarks. Thus, the assassination of President Popov would send a signal to the world that Cuba is not a country to be trifled with.

"But why, in the name of Allah, would you want to assassinate President Trimmer? Our intelligence reports say this about President Trimmer as the American commander-in-chief: He has made drastic cuts in the budgets of the American armed forces. He virtually destroyed the morale of the American fighting men by trying to make them live in close quarters with homosexuals. He insists on putting women into situations where their presence is a hindrance to combat effectiveness. In order for women to 'qualify' for positions requiring physical strength and stamina, the traditional, time-tested combat standards have been lowered. Inevitably, sexual scandals, from general officers to privates have occurred and the radical feminists are using these episodes to undermine the authority of those in charge. The vaunted Drill Sergeant, the last vestige of iron discipline in the American armed forces, is being emasculated. Trimmer's misadventure in the Balkans may well destroy NATO, just the way Mikhail Gorbachev destroyed the Warsaw Pact.

"Personnel turbulence is at an all-time high. Talented junior officers, many from the American service academies, resign their commissions just as soon as their obligated service is served. For a change, one American general had the guts to admit that a huge number of America's front-line aircraft do not have sufficient parts and skilled mechanics to keep them flying. Record numbers of senior officers are opting to retire early rather than stay on for full careers. Many who do stay in service are either driven by promotion-centered dishonesty or are second-rate in other ways.

"The American forces that performed so well in Desert Storm are but a shell of what they were. An entire front-line infantry division was recently found to be incapable of going to war. As a result, we felt free to move against the Kurds in northern Iraq because we are aware of what President Trimmer has done to the once mighty forces of the Gulf War. Every month or so we thumb our noses at the United States by refusing to cooperate with that cursed UN weapons inspection team. Ultimately, we out-maneuvered Trimmer and whenever we choose to allow the UN inspectors into our country they are of no value to their masters.

"Moreover, President Trimmer is signaling to the world that he thinks so little of his military forces that he has turned them into some sort of sociological experimental laboratory. Trimmer sees his military as a Peace Corps carrying rifles. And, he is so weakened by his sexual peccadilloes and cover-ups that we see him as merely a likable, but ineffectual, buffoon.

"You want to kill President Trimmer? With all due respect, Comrade Raoul, have you lost your mind?" asked Tarik Hussein.

Instead of letting Raoul continue the briefing, Fidel took the floor to handle the questions of Tarik Hussein. Sensing Fidel was about to launch into one of his famous tirades, Raoul, who was sweating under his hood, took the opportunity to sit down.

But, as usual, Fidel surprised him. Instead of ripping into Tarik Hussein, Fidel said: "Gentlemen, you have listened hard and well this morning. And now, because it is noon and the heat is beginning to make our meeting place uncomfortable, we will move down to the beach where we will enjoy some traditional Cuban sandwiches followed by a nice siesta. When the sun begins to settle down behind the mountains of Puerto Rico to our west, we shall reconvene around this table in comfort of the always-reliable on-shore breeze.

As the foreign dignitaries followed Fidel and his guards down to the beach, Raoul reflected on the morning: *Comrade Fidel is going to ask them for a great deal of money and this deal is far from made.*

Chapter Eight

January

The Oval Office

With her newly-acquired Oxford accent, the President's appointments secretary announced,"Mr. President, Mr. Winthrop Sinclair the 3d, the Secretary of Interior, is here for his appointment."

"Send him in," said the President.

Looking as if he just stepped out of the pages of an Orvis catalog, the Secretary of the Interior crept in on what President Jim Bob Trimmer liked to tell Eddie Briccone were little cat feet. Motioned by the President to a chair beside the presidential desk, the Secretary of Interior said: "Mr. President, I understand you are heading out west next Labor Day for some fly fishing with the Russian President."

"Jesus, Winthrop. Can't anybody keep a fucking secret around here? Who told you that?"

"Mr. President, Washington is a porous place. When my grandfather was Secretary of State, he used to say…"

"Winthrop. You've told me that story ten times already. So, why do you need to see me?"

"Very well, Mr. President. It is my understanding that you will actually be engaged in fly fishing in Colorado."

"No, Winthrop. I'm going to bungie jump off the fucking Royal Gorge. Come to the point."

"My point is this, Mr. President. If you actually do catch a fish, we, at Interior, are hoping that you will practice 'catch and release.'"

"Hell, no. If I catch one of those little bastards, I'm going to keep it and have the chef cook it."

"Mr. President, that's why I asked for this appointment. With all due respect, Mr. President, I can see there is a need to sensitize you to some rather important environmental concerns."

"Okay, Winthrop, I'll tell the media that I'll release any fish I catch. But I'm telling you if I catch a trout, I'm going to eat it."

"As you wish, Mr. President. But what if someone sees you keeping a fish?"

"The Secret Service tells me the stretch of the Colorado River where I'll be fishing is so protected from view that I can do anything I want."

"Very well, Mr. President, but there's a whole range of environmental issues I need to take up with you before you fly out to Colorado."

"Such as?"

"The reintroduction of wolves and lynx into Colorado is a good place to start."

"Why in hell do you want to do that? Don't wolves and lynx eat cattle and sheep?"

"Mr. President, let me back up. We in the environmental movement think it's time to be realistic about those ranchers who graze their cattle and sheep up in our beautiful scenic areas. They are following a way of life that must come to an end."

"Those ranchers have been in the Rockies forever. Why do you want to pick on them?"

"All those cattle, sheep, horses and cowboys detract from the scenic beauty of the Rockies. They're rough, mostly uneducated people, Mr. President."

"You mean they don't belong to the Sierra Club?"

"They hate the Sierra Club, Mr. President. Their time has come and gone. They are an anachronism. Every time we try to set aside land and put it off limits, they oppose us."

"Since you're always trying to raise the fees they pay for grazing on public lands, I can't say as I blame them."

"They pay a pittance in comparison for the benefits they get from grazing on public land."

"Winthrop, we've always had a cheap food policy in this country. You raise those grazing fees too high and the consumer lobby is going to raise hell with me. How'd you like to have to pay a dollar more a pound for steak or lamb.?"

"I don't eat meat, Mr. President. I'm proud to say I'm a vegetarian."

"Somehow, I'm not surprised to hear that. So, what do you want me to say while I'm out in the Rockies?"

"If at all possible, Mr. President, we'd like for you to follow Vice President Holzhalter's line on environmental concerns."

"Such as?"

"Get the farmers and ranchers out of the scenic areas, reintroduce the wolves and lynx, restrict hunting in general, take away their guns, do away with private property rights along the river banks, put a stop to all logging and mining, limit the places where people can drive in the mountains. But, above all, Mr. President, you must help us have more land set aside under what we are calling, The Conservation and Reinvestment Act."

"I've read your legislation, Winthrop, and you ought to call it: The Condemnation and Relocation Act. If you get your hands on $43 billion over the next 15 years to buy up more land and put it off limits to the public, you'll be condemning the land of lots of hard-working Americans out West. I know how you guys operate."

"But, if we get it through Congress, you will sign it won't you, Mr. President?"

"Hopefully, it won't come to my desk for signature while I'm still here. Holzhalter will sign it in a heartbeat. But I'm curious about something, Winthrop. How in the hell are working people going to go on vacation in the mountains if you cut off their vehicle access?"

"They should not have vehicular access. If they want to see these scenic areas, they should hike into the wilderness with their backpacks. That is what my family has done for over a century."

"Winthrop, are you nuts? What about Joe Six-Pack, the Detroit autoworker, who only has two weeks vacation and he wants to load up his family in his RV and show them the glories of the Rocky Mountain West?"

"Joe Six-Pack, as you call him, does not deserve to see the glories of the mountains if he wants to see them through the windshield of his RV. In fact, RVs are an abomination. They should be banned, as well."

"Winthrop, how do you see the Rockies?"

"My family has been vacationing in the Rockies since the late 19th Century. In the early days, we went from New England by train to the Broadmoor Hotel where we spent the entire summer. Great-Grandpapa used to hike Pike's Peak before they built that blasted highway to the top. The Pike's Peak road is a perfect example of what I'm talking about, Mr. President. It should never have been built."

"Yeah, Winthrop, but how many people would have been able to gaze across 'the fruited plain' from the top of Pike's Peak without that road?"

"You are taking the side of the masses in this, Mr. President?"

"Winthrop, if I don't represent the masses, who the hell do I represent?"

"That is fine political rhetoric, Mr. President; however, let us be frank. If we run this country for the benefit of the masses, they will ruin it."

"Winthrop, did anyone ever tell you you're are an elitist asshole?"

"Mr. President, I resent your language."

"Look, Winthrop, I needed the support of all you environmentalist wackos to get elected and reelected. I've paid you and them off by putting you in charge of Interior, by letting you take away the control of airspace over the national parks from the FAA, by letting you fool around with those fucking wolves in Yellowstone, by letting you put those stupid Spotted Owls before jobs for loggers and by using some obscure quirk in the law to enlarge many of the National Monuments without the consent of Congress or anyone else. So now, what have you and your fumble-footed park rangers done? You failed to control a fire you set on purpose in Yellowstone National Park.

"I was just out there and it still looks like shit and will for decades to come. Anyone who isn't brain dead knows that when forest fires get that fucking hot they sterilize the ground. All your propaganda about how the Yellowstone fires will rejuvenate the forest is bullshit and you know it. Yellowstone may come back, but you and I won't get to see it.

"Then, you set off one of your fucking 'prescribed burns' near Los Alamos that almost destroyed our atomic weapons laboratory. To make matters worse, your dumb ranger who authorized the burn, said he'd do it again. You know, Winthrop, I'll bet you and your rangers have polluted the atmosphere more than Andrew Carnegie and his fucking steel mills ever did.

"Winthrop, if you are serious about locking up more of our scenic wonders so Joe Six-Pack and his family can't see them through the windshield of their RVs, then I've got to get you to call off your land-grabbing dogs or Vice President Holzhalter won't have a chance to be my successor. I've already locked more land away from Joe Six-Pack than Teddy Roosevelt and that part of my legacy is secure. But I'm going to can your ass and send you back to the Broadmoor or Choate or wherever the hell you spent your private-school boyhood if you don't knock off your land-grabber rhetoric until we can get that dumb sonofabitch Holzhalter elected."

With trembling lips, Winthrop Sinclair announced, "Mr. President, I resent your characterizations of Vice President Holzhalter and of my department and me. I will leave my resignation on your secretary's desk as I leave."

"No, you will not. You will go back to Interior and do your job until I tell you to quit. But knock off this goddam lock-up-America-from-the-taxpayers-crap. I'll support 'catch and release,' I'll even let you have a public debate about those fucking wolves and even those poor lynx that are starving to death out in Colorado. But I will not let you alienate Joe Six-Pack who counts for one hellava lot more votes than you and your Chablis and Brie environmentalists."

"We Chablis and Brie environmentalists, as you call us, put a lot of money into your presidential campaign, Mr. President."

"That's true, Winthrop. But dollars aren't votes and don't you forget it. I got more votes from people who drink beer and eat brats out of their RVs than I got from those Harvard coupon-clippers who sip Chablis and eat Brie off the tailgates of their Volvos."

"I can see where your loyalties lie, Mr. President."

"Winthrop, the first duty of a politician is to get elected. The second duty of a politician is to get reelected. Now, I've done both. I can't run for this office again. So, you and the tree huggers and Bambi lovers can take a fucking flying leap.

"The problem with you enviro-nuts is that you take a wonderful-sounding idea like 'wilderness' and turn it into a bureaucratic nightmare. You won't let anyone into the areas you've locked up so they can take out all the deadfall and other fuel that piles up and then, when the fucking forest catches fire, your stupid rules prohibit the use of mechanized fire-fighting equipment and even if fire-fighting equipment is allowed in there are no roads to move it. The nation loses millions of trees, the animals lose their habitat and the air gets polluted. I swear, Winthrop, you tree-huggers are bigger enemies of the environment than the logging and mining companies.

"Take a look at how the Europeans manage their forests. Have you ever heard of a forest fire in Germany? Of course not. The place is covered with forests and no fires. You know why, Winthrop? Because, if a tree falls in a German forest, they let someone in there to harvest that tree for firewood or to make particleboard or something useful. They don't let fuel build up in their forests.

"If you enviro-nuts didn't have shit for brains and such hatred for our common folk who just want to drive out West and see a bear or a moose, you could understand what I'm talking about," said President Trimmer.

By now, Secretary Sinclair's face was red and his eyes were welling up with tears of rage and his lower lip was trembling uncontrollably. Alleged to be able to feel the pain of others, President Trimmer could see he had been too rough.

"But, I'll tell you what, Winthrop. I can see you're upset. I'll make you a deal. While I'm out in Colorado catching and releasing all those fucking trout, you and your family can come out over the Labor Day weekend and stay for a day or two. I'll even send Air Force One to come fetch you and your family."

Fighting to regain control of himself, the Secretary took several deep breaths before he answered.

"That would be very nice, Mr. President. I have an old bamboo fly rod that my grandfather gave to me. I would love the opportunity to show my son how to use it."

"Then, we are agreed, Winthrop. Sometime during my fishing vacation, I'll look forward to seeing you and Mrs. Sinclair and what's your son's name?"

"His name is Winthrop, too, Mr. President. Actually, he's Winthrop Sinclair the fourth."

"Yes, Winthrop. Somehow, I should have known that. Good Day, Winthrop."

CHAPTER NINE

January

Vieques Island, late afternoon

The Iranian, Iraqi and Red Chinese "delegates" were chatting among themselves when Fidel reentered the briefing hut. Quickly, they resumed their places around the table and Fidel began:

"I trust you gentlemen enjoyed your lunch and your siesta," opened Fidel. "But now, let us pick up where we left off this morning when there was a question about the wisdom of getting rid of President Trimmer.

"Comrade Tarik, you raise some very valid points. Everything you say is true and we are grateful for the harm President Trimmer has done to his military establishment. We must, however, look to the future.

"The political pendulum in the United States sometimes makes very wide swings. In 1994, the Americans placed the conservatives in charge of their congress for the first time in 40 years. It was as if they decided to sober up after 40 years of binge-taxing and binge-spending, mostly spending.

"Yet, when it became apparent they could not have their spending cake and eat it too, they blinked. Even the modest spending reductions proposed by the conservatives did not find favor. The United States, in many ways, is moving down the same path that destroyed the Greek and Roman Empires.

"This morning, in my introduction, I spoke of the return of Vieques Island as a precursor of things to come. It was on the basis of what I see as America's internal rot that I made my prediction of the demise of the Great Satan. Internal rot is the key.

"That is why this attack must be made to appear as an act of domestic violence rather than foreign-sponsored terrorism. Faced with an external threat, all nations have a tendency to pull together. Look what happened when the United States bombed North Vietnam and when President Trimmer used missiles and bombs on Yugoslavia. The resistance of the people under attack grew stronger rather than weaker.

"But the end of the Cold War proves my point. If the Cold War were still on-going, not even the Americanos would be stupid enough to elect a James Robert Trimmer," said Castro, jabbing the air with his cigar again for emphasis.

Raoul shifted in his chair thinking how much he enjoyed it when Comrade Fidel got really wound up as he was now. Fidel was standing now, his earlier apparent fatigue a thing of the past.

"Politically, the Americans are like children," Fidel continued. "They do not understand socialism. Nor do they have any conception of how socialism, properly implemented, can benefit humankind. Beginning in the 1960s, the American Establishment capitulated to radical individualism that appealed to the so-called 'flower children' of the 1960s who devoured the writings of Kinsey, Hefner, Camus, and Sartre while living on drugs, birth-control pills and penicillin.

"So, you see my comrades, the seeds of the North American destruction lies within this generation of baby-boomers who, in the 1960s, were looking for an excuse to use drugs and engage in licentious sexual behavior. They made the war in southeast Asia their excuse. 'Make love, not war,' was their mantra.

"In actual fact, many of the young males of the 1960s were simply afraid to fight in Vietnam or just didn't want to be inconvenienced. So, the pampered American college youth of the 1960s waged their rebellion against the Old Order—the order which had defeated Germany twice, Japan once and had drawn a line in the sand against the spread of Marxist-Leninist socialism.

"For example, during World War II, Harvard lost 691 of its alumni in the effort to defeat Hitler and the Japanese. But from the Harvard classes of 1962 through 1972, only 12 of their alumni died in Vietnam. During the same period, Princeton lost six men and MIT only two. Ironically, some of those who avoided service in Vietnam were the sons of the so-called 'best and brightest' of the Kennedy and Johnson Administrations who led the American government deeper and deeper into the Vietnam War.

"In the end, these foolish, spoiled youth became our allies—'useful idiots,' as Lenin used to say. Their civil disobedience weakened many of the basic institutions that created the American Colossus. Just look at the rampant rise of illegitimacy, drug use, venereal diseases of all kinds to include AIDS, plus street crime and a general decline in academic and moral standards. Teachers and professors were afraid to grade students against any kind of standards of academic rigor. I recall with both affection and amusement how, at so many American colleges, the inmates were running the asylum—and, in some cases, continue to do so."

Pausing for effect, Fidel was rewarded with a burst of both laughter and applause from his tiny audience. Fidel paused to drink a shot of Metaxis offered by Raoul.

"I alone," Castro continued, "of those among us can speak from successful experience at weakening the Americanos. It was I who created the Cuban Committee of Solidarity with South Vietnam. It was I who brought Huynh Van Ba to Cuba to meet with young Americans so he could instruct them on how to conduct anti-war demonstrations in the U.S. and abroad. I arranged for the meeting between the U.S.

Weathermen with a delegation from North Vietnam and the Viet Cong in Havana which led to Chicago's 'Days of Rage.' And, it was I who arranged for Jane Fonda to go to Hanoi to help demoralize the POWS in the so-called Hanoi Hilton.

"At the same time, a young, James Robert Trimmer, was supposed to be studying abroad at Oxford. Instead, he was helping to organize rallies and demonstrations in England and the Scandinavian countries for the purpose of undermining the American foreign policy and the war effort in southeast Asia.

"So, when I tell you your investment in this mission is well-warranted, I speak from experience. If there is anyone in this room who has had more success at sticking his thumb in the eye of the Americanos, let him speak now!"

With his beard now flecked with spit and his brow covered with sweat, Fidel Castro might as well have been speaking before thousands of people in downtown Havana. With that virtually impossible to teach sixth sense possessed by great public speakers, Fidel Castro sat down, dropped his voice and continued:

"The Reagan Revolution stopped them for a time. But now my children of the 60s are back and they have seized the reins of power in higher academe, in the public schools, in government offices, on the factory floor and even the Casa Blanca itself. They continue where they left off in the 1960s to create a society with no restraints on individual pleasure, no concept of law and order, no concept of duty to the state or duty to anyone to include the unborn and the elderly. The fact that a known abuser and exploiter of women can remain in the White House proves my point. The inmates have, indeed, taken over the asylum.

"They want their bread and circuses today and are willing to let their children and grandchildren inherit a crushing tax burden—a burden so heavy it may someday, we hope, lead to financial collapse, chaos and, eventually, anarchy.

"But let me save that complete lecture for another time. It is, however, our belief that President Trimmer, by his disgraceful personal behavior and his clumsy attempts to cover it up, has, in the long run of history, disgraced himself and his party beyond redemption. His recent impeachment by the U.S. House of Representatives, will eventually weaken the Left and strengthen the Right.

"Comrades, you can be assured the Americanos will, in the future, make double sure they don't elect a person of such weak character again to such a high office. For that reason, it is almost certain they will elect a conservative with strong religious convictions and a clean record in both personal and official matters.

"We must intervene to keep that from happening. We must take steps to insure the succession of Vice President Holzhalter to the Oval Office. And, here is why:

"In the 20th Century major efforts were made by strongly-led regimes from both the right and the left to destroy capitalism and they all failed. Two World Wars and the Cold War could not stop the economic and resulting military might of the United States. Our former ally, the Soviet Union, destroyed itself in the effort and disintegrated.

"We are proposing a new way of destroying our neighbor to the north. We must destroy free-market capitalism because it is the engine that produces the huge armies, navies and air forces of the Americans. By my calculation, environmental extremism is the only way that the forces of socialism will be able to defeat the capitalist menace.

"If you peel back the layers of the environmental movement, strip off the front groups and their unrealistic, simplistic idealism, the primary motive of the environmental or Green Movement is the destruction of capitalism. If you lock up a nation's natural resources and make them unavailable, you gut that nation's ability to function effectively on the world stage.

"Believe me, I have virtual, first-hand knowledge of this subject because we have our agents working within many of these environmentalist groups.

"Therefore, by assassinating President Trimmer, we prevent the kind of shift to the Right we think Trimmer's disgraceful behavior will provoke. Vice President Holzhalter will get the sympathy and support of the electorate and be elected in his own right and, perhaps, reelected. In the end, we get an environmentalist president in place for a long time who will, within a decade, set in motion environmental policies leading to the demise of the United States as an economic power. And, once the United States is crippled economically it will be crippled militarily.

"Finally, this assassination operation is our way of thanking President Trimmer for all the work he and his wife have done on behalf of the socialist cause for so many years."

"Excuse me, Comrade Fidel," interrupted Son Yat Soo. "You are going to thank President Trimmer by killing him?"

"Si, Comrade. In historical terms, Trimmer's personal behavior has made him a domestic and international laughing stock. Even some of the people of his home state resist the idea of a Trimmer presidential library being located there. A committee of that state's association of lawyers wants him disbarred from practicing law in that state.

"The only way Trimmer can have a chance of recapturing some of the popularity he once enjoyed, is for him to die as a martyr. As the waters rushing down the Colorado River from the burst Lake Granby High Dam sweep him away and he understands he is about to drown, he will not want to die. Yet, dying is the only way he can achieve a place in history that is not solely that of a fornicator and prevaricator. Our sources tell us that Mrs. Trimmer, although she will play the bereaved widow and try to remind us of Jackie Kennedy, will be greatly pleased. Gentlemen, what we are about to do is simply our most profound way of saying gracias to both of them.

"Finally, and I must confess that this is a matter of Cuban pride, it has been almost 40 years since I played a role in a presidential assassination.

"As you know, the Kennedy brothers ordered the CIA to carry out my assassination. The CIA came up with some silly devices and schemes that proved totally ineffective. Actually, I was always more concerned about the Cosa Nostra.

"As I'm sure you are aware President Kennedy and one of the Cosa Nostra bosses had a common mistress. Not that she looked common. In fact, she was rather attractive.

"Using her as a go-between, the Kennedy brothers tried to enlist certain members of the Cosa Nostra to effect my elimination. Then, for some reason we do not fully understand, Robert Kennedy ordered an all-out war on the Americano Cosa Nostra.

"Robert Kennedy's sudden anti-mob crusade broke a long-standing agreement between his father, Joseph P. Kennedy, and the Cosa Nostra that went back to the days of Prohibition and Joe Kennedy's rum-running operations. Say what you will about the Cosa Nostra, but they do live by their Code. As a rule, they do not attack law enforcement officials. But once the Cosa Nostra works out a mutually agreeable arrangement with a law enforcement official, or a person with a great deal of political influence, it is regarded, by the Cosa Nostra anyway, as a sacred bond between them. In fact, the Americans make a joke about it. They say an honest politician is a politician who, once bought, stays bought.

"The Cosa Nostra reserves its harshest violence for those who betray it. So, when Bobby Kennedy sent the FBI after the Cosa Nostra, the Cosa Nostra felt betrayed. From that time on, the Kennedy brothers were marked men.

"Therefore, given the attempts by the Kennedy brothers to have me killed, we were most happy to assist the Cosa Nostra when the time came. The rest, as they say, is history.

"With the succession of Lyndon Johnson to the American presidency, we gained a man, like Trimmer, with absolutely no talent for the role of commander-in-chief. His befuddled attempts, and those of Secretary of Defense Robert McNamara, to micro-manage the Vietnam War prevented what should have been a relatively easy American victory in Vietnam. Instead of victory, Johnson and McNamara prolonged the conflict. Their ineptitude cost the Americans so many lives that many Americans lost heart and civil discord swept the land. Again, let me remind you of the role played by me, Huynh Van Ba, Jane Fonda and other soldiers of the socialist Left.

"Indeed, we came close to seeing the anarchy we know is the penultimate step before America's final collapse. America's current astronomically high national debt began when Lyndon Johnson tried to finance the Vietnam War without raising taxes. Instead, he drained the resources of the American military at home and in Europe. Eventually, he borrowed more and more money. He set off an inflationary cycle that caused Richard Nixon to impose wage and price controls. President Ford and Carter all went down under the burden of inflation. Reagan inherited an inflated economy and a hollow military.

"But Reagan was lucky. Thanks to a botched assassination attempt—please note the historical importance of even failed attempts at assassination—President Reagan gained the popular support he needed to revitalize the American military while launching the United States into almost 100 months of upward economic activity. This is just another example of what I call: Americano assassination politics.

"So, in summary, let me say we may have lost our Soviet sponsor and the major market for our agricultural products. We may have been hit by hurricanes and poor crop years. We may be experiencing severe economic problems. But, through it all, we have remained loyal to our Marxist-Leninist principles and devoted to world revolution. We are bloody, but unbowed. And, with your help, I can still remove one American president and put someone in his place who will cause even greater damage to the Great Satan.

"Have I made myself clear, Comrade Hussein?" concluded Fidel with a flourish.

"Indeed, you have," said Hussein. "And, may I add, your analysis of the political past, present and your predictions for the future are absolutely brilliant."

"Thank you, Comrade," said Fidel. "Now, Comrade Raoul, please continue."

Raoul resumed his place behind the lectern but he could see that Tarik Hussein was still being more diplomatic than actually convinced.

"Thank you Comrade Fidel," said Raoul. "But perhaps there are more questions before I continue?"

"Yes," said Tarik Hussein, "but only a few of a somewhat tactical nature. I would assume your survey crew would only be a few men and yourself. How could such a small force be able to wreak havoc on such a large scale?"

"My men will be divided into four teams. One for the Adams Tunnel, one for the Lake Granby Pump Plant, one for the Moffat Tunnel and one for The Grand Ditch. Each team will carry out a detailed reconnaissance of its objective and then formulate a precise plan to accomplish its destruction. I, and my deputy, who is a structural engineer, will personally review these plans to make sure they represent the simplest and most effective way to accomplish the simultaneous destruction of these installations," said Raoul.

"Comrade Raoul, you forgot the Lake Granby High Dam." said Hussein.

"Not at all," continued Raoul. "The Lake Granby High Dam will be my personal responsibility, Comrade Hussein.

"Timing will be of the essence there. For example, before I destroy the dam and, consequently, eliminate the Presidents of the United States and Russia, I must be certain the other attacks have gone off as planned. Otherwise, all of the focus will be on the Lake Granby High Dam and that would unmask our plan. Because the Granby Pump Plant is within sight of the Lake Granby High Dam, I will be able to hear that explosion plus observe the collapse of the structure. The two water tunnels are, however, too far away for me to hear those blasts. Fortunately, cellular telephone service in that area is excellent and my men will be able to communicate with me by that means," said Raoul.

"You appear to have thought of everything, Comrade Raoul. But tell us what you can about the qualifications of your men?" asked Hussein.

"All of them are Latino; however, all have lived in the United States at one time or another. In addition, before the break-up of the Soviet Union they received training by the KGB outside of Moscow. Almost all are fluent in American English to include the latest slang expressions. Although most of them have engineering backgrounds, they are not academic types. They are fit, trained in the martial arts, and are experts with firearms and explosives. One of my men is an expert helicopter pilot," said Raoul.

"And what about you, Comrade Raoul?" asked Mr. Gobanifar?

"Well, I'm not as young as I was when I served with Che Guevara and assisted with the writing of Che's classic treatise on guerrilla warfare. But, following the death of Che, Comrade Fidel saw to it that I was slipped into the United States and enlisted in the United States Army. After the usual training, I was shipped to Vietnam and assigned to the 1st Air Cavalry Division.

"Initially, I was assigned to an Infantry company where I learned many useful combat skills. Toward the end of my year in Vietnam, I was offered a job as a door gunner on a helicopter if I would extend my tour. During that time, Comrade Fidel sent word that I was to get away from the Americans and rendezvous with our comrades in the North Vietnamese Army.

"My opportunity came when our helicopter was flying a mission along the Cambodia border. Without being seen, I unscrewed a hydraulic line forcing my aircraft commander to make a precautionary landing in a jungle clearing. While he, the pilot and the other door gunner were examining the hydraulic line, I shot them with my service pistol and took off into the jungle.

"The rest was easy. Using map and compass, I found my North Vietnamese comrades. A month later, I was in Hanoi where I helped interrogate American prisoners in the so-called Hanoi Hilton. But, back in Vietnam, the Americans just thought I was just another MIA," said Raoul.

Raoul detected a slight shift in the body of Son Yat Soo and he knew what Soo was thinking: So, this man is actually the infamous Carlos. The man the American POWs feared and hated even more than their North Vietnamese captors. Raoul's suspicion was confirmed when Soo said, "Comrade Raoul, would there be any chance of your being recognized because of your role at the Hanoi Hilton?"

"Not in Grand County. Currently, there is only one former POW from the Hanoi Hilton living in Grand County of whom we are aware and I will explain his situation in a moment.

"There are, however, a number of other Vietnam veterans. In fact, this is another bit of good fortune. Someone I knew of by reputation only in my old brigade has retired there. He happens to be one of the leaders of the rangeland rebels. His name is Charles Lee. What makes Lt. Colonel Chuck Lee, U.S. Army, retired, of interest is that Senor Lee is a descendent of one of the women forced to work in the brothels frequented by the Oriental labor gangs digging The Grand Ditch."

"Does he look Chinese?" asked Comrade Soo.

"Although Captain Lee commanded a company in a sister battalion, we never met. I only know his company had a fine, fighting reputation. But we hope Senor Lee harbors some resentment because of the way the Oriental workers were exploited up on The Grand Ditch.

"However, Senor Lee's anger concerning his government's lack of concern for the Hmong people may be of even greater use in our recruitment of Senor Lee," said Raoul.

"Perhaps," interrupted Comrade Soo, "our comrades from Iran and Iraq are not familiar with the plight of the Hmongs."

"Thank you, Comrade Soo," said Raoul. "The Hmongs are an ancient people living mostly in Laos. During the Vietnam War, the American CIA, with help from members of the U.S. Special Forces members such as Charles Lee, trained the Hmongs to fight against the North Vietnamese Army. Mr. Jerrold Barker Daniels led the CIA effort. According to our intelligence sources, Charles Lee was one of Daniels' key officers. Lee became so emotionally involved with the Hmongs that when the Americans pulled out of Laos, he refused to abandon them. Apparently, CIA operatives had to slip into Laos, kidnap Charles Lee and detain him in a military hospital in Hawaii.

"Although some effort was made by the Americans to help the Hmongs immigrate to the United States, we understand that Charles Lee and his colleagues feel the U.S. Government did not do enough to protect the Hmongs from the retribution so rightly visited upon them by the victorious North Vietnamese Army. We hope to exploit Senor Lee's anger over the treatment of the Hmongs and, of course, exploit his feelings over the cruel treatment of the Orientals who built The Grand Ditch.

"In addition, Mr. Lee has a close friend living in Grand County who was once a pilot for Air America—the airline owned by the CIA. This pilot's name is Louis Leclerc. Mr. Leclerc was a POW in the Hanoi Hilton. Fortunately, he was captured sometime after I returned to Cuba.

"Their experiences in life, and especially in Vietnam, Cambodia and Laos, suggest to us that both of these men are vulnerable to manipulation. Using the thread of our common service in Vietnam, I plan to ingratiate myself with Colonel Lee and Mr. Leclerc and put them and their colleagues, unwittingly, into our service," said Raoul.

"And then you will kill them," said Gobanifar.

"That is correct," replied Raoul. "We will kill them and their bodies will be found in the rubble of our targets. These men who lived their lives as patriots, will go down in history as traitors while a President, whom men like Charles Lee and Louis Leclerc would deem a traitor, will be hailed as a martyr. The supreme irony," opined Raoul.

Lighting a Turkish cigarette, Hussein said, "The destruction of the water-diversion systems and the communications systems, while of great importance, seem somewhat mundane compared with your plan to assassinate the American and Russian presidents."

"Such a master stroke depends upon reliable intelligence, excellent timing and a degree of good fortune. We think the Soviet American Summit on the American Labor Day is a virtual certainty; however, one can never be certain when it comes to international affairs. But, we shall be ready to take advantage of this opportunity should it present itself. With or without the visit of President Popov, we plan to give the Americanos more of a Labor Day celebration than they expect," said Raoul.

"Please forgive me and do not take this as a sign of a lack of enthusiasm on my part, Comrade Raoul," said Tarik Hussein, "but we are talking about a great deal of money to finance your operation. We know how effective Comrade Castro was with the anti-war movement and the assassination of President Kennedy, but do you have any kind of experience with terrorist acts within the United States?"

"Yes, as a matter of fact, I do. On the east side of the Continental Divide near Estes Park, Colorado, is what is known as the Flatiron Pumping Plant. On December 13, 1995, I was able to single-handedly cause an explosion inside this pumping plant and get away undetected. To this day, the authorities of Northern Colorado Water Conservancy District, which operates the plant, do not know the exact cause of this explosion. They blame it on a lightning strike. At least that's all they have told the American public.

"Actually, it takes very little to cause a major power outage. Just recently, a small bird, a magpie, flew into the transformer station at the Lake Granby Pump Plant and crossed two wires. Electrical power was out between the two towns of Grand Lake and Granby for about two hours. If a stupid bird can do that, just imagine what a highly-trained team of terrorists can do.

"Even more recently, I was able to slip into another pumping station at a place called Windy Gap, turn a few valves and cause it to flood. The station had to be shut down for a brief time.

"But my main point is this: In both cases, I was able to slip in and out without detection. With only a rudimentary knowledge of the electronic circuitry of the Flatiron Pumping Plant, I was able to cross-wire it in such a way that its engines and turbines exploded. The Flatiron Pump Plant was out of action from December, 1995, until September, 1996. Turning some valves at Windy Gap was simpler, but less lasting.

"Comrade Hussein, you asked for proof of our ability to accomplish a daring and dangerous mission and not get caught. I offer the destruction of the Flatiron Pumping Plant and the sabotage of Windy Gap Pump Plant as proof," concluded Raoul.

At that point, Fidel smashed the soggy remains of his cigar in his ashtray and stood up.

"Gentlemen, if you still harbor any doubts about our ability to carry out this operation, let me remind you with what I feel is justified pride that I have been able to beat President James Robert Trimmer like a drum. A recent example is how I forced the Trimmer Administration to do my bidding with regard to the unfortunate little boy whose traitor-bitch of a mother tried to place him in the grubby hands of his capitalist relatives in Miami," said Fidel.

"Yes, comrade Castro," said Tarik Hussein, "we have been wondering what strange power you have over President Trimmer and his Attorney General?"

"I have the ability to cause a great deal of trouble for President Trimmer just like I did for former President Carter," said Fidel. "When I emptied my prisons of the criminally insane and sent them from the Port of Mariel to Florida, the presence of the so-called *Marielitos* was going to cause President Carter to lose support in the State of Florida. In order to win reelection, Carter desperately needed Florida's votes in the American Electoral College.

"So, Carter begged his friend, then Governor Trimmer of Arkansas, to take the *Marielitos* into Fort Chaffee, Arkansas. Governor Trimmer took in the *Marielitos*. But they continued to riot and cause problems. In fact, the *Marielitos* caused Trimmer to lose his own gubernatorial reelection bid and, as a result, Trimmer learned to fear what I can do.

"It was his fear of Fidel that caused Trimmer to change the Cuban Adjustment Act of 1966, an act written to encourage Cubans to defect to the United States. As originally written, that law said any Cuban reaching American territorial waters had an absolute right to file a claim for political asylum. Secretly, through his personal lawyer go-between, I let Trimmer know that I did not like the way that law was written. So, Trimmer issued an executive order in 1994 that says Cubans must actually touch their feet to American soil before they can apply for asylum. That executive order did much to discourage the defection of those misguided Cubans who think that a 90-mile voyage to Florida will land them on the capitalist easy street.

"Moreover, Trimmer is deathly afraid that I will launch another wave of *Marielitos* into Florida just prior to the upcoming presidential election. That could cause Vice President Holzhalter to lose Florida and that could throw the entire election to the Republican presidential candidate. Of course, I would never do that because we want Holzhalter elected. But Trimmer doesn't know that.

"If the Republicans come to power, the normal functions of the so-called American Rule of Law will be restored and Trimmer's unconstitutional and criminal activities will be subjected to the light of day. In terms of moral leadership, a panel of distinguished historians has already rated Trimmer as the worst American president, even below Richard Nixon. Trimmer is a sinking ship and he knows another wave of *Marielitos* can send him even deeper into the historical depths and could even land him in prison.

"So, you see gentlemen, Fidel Castro has the power to change the outcome of both state and national elections in America and President Trimmer knows that full well. When I say: Jump! President Trimmer asks: How high? Also, this pathetic person is so worried about his place in history that he wants to normalize relations with Cuba as part of his so-called legacy.

"Trimmer knows his friends in the liberal media will applaud such an action because they have always been admirers of communism, at least in theory, if not in practice. Trimmer also knows the liberal college professors will rush to write the first histories of his time in office. They, like the mainstream American media, will praise him for restoring normal relations with Cuba. Of course, I will be happy to normalize relations with the United States because of what that means in terms of economic benefits for our economy. But, at the end of the day, I and my Marxist-Leninist regime will still be in charge of the Cuban people. Once again, Trimmer will have sold out and he will do so for just a few favorable lines in the initial histories of his time in office.

"Also, I am pleased to point out that my insistence on the return of the boy to his Cuban father set off riots in Miami and it caused strife between the White, Black and Latino populations of southern Florida. In fact, I am amused at how poorly the Cuban defectors in Little Havana, as they call it, put forth their demands for the little boy to stay in Florida.

"Instead of waving American flags, they waved Cuban flags. Instead of holding up posters in English, they wrote them in Spanish. Instead of shouting Freedom, they shouted Liberdad. The English-speaking American public could not understand who they were and what they wanted. Of course, my secret agents in Little Havana played a role in duping the stupid defectors into sending such mixed messages. In fact, the lawyer the Miami Cubans hired to represent the little swine in court was actually one of President Trimmer's henchmen. Naturally, he bungled the boy's defense and we have him now in a reeducation camp.

"Remember, my Comrades, the United States has always had the military power to crush me and my revolution like a Palmetto bug. President Kennedy botched the best chance they had when he refused to provide sufficient air cover for the abortive landing at the Bay of Pigs. Then, I played Kennedy for a fool during the Cuban Missile Crisis by extracting a pledge that the United States would never, ever invade my country again.

"Comrades, I am but one man on a tiny island and yet I have made the Americanos dance to my tune. No world power worthy of the name would have permitted any foreign power to establish a major forward base for communism just 90 miles from its mainland.

"Think of it this way: Cuba is like a huge aircraft carrier floating just off the American coastline. Would the United States have permitted the Russians or the Chinese to park such a formidable weapon so close to its shores for 40 years? I think not.

"But I have been able to launch a variety of weapons against the United States for decades from my island aircraft carrier. Cleverly, I have chosen weapons of subversion, intelligence gathering and psychological warfare against which the Americanos have no defense. I knew better than to attack them with missiles or cannons because, as I said before, they would smash me like a bug. I kept the level of my attacks just below the threshold that would provoke a military response that would be beyond our ability to defend against it. As a result, I have made the Americanos look like the fools they are.

"What Comrade Raoul and I are proposing to you today is just one more, and, perhaps, my final, slap into the face of the United States of America. As history records, I have done it before and, working together, we can do it again.

"Now, comrades, unless you have further operational questions for Comrade Raoul, I suggest we move on to how this project will be funded.

"Seeing no hands raised, we want to thank Comrade Raoul and tell him that we wish him and his Team PEMEX well," said Fidel.

When Comrade Raoul was gone, Fidel quickly relieved each of his visitors of $10 million dollars, passed around a box of Cuban cigars and opened a bottle of Metaxis. With a twinkle in his eye, Fidel declared the Laws of Islam and Christianity not in effect on Vieques Island. A selection of attractive women was paraded before them. And, by midnight, all four men were pleasantly drunk and in bed.

CHAPTER TEN

Dark riders are coming, by the rustler's moon, while the wannabes watch cowboy cartoons. As they're sub-dividin' ranch to ranchettes, some humans are residin' with the hangman of debt. Ride Rangeland Rebels. Ride to beat the devil.

—Michael Martin Murphey

Roberto Chavez and his family are typical of blue-collar people in Grand County or any of the resort areas who must work several jobs to make ends meet. Roberto's father and his father before him were reasonably successful truck farmers in the days before World War II. Their high-altitude lettuce and spinach were in great demand at some of Colorado's finest restaurants and hotels, including the famous Broadmoor Hotel in Colorado Springs.

Bit by bit, Roberto's grandfather was able to add to the family land holdings until his family, his children and their children could make an adequate living off the land. In fact, Roberto felt able to splurge one October by taking his wife on a trip to Bad Toelz, Germany, where, in the early 1960s, Roberto served with Chuck Lee in the 10th Special Forces Group. Following a Special Forces reunion in Bad Toelz, Roberto and Maria did the usual tourist things, to include a trip through the Black Forest.

That was where Roberto got the idea to go into the timber business. Maria pointed out how she didn't see any fallen trees within Germany's pristine forests. If a tree died or the wind blew it over, someone must be coming into the forests and removing the debris. Roberto told her that was why forest fires are virtually unheard of in Germany.

Roberto made the acquaintance of a local *Forstmeister* who explained how gleaners are allowed to come into the forests to remove unwanted tree debris. Much of it is used by the locals for firewood. Some of it, however, was sent to processing plants and converted into particleboard and other wood-based products.

Eager to broaden the family business beyond lettuce and spinach, Roberto and Maria were looking for another activity. After all, a lettuce blight just prior to World War II wiped out the original growers of Granby lettuce. Diversification seemed the logical thing to do. Roberto and his wife felt they saw an environmentally sound way of getting into the timber business.

Yet, Roberto wanted no part of the practice of clear-cutting timberlands. Some logging companies think the only way to make a profit is to level the forest by clear-cutting—a practice abhorred by environmentalists, conservationists and anyone with a lick of common sense.

Instead, Roberto wanted to harvest the millions of Jackstraw Pines that fall during high winds or are killed by Pine Beetles and other tree-killing pests. This dead-tree litter is of no benefit to the forests. The animals have plenty of cover even without the fallen trees. Besides being a wasted natural resource, the dead trees provide fuel for forest fires, which destroy hundreds of thousands of healthy trees and pollute the atmosphere with smoke.

After their return from Germany, it took Roberto some time to find a market for trees that had lain in the forest for so long that they were no longer suitable for construction lumber or for furniture manufacturing. But his determination paid off and he found a buyer who had a process that could grind up the trees to not only make particleboard but also use the deadfall to make a new form of heat-saving and sound-deadening insulation.

Removing the fallen trees from the forests was not easy. But Roberto figured out a way to put extra-large tires on all-terrain vehicles and skid the logs out to where they could be loaded on trucks and sent to market. Roberto invented a large rake to mount on the rear of his ATVs. After the deadfall was skidded out of an area, the area was raked to remove the skid marks and to clean up any unsightly debris. After a Chavez crew gleaned an area, it looked as pristine as the German forests and the fire danger was greatly reduced.

Getting his timber business started required capital. None of the conventional lending agencies wanted anything to do with anything that sounded like logging. Not if they didn't want the Trimmer Administration to fill their offices with federal bank regulators. So, Roberto had to borrow the needed capital from Chavez Farms. After a decade of investment and hard work, Roberto and his sons were beginning to show a modest profit. Then disaster struck.

A consortium of environmentalist and animal rights groups filed a law suit in federal court seeking an injunction against all logging operations in northwestern Colorado. The purpose of the lawsuit was twofold: to stop clear-cutting operations and to prevent the logging of trees which might be used as habitat by Spotted Owls and other endangered species.

Ironically, the timber being harvested by the Chavez Timber Company was deadfall, not clear-cut and no one, to include the Colorado Department of Wildlife, the U.S. Forest Service and the U.S. Park Service had ever seen a Spotted Owl anywhere in Grand County and certainly not in a tree lying on the ground. Nevertheless, a federal marshal came to the Chavez Timber Company and served a cease-and-desist order on Roberto, Maria and their two sons. Unable to operate, Robert could not make his payments to Chavez Farms just at the time an even greater disaster befell the Chavez family.

Roberto's father died and Roberto wept. But when Roberto got the bill for the estate taxes, he wept some more. Now, he had not only lost his father, it would be necessary to sell much of the land suitable for truck farming to pay the estate taxes.

Fortunately, Roberto and Maria were able to hold on to almost 100 acres of bottomland. The cattle market was experiencing one of its periodic, but brief, highs and they took the money they had left and bought cattle. When calving time came, they spent many a sleepless night caring for the cows as they gave birth. When one of the cows died, Maria and children used a baby bottle to feed the orphaned calf.

When time came to market their first steers, the market was still high and it looked like all their hard work would pay off. They used every dime of their cattle profits to improve their herd, fix the barbed-wire fences and improve the pasture. That was their mistake. They didn't understand capital gains taxes. When tax time came, they didn't have any funds available to pay them. The IRS insisted on payment and, when they couldn't pay, the IRS seized their livestock and other assets.

Thus ended what had been a wonderful story of an immigrant family trying to make good in America. The Chavez family found themselves living in town and working for wages.

The best Roberto could do was to hire out as a part-time cowboy for one of the local dude ranches and to work part-time helping Chuck Lee with his martial arts school and outdoor guide service. The descent from Patron of his own business to working as an employee for others embittered Roberto Chavez against big government. He and his family tried to live the American dream and almost succeeded only to fall victim to a system they felt only rewarded faceless bureaucrats and heartless lawyers.

Roberto took to spending more time with Chuck Lee and drinking more than he should. Maria had to work at a local motel making beds. It upset Roberto's sense of machismo to have his wife work outside the family. They began to quarrel. His sons were jailed for drinking and fighting and he had to go over to the county jail in Hot Sulfur Springs and bail them out. The local paper reported all the details of their arrest and subsequent trial.

Chuck Lee, of course, stood by him. Together, they nursed the bruises life handed them while they nursed their long-necked beers at Happy Jacques. Deep in their cups and waxing philosophical, they concluded that Americans can withstand almost any kind of physical hardship and suffering, just as they had in Vietnam, Laos and Cambodia; however, Americans cannot, and should not, tolerate unfairness. Given the chance, they would strike a blow for justice. Someday.

CHAPTER ELEVEN

The Grand County Board of Commissioners meets on Tuesdays in the Grand County Court House located in Hot Sulphur Springs, Colorado.

Typically, the hearing room is empty except for the three commissioners, the county manager, the county attorney, a secretary and, perhaps, some officials from the various county departments. This day was different. The hearing room was packed.

Some people were there to air grievances of one kind or another. Some were applicants for various types of permits or to ask the commissioner to fund their pet projects, but almost all were there to learn more about the Mexican company that wanted to explore the county for natural gas.

Like most mountain counties, the fight between the pro-growth and the anti-growth elements was on going. The pro-growth side was there to urge the commissioners to issue permits for gas exploration, for mining, for logging, for more golf courses, more housing and for any enterprise that might create more wealth for the landed gentry and to create more wages for those working for wages.

The anti-growth side was there to urge the commissioners to vote against any proposed activities that would somehow diminish their "quality of life." Some of these were grizzled old-timers who wanted the pristine beauty of Grand County to remain unspoiled. Some were wealthy newcomers to the county who met the definition of the environmentalist:

"someone who already has a second home in the mountains." Some were bearded, wild-eyed radicals still living in the 1960s who didn't have a pot to pee in or a window to throw it out of. They were born economic losers and, knowing that, didn't want to see anyone else get ahead either. Together, they made common cause.

When word got out that the Mexican oil company, PEMEX, would be going before the commissioners asking, under the terms of the North American Free Trade Agreement (NAFTA), for permission to do exploration work, a full hearing room was assured.

Senor Raoul Aredondo-Garza, who signed in as the "chief geologist" for Petroleos Mexicanos (PEMEX), was asking for an opportunity to explain to the commissioners the purpose, method and scope of the geologic survey he and his crews would be conducting throughout the county. Under the terms of NAFTA, PEMEX needed no permit from any county or state government to conduct its explorations. Permissions were, however, needed from private landowners who, for the most part, were eager to allow any oil and gas company to come on their land and, perhaps, make them rich. Although about 70 percent of Grand County consists of federal lands of one sort of another, there was no shortage of private landowners who would be happy to grant PEMEX whatever it needed.

Still, the county board had a role to play. Blasting permits would be needed plus there was the matter of safe storage of the explosives brought into the county by PEMEX. A county building inspector would have to certify that the explosives were properly stored.

Also on the agenda was: Dr. James Buckley "Buck" Madison who was appearing to see if something could be done to fix the landing lights at the Granby Airport. It seems the prairie dogs had a taste for the electrical wiring. Dr. Madison was also there to ask the county to recognize the need for a heated, maintenance hangar at the airport. He was accompanied by his lovely wife, Dolly, who, like her husband, was a pilot.

Because they had only lived in the county for about a decade, the Madisons were relative newcomers. But, early on, they noticed a not-so-subtle tension between the western and eastern sides of the county. The reasons for this remained a mystery to the Madisons until they read the writings of Dr. Robert Black who explained in his book *Island in the Rockies,* the historical reasons behind the tension.

In 1803, when the French sold the Louisiana Purchase to President Thomas Jefferson, no one knew the exact whereabouts of the western boundary of the land being acquired by the United States from France. Nor, did anyone know the exact boundary of the Spanish Empire to the west. So, for many years no one knew for sure if large portions of Grand and Summit Counties were part of the United States or part of the Spanish Empire.

A joint American-Spanish boundary commission arrived at a temporary solution by drawing a north-south line between the United States and Spain at the town of Parshall. The effect of the commission's decision was to split Grand County into American Grand County and Spanish Grand County. Therefore, for 20 years, the towns of Winter Park, Fraser, Granby, Grand Lake and Hot Sulphur Springs were in the United States while the towns of Kremmling and Troublesome remained a part of the Spanish Empire.

But an even greater division than geo-politics splits Grand County east and west and that is geography. A five-mile stretch along the Colorado River called Byers Canyon offers some of Colorado's worst winter driving conditions. The sun never shines on portions of Byers Canyon leaving the road caked with ice. If they can find a way to avoid driving Byers Canyon in winter that is what the locals do. As a result, communications and commerce between eastern Grand County and western Grand County are greatly diminished.

Like the boy who lived on "the morning side of the mountain," and the girl who lived on "the evening side of the hill," any romance between the two sides of Grand County was, at best, strained.

Understanding the effects of history and geography on their sur-
roundings led Buck and Dolly to be more philosophical about Grand
County's east-west politics. But both of them were hopeful recent
changes in the make-up of the county board and a new, and highly
effective, county manager would loosen up some funds for needed
repairs and improvements at the Granby Airport where they kept their
airplane.

Also, there was an agenda item dealing with a proposed cattle-driv-
ing trail. Motorists were complaining about the spring ritual of cattle
being driven along U.S. Highway 40 from their winter confinement to
summer pastures. The ranchers were proposing the creation of an
unpaved trail from Granby to Kremmling that could also be used in
winter for snowmobiling and cross-country skiing. The environmentalists, represented by Professor C. Ambrose Coleridge of the University of
Colorado at Boulder, were present to oppose the cattle-trail project.

A local developer was on the agenda to ask the county to open a road
between U.S. Highway 34 and Colorado Highway 125. Several ranchers
and homeowners felt they would be adversely affected by the road and
they were present to voice their opposition.

Lou Leclerc was there to protest the valuation the county assessor was
placing upon his cabin that bordered Rocky Mountain National Park
near Grand Lake. Lou built the cabin himself from logs he felled on his
own land. Over the years, Lou added more rooms until the cabin had
two bedrooms, an inside bath connected to a septic system and a lean-to
garage where he kept a snowmobile and an all-terrain vehicle.
Otherwise, the cabin would be accessible only by foot or snowshoes or
cross-country skis. Each time the cabin was reassessed by the county, the
valuation went up. Lou could not understand if the county played no
role in the creation of what was now a sturdy, albeit not very attractive,
home why should the county profit from his hard labor? With no children, other than those he may have sired in southeast Asia and didn't

know about, Lou was not keen on giving his money to support what he called a bunch of snot-nosed vandals.

A delegation of self-appointed, civic-minded citizens was there to ask the county board to try, once again, to get the Denver-owned (and thus, tax-exempt) Winter Park Ski Resort to pay some taxes to the county. The delegation wanted to know why the ski area was supposed to pay over $2 million a year in taxes to Denver, but refuses to pay any taxes to Grand County?

There to counter those who wanted the ski area to pay taxes were some ski area executives who came to remind the county board that the ski area was the county's largest employer and brought a great many sales-taxable, ski-tourist dollars into the county.

Chuck Lee was there to press his case for a liquor license for the health-juice bar he operated as part of his martial-arts school in Granby. Currently, the bar served only health drinks and vegetable juices. But some of his patrons were more interested in beer. Given Chuck Lee's reputation as a no-holds-barred fighter, some of his neighbors were not in favor of his petition; however, they were prudent enough to post their concerns with the local newspaper's anonymous call-in, hot-line rather than risk a physical confrontation with Chuck Lee. Chuck's sidekick, Roberto Chavez, was there as well.

After the hearing room was packed, the three county commissioners filed in. Mr. Frank Wheeler, the current chairman, represented the western part of the county and lived in Kremmling. Mr. Bob Plummer, represented the Winter Park area in eastern Grand County and Mr. Ned Selak represented Granby which is also in eastern Grand County.

Chairman Wheeler cleared his throat to announce, "The first agenda item is to hear a presentation from Mr. Raoul Aredondo-Garza, the representative from PEMEX which, as I understand it, is the national petroleum company of Mexico. Mr. Aredondo, if you would please come forward and take a chair here at the table."

Taking the seat indicated by the chairman, Raoul, in his flawless, accent-free English, began his presentation:

"Gentlemen, as your chairman stated, I am Senor Raoul Aredondo-Garza; however, I hope you will all become my Americano friends someday and just call me: Raoul or even Ralph, if that pleases you. I am a geologist for PEMEX, the Mexican national oil company. As you may be aware the North American Free Trade Agreement or NAFTA, makes it possible for our two countries to work together on the development of oil and gas resources in a way never permitted before under previous treaties.

"Part of the NAFTA agreement allows your oil and gas industry to explore for oil and gas in Mexico and, in like measure, Mexico can explore for oil and gas north of our common border.

"It is the belief of the PEMEX geologists that Grand County may be the site of a considerable amount of natural gas. My company, PEMEX, has entered into a joint venture with an American oil company under which PEMEX does the geologic survey. If we find enough natural gas, the American company will come in and do the drilling."

"Let me stop you right there, Mr. Aredondo," said Chairman Wheeler. "Why doesn't the American oil and gas company do its own geologic survey?"

"It is a matter of cost, Mr. Chairman," replied Raoul. "My crews work for much less money than American crews."

"But don't you have to pay premium wages for what I understand is highly technical work?"

"Actually, the work itself does not require highly trained workers. I, of course, am a geologist and I work inside the PEMEX control truck monitoring the sensing devices and recording the data. My crew members, on the other hand, have much simpler duties."

"What, exactly, do they do?"

"Their job is to place what we call geophones or geopods out at a distance from the monitoring truck. Each geophone is connected to the truck by an electrical cable. So, you see it doesn't take great skill to set out the geophones, connect the cables and, when we are done, put the geophones and the cables back in the truck."

Reaching down into what was obviously originally manufactured to be a bowling ball carrier, Raoul came up with an orange-painted geopod and placed it on the table.

"As you can see, Ladies and Gentlemen," explained Raoul, with a gallant nod toward Dolly Madison, "a geopod is quite small. We put them out in a certain array, we cause the earth underneath them to vibrate a small amount, we take our measurements, we put the geopods back into our vehicles and we go to the next location and do it all over again. After a few months, we return to Mexico."

"Mr. Aredondo," pressed the chairman, "let's hear more about the part where you cause the earth to vibrate a small amount. Please explain how you do that."

"This is the part, Mr. Chairman, where we need to have your permission because it requires the use of small amounts of explosives. You see, once we have the geopods in proper array around the monitoring truck, we dig a hole down to a certain depth in the center of the geopod array. We place a precise amount of TNT into the bottom of the hole. Observing all safety precautions, we set off the TNT in the holes. The TNT sends shock waves into the ground. These shock waves are monitored inside the PEMEX truck by highly sensitive seismic-measuring instruments. These instruments record their data on special paper mounted on rotating drums.

"After the data are recorded, the data along with the precise location of the test site are sent to PEMEX headquarters in Mexico City where highly skilled specialists study the data."

"And what are you looking for in all this data, Mr. Aredondo?"

"We are looking for what we call geodomes or anticlines. Geodomes are generally found where several rock strata come to an underground apex. Natural gas has a tendency to flow upward into these structual traps where it can be tapped and collected."

"Now Mr. Aredondo," cautioned Wheeler, "I think you need to know right up front that we don't want a bunch of oil wells sticking up ruining the beauty of Grand County. And, we sure don't want a bunch of sludge pits of oil and such spoiling and polluting our waters."

"That is the beauty of natural gas as opposed to oil, Mr. Chairman. We need very small drilling rigs. Once we drill into the apex of the geodome, the drilling rig is removed and a very short tower of valves called a 'Christmas Tree' is placed over the well. The Christmas Tree is used to regulate the flow of the natural gas into an underground pipe to a central collecting station.

"From there, it goes into the nearest interstate gas pipe line and is sold to consumers. In my brief stay in your beautiful county, I notice most of the homes have propane tanks sitting outside. Should we find the natural gas we hope to find, this will be a blessing to many of your residents who are currently paying a high price for propane and, of course, we think underground natural gas for heating and cooking is safer than propane. And, forgive me for saying so, we think the underground gas lines are much more attractive than having aboveground propane tanks sitting around everywhere.

"We, at PEMEX, understand your concern for the impact the drilling and production operations will have on the beauty of your county. Let me assure you the Christmas Tree installations are only about ten feet tall. The gas producers will construct an attractive house around the Christmas Trees to hide them from view. In addition, they will plant trees and scrubs around the little houses. All of these requirements are now codified in U.S. law. In fact, I have a short video showing a gas-well installation in the before, during and after stages of the process. With your permission, I would like to show it to the board and the audience at this time."

"How long is it?"

"Only two minutes."

"Well, okay," said Chairman Wheeler.

The county's only concession to modern presentation methods was a wobbly cart bearing an old TV and a VCR. Aredondo slipped his video in the VCR, turned on the TV and hit the "play" button on the VCR.

Buck Madison recognized the clip. It was actually an edited version of a TV commercial done up in Wyoming by an American oil company. Apparently, Aredondo removed the logo of the American oil company which, in the original, appeared at the beginning and at the end of the commercial.

Too slick, Buck thought to himself. *This act seems a bit too polished.*

"I must say that piece of land in your little film there looked better when you got done than it did before that well was drilled," said Chairman Wheeler.

"Thank you, Mr. Chairman," said Aredondo.

"And what does Grand County get out of these explorations, besides these little houses, some trees and these holes being dug around our county?" asked the chairman.

"PEMEX and its American drilling and producing partner will pay Grand County $1,000 for every seismic test shot we make. The landowner where we find natural gas will receive 1/16th of the profits from each producing well for as long as they produce. As an override, PEMEX and its American partner will pay Grand County a 1/32 share of the profits from each producing well."

"Are we talking very much money, Mr. Aredondo?"

"We are talking at least $1 million a year in revenues going directly into your county treasury, Mr. Chairman. Indirectly, your county will realize much more money than that because your fortunate landowners will be making and spending more money in the county."

"I can't imagine any landowner refusing to let your men on his or her land," said Chairman Wheeler, "but what if someone won't let you on their land?"

"There is such as thing as a 'forced pool' whereby even those who do not wish to cooperate with us are still compensated. You see, Mr.

Chairman, the oil and gas pools were there before the landowners came and surveyors measured lines on the ground to mark off one person's property from that of another person. These pools underlie many, many properties and we intend to see that all property owners whose land is on top of natural gas pools are compensated. Of course, those who cooperate with our exploration efforts will be compensated even more," said Raoul.

With over 70 percent of Grand County composed of non-taxable public lands plus the big ski resort getting a free ride with regard to paying county taxes, all three commissioners leaned forward to hear more from Mr. Aredondo.

"Assuming we vote to give you the permits you need to carry out your gas explorations, Mr. Aredondo, how long will all this take?" asked Commissioner Plummer.

"We would like to begin our field work just as soon as the 'mud season,' as you call it, is over. We understand mud season begins toward the end of May. So, I would think, with luck, we will all be out of here by the holiday you call Labor Day."

"So how soon can we expect the rest of your crew to arrive here in Grand County?" asked Commissioner Selak.

"Very soon, Commissioner Selak, because we have many things to do to prepare. If you will grant us the permissions we need, we plan to rent a large house to the west of Shadow Mountain Lake," said Raoul.

A frown formed on the face of Chairman Wheeler. "Does that mean all your work will be done on the east side of the county?" he asked.

"Oh no, Mr. Chairman, we will be exploring the entire county; especially, around the Kremmling area. We'll be renting motel rooms and eating many of our meals in Kremmling.

"And how soon do you think you'll be spending all this money in Grand County?" asked Chairman Wheeler.

"We'll be here within 30 days. In other words, before the end of May," said Aredondo.

"Just how many people are we talking about and how much equipment?"

"We will have four panel trucks, a jeep for me and a Bell Huey helicopter. To do the work, I'll have about 19 people, including myself."

"And you say you've already found a place to rent?"

"Yes, we found a suitable place. It's the old Koch Ranch. There's a main house for me and my staff and a bunkhouse for our crews. There's plenty of room for our helicopter, places to park our vehicles and the storage sheds we need."

"Sounds as if you're pretty well organized already," Mr. Aredondo. "What's the helicopter used for?"

"The helicopter we need to guide the panel trucks to their locations. Sometimes, we will have to engage in off-road operations and the helicopter can be quite helpful. Rather than run our trucks back and forth overland to our compound, we'd rather use the helicopter because it doesn't damage the terrain. In addition, we will be establishing a PEMEX office in Denver for administrative purposes and for routing our data to Mexico City. The helicopter will save us a two-hour drive over Berthoud Pass."

"You PEMEX fellas must have a lot of money," said Plummer.

"Gentlemen, we are prepared to make a lot of money for Grand County. All we need is permission for the explosives, the cooperation of local governments, some nice publicity in your local newspapers so people will understand what we are doing and, of course, some good western hospitality for a small group of people of foreign origin who are going to be far from home for several months. We promise to make as light a footprint on your beautiful county as possible and to leave it almost the way we found it. If we are fortunate to find natural gas in recoverable amounts, those small plantings are all you will ever see on your landscape. We think the millions of dollars your county will receive in royalties will more than make up for any inconvenience we may cause during our brief stay here."

"You say all of your men are of foreign origin. All Mexican, I suppose?"

"Yes, Mr. Chairman. We are all Mexican."

"Do your men speak English?"

"Actually, my administrative assistant is a female and she also serves as our cook. As to your question about language. Some speak English better than others and some of them speak your language quite well."

"I notice your English is perfect, Mr. Aredondo."

"Thank you. I had the good fortune to study in Switzerland from the time I was a small boy giving me the advantage of fluency in English, German, French, Italian, and, of course, Spanish is my cradle language. But, enough about me. Mr. Chairman, do you or any of your colleagues or does anyone in the audience have any questions about the operation that PEMEX proposes?"

Looking at his colleagues and seeing no interest in additional questions, Chairman Wheeler said, "Thank you for your testimony, Mr. Aredondo. Looks like you've told us what we need to know. We'll take up your requests next Tuesday during our regular commission meeting and take a vote. Just leave the clerk a phone number where you can be contacted and we'll let you know what we decide. Thank you."

Knowing the county's need for money, Raoul Aredondo had no doubt about the outcome on the vote the following Tuesday. He left Hot Sulphur Springs in high spirits.

CHAPTER TWELVE

"Our next agenda item," said Chairman Wheeler, "is to take public comment on the proposed cattle trail between Granby and Kremmling. The next person to testify then will be Professor C. Ambrose Coleridge. Professor Coleridge, please come forward and take a seat, state your name, tell us who you represent and then tell us what's on your mind."

Earlier that morning Professor C. Ambrose Coleridge locked his bachelor apartment close by the campus of the University of Colorado at Boulder, got into his Volvo station wagon and set off for Grand County. Seated behind the wheel, he looked into the rearview mirror and adjusted his polka-dot bow tie. Noting with satisfaction the way his tie went with his tweed jacket and checkered button-down oxford cloth shirt, he settled back to enjoy the splendid scenery—the foothills of the Rockies to his right, the Great Plains spread out to his left.

Heading south on Colorado 93, he made a face as he passed by the Rocky Flats Arsenal, the place where the plutonium triggers for America's nuclear arsenal were made during the Cold War.

The Cold War warriors made a dog's breakfast of that, Coleridge thought to himself. And on this subject Professor Coleridge was quite correct. The private corporation charged with the operation of Rocky Flats had made a mess of things. Yes, Rocky Flats provided the plutonium triggers for the nuclear weapons deployed during that nightmare part of history when the United States and the Soviet Union faced each other like two scorpions in a bottle or, as the nuclear theorists, in their Strangelovian jargon called it: mutual assured destruction or MAD. But the private firm botched its responsibility to prevent leaks of radioactive materials. Indeed, the mismanagement of Rocky Flats inspired much of Professor Coleridge's environmental activism.

Coming to Interstate 70, Professor Coleridge turned right and began the long, westward climb into the foothills and over the Continental Divide. Winter snows still blanketed the higher slopes of the Rockies. Tons of snow packed the deep bowls that meant Clear Creek would, once again, get out of its banks on its way to Golden. Shortly after Easter, most of the ski resorts would shut down for the year although the Mary Jane side of Winter Park would probably operate until Memorial Day and Arapahoe Basin would, no doubt, stay open well into June. Despite recent snows, the roads were clear and the professor expected a comfortable, scenic drive over Berthoud Pass and on to Hot Sulphur Springs.

A long-time member of the Sierra Club, the Caucus of Environmental Voters and a secret member of the radical Earth First!, C. Ambrose Coleridge felt he was at the cutting edge of saving the planet from everyone else.

To C. Ambrose Coleridge, Mother Nature was casting her pearls before these undeserving swine in their RVs and their snowmobiles. Only those who were willing to hike into wilderness areas with packs on their backs were deserving of seeing the beauties of the national forests and parks. The idea of those blue-collar, Joe-six-packs loading up their families in their bourgeois, gas-guzzling RVs to view the splendor of the Rockies was anathema to C. Ambrose Coleridge. On his office wall, was an autographed photo of his idol, Secretary of the Interior, Winthrop Sinclair III.

Professor Coleridge was active in a number of causes dear to the heart of the liberal establishment. He worked hard on the pay and allowances committee of the American Association of University

Professors as part of their constant battle to increase professorial pay, to reduce classroom hours and to combat any attempts to do away with the tenure system. He was an active member of the American Civil Liberties Union and a heavy contributor to the ACLU coffers. After all, only the ACLU was willing to take an active role in trying to protect the North American Man-Boy Love Association or NAMBLA, as it was called. As a covert, but practicing member of NAMBLA, Professor Coleridge had good reason to support the ACLU.

A public hearing in Hot Sulphur Springs was the professor's more immediate concern. Because of his prominence in the environmental movement, Professor Coleridge had been asked by the Sierra Club to go to Grand County to testify against a proposed cattle trail which, no doubt, would be used by the dreaded snowmobilers.

According to the briefing sheet provided by the Sierra Club, the current practice was for ranchers to drive their cattle along US Highway 40. This practice, however, caused traffic delays and could be a safety hazard both for the cattle and for motorists. In an attempt to keep down the traffic delays, the cowboys were limited to moving the cattle for only a few hours beginning at dawn and then having to stay with the cattle in a pasture to await the next dawn to resume the drive. A cattle drive that should only take one day at most was then strung-out over several days. The proposed multi-use trail would solve the problem and the trail would be available almost all the time for use by hikers and, in winter, available to cross-country skiers and snowmobilers.

Professor Coleridge's hatred of snowmobilers knew no bounds. Snowmobiles were the smelly, noisy steeds of pot-bellied, beer-swilling, blue-collared, poor-white-trash crackers of the worst sort. He didn't care if snowmobiles were useful in carrying injured people from the outback to medical care. They shouldn't have been in the outback to begin with.

Not that Professor Coleridge was totally opposed to outdoor sports. He and his university colleagues were fond of donning their Nordic sweaters and knickers and then stepping into their cross-county skis for a few turns around a well-manicured track after which they would repair before the fireplace of a cozy lodge and enjoy some hot-mulled wine. Their embrace with nature concluded, they would jump in their Volvos and Saabs and return to Boulder. If snowmobiles did have a place, it was only to groom tracks for cross-country skiers. Other than that, they should be banned.

The linoleum-tiled floor and the olive-drab walls of the hearing room at the Grand County Courthouse did not seem a friendly place to Professor Coleridge. Seated behind a well-worn wooden table, the three county commissioners wore western shirts under leather jackets. All wore cowboy boots. Not a good sign. Except for a very attractive blond in maybe her late 40s, all the others in attendance seemed rather rough. Professor Coleridge's bow tie and the tweed jacket with the leather patches on the elbows set him apart.

"Look at that prick from the People's Republik," whispered Lou Leclerc to Chuck Lee and Roberto Chavez. "He looks like he's got a cobb up his ass and a persimmon in his mouth. Bet he has to squat to pee."

Chuck Lee was about to offer his own scathing commentary when Dolly Madison turned around from her front-row seat beside Buck and gave all three of them a disapproving look.

Chairman Wheeler continued, "In addition to Professor Coleridge, I see we have representatives of the US Forest Service, the Bureau of Land Management, the Colorado Department of Transportation, the Colorado Department of Wildlife, the Colorado Guest Ranch Association, plus several ranchers and, of course, other interested members of the public.

"So, Professor Coleridge, we'll let you begin."

"Thank you Mr. Chair," began Coleridge only to be interrupted by Chairman Wheeler.

"Just so we understand each other up front Professor Coleridge, I am a person, not a chair. Up here we say: Mr. Chairman or Madame

Chairwoman, as appropriate. You can even call me Frank if you like. But please spare us the politically-correct gobbledygook. Okay?"

"Yes, Chairman Wheeler, I'll try to keep that in mind. I am Professor C. Ambrose Coleridge and on behalf of the Sierra Club and other environmentalist groups, I am here today to speak in opposition to the proposed multi-use trail between Granby and Kremmling.

"We feel such a trail will detract from the natural beauty of your fine county but will also result in uses that will be deleterious to existing wildlife habitat. Specifically, if we understand the proposed uses correctly, that snowmobiles will be permitted to use the trail in winter. They will frighten the deer and elk causing them to expend their limited energies unnecessarily and result in the needless deaths of many of these animals.

"Moreover, the creation of this trail to facilitate the cattle industry only serves to perpetuate the cattle industry."

"Excuse me for interrupting, Professor," said Chairman Wheeler, "but what is wrong with perpetuating the cattle industry?"

"Commissioner Wheeler, study after study shows the health dangers of eating red meat. Cattle trample the grasses thereby causing soil erosion, they consume voluminous amounts of water and grass which causes them to emit enormous amounts of methane gas. The methane gas fouls the atmosphere and their excrement fouls the streams."

"Excuse me, Mr. Chairman," interrupted Commissioner Selak, "by excrement, Professor, I assume you are talking about bullshit. Only I suspect you folks down in Boulder would call it male bovine excretia. And, with all due respect, let me suggest that you are full of male bovine excretia if you think this group of elected officials is opposed to cattle ranching in Grand County. Professor, some of our people, to include my own family, have been ranching up here for almost 150 years."

"And with all due respect to you, Commissioner Selak," said Coleridge, "then I think it is time to suggest that ranchers find something better to do with their lives."

"And what would you suggest we learn to do with our pitiful, little lives?" asked Selak.

"Open some shops for tourists. Make pottery. Paint those Elvis-on-velvet pictures of which you people seem so fond. Learn to make espresso, cafe-au-lait, anything but cattle ranching."

At this point, a number of the ranchers in the hearing room were wishing for a rope, a tall tree and for the sheriff to be out of town. Unknown to Professor Coleridge, Hot Sulphur Springs was not a stranger to vigilante justice. In 1883, Texas Charlie Wilson, rode into Grand County and proceeded to bully people with an array of firearms. By 1884, the good people of Hot Sulphur Springs decided Texas Charlie Wilson was beyond earthly salvation.

Tuesday, December 9, 1884, dawned clear and mild for that time of year. As Texas Charlie swaggered down the street with two of his fellow bullies and a lawyer from Denver, a hail of gunfire cut down Charlie. Almost immediately 15 men carrying a variety of firearms emerged from a prominent building to make sure Texas Charlie was dead.

His body was immediately carried to a makeshift coroner's office where an inquest was held on the spot. Eleven of the town's finest people were called to testify. Amazingly, no one had seen the shooting although some of the witnesses had heard a "discharge of firearms." The case was closed for lack of evidence.

"Professor," said Selak, fingering the nitro-glycerin pills in his vest pocket and wondering if he should take one, "you are treading on pretty thin ice. Are you sure you want to tell us more about how our cattle use up the water and foul our streams?"

"Yes, I would. Water from the mountains is badly needed in the populated parts of Colorado. It is needed for growing vegetables, for drinking, for electricity and for sanitation."

"You mean you need the water down in Boulder and Denver more than we need it up here where it snows and rains?" asked Commissioner Wheeler.

"That is correct. And that view is perfectly democratic. The majority of the people are down along the Front Range while only a comparative handful live up here. The water belongs to the people."

"So, you're saying we're not people up here in the mountains?" asked Selak.

"Well, you are people. But you are just a fraction of the people. You couldn't possibly use all the snowmelt and rainfall you get up here. That's why there are all these tunnels and other water diversion projects—so the water can get to the majority of the people where it is really needed.

"You mean so the majority can water their over-fertilized and manicured lawns every day and wash their cars and fill their swimming pools and the golf courses can maintain their nice, bent-grass greens?" asked Commissioner Selak.

"Well, people do have a right to keep their properties as they please," countered Coleridge.

"Yeah. Well, we think we have right to our lives up here and we don't muck up the environment with a bunch of lawn chemicals. And, what's more, you talk about snowmobilers running the deer and elk and, I admit, that's not good. But who the hell do you think feeds the deer and elk toward the end of winter when their fat supplies run low? I'll tell you who feeds them. We ranchers let the deer and elk into our pastures and feedlots and we give them the feed they need to make it through those last weeks of cold weather. And, if we try to get reimbursed for saving those animals, filling out all the paperwork takes more time than it is worth."

"You should not be feeding the deer and the elk. That upsets the balance of nature. We in the environmental movement are taking steps to prevent any future feedings of these animals," said Coleridge.

"Then let me suggest that you don't show your pasty face on my land when my ranch hands and I are doing the decent thing by feeding the deer and elk or we'll blow your ass off!"

The hearing room erupted with shouts of support for Commissioner Selak's threat causing Chairman Wheeler to pound the table with his gavel.

"That's enough! Order! We will have order!" yelled Wheeler until all the hooting and hollering from the crowd settled down.

"Well, Professor Coleridge," said Chairman Wheeler, "you've made your position quite clear and I think you have gotten an idea of how some of our residents feel as well.

"Unless other commissioners have questions or comments, we will simply thank you for coming up here to enlighten we common folk with your views. Let me suggest you proceed without delay back to the People's...excuse me, back to Boulder. We sure wouldn't want anything untoward to happen to you."

"I am accustomed to being vilified for my beliefs, Mr. Chairman."

"Before you go, Professor. Would you answer a few questions totally unrelated to the subject of this hearing?" asked Commissioner Selak.

"I suppose so."

"Alger Hiss. Innocent or guilty?"

"Innocent."

"The Rosenbergs. Innocent or guilty?"

"Innocent."

"Abortion. Pro-abortion or pro-life?"

"I'm pro-choice."

"The Cold War. Whose fault? The USSR or the US?"

"I don't see how that is related to this hearing."

"I told you it wasn't related. But I'll bet you voted for George Bush and Bob Dole."

"Of course not!" Coleridge blurted out.

Professor Coleridge turned crimson as he realized he had allowed this country bumpkin of a county commissioner to goad him into revealing for whom he voted, something he would only have told within his own circle of liberal friends.

"Again, thank you for your testimony," said Chairman Wheeler. "You are excused."

Coleridge was furious with himself for being made a fool of in front of a bunch of poor, white, trailer-trash rednecks, as he liked to call people who lived outside his world. By the time he stopped to buy gas, Professor Coleridge was still shaking with anger from his treatment in Hot Sulphur Springs. Yes, he and his colleagues would show these local yokels a thing or two. He'd send some of his Earth First! friends to pour sugar in the fuel tanks of log-transporters, backhoes and other earth-moving equipment.

The gas paid for, Coleridge drove along US 40 by the Sol Vista at Silver Creek Ski Resort in the direction of Berthoud Pass. Soon, he was passing the Winter Park and Mary Jane ski areas on his right and, shortly thereafter, was steering his Volvo wagon up through the series of switchbacks leading toward the pass. Three switchbacks below the summit, he saw a young snowboarder hoping to hitch a ride to the top.

Young people with little money used hitch hiking as a means for skiing or snowboarding when broke. Once on top, they would slide down until they came once again to Highway 40 and, hopefully, another motorist willing to give them a lift back up.

"I'll take you to the top," Professor Coleridge told the boy as he motioned for him to get into the Volvo wagon.

"Thanks a lot, Mister," said the boy, placing his snowboard in the back. "I've really been lucky today. This is my fifth ride up."

"You've been at this all day?"

"Yeah, it's a blast."

"Aren't you supposed to be in school today?"

"Yeah, but with all this fresh snow and sunshine I can't see being inside."

"How do you expect to graduate if you don't attend school?"

"You mean so I can get a good job?"

"Precisely."

"The only jobs up here are making beds and waiting tables or maybe being a lift attendant."

"Then, I take it you are not interested in going to college someday?"

"Heck no. A college degree means I have to live down in Denver or somewhere. Aren't many college jobs up here. I just want to get a job around here so I can help my Mom."

"Very commendable young man. I'm sure you'll do just that. What about your father?"

"Oh, he split last year."

"So, when are you supposed to be home."

"As long as I get home by dark, I'm okay."

"I see. How old are you my boy?"

"Thirteen."

"What's your name, Mister?"

"Ah, ah, George. What's yours?"

"Troy."

"Well, Troy. Here we are, the summit of Berthoud Pass. Tell you what. Let's park the car over here out of the way and you can repay my kindness by answering a few questions about snowboarding. I've only done cross-country skiing so anything you could tell me about snowboarding would be most appreciated.

"And while you're telling me all about snowboarding, we can share some delicious hot cocoa from my thermos. It will only take a few moments to prepare a cup for you."

The professor got out of the car, went to the back and opened the tailgate. In a few moments, he presented Troy with a cup of cocoa."

"How's that?" the professor asked.

"Kinda bitter, but it's good and hot," said Troy.

"It's a special dark-roast blend. That's what makes it bitter. Now tell me why you like snowboarding," said Professor Coleridge, as he watched the boy pass out.

Chuck, Lou and Roberto were drinking at Happy Jacques when the bartender told Chuck he had a call. Picking up the receiver all Chuck could hear was his sister's hysterical sobbing."

"Sis, is that you?"

"Oh thank God, Chuck. Something terrible has happened to Troy. He's been…God, I can't say it."

"Sis, get a grip. Is he alive?"

"Yes, he's alive. But he's been…He's been raped."

"Is he all right?"

"He tells me he's bleeding. But he won't let me look. He's locked himself in the bathroom and he's crying."

"Okay. Adrienne, try to stay calm. Have you called the Sheriff?"

"No, you're the first one I called. Should I call the Sheriff?"

"No. Wait till we get there. I've got Lou and Roberto with me. We'll figure out what to do when we get there."

Half an hour later, Chuck got Troy to open the bathroom door while Lou and Roberto tried to comfort Adrienne. After awhile, an ashen-faced Chuck came out of the bathroom.

"He was raped all right. I cleaned him up and the bleeding's stopped. I found some stuff for hemorrhoids and put it on a sanitary napkin and he's in there sitting on that. I made him take a couple of pain pills. Physically he'll recover. But mentally, it's going to be tough. He keeps telling me he's so ashamed."

"Does he know who did it?" asked Lou.

"He says some older guy in a Volvo wagon picked him just below the summit of Berthoud Pass about mid-afternoon," said Chuck.

"What was he doing up on the pass on a school day?" asked Roberto.

"Playing hooky so he could hitch rides up to the top of Berthoud pass and snowboard down," said Chuck.

"He's been a mess ever since the divorce," said Adrienne.

"You're still better off, Sis," said Chuck, "if that sonofabitch ever hits you again, I'll kill him."

"You almost did," said Roberto. "If I hadn't pulled you off, you would have killed him."

"So what are we going to do about Troy? What are we gonna do about the rapist? Call the Sheriff?" asked Lou.

"Oh God, Chuck," said Adrienne, sobbing. "He's so ashamed now. Do we have to call in the police? It'll get in the paper. You know how they print everything like that. Oh God. Oh God."

"Pardon my French, Adrienne," said Lou." "but even if the police catch this motherfucker, he'll just walk because some fancy lawyer will get the trial moved to Denver and a liberal-ass judge will just slap him on the wrist and let him go."

"Chuck, go ask him if he can remember anything about this guy," said Roberto.

In a few moments Chuck came back into the living room.

"He was about 50 years old. He was wearing a bow tie and a tweed coat. He was driving a Volvo wagon and he said his name was George. That's all he can remember right now," said Chuck.

"George, my ass," said Roberto. "That was that Professor Coleridge we saw this morning at the court house."

"Wait a minute, Sis, we'll be right back," said Chuck. After a brief conference outside the trailer with Lou and Roberto, Chuck came back in alone to talk with Adrienne.

"Here's the deal. I know a lady who will give Troy some counseling at no charge. She'll just do it because she and her husband are good troops. Buck Madison and I go way back. She'll give you some counseling too, Sis."

"Dolly? I know her. Everyone loves Dolly. Please call her, Chuck."

"Meanwhile, we don't think it will do Troy any good to call the police. Just more trauma for him. If he can hack it, he ought to go back to school. If not, tell the school he's sick and keep him home a day or two."

"But what about the creep who did this to my boy, Chuck?"

"We think we can find him and help him pay his debt to society. But you'll have to keep your mouth shut."

"Oh Chuck, please don't kill anybody. I couldn't bear to lose you too."

"Nothing like that, Sis. But I guarantee you he's raped his last victim."

CHAPTER THIRTEEN

It took Chuck, Lou and Roberto about two hours of steady work to pull together the supplies they needed. As former members of a U.S. Special Forces "A" Team, both Chuck and Roberto possessed the mandatory expertise in the basic Special Forces skills: weapons, engineering and demolitions, communications, medicine, operations and intelligence plus at least one foreign language. Prior to becoming a commissioned officer and an "A" Team commander, Chuck Lee's military occupational specialty (MOS) was 18C, making him an expert in demolitions. First Lieutenant Roberto Chavez was his executive officer. In fact, as an enlisted man, Roberto completed the 57 weeks of training required to hold MOS 18D, the medical specialist. This would be a mission made to order for Roberto Chavez.

At 0400 hours, a maroon, mini-van pulled into the driveway of Professor C. Ambrose Coleridge's duplex apartment in Boulder and parked beside a Volvo station wagon. Three men in dark street clothes, and wearing surgical gloves, walked quietly over to the Volvo. Lou Leclerc slipped a piece of flexible steel in between the driver's side window and the doorsill. In moments, the door was open.

Then the three men moved to the apartment building and made sure they were in front of the correct door. Lou took out a leather wallet full of picks, selected one and picked the lock.

A rag laced with chloroform rendered a struggling C. Ambrose Coleridge unconscious. Without a sound, his inert shape was carried outside and placed into the mini-van.

Inside the mini-van, the windows were taped so no one could see in or see out. Coleridge's pajama sleeve was pushed back. Roberto injected enough sedative to render the professor unconscious for several hours. Next, he was stripped naked and tied face up on a wooden plank suspended across the flattened rear seats.

A surgically-gloved hand grasped his penis and pulled it sharply toward his navel. Another gloved hand applied three strips of surgical tape to hold the penis up and out of the way. Next, an emissis basin that had been lined with plastic food wrap was placed under his scrotum.

Neatly arranged nearby were sponges, sulfa powder, alcohol, iodine, pliers, suturing materials and a scalpel.

While Lou held a portable spotlight, Chuck stood by to act as a surgical assistant. Roberto took the scalpel out of its sterile wrapper and positioned his hands over the exposed scrotum. Deftly, he made a vertical incision over the left testicle. Blood gushed from the wound but Chuck quickly applied a sponge. Even so, some blood dripped down into the emissis basin.

Opening the incision until he could insert his index finger into the scrotum, Roberto hooked it around the testicle and pulled it forward and out of the scrotum which quickly collapsed to fill the void. Taking the same pliers used by ranchers to convert bulls to steers, he snipped off the testicle and dropped it into a baggie held by Chuck.

Roberto sifted some sulfa powder onto the wound. Then, Chuck taped a sponge over it. Roberto shifted position slightly to address the right testicle. Again, a precise incision opened the right side of the scrotum. More blood appeared and, again, Chuck applied a sponge. The right testicle was pulled from the scrotum, snipped off and dropped into the baggie.

Yellow and blue do make green, thought Chuck, as he closed the baggie.

Roberto dropped the scalpel and the pliers into the emissis basin, dusted on more sulfa powder and Chuck handed him a surgeon's needle already threaded with suturing material. Roberto began at the top of the incision over the left testicle and quickly sutured downward until the entire wound was closed. Moving again to his right, he did the same over the right side of the scrotum. The wound sites were washed with an iodine solution and dried. Sterile gauze was placed over both wounds and taped in place with surgical tape.

The procedure completed, the unconscious figure was dressed again in his pajamas. While Roberto and Chuck deposited the operating detritus in a hazardous materials disposal bag, Lou placed a bag of ice in the driver's seat of the Volvo Wagon and then taped the baggie full of balls to the professor's rear-view mirror.

I'll bet the professor hates those fuzzy dice we rednecks hang on our rear-view mirrors, thought Lou. *He'll like this pair even less.*

Walking back to the mini-van, he informed Roberto and Chuck the Volvo was ready. Together, they carried the child molester to his car and placed him in the driver's seat, securing him upright with the seatbelt and shoulder restraints. Not having a key to get the window on the driver's side to come down and not wishing to take the time to hot-wire the car, they simply left the driver's door slightly ajar.

As quietly as it came, the mini-van slipped away just as the sun was beginning to cast its first light out over the Great Plains.

A few hours later, neighbors called the police to report a man shrieking from inside his parked car. The police came and called for an emergency medical team. While they were waiting for the ambulance, they found the apartment door wide open and walked in.

Two police officers found a nest of pornographic materials. Most of the photos showed men having anal and oral sex with young boys. University police were called to the apartment where they took photographs of the evidence of pedophilia along with photographs of some correspondence bearing the letterhead of NAMBLA. Next to a computer, they found a long list of websites specializing in pornography.

In his hospital room, when he was more cogent, the victim could not remember anything at all except waking up in his car sitting in a pool of cold water and the slow realization of what had happened to him. The Boulder Police were unable to find a single clue. No prints, no hair, no fibers, no nothing. Obviously, the people who castrated Professor Coleridge were consummate professionals.

Given the record of the Boulder police and the district attorney for failing to apprehend and convict criminals even when they have evidence, both the police and the district attorney were delighted when Professor Coleridge expressed no interest in pursuing the matter. The professor's only interest was in keeping publicity to a minimum.

But the university police turned over the evidence of pedophilia and involvement with NAMBLA to the University authorities. Shortly thereafter, Professor C. Ambrose Coleridge tendered his resignation from the faculty for "health reasons" and left Boulder without leaving a forwarding address.

Following their return to Grand County, Chuck, Lou and Roberto, slept almost all day. But in the evening they met at Happy Jacques to hold their post-mission critique. Since they couldn't think of any ways to improve upon their "operation," they said to hell with it and got rip-roaring drunk. The other patrons couldn't remember when they had seen the trio in such good spirits.

CHAPTER FOURTEEN

With his crew, vehicles, equipment and helicopter neatly assembled at the old Koch Ranch. Raoul called the members of Team PEMEX together for a formal mission briefing. For security reasons, they sat out in the open on bales of hay arranged in a semi-circle facing away from the sun. Raoul stood so he could face them.

"Our first task," announced Raoul, "is to convince the people of Grand County that we are what we say we are: geological surveyors looking for natural gas deposits.

"Our second mission is to make friends with local members of the Sagebrush Rebellion and recruit some of them to help us destroy four targets: the Adams Tunnel, the Moffat Tunnel, the Lake Granby Pump Plant and The Grand Ditch. But our most important mission to assassinate Presidents Trimmer and Popov by destroying the Lake Granby High Dam at precisely the correct time.

"Finally, we want to escape successfully leaving the local Militia, if you will, to take the blame.

"Five days a week, we will conduct survey operations all over Grand County. But every evening we will be in the local bars looking for recruits. On the weekends, we will travel around doing the things tourists do. Of course, these 'tourist' trips will be related to our missions.

"Here are your assignments:

Team Adams: Francisco and Miguel

Team Moffat: Pancho and Salvador initially; however, Regina may be needed, as well.

Team Pump: Antonio and Felipe

Team Ditch: Only Juan for now. But I hope to be able to recruit a couple of gringos to attack this lower-priority target.

The security force will consist of: Arturo, Ernesto, Jorge, Julio, Manuel, Ramon, Ruiz, and Sancho.

"Of course, I alone, will be in charge of the destruction of the Lake Granby High Dam."

"Living in the main house with me will be Regina, Federico and Jose. The rest of you will live in the bunkhouse. Regina will act as our base station radio operator and computer expert. Regina will also cook our breakfasts and look after me. If you think that means what you think it means, it does. Anyone who looks twice at Regina will be shot. Do I make myself clear?

"We will take our mid-day meals in the local restaurants close to wherever we are working. Our evening meals will be taken in local bars and restaurants. That way, we maximize our chances of approaching recruits. Keep your food and drink receipts and turn them into Regina for reimbursement.

"If anything happens to me, Federico takes command.

"D-Day is set for Labor Day. H-Hour is tentatively set for 0700 hours, but that will depend on President Trimmer's schedule. We need him to be down in the valley of the Colorado River, either fishing or attending some kind of Labor Day celebration. In any event, H-Hour will be adjusted accordingly. But I am thinking the earlier in the day the better because that will give us more time to make our escape.

"I expect each team to conduct a proper reconnaissance of its objective and be prepared to brief me on how you will accomplish your missions not later than 30 days from now.

"Are there any questions?"

"Senor Raoul, what is the plan for our escape? The Huey helicopter can only carry 12 of us. We have 18 men here plus Regina."

"That's why we have a twin-turbine helicopter. It can carry a full load even on the hottest days. But your question is excellent. Be advised, by the time we get to D-Day, I will have sent many of you on ahead to a Cuban ship lying in Vancouver harbor. If everything goes as planned on D-Day, the only team members remaining here will be from Team Adams, Team Moffat, and Team Pump. Counting myself, Regina, Federico and Jose to pilot the helicopter, that makes nine. Add on three security men and that brings the total up to 12.

"The PEMEX signs on the sides of your trucks are magnetic. Before departing for Canada, you will remove the PEMEX signs and replace them with magnetic signs which we already have on hand. They say: 'Joe's Plumbing,' 'Hank's Electric,' and the like. I also have Montana license plates for each vehicle. You will remove the special NAFTA license plates you used to cross into the States and replace them with Montana plates for your drive into Canada," said Raoul.

"One more question, por favor, Jefe," asked Ramon.

"How will we get our mail while we are here?"

"You won't. We'll all be out of here by early September. Being out of contact with our loved ones for a few months is just one of the many prices we all have to pay if we are to see the triumph of our glorious revolution.

"But I promise to make your stay here as pleasant as possible. We are well funded. I am pleased to tell you that, if we are successful, a large sum of money has been set aside for each of you. You will never have to work again. Plus, while you are here, you will have all the money you need to eat and drink on the local economy and to buy drinks for the gringo friends we are going to make.

"If we maintain our discipline, watch what we say and make no slips of the tongue, we will do our jobs and escape without notice," said Raoul.

"But how do we carry out our assignments if all our vehicles have departed for Montana prior to D-Day?" asked Manuel.

"The plan calls for the use of a gringo pickup for the attack on The Grand Ditch. I will, however, need a pickup of my own for the Granby Dam attack. I have already located a used-truck lot with no security whatsoever. The lot will be closed for Labor Day. So, before dawn on Labor Day one of you will be tasked to hot-wire a suitable pickup and bring it here for my use. We made up a magnetic sign that looks like the signs on the sides of the vehicles belonging to the Northern Colorado Water Conservancy District. The stolen pickup will not look out of place should anyone drive by.

"Once I get the explosive charges in place inside the dam, I simply connect the electricity to the circuit, set the timer for the explosive charges, leave the truck to be destroyed along with the dam and walk northwest along Grand County Road 6 to a clearing near Sunset Point where Jose will pick me up in the helicopter and bring me back here. When all 12 of us are assembled, we fly south to New Mexico to a remote location where we will find a fuel bladder and a wobble pump. After we refuel ourselves, we fly beneath the gringos' radar coverage into Mexico. You may recall when a U.S. Air Force A-10 fighter made an unauthorized flight from Arizona to Colorado that it took the American authorities almost a month to find the crash site.

"Now, any final questions?" asked Raoul.

Federico and Regina watched Raoul's performance with admiration. He had Team PEMEX in the palm of his hand.

"Good," said Raoul. "Now on our first full evening here at the Koch Ranch, I have a treat for everyone. I had Regina go to one of the local markets and buy plenty of hickory-smoked chickens and a pound of hickory-smoked ribs for every man here. On top of that, Regina has prepared Cuban rice and beans and all of the other foods we love so well. Plus we have enough rum, cokes, limes and ice to fill Lake Granby. Of course, I exaggerate. So, amigos, eat, drink, but keep your hands off Regina. Sleep late tomorrow and rest. The day after tomorrow we begin our work."

CHAPTER FIFTEEN

Toward, the end of the ski season came one of Dolly's least favorite times of the year. Not only was it mud season, it also meant the approach of the annual 10th Colonial Parachute Regiment Memorial Dinner. First of all, it would take Buck away for one evening in mid-March while Buck and the other locals who had served together in 1st Air Cavalry Division in Vietnam planned the affair. The planning meeting always took place in the backroom of Happy Jacques Saloon. And then, there would be the actual dinner in the main dining room of Happy Jacques. The dinner was always held on May 7th, in memory of the fall of the French garrison at Dien Bien Phu.Thanks to the ever-vigilant Grand County Sheriff's Department, a "driving under the influence" ticket was an almost certainty for anyone who tried to operate a motor vehicle after drinking all those innumerable toasts to the fictional characters of the 10th Colonial Parachute Regiment. That meant, and it was the only time each year she had to do it, Dolly would have to drive over to Happy Jacques and retrieve her Buck.One of the stranger aspects of this annual dinner was the fact that the mythical 10th Colonial Parachute Regiment never even served a mythical tour in Vietnam. Long after the French Paras of Vietnam were defeated at Dien Bien Phu and returned home to metropolitan France, the 10thColonial Parachute Regiment was formed in the mind of the French journalist/novelist, Jean Larteguy, and deployed, not in Vietnam, but to Algeria.

As fans of Jean Larteguy know so well, the 10th Colonial Parachute Regiment only existed in the pages of two of his novels: *The Centurions* and *The Praetorians*. But, The *Centurions,* published in English in the early 1960s, became a virtual Bible for young American officers preparing themselves for their first tour in South Vietnam. By 1965, it would be difficult to find an officer of the combat arms who had not read Larteguy's fictional, but highly accurate account, of the plight of the survivors of the French defeat at Dien Bien Phu, the horrors of their imprisonment at Prison Camp Number One and how they later applied the lessons learned from their North Vietnamese captors against the Algerian rebels.

The reading of *The Centurions* was actively pushed by the Infantry School at Fort Benning, Georgia, because the highly readable novel illustrated so well the political mistakes made by the French government in Indo-China, the ensuing military mistakes made by the French military and the methods used so successfully by the Viet Minh to drive the French out of Indo-China.

By exposing as many young officers as possible to the lessons the French should have learned, it was hoped the American military would not make the same mistakes. But the effort went awry.

Apparently, only the young American officers in the jungles, rice paddies and mountains of South Vietnam bothered to read and understand the lessons of *The Centurions* and *The Praetorians*. For sure, President Lyndon Johnson and Secretary of Defense, Robert S. McNamara, did not read them or, if they did, they sure didn't understand what Larteguy was trying to say. How ironic that so many young Americans went to Vietnam knowing what mistakes not to make and then were forced into making them by their so-called superiors in Washington. For Buck Madison, his dog-eared copy of *The Centurions* was almost as important to him as his equally dog-eared copy of *The New Testament*. In fact, Buck and his fellow officers in the 1st Air Cavalry Division's 2d Battalion of the 5th Cavalry got so involved with the French officers described in *The Centurions* that they began to assume the persona of Larteguy's characters. It all probably started as a joke, this business of assigning to themselves some of the names of the characters in the book, but it soon took on a life of its own. In fact, the game went so far that the battalion commander, some of his staff and all of the company commanders began, much to the dismay of the division signal officer, to call each other by their "Centurion" names when speaking to each other over the battalion radio network.

Their battalion commander was, in fact, descended from an aristocratic French family some years back and so he took the name Jacques de Glatigny. Why? Because Jean Larteguy's character, Jacques Glatigny, was a French aristocrat. Coincidentally, the mythical de Glatigny spent a great deal of his service as an aide-de-camp to a very senior French general officer—a fact which just happened to mirror the career pattern of Buck's battalion commander.

Pierre Raspeguy, who was played by Anthony Quinn in the Hollywood movie version of Larteguy's follow-on novel, *The Praetorians*, matched up rather well with Major Sword, the battalion operations officer. By the time Major Sword joined the 2d Battalion of the 5th Cavalry Regiment, he was on his third tour in Vietnam. During his first year in country, he served as an advisor to the Vietnamese Airborne Division. This put Sword in contact with a bunch of ex-patriot French Paras who had returned to Vietnam to be with their Vietnamese wives and children and liked to spend their free time hanging around the Vietnamese airborne units. The tall tales of the retired Paras fascinated Major Sword who was in the process of developing an intense hatred for the Viet Cong and the North Vietnamese Army. It was Major Sword who was the driving force behind the transformation of the very real 2d Battalion, 5th Cavalry into the mythical 10thColonial Parachute Regiment.

But the most interesting of the Larteguy characters brought to life within the 2d Battalion, Cavalry, was Julien Boisfueras. Chuck Lee, one of Buck Madison's fellow company commanders, was a perfect match for the Boisfueras character. Both the imaginary Boisfueras and the real Chuck Lee had a gift for mastering obscure languages and dialects. They knew how to go native and win the hearts and minds of their adopted hosts. Both the mythical Boisfueras and the very real Chuck Lee were masters of the martial arts, dead shots with small arms and had forgotten more about small-unit tactics than Sun Zsu and Che Guervara ever knew. Both Boisfueras and Lee could be kind one minute and ruthless the next. Choose any weapon or bombination of weapons or care-handed, both men could take on multiple opponents and slay them and, if deemed psychologically useful, kill all their friends, relations and sympathizers as well. They were the epitome of what the United States Special Forces tries to train its "A" Team leaders to be able to do: recruit, train and employ effectively an entire regiment of combat-ready gueril-las.At first, the aristocratic battalion commander looked down his long nose at Chuck Lee and once confided in Buck that he wasn't sure a "snake-eater" like Chuck would do well as the commander of a regular infantry unit. He worried that a captain whose only "official" soldiers had been in a 12-man "A" Team would not be up to commanding the five other officers and 164 enlisted men supposed to be assigned to a regular Army infantry company.

But in a matter of days, Captain Lee won the hearts and minds of his officers, NCOs and enlisted men.

Within two weeks, Chuck Lee led them through a series of brilliant engagements that inflicted heavy losses on the North Vietnamese without the loss of a single GI.Also within weeks, Chuck Lee and Buck Madison, as fellow company commanders, were on their way to becoming the fastest of friends. Buck, who was innately orthodox in his tactical thinking was fascinated by Chuck Lee. Buck always said that watching Chuck was like watching a Cobra get ready to strike. But finding something to strike was often a problem.

Not because the 1st Air Cavalry Division didn't know where the enemy was, it was because of screwball political restrictions.

The NVA had its sanctuary in Cambodia from which it would periodically emerge, strike some American patrol or night defensive position or firebase and then quickly melt back into the safety of Cambodia.

Despite aggressive patrolling and imaginative use of airmobile operations, the 1st Air Cavalry Division was often reacting too late to the NVA's incursions and then finding itself helpless to pursue the enemy into Cambodia.

Without asking anyone's permission, Chuck Lee carefully selected and trained two-man teams to lie concealed at strategic points along the river separating South Vietnam from Cambodia. This was in total violation of a division directive that decreed 1st Cavalry troops were never to operate in less than company-size units along the Cambodian border and that all divisional troops must always operate within the range of the Division's organic 105-millimeter howitzers. As Chuck Lee was found of saying:

"Rules are made for people who don't know what they are doing."

If we were to get the war over with and with minimum U.S. losses, Chuck Lee knew he needed better intelligence on the movements of the 9th NVA Division than was available from the normal intelligence sources of U.S. Forces, Vietnam. He also needed better, more powerful radios and many more M-60 machine guns.

During one of those rare rest periods given to the rifle companies in his battalion, Chuck asked for and received a three-day pass to go to Bien Hoa, a huge base camp near Saigon. Chuck went to see his brother, who was the Vietnam era equivalent of Sergeant Bilko. Just as his pass was about to expire, Chuck showed up at the Plei Me Special Forces camp south of Pleiku with a "borrowed" five-ton truck full of radios, machine guns and those nifty little Special Forces ponchos. Everyone had the good sense not to ask where or how he got them. In fact, Chuck Lee had enough liberated tools of war to not only re-equip his Charlie

Company but Buck Madison's Delta Company as well. With a PRC-25 radio and a M-60 machine gun for each of their squads, the two rifle companies had more firepower than two NVA battalions.

"Now," as Chuck Lee was also fond of saying, "all we need are some Gooks." Even though of partial Oriental ancestry, political correctness was not one of Chuck Lee's long suits.

Jonathan Winslow, one of Buck's lieutenants came from a long line of northeastern American blue bloods who typically went to Harvard and then on to Tufts where they studied at the Fletcher School of Diplomacy and then onto careers in the U.S Foreign Service. The name Winslow dominated the list of FSOs who attained the rank of ambassador.

Lt. Winslow possessed both language and political skills. He was fluent in French, a fact that endeared him to the battalion commander who once taught French at West Point. Lt. Winslow was given the name of Lt. Marindell, one of Larteguy's characters whose political skills were more than a match for the North Vietnamese when Marindell and his colleagues were POWs. Both de Glatigny and Marindell liked to play cribbage and, despite the vast differences in the their rank, status and age, it was not unusual for Lt. Marindell to spend part of an evening outside de Glatigy's tent playing cribbage with his battalion commander.

Roberto Chavez, one of Chuck Lee's lieutenants, was given the French name of Lt. Merle because Roberto, like Merle, was so decent and caring. In *The Praetorians*, Lt. Merle is captured by the Algerian rebels, killed and his body horribly mutilated. No one liked to talk about the fate of Lt. Merle.

Lou Leclerc was the only one of the local Vietnam veteran's inner circle who was not an original member of the 2d of the 5th's Larteguy Legion. Lou had only been with Buck, Chuck, Jonathan and Roberto on one occasion and that was at Ducco and that was literally by accident.

Chuck Lee's Charlie Company and Buck Madison's Delta Company had been playing out one of their hammer and anvil maneuver schemes near Ducco when the 9th NVA Division decided it had had enough of those two American companies and came across the river from Cambodia in force. The commanding General of the 9th NVA Division sent the entire 33d Regiment to find Chuck and Buck and destroy them. Pressed like they had never been pressed before, Chuck and Buck fell back on the U.S. Special Forces Camp at Ducco, surrounded the camp and faced outward to meet their fate. It became an all-out pitched battle right up along the Cambodian border.

The nice thing about the Ducco camp was its dirt runway capable of handling the C-123 cargo aircraft. But the NVA massed so many anti-aircraft weapons around Ducco, the runway became littered with shot-up C-123s. When ammunition, medical supplies and rations ran low, Chuck and Buck turned to the CIA's Air America. Again and again a certifiably crazy Helio-courier pilot braved a curtain of enemy fire to fly into Ducco, drop off critical supplies and fly out again.

Predictably, the pilot, a wild man named Lou Leclerc, flew one too many sorties into Ducco and his Helio-courier was shot out from under him. Brushing some mud from his Flying Tiger leather jacket and stuffing his trademark white scarf in his pocket, Leclerc walked over to Chuck Lee, saluted and reported for duty as a rifleman.

As it turned out Leclerc was not only a pilot extraordinaire, he was also a crack shot. Rummaging around in a tunnel underneath the S.F. team house, Leclerc found a Browning .50 caliber machine gun fitted with a sniper scope. A .50 caliber with sniper scope in the hands of an expert is an awesome weapon. It is fired single shot with devastating effect on the person it hits and creates big morale problems for the bystanders who are spared.

Noticing the camp's water tower stood about twenty feet above the camp but was rendered useless by a hail of NVA gunfire and was, therefore probably of no further interest to the camps' attackers, Leclerc waited until the cover of darkness and then hauled the big machine gun up into the water tower.

If the NVA had known he was up there, they would have made quick work of him. But the tower was large enough that Leclerc had room to set up the machine gun in such a way that the barrel did not protrude outside the tower.

It was dark back in the water tower and Lou could not be seen from the outside. As long as he didn't fire at night, it was virtually impossible for the NVA to know where Lou's lethal fire was coming from.

Each time the NVA officers would organize another dawn assault on the camp and move into their attack positions, Leclerc would figure out who the NVA lieutenants or captains were and drop them in their tracks. One minute they were ready to lead their troops. The next minute their heads were missing. If one person could be credited with preventing the Ducco S.F. camp from being overrun, it was Lou Leclerc.

But since Lou worked for Air America and didn't officially exist, he would not be getting the Distinguished Service Cross he so richly deserved. This fact was not lost on Chuck Lee and Buck Madison who adopted Lou as one of their own and made him an honorary member of the 2d Battalion, 5th Cavalry and, more importantly, a member of the 10th Colonial Parachute Regiment. But since Lou already had a French name and was a legend in his own right, no one felt it appropriate to assign Lou the name of one of Larteguy's characters. As always, Lou stood alone and was proud of it.

The most intellectual of Larteguy's characters was Captain Phillipe Esclavier. The most intellectual of the captains serving in the 2d Battalion, 5th Cavalry was James Buckley "Buck" Madison. Buck was a descendent of James Madison who, among our Founding Fathers, was thought to be one of the best thinkers. Both quiet, thoughtful and intro-spective, Esclavier and Buck were a perfect match.

One of the purposes of the planning meeting was to decide who would play the role of Colonel Raspeguy and give the main speech at the annual dinner. They had lost track of Major Sword. They knew the location of their former battalion commander, but even if he could be persuaded to come all the way from the east coast to attend, he didn't have the temperament to play the rough-and-tumble Colonel Raspeguy.

Buck didn't know why the planning group went through the charade of trying to pick someone to play Raspeguy because it always came down to one of their number and that was Chuck Lee. Each year, after considerable arm-twisting, Chuck would agree to drop his role as the wily Julien Boisfueras and make the Raspeguy speech.

Buck, as the smooth and well-spoken Esclavier, always served as the presiding officer or "Mr. Vice" of the dinner. It was Buck's duty to arrange for an honor guard to post the Colors and for a Piper to play a medley of regimental tunes. The hands-down favorites were Scotland the Brave and Amazing Grace. Then, it was Buck's duty to introduce everyone in attendance by their "Centurion" names and then lead Larteguy's Legion in a round of toasts which included a long list of military heroes and, of course, toasts the memories of the fallen members of the 2d Battalion, 5th Cavalry and the 1st Cavalry Division and to all those who had been killed or wounded in Vietnam, Laos and Cambodia. The final toast would be to the officers and men of the 10th Colonial Parachute Regiment. Notably absent from the list of those being toasted would be the current commander-in-chief. Instead, they would substitute former British Prime Minister Margaret Thatcher for President Trimmer on the grounds that Dame Thatcher had more balls.

Following the initial toast would be the thick slabs of rare prime rib and, after that, the speech by Colonel Raspeguy which, by that time, was generally incoherent in both its delivery and reception. But since everyone already knew Raspeguy would spend his allotted time railing against traitors, draft-dodgers, wimps, weak-kneed politicians and end up praising the virtues of the warrior class, the fact that Colonel Raspeguy slurred his words and the fact his audience was hearing-impaired by alcohol made the matter moot.

After Raspeguy received his annual standing ovation, the group would get down to some serious drinking.

At the stroke of mid-night, Dolly would be parked out front and Buck, who always kept his wits about him, would give his buddies a goodnight embrace and come out to the car so Dolly could drive him home.

Although Dolly thought them all insane, she also understood their need to relive, even in this zany way, what had been the most intensely emotional times of their lives. While others ran off to Sweden or Canada or Oxford or sought other ways to avoid serving when duty called, they had not. They did their duty under incredibly difficult circumstances which had been made even worse by unfaithful politicians and self-centered cowards whose demonstrations and protests prolonged the war and caused thousands of additional casualties on both sides. Dolly understood their hurt and she understood their love for each other. As long as the 10th Colonial Parachute Regiment only came back to life once a year, Dolly could handle that.

Chapter Sixteen

Raoul's plan to recruit the local rebels he needed was simple: hang around the watering holes where the natives come to drink. Most often that was the bar at Happy Jacques located on the road between Lake Granby and Shadow Mountain Lake although, sometimes, they drank at Doc Lee's Saloon in Grand Lake.

Jacques de Bois was a descendent of the French trappers who were the first whites to live year-round in Grand County. Despite all the references to Native Americans on the maps such as Arapaho National Forest and the Indian Peaks Range, the book on Native American history in Grand County would be very thin.

The Indians gave two reasons for not spending much time in the high country. The first reason is more romantic than factual. The Indians claimed God lives in the high mountains and to spend too much time up there is to commit a sacrilege.

The second reason is probably closer to fact: in the early days, it was just too cold to spend the winter in Grand County.

But cold was taken in stride by the French trappers and other mountain men who made the high country their year-round home. Besides, the winter gave them the best furs to trade when the warmth of spring made it possible for them to travel to pow-wows and rendezvous to sell their wares.

The interior decor of Happy Jacques reflected his French trapper heritage. The heads and stretched-out skins of local big game adorned the walls. Elk, deer, bear, pronghorns and Rocky Mountain Bighorn Sheep were everywhere. Enough weapons were strapped to the ceiling to start a small war. Old cowboy boots, bits, and bridles were mixed in with the rifles and pistols on the wooden ceiling. Peanut shells and other debris covered the rough plank floors that Jacques swept out once a week whether the patrons thought it needed it or not.

One side of the place was given over to a u-shaped bar, a small dance floor, and a place to shoot pool. Neon beer signs hung in the two windows across from the bar. The window frames showed signs of frequent repair. It was not unheard for one patron to throw another patron out a window. The other side of the one-story building held a dining room and a cashier's stand. Behind the public areas was the kitchen.

Raoul and Federico decided the PEMEX invasion of Happy Jacques would take place in small groups. Raoul and Federico would be the first to venture into what they referred to as "red-neck heaven." Slowly, they would bring some, but probably not all, of the PEMEX crew into the social circle at Happy Jacques.

Time was on their side. They could bring in different crewmembers and see who might be simpatico with the locals and who might have problems. If needed, they could bring in Regina who claimed that given a dark, secluded corner, she could make any man forget mother, wife, home and country.

Separated by skin color, language and background from the regulars at the bar, the terrorists had only one card to play and Raoul knew how to play it.

They went into the bar side first and sat at the bar near the telephone. If trouble broke out, Raoul figured they could call back to the PEMEX compound for reinforcements. But the bar was almost empty. A couple of grimy workmen were having a snort before going home. Two women were on the other side of the bar. They were smoking and joking and coughing that boozy, croupy cough that comes from heavy smoking and drinking.

On that first night, Raoul spotted a light-skinned Latino coming in the back door. He was dressed like a ranch hand. Raoul scanned his memory bank of photographs supplied by the Cuban Intelligence Directorate and came up with: Roberto Chavez.

"Hello," said Raoul, extending his hand, "My name is Raoul Aredondo. I'm with that gas exploration crew."

"Howdy, Raoul," said Roberto, with a firm handshake, "I'm Roberto Chavez."

"And this is my main man, Federico Perez," said Raoul, "but everybody calls him Freddie."

"Hi, Freddie," said Roberto, shaking hands.

"Can we buy you a drink?" asked Raoul.

"Sure. Thanks."

"What'll it be?"

"Coors Light. That's all I drink."

"Trying to get back some of the local water that way?"

"Actually, Coors isn't made from Grand County water."

"It's not?"

"Nah, it comes out of Clear Creek. Clear Creek starts on the Denver side of Berthoud Pass and flows down to Golden."

"Coors pumps the water up out of the creek?" asked Federico.

"Actually, Coors comes out of springs deep under the town of Golden. Otherwise I wouldn't drink the stuff."

"I take it then that Clear Creek's polluted," said Raoul.

"It runs right alongside I-70 for miles. Wadda you think?"

"It's polluted. Are you a rancher?" asked Raoul.

"Work for a rancher part-time now. Used to own my own ranch. But the government took it. So, I help a friend with his martial-arts school and outdoor guide business part-time."

"Martial arts. I haven't done any of that since I was in the U.S. Army," said Raoul.

"The U.S. Army?" asked Roberto. "I thought you were Mexican."

"I am now, but I was with the 1st Cav in 'Nam," said Raoul.

"No shit. My buddy and I, the one with the martial-arts school, we were in the 1st Cav. When were you there?"

"In 1966 and 67."

"Where?"

"Everywhere between the Song Ba and Ducco."

"Holy shit. That's where we were. Which outfit?"

"1st of the 5th Cav. How about you?"

"2d of the 5th Cav. Hey, sister battalions. How 'bout that!" What about Freddie here?"

"Oh, he wimped out. He was always back in the big base camp at Bien Hoa pecking at a typewriter for *The Stars and Stripes*," said Raoul.

"Hey, watch your mouth," said Federico, "I broke several nails pecking on that typewriter. It wasn't even electric."

"Well, Freddie," said Roberto, "a lot of folks would have preferred to be back in Bien Hoa rather than getting shot at in the jungle. At least you served. Not like our draft-dodging, wimp El Presidente."

"I figured if I didn't go to Vietnam, then some poor bastard from Hope, Arkansas, would have to take my place," said Federico with a grin.

"Freddie, I like your style," said Roberto, giving Federico a high five.

"Actually, we should not be making jokes about President Trimmer and Vice President Holzhalter. It's not right for us to say anything," said Raoul.

"Why the hell not? It's the truth, ain't it?" countered Roberto.

"Well yes, but we've got these good jobs in Mexico and we don't really live here anymore."

"But you are U.S. citizens. Right?"

"Used to be. We had to give that up to work for PEMEX. So, you see, it's not right for us to make comments. We're here to make friends, not enemies."

"You won't make any enemies in this place. Hey, I can't wait for you to meet Chuck Lee. He's the one from the 2d of the 5th like me."

"We would like to meet your friend, Chuck Lee."

Chuck Lee did not come into Happy Jacques that evening. He was over at his sister's house beating the crap out of his former brother-in-law.

"I told you if you ever hit my sister again that I'd make you wish you were never born," said Chuck, as he kicked Lloyd Garvey for about the 30th time in the stomach. But to the casual observer, Lloyd Garvey appeared unharmed. Where Chuck Lee was inflicting pain was covered by Garvey's shirt and jeans.

"You are the lowest life sonofabitch I've ever seen. You couldn't whip a 97-pound weakling. But you sure think you can beat up my sister," said Chuck Lee.

Then, grabbing the sobbing Garvey by the front of his shirt, Chuck pulled him to his feet and beat the back of Garvey's head against the wall of the house trailer. "Listen to me, you cocksucker, if you miss another child-support payment, I'm going to stick a cattle prod up your ass and turn it on. And, if you lay a hand on my sister again, I'm going to kill you with my bare hands."

With that, Chuck Lee dropped Lloyd Garvey to the floor, opened the door of the trailer house and kicked him out into the snow. "When I finish visiting with my sister, you better not still be out here—you miserable sack of shit."

While her brother was punishing her former husband, Adrienne Lee Garvey lay on the coach nursing her bruised face and applying a bloody wash rag to the corner of her mouth. Chuck rummaged around in the bathroom and found some alcohol and applied it to Adrienne's face with his bandana.

"Oh Chuck, thank God you happened to stop by. He might have killed me."

"What caused that bastard to come here?" asked Chuck.

"My lawyer wrote him about missing the child-support payments for Troy. That set him off."

"Where's Troy?"

"Working down at The Furniture Store. He's doing what he can after school to help out."

"He's a good kid. Hopefully, he got all your genes and none of that scumbag father of his."

"Well, at least Lloyd has a good job at the pump plant."

"Yeah, the pay's steady and the benefits are good. But that asshole doesn't do a goddam thing."

"He told me he was in charge out there."

"In charge, my ass. He sits in the pump plant all alone from about mid-night to dawn when every thing is shut down. I've got a buddy on the day shift who says they have to wake him up when they come on duty at eight."

"Then that's why he has time to come over here in the daytime."

"Not anymore. If you even see him within 100 yards of this place, you call me."

"Do you think he'll go to the Granby Clinic and report you?"

"Nah, I made sure I didn't break anything. Just pain. I inflicted a lot of pain. Besides, he knows I will kill him if he goes to the sheriff."

"Chuck, I guess I've spoiled your evening over at Happy Jacques."

"No problem, Roberto, Lou and I spend too much time over there anyway. Does me good to have a health night."

"Chuck, I can't thank you enough for your help."

"No problem. That's what big brothers are for."

Lloyd Garvey was gone when Chuck opened the door to the house trailer. *Damn, I was hoping I could kick him some more,* thought Chuck.

By now, Raoul, Federico and Roberto were on their sixth beer. "Well, looks like Chuck ain't coming tonight," said Roberto. "Too bad. I know we all got a lot to talk about. Maybe we can all get together when Lou Leclerc's here too."

"Who is Lou Leclerc?" asked Federico.

"Lou is another Vietnam buddy. Well, sort of. He flew for Air America. Some kind of hush-hush CIA-type shit. If you can believe 'em, he's got some great flying stories. Make you wet your pants just to listen to him. He and Chuck are real close. They even served together over in Laos working with the Hmongs."

"How'd you get the name Roberto?" asked Federico. "Are you Latino or Italian or something?"

"My father's people came from Mexico and my mother is Italian."

"Were you born in Mexico or Italy?"

"Italy. My dad joined the U.S. Army in World War II and got his citizenship. He was good with languages so he was an intelligence agent in Italy. That's where he met my mother and where I was born. After the war, we moved to the States."

"Do you speak any Spanish?"

"Spanish and Italian. But I don't get much practice with either language up here. When Chuck Lee and I were in Special Forces, Spanish was our language specialty. When we operated in South America, we even learned several dialects. If you like, we can speak Spanish instead of English."

"Oh no," said Raoul, "we have to do our business up here in English. You would not be doing us any favors by speaking Spanish. Total immersion is the only way to learn and to maintain a language skill. We need to think in English, not Spanish."

"You're right," said Roberto. "That's why so few Americans can speak a second language. Our schools keep pushing a nutty concept they call: "bi-lingual education," even though it rarely works. It's more of a handicap to Latinos than a help. In fact, it's a handicap for Anglos."

"For Anglos, as well?" asked Federico.

"Yeah. Every Anglo I know has taken French or German or Spanish in school and I don't know a one who can speak a foreign language," said Roberto. "So, studying a language just part-time doesn't work. It's all or nothing and our young Hispanics would be a lot better off if we just let them jump into English flat-out and skip the crippling effect of bi-lingual education."

"You said your friend, Chuck Lee, can speak Spanish. Is he Hispanic by chance?" asked Raoul.

"Chuck's all kinds. He's Chinese, Swedish, Hispanic and American."

"Was he born overseas like you?" asked Frederico.

"Nah. Chuck was born down in Denver. He grew up speaking Spanish. They didn't have bi-lingual education back then. So, it was sink or swim for Chuck and he swam. As a result, his English is really good.

"Chuck's Chinese and Swedish heritage has to do with something we call: The Grand Ditch. If you guys are here tomorrow night, I'm sure Chuck, and maybe Lou, will be here. I'll get Chuck to tell you the story about the foreign workers who built The Grand Ditch."

"Okay, tomorrow night it is," said Raoul. "It's time to sky out of here. We must get going back to our lager. At oh-light-thirty we'll have to gaggle up and keep looking for natural gas."

"Sky up. Lager. Oh-light-thirty. Gaggle. Haven't heard that 1st Cavalry lingo for ages. Thanks for the beers," said Roberto as he made his way somewhat unsteadily for the door.

CHAPTER SEVENTEEN

Jonathan returned in the spring to continue checking on the preparations for the presidential visit. As usual, he stayed with Buck and Dolly.

After dinner one evening, Dolly drove into town to spend some time with Chuck Lee's nephew and try to help him overcome a personal trauma that Dolly never discussed with Buck or Jonathan.

Buck and Jonathan took the occasion to take their after-dinner drinks out onto the deck so they could watch the fading sunlight play across Lake Granby and on the Continental Divide. It was one of those magical times when the alpenglow shines across Knight Ridge and up onto the craggy outline of Abe Lincoln regarding the Heavens.

"Do you ever wonder what President Lincoln would think about the state of our nation in these times?" asked Buck.

"More often than I care to acknowledge," said Jonathan.

"Why's that?"

"Because I think we are in a state of national emergency only most of us don't know it."

"What kind of emergency? You mean like the emergency faced by President Lincoln when he felt compelled to impose martial law and revoke some of our fundamental rights such as *habeas corpus* protection?" asked Buck.

"No. I think this emergency is just the opposite of what Lincoln faced. President Lincoln felt he had to assume dictatorial powers in order to save the Union. Lincoln was convinced a strong Union was the only way to preserve the Bill of Rights and the Constitution."

"Sort of like we have to destroy this village to save it?" asked Buck.

"Something like that only the consequences were much more serious. Lincoln assumed dictatorial powers because he felt the end justified the means."

"It also helps if you win the war," said Buck. "If the South had won or, more likely, the result had been a stalemate, Lincoln's assumption of dictatorial power would not smell so good today. And then, John Wilkes Booth made him a martyr to boot."

"Yes, it's often better to be lucky rather than smart."

"Oh, I think Lincoln was both smart and lucky," said Buck.

"If there had been a presidential protective detail back then, I don't think my predecessor would have thought that Lincoln and he were lucky," said Jonathan.

"Okay, Jonathan, what's your point? You think the country is so screwed up that President Trimmer needs to assume dictatorial powers?"

"Just the opposite. I think the government has become so imperial and so all pervasive in the lives of the people that we are about to be faced with a national emergency in the form of a popular uprising against the federal government."

"Why not against all government, why not state and local as well?"

"Because it is the power of the federal government that is running amuck."

"Give me some examples."

"Take Waco. The local sheriff had been to the Branch Davidian compound several times. Each time, he was received with courtesy and respect. If the Bureau of Alcohol, Tobacco and Firearms or the FBI had a problem with David Koresh and his followers, all they had to do was give that warrant or whatever document they wanted to serve to the local sheriff and he would have gone out there and served it. Even if it had been a search warrant, my sources tell me the local sheriff would have been let in to look around. But no, the BATF decides to stage a military-style assault."

"Wasn't the BATF budget about to come up for congressional review just before the assault?" asked Buck.

"Absolutely. The BATF assault was a showboat operation aimed at getting more money out of the Congress. Those federal officials were so money-hungry they went ahead with the assault even after they were dead certain they had already lost the element of surprise."

"Dead was right," said Buck. "It cost them the lives of several agents who, as individuals, were probably very good men. Clearly, they were just pawns on the larger budgetary chessboard in Washington."

"Washington is the problem," said Jonathan. "Washington is our national emergency and I just wonder how much longer the people will tolerate these abuses by the federal government."

"Ruby Ridge comes to mind as maybe the quintessential example of the FBI running amuck," said Buck.

"Correct. There you had the FBI and the BATF going out of their way to get Randy Weaver to saw off the end of a shotgun as a favor to a BATF plant. Pure entrapment.

"Sure, Randy Weaver was a loud-mouth bigot. But he and his wife and his older son, their baby and their dog could have stayed up in those mountains forever and never had an impact any farther than the range of Weaver's loud mouth. Instead, the FBI decides to make a federal case out of Weaver's bigotry. They killed, make that murdered, his son and his wife. All in the name of shutting up a loud-mouthed, white supremacist.

"Have you ever noticed how the media handles Randy Weaver? They always tag him as 'White Supremacist Randy Weaver'. It's like that was the name his parents put on his birth certificate," said Buck.

"Well, he was a white supremacist," said Jonathan. But his treatment by the federal government is just another example of federal law enforcement riding in, murdering citizens and riding off into the sunset. If the local sheriff had done what the FBI did at Ruby Ridge, the sheriff would have been recalled. But you see with we Feds there is almost no account-ability for our actions as there would be with local law enforcement offi-cials who have to stand for election or reelection. The BATF and the FBI are like Paladin. They ride in, they ride out. Unaccountable."

"What about the Department of Justice?

"Pure politics, Buck. The Attorney General says she was assured by the FBI experts that the gas to be used on the Branch Davidians would not harm children or pregnant women. Obviously, that was wrong. She claims the FBI told her that Koresh was beating the children. Follow-up analysis finds that notion had no basis in fact and was pure speculation by 'someone' in the FBI. Despite all her claims that the safety of the those children was her primary concern, she never lifted a finger to punish those FBI officials who gave her bum information on the effects of the gas or pushed her over the edge with the bogus claim that Koresh was beating the children inside that compound."

"So, she had to destroy those children to save them?"

"Yes, and what is so amazing is that she got away with it. As usual, they call in some unemployed former Senator or whatnot, to hold hear-ings to whitewash the whole affair. But they always wait until the TV images of what actually happened have faded from the memory of the gum-chewing public. By that time, nobody gives a rat's ass anymore because the passing parade has moved on to some other outrage either here or abroad."

"Why didn't your boss ask the attorney general for her resignation?"

"He and his advisers figured that because Koresh was some kind of fundamentalist, religious nut that the media—most of whom admit they never go to church—would continue to claim the destruction of the Branch Davidians as justified. Turns out, he was correct. Listen care-fully to media accounts of the final assault on the Branch Davidian compound and notice how the media says 'a fire broke out'. It's like it was spontaneous combustion. They gloss over the fact that the Feds drove a tank into a compound which they knew, in advance, had gallons of combustible materials sitting around. When a tank goes ripping through electric lines in the walls and its metal tracks are making sparks and it has a very hot exhaust system, you have a recipe for setting off whatever flammables that are present."

"Okay. You've given me two glaring examples of federal abuse of the police power. Now, Jonathan, explain this national emergency you see on the horizon."

"Let me begin by asking Professor Buck Madison to tell me what the American Revolution was all about."

"I'm not sure why this is necessary and, besides, you've heard my lecture on this subject many times before when we were lying out under the stars in Vietnam."

"Yes, Buck, I've heard it. But I want you to lay it out once more before I deliver the punch line to my description of the crisis that lies ahead."

"Okay. Most people don't understand the fundamental difference between the French Revolution, the Russian Revolution and the other 'traditional revolutions' and the American Revolution.

The French Revolution, the Russian Revolution, and the revolutions that overthrew colonial empires around the world were aimed at the destruction of the Old Order. The fighters in those revolutions were sick and tired of being oppressed, thrown in jail, murdered and, in general, being denied any opportunity of climbing up the economic ladder. Sadly, most people think the American Revolution was the same sort of revolution but it most decidedly was not.

"Our Founding Father started the American Revolution because they loved and adored the institutions of the Old Order in England. They loved the protections of the *Magna Carta* and the English Common Law as they had evolved and were being practiced back in England.

"Our beef with King George was that we in the American colonies were being denied the benefits provided by the Old Order in Merry Old England. We wanted more of it, not less. The 'unalienable rights' penned by Thomas Jefferson and the committee that drafted our Declaration of Independence were rights being enjoyed by our English cousins. Our Declaration of Independence is actually a love song dedicated to those rights and our desire to be able to enjoy those rights on the North American continent.

"If King George III had not been so incredibly stupid and had let the American colonists enjoy the same rights as his subjects living in England, we would still be saluting the Union Jack, stopping for tea at 4:00 p.m. and dressing for dinner."

"Well said, Buck," agreed Jonathan. "So what I am suggesting now is that we are about to see a second American Revolution. I think the American people still love those same rights so revered by Thomas Jefferson and the other Founding Fathers. But I think our federal government has grown so imperious and imperial that it is taking the place of King George and his advisers. I think the American people want government to do two things: provide an effective national defense and make them be able to feel safe in their homes and on the streets."

"Jonathan, I wish I could agree completely with your last statement, but I can't. I see too many people who think the government owes them a living and they'll vote for any snake-oil politician who will promise them a lifetime of free lunches."

"Okay, Buck, I'm afraid you have me there. But I also think there are a lot of truly caring and responsible people who are coming to see the federal government as oppressive and as the mechanism that is denying them their 'unalienable rights' as described in the Declaration of Independence and as codified in the Bill of Rights and in our Constitution.

"I think a lot of us see 'judge-made law' as a corruption of the democratic process and the destroyer of what the Founding Fathers intended in the Constitution and the Bill of Rights. The Founding Fathers never intended for the people to fear their government. They thought the government ought to fear the wrath of the people if the government screwed things up or overreached its powers. The Constitution tells the federal government what it can do. The Bill of Rights tells the federal government what it cannot do. The people are supposed to be sovereign, not a bunch of faceless assholes in Washington, D.C. or some liberal dipshit judge who cares more about his or her social agenda than upholding the law.

"I can give you dozens of examples where the people in several states have voted overwhelming for what they felt was a needed reform only to have it set aside by a single judge who just doesn't happen to agree with a majority of the people. And, it doesn't seem to do any good to elect people to state legislative bodies or to Congress and tell them to pass laws in accordance with the will of the people because some liberal judge will just set them aside and when these matters reach the Supreme Court all too often an unelected, committee of nine, black-robed lawyers will tell the people to go stick it up their rectums, or whatever the Latin plural is.

"Add to those irritations the excesses of the federal government. The Presidency, and I see it everyday, has grown far beyond the wildest dreams of Julius Caesar, a Louis XIV, a Napoleon, a Mussolini or even an Adolph Hitler. The tax dollars we are spending to operate Air Force One, which is really just a giant political pay-off machine, are ridiculous. I just read an editorial in an aviation magazine where the editor claimed the average cost of an Air Force One mission is $17 million dollars. I'm right in the middle of all the Air Force One missions and that figure sounds about right to me. The VC-25A that they use only carries 70 passengers and a crew of almost 30. That's about $170,000 per seat.

"If a President, or any President, not just this one, has a whim to play golf somewhere, we spend enormous amounts of money to make the golf outing secure. I'm not at liberty to tell you what my budget is, but it would knock your socks off Buck if you knew. We just took a trip on Air Force One to India, Pakistan and Bangladesh that cost you and me between $50 and $60 million dollars. The trip had no purpose. No treaties or agreements had been worked out in advance by the Department of State and no treaties or agreements were signed. POTUS just wanted to take a bunch of his relatives and heavy-hitter contributors on a lame-duck joyride at taxpayer expense. We just did another trip to Russia for no purpose other than for Trimmer to go begging for some crumbs from Popov's table. Popov knows Trimmer is the lamest of lame ducks and the only reason Popov is coming over here to Camp Hope is because Popov really does like the outdoors and, I'm told, that he's a hellava good fisherman.

"You know, Buck, I think the American people just want a President who goes to work everyday in his home office which we call the White House and doesn't use the Oval Office for a brothel. For almost eight years now, we have hardly spent any time at all around the White House. Instead, we are constantly out on the road, doing political fund-raisers or visiting some exotic places or holding economic summits which are just venues for a bunch of world leaders to booze and eat it up at their taxpayers' expense. Buck, it's bullshit and I'm ashamed to be such a key part of it."

"Then, you should quit, Jonathan."

"I'm going to do just that. But I'm not finished with my little speech here. Buck, I think the American people can withstand most any kind of hardship; however, I do not think they will tolerate what they feel is unfairness. If they think the system is stacked against them, I think they will resort to violence in an effort to regain their lost freedoms."

"In short," said Buck, "you think Oklahoma City was just the tip of the iceberg."

"The Oklahoma City bombing was an overreaction by a brain-less jerk. But I think that bombing was just the precursor to a long string of bombings and other acts of violence which will be carefully designed to make a political point; however, without killing anyone."

"If I understand the tenor of your remarks, you could find some sympathy for those who might take up arms or bombs against the current regime? asked Buck."

"I wouldn't go as far as sympathy, Buck. But I can understand how they feel. And, if they really knew the kind of self-serving, power-mad bullshit that goes on, the revolution would start today, not sometime in the future.

"The people I have to deal with everyday don't give a shit about anything except power and the perks of power. Trimmer spends most of his time figuring out whom he can screw and how to get out of the other times he got caught with his pecker in the wrong place. His political handlers call most of the shots, except for the shots called by FLOTUS. Just now, as the military's spare-parts shortage starts to come out, are we beginning to see how our national defense was cut back in order to give some other draft-dodger a government social-program handout. Everyone thinks the Cold War is over and we can get away with these military cutbacks, but I get to see bunches of intelligence reports and the world is just as dangerous, if not more so, than when the Soviet Union had two kopecks to rub together and a superb nuclear force. God knows who has control of many of those nukes or how many of them have been sold to Iran, Iraq, Red China or to just a bunch of Ian Fleming's Blofeld types.

"Basically, our country is being run, if you can call it that, by three women. When FLOTUS bothers to speak to Trimmer, she tells him what to do and how to do it. When it comes to foreign policy the old broad he appointed SECSTATE consistently lets her personal feelings overcome her judgment. She got this hard-on for Milosevic and thousands of innocent people died because of it. The attorney general gives the order to gas a compound full of innocent kids and they're toast. A mother drowns trying to get her kid out of Cuba and into the United States and she never bothers to ask the kid what he wants. Meanwhile,

Trimmer is AWOL as usual dicking around with some newsie or intern or campaign worker.

"Are you suggesting that Ernst Stavos Blofeld actually exists?"

"Not by that name. But there are arms merchants out there who could possess enough doomsday weapons to pose a credible threat. Nuclear blackmail would occur to them at some point."

"Meanwhile, we have real problems and real enemies that need to be dealt with," suggested Buck.

"Yes we do, Buck. And, when the pendulum swings too far to the left, it always provokes a reaction to the right. Look at Germany after World War I. Things went so far to the Left in the Weimar Republic that it made possible the horrors brought on by Hitler. After 300 years of oppressive reactionary rule by the Romanovs, the result was 73 years of wild-eyed, bloodthirsty communism.

"It's happening right under our noses. Trimmer and the Left are going to provoke a reaction by the Right. My staff is gearing up for it right now. I can't say much about it. But the problem is when we gear up to deal with these sorts of threats we always add another layer to the federal police forces. We continue to create the organs of power that can be used to rob us of our freedoms.

"Buck, highly trained physicians accidentally kill far more people each year than random gun violence yet the bad doctors rarely lose their medical licenses. But if some neglected, self-hating kids mow down their schoolmates, the gun-grabbers want to lock up my personal protection firearm and yours."

"I agree, it's crazy," said Buck.

"Exactly, Buck. A good example is this craziness of detailing the military to deal with the drug war. That should be a function of the civil police. When you start putting the military into the drug war, you start down the slippery slope of having the military enforce civil law. In essence, you begin the suspension of civil control. Moreover, it puts the military in a position to be corrupted by the drug lords. Mark my words, we'll soon see cases of military officers and NCOs being court-martialed for taking drug money."

"So, Jonathan, where do we go from here?"

"We go to bed and hope to have a better day tomorrow," said Jonathan.

CHAPTER EIGHTEEN

Team Moffat

Salvador and Pancho spent the morning gambling in Central City and Black Hawk. Salvador, with his engineering degree from Moscow State University, thought he had a sure-fire system for winning at Blackjack. Pancho, with his degree in sociology from Moscow's Patrice Lumumba University, had no talent for statistical odds. He played the slot machines. Neither man won any money. In fact, they lost. But they really didn't care. After all, it was expense money given to them by Raoul.

After lunch, they drove their pickup north along Colorado Highway 119. When they came to a sign that said East Portal, they turned west down a rough road that eventually led to the East Portal of the Moffat Tunnel.

In the glory days of the railroad, East Portal was a busy place. Today, the area around East Portal is home to a handful of track inspectors and gandydancers who inspect and repair the 6.2 miles of track that run through the Moffat Tunnel.

Yet, visitors come and go unnoticed if they are carrying fishing gear because the outlet of the Moffat Tunnel's water bore is a popular fishing spot. Night and day water taken from the Fraser River watershed on the west side of the Continental Divide near Winter Park comes cascading out of the tunnel's water bore. Just to the right of the water outlet is the black, soot-encrusted facade of the train tunnel.

Salvador and Pancho parked their pickup, extracted their fishing gear and food from its camper shell and took up residence beside the rushing waters.

They had no more luck fishing than they did gambling. No matter. Their investment in time began to pay off when a man in a sport utility vehicle drove across the railroad track and parked his car by a small door just to the left of the train tunnel portal.

The man produced a key, unlocked the door and went inside where he remained for what seemed like an eternity to Salvador and Pancho. Then, just before dusk, the man emerged from the door, got into his vehicle and drove away.

"Probably, the engineer who looks after the tunnel," observed Salvador. "Let's have our dinner."

As they ate their sandwiches and drank their Coronas, the huge door to the East Portal opened, without warning, like a giant garage door. In a few moments, an Amtrak passenger train came out of the East Portal headed for Denver and points East. Shortly thereafter, the giant door descended and the entrance was closed shut.

They were just about to finish their meal when the smoke-evacuation fans on each side of the tunnel entrance began to wail like banshees. They were so startled by the noise that they dropped their sandwiches in the dirt. In fact, the noise was so intense they had to cover their ears with their hands.

Pancho picked up the remnants of their meal and threw them into the rushing waters. They returned to their fishing only to be interrupted an hour later when a freight train approached the tunnel from the east. Suddenly, the giant door rose up again into its receptacle inside the East Portal. Not long after the train disappeared into the tunnel and the gate came down once again, the smoke-evacuator fans began to bellow.

"Dios," said Pancho, "I'd hate to be one of those railroad workers living over in those row houses. Those blowers must drive them crazy."

After dark, Pancho stood watch as Salvador walked over to the door used by the tunnel engineer and picked the lock. Inside, to the left of the entrance, was a small office with a glass wall looking into a much larger control room. Centered on what must be the engineer's desk was a desktop computer. It was running. The screen depicted the layout of the tunnel. On the right margin of the screen were what appeared to be real-time readings of the temperature, air pressure, air quality and other environmental factors inside the tunnel.

Entering the government-green control room they saw dozens of dials and gauges neatly recessed into an imposing control panel. Above the control panel they found the answers to their long list of questions.

Stretched across the breadth of the control panel was a complete diagram showing both the train tunnel and the water bore. Pancho produced an instant camera from his pack, focused on the huge diagram and shot an entire roll of film. Meanwhile, Salvador looked through the engineer's desk and at all the reference manuals neatly shelved against the office walls.

Adjacent to the control room was a much larger room lined with row upon row of electrical busses and circuit breakers. The gang switches on the circuit breaker panels were so large it would take a fairly strong person to pull them open or push them shut.

Clearly, the dials, gauges, electrical busses and the circuit breakers were old technology. No doubt in the early days of the Moffat Tunnel it must have taken a crew of several men to monitor, operate and maintain this equipment. But someone had made the entire operation less labor intensive by clever use of computerization. Possibly the man they had seen earlier in the day.

With a practiced eye, Salvador traced a network of wires which were obviously part of a retrofitted computer system. Apparently, the operation of the railroad tunnel and the water bore could now be monitored entirely from the engineer's desk, and possibly, even from a remote location.

Suspecting the maze of rooms was connected to the railroad tunnel, they kept opening doors until they unlocked one that gave them access to the tunnel and the railroad tracks.

"Sure smells of soot and oil," said Pancho. "A white, tropical suit wouldn't last five minutes in this place. Try not to bump against anything."

Walking into the tunnel another 50 feet, they discovered the inlets for the smoke-evacuators. There was one on each side of the train tunnel. Both inlets were covered with giant, soot-laden, movable dampers.

"Can you imagine being caught in front of one of those dampers when those giant fans turn on?" mused Salvador. "You'd be pinned like a fly on a kitchen drain."

"Si, amigo," said Pancho, "so let's get out of here before that happens to us."

Retracing their steps, Salvador and Pancho were careful to leave no evidence of their visit. After relocking the door they packed away their gear and departed for the PEMEX compound at the Koch Ranch.

The next morning Team Moffat met with Raoul and Federico in the main house to discuss the results of their reconnaissance. Regina handed everyone mugs of fresh coffee and then sat down to listen to what Salvador and Pancho had to report.

"These instant photographs are excellent," said Raoul. "They show the entire layout of both the water bore and the railroad tunnel. Did you have any difficulties?"

"No, Raoul," said Salvador. "There appears to be only one person to oversee this mammoth tunnel complex. Once he locks up and goes home, it seems there is not a single human between the East Portal and the West Portal."

"Did you observe any trains?"

"Si, Raoul," said Pancho. "The first train we saw was a passenger train going from west to east. We knew something was coming because the huge door to the East Portal opened suddenly. It scared the shit out of me."

"Did the door remain open?"

"No, the door came down again shortly after the train cleared the tunnel.

"Then what happened?"

"These huge blowers began to evacuate the smoke the train left in the tunnel. There's a blower on each side of the East Portal. They make a terrific noise. It's so loud you have to hold your hands over your ears. It must scare the fish because they sure didn't bite."

"How long did these blowers operate?"

"It seemed like forever, but I suppose it was only 15 minutes."

"What else happened?"

"Later, a train came from the east."

"What about the gate?"

"This time we had some warning because we could hear the train before we saw it. It rattled a lot so we knew it was pulling empty coal cars. The huge door rose again and the train passed into the tunnel. After a while, the door came back down and the blowers switched on again. Terrible racket."

"Is there a similar gate at the west end, the Winter Park end, of the tunnel?" asked Federico.

"No. The only gate is at the east end," said Salvador. "Evidently, only the one gate is needed. And it is only there to provide a seal so the smoke-evacuation blowers can do their work."

"Is there someone to operate this gate?"

"No," said Salvador. "When we got inside, we looked for a gate opening and closing mechanism. We could not find one, so we looked along the tracks and we found a switch. When a westbound train passes the switch it triggers the door-opening mechanism. We didn't see it, but there must be a similar switch inside the tunnel for use by east-bound trains."

"So, how do they prevent two trains being in the tunnel at the same time?" asked Raoul.

"According to the big diagram shown on some of the instant photos," said Salvador, "there is a central control headquarters in Omaha, Nebraska. Evidently, they have the means to control which trains use the tunnel and when."

"Is there anyway we can know, in advance, when these trains will be using the tunnel?" asked Federico.

"Si. We found a computer running in the control room," said Pancho. "The screen showed a model of the tunnel and was showing what appeared to be a real-time depiction of what was happening inside the tunnel and at the approaches to the tunnel."

"That's fine," said Federico. "But real-time doesn't give us enough advance warning. It doesn't tell us the train schedule so we can time the attack on the tunnel."

"True, I am hoping Regina can help us with that part," said Pancho. "We think it may be possible for her to hack into the computer system. If she can do that, she should be able to obtain the schedule for the trains."

"That explains why the engineer can leave the tunnel for periods of time," said Raoul. "He must be able to monitor the tunnel from a Denver office or even his home or from anywhere where there is a telephone for that matter."

"If so, that could be a problem," said Pancho. "What if we are preparing the tunnels for destruction and this engineer person happens to check his computer?"

"Any ideas, Salvador?" asked Federico.

"I looked in all the desks and at all the book shelves. On one shelf, I found a bunch of computer software," said Salvador. "In that same place, I found the diskettes and the operating manual for the software that allows one computer to assume control over another computer by what the layman would call: remote control. I know this software because I'm not really a computer expert so I have to have lots of help. The guy who helps me back in Havana got tired of having to come over to my office to fix my screw-ups. So, he installed this program on my machine. It allows him to take control of my computer over the phone from his house. If they have this software loaded into the computer for the Moffat Tunnel, then I'll bet Regina could gain control of that computer's operating system."

"Regina, do you think you can blind the engineer or anyone else who might be checking the monitor by inserting a screen that makes everything in the tunnel appear normal?" asked Raoul.

"Si, Jefe. I've done that before. It should be no problem," said Regina as she refilled their coffee mugs.

"Okay," said Pancho. "So that buys us the time to prepare the charges. But frankly, I'm not sure we know enough about demolition to know where to place the charges."

"That's why we have Federico, our expert engineer," said Raoul. "It is his job to review all of the plans to make sure we obtain maximum damage while using the minimum amount of explosives.

"But because we are hoping to have help from the gringos, whatever we do has to focus on the water tunnel rather than the railroad tunnel. We need to convince our gringo friends that their actions will stop the diversion of their water from west to east and, this is very important, while not hurting or killing anyone. Otherwise, unless we could be so fortunate to find another Timothy McVeigh, we won't gain their cooperation," said Raoul.

"Jefe, although I haven't had time to make a complete study of these photographs of the tunnel layout," said Federico, "I think I have an idea that will fit within the parameters you desire.

"Look here at this side view of the tunnels. The entrances at both ends of the tunnels are approximately the same elevation above sea level. But notice how the tunnels rise up in the middle to what they show on the diagram as the Apex.

"The only way for the water in the water bore to make it over the Apex and start flowing down toward Denver is for that water to be under pressure from the Winter Park side. Correct?"

"Si," said Pancho. "We found this huge water pipe that runs downhill from the Winter Park Ski Area. The source of this water is evidently high enough above the tunnel that the water is under enough pressure to force it up and over the apex. So, there is no need for a pumping station." (See: *www.thegrandconspiracy.com*)

"Now," continued Federico, "note how the two tunnels lie side-by-side running absolutely parallel. But they are connected every so often by passageways which they show here on the diagram as 'Refuges.'"

"That's because the water bore was dug first," said Salvador. "After the water bore was completed, they blasted out those cross-tunnels or 'Refuges' over to the much-larger railroad tunnel."

"This means all we have to do to gain access to the water bore is get one of those railroad handcars or put a railroad adapter on a pickup truck and drive up the railroad track to a point near the Apex. Of course, at a time when no trains will be coming through for some time," said Pancho.

"The diagram shows they start counting these cross tunnels or refuges at the East Portal," said Federico. "So, the first one is Refuge 1. At the Apex, we find Refuge 8. But look just on the west side or the Winter Park Side of the Apex and you see Refuge 11. It is slightly downhill from the Apex.

"So let's say we can get a gringo to drive up from the Winter Park side to Refuge 11. He moves the explosives on a hand dolly through Refuge 11 and places them against the side of the water pipe.

"He sets the timer so that he will have time to get back out of the tunnel at Winter Park's West Portal before the explosion at Refuge 11 goes off.

"Now, follow this scenario with me. The explosion blows a huge hole in the side of the water bore at Refuge 11. The water, which is under pressure from the Winter Park side, takes the path of least resistance which means instead of trying to run uphill to the Apex, over the Apex and then down to Denver, it will rush sideways through Refuge 11 and into the train tunnel. Gravity then pulls the water down the train tunnel and back toward Winter Park.

"So what good will that do us?" asked Raoul. "The water will just flood the area around the base of the Winter Park ski area."

"Be patient, por favor," said Federico. "We set off another explosion that blocks the West Portal of the Moffat Tunnel.

"What about the gringo?"

"Ah, once Salvador and Pancho blow the west end of the tunnel shut, the gringo cannot get out. He will drown. When his body is found, he will be blamed.

"But, I digress. Again, the water, still under pressure from the Winter Park side, keeps crossing over from the hole in the water bore through Refuge 11. When this water runs back downhill to the point where we have blasted the West Portal shut, it will begin to back up the railroad tunnel.

"The railroad tunnel will continue to fill until the water level reaches the Apex at Refuge 8. At which point, it starts running down toward the closed tunnel entrance at the East Portal. Eventually, the railroad tunnel will be filled with water, almost from portal to portal.

"But, at some point, the water pressure against the wooden gate at the East Portal will become so great it bursts the gate wide open. Yet, something more important will happen before the gate collapses. The water will build up at the east end of the tunnel until it floods the evacuation blower buildings, the electrical buss room, the control room and the engineer's office." said Federico.

"But I don't think mere flooding is sufficient destruction at the east end," said Raoul.

"True. But here is the best part. A few days before D-Day, we send Salvador and Pancho back into the east end of the tunnel. They told us that there is a wide place inside the tunnel where the smoke-evacuation blowers have their air dampers. A perfect place for Salvador and Pancho to set explosive charges hooked to a detonator designed to be set off only if submerged in water. Basically, the positive and negative leads for the detonator are left about an inch apart. But, when the leads become submerged in water, the water bridges the distance between the two leads and closes the circuit. Boom!"

"I see," said Raoul. "A water-triggered device could be put in place well in advance of D-Day. If everything we have planned to happen at Refuge 11 takes place, the water will eventually rise at the east end of the tunnel to the point the water-trigger makes contact. As you say: Boom! We will have destroyed both ends of the railroad tunnel but we only had to operate from the Winter Park side. Brilliant, Federico, brilliant!"

"It is nothing, Jefe. Without the excellent reconnaissance by Salvador and Pancho and Regina's Internet research, we would not have discovered this simple method of accomplishing the mission of Team Moffat."

"But there is one more benefit coming from this mission," added Pancho.

"What's that?"

"I found this piece of black, 5/8-inch cable lying beside the track in the railroad tunnel. There are four bands of this cable running along the sidewall of the railroad tunnel. Look, it says 'optical fiber cable' on the side. As you can see, it has filaments coated in blue, green, brown and white covering on the inside. These are the fiber-optic cables that MCI and Qwest and other telephone carriers use. When the Moffat Tunnel blows, both the MCI and the Qwest networks west of the tunnel will cease to exist," said Pancho.

"Amigos," said Raoul, "My confidence in you has been more than justified. Until this briefing, I thought the Moffat Tunnel would be our greatest challenge. But with the clever fieldwork of Salvador and Pancho, the engineering brilliance of Federico and the computer expertise of Regina, I have every confidence in Team Moffat.

"Now, all that remains is to recruit a gringo to set the explosives by the water pipe at Refuge 11.

"Regina, fetch that bottle of Mount Gay from the kitchen. Let's all have a Cuba Libre!" said Raoul.

CHAPTER NINETEEN

For the true working class of eastern Grand County, the place to be on Saturday night is Happy Jacques. Starting at 4:00 p.m., Jacques de Bois and his staff put out trays of Buffalo-style chicken wings, baby-back ribs, salsa and tortilla chips. Extra bartenders make sure no one waits for their longneck beers or for shots of tequila with lime and salt.

But, as the evening wears on, the tension level begins to rise in anticipation of the first fistfight of the night. In the old days, when mining and logging were still viable in Grand County, the fighting was more mixed. Sometimes, it would be the miners against the loggers. Other times, it would be the miners against the cowboys or cowboys versus loggers.

But now, the miners are gone and few loggers are left. But thanks to America's love affair with beef and thanks to America's infatuation with the Old West, the cowboys manage to survive, although some who appear to be cowboys are merely truckers trying to look like cowboys.

The real cowboys, however, are easy to spot. They wear spurs on their boots, chaps over their blue jeans and, sometimes, even six-guns. But Jacques makes them hand over their six-guns at the door. Also, the real cowboys smell of saddle leather, hay, manure, and cheap after-shave liberally applied.

These days there are two types of cowboys. The ones who live on working ranches where the sources of livelihood are cattle and hay farming. The other cowboys work on the five dude ranches for which Grand County is famous.

A typical fight scenario begins when one of the working-ranch cowboys taunts one of the dude-ranch cowboys with some remark suggesting the only way they keep their jobs is by sleeping with their guests. Some dude-ranch cowboys are more sensitive to the reputations of their guests than others and these are more likely to take offense and want to fight.

Most of the fights are one-on-one; however, if a cowboy of either stripe decides the fighting is too one-sided, he might join in to try to balance the scales of justice. Unfortunately, someone else may have a different vision of justice and, before you know it, a dozen combatants may be out on the small dance floor punching, kicking, biting and gouging each other.

Jacques has a great sense of how long to allow these antics to go on before he pulls out his own six-shooter from behind the bar and fires it into the ceiling. But tired of having to repair a leaky roof, Jacques has fallen onto the bogus practice of loading that particular six-shooter with blanks. So far, his drunken patrons have not caught on. Or, at least they pretend to not have caught on.

Another order-restoring tactic is for Jacques to order a free round of beer for everyone who quits fighting. This makes everyone happy. It keeps down the furniture repair and replacement costs. The working-ranch cowboys have gotten their exercise. They've also got another tale to tell when they get back to the ranch house and something to talk about all week while they are out tending cattle, repairing fence or using their shovels to improve the small irrigation ditches that supply the watering holes. The dude-ranch cowboys use their bruised faces and scraped knuckles to advantage in telling their female guests how well their honor was defended. The non-combatants go home happy because they've been treated to live entertainment.

When Raoul and Federico arrived at Happy Jacques, Chuck Lee, Lou Leclerc and Roberto Chavez where already occupying a booth.

"Hey, guys," said Roberto, "there's the two dudes from PEMEX I told you about. Let's invite 'em over."

Seeing Roberto wave his hand, Raoul and Federico walked over to the booth. Roberto introduced them as Raoul and Freddie and suggested they all move out to a larger table.

"Please allow us to buy a round of drinks," said Raoul, when they were seated. "Roberto made us feel most welcome the other evening and we are most grateful."

"Long way from home, huh?" said Chuck.

"Mexico City, actually," said Raoul. "But some of our crew are from all over Mexico.

"How many you got?" asked Lou.

"Just under 20. But that includes one woman."

"A woman. What does she do?" asked Chuck.

"She's my assistant," said Raoul. "She does our paperwork and cooks breakfast for the crew."

"Where do you eat the rest of the day?" asked Lou.

"The crews are always out somewhere in the daytime, so they eat in cafes and saloons around the county," said Raoul. "But speaking of eating, we are thinking of having a little fiesta at our place. Regina, that's the woman, she can make wonderful Mexican food. Maybe you gentlemen would like to come over some evening?"

"Sure," answered Chuck for all.

"I hear you guys are renting the Koch Ranch," said Lou.

"Yes. It suits our needs. We have the bunkhouse for most of the crew. Freddie, Regina, our helicopter pilot and I live in the main house where we have our offices. Plus, we have the barns to store our vehicles and our supplies."

"Which one flies your Huey?" asked Lou.

"Oh, that's Jose," said Raoul. "He's a very good pilot."

"Use to fly a bit myself," said Lou.

"Helicopters?" asked Freddie.

"Choppers, light planes, jet fighters, transports, you name it." said Lou.

"Roberto told us you had some exciting times in southeast Asia," said Raoul.

"Yeah, Chuck and Roberto here, we all did some shit over there in the old days. Roberto says one of you guys was with the 1st Cav. Which one?"

"I was with the 1st of the 5th Cav in 1966-67," said Raoul.

"No shit? Chuck and Roberto were with the 2d of 5th. But I did fly in some supplies to them at Ducco a couple of times," said Lou.

"How come you were with the 1st of the 5th but now work for Mexico?" asked Chuck.

"For people in positions like Federico and me, PEMEX pays very well," said Raoul. "But the Mexican government reserves the best jobs for Mexican citizens. So, Freddie and I gave up our U.S. citizenship and moved to Mexico."

"Freddie too? Were you in the Army like Raoul?" asked Chuck.

"Yes, but I was only in a support unit. I never saw any action," said Freddie.

"Too bad," said Chuck.

"So, gentlemen, what do you think? Although the rest of our crew isn't so good with English, they are eager to learn. So, we would consider it a great honor if you gentlemen could come over some evening for Mexican food and beer. How about it?" asked Raoul.

"Can we bring anything?" asked Chuck.

"No. Just your appetites and thirst. How about a week from tonight?"

"Well," said Lou, "we kinda like to be here on Saturday nights. You never know what those crazy cowboys may do. But how about next Friday night? Would that work?"

"Certainly," said Raoul. "Friday night it is. Say about 7:00 p.m.?"

"Done," said Chuck. "We'll be there. May we bring some flowers for your senorita?"

"Regina would love that," said Raoul.

With those arrangement made, Chuck, Robert and Lou explained to Raoul and Freddie the protocol for watching fights at Happy Jacques without getting drawn into them.

"The secret is your eyes," said Lou. "When the cowboys come prowling around looking for a fight, don't make eye contact with them. And, for God's sake, don't eyeball their women. We just keep talking among ourselves and don't pay them any attention. But, once they start fighting, you can watch them all you want. Just don't appear to take sides."

"Do you guys ever choose to get into these fights?" asked Raoul.

"Not me," said Lou. "But Chuck and Roberto here are experts in the martial arts. One time, some cowboys made the mistake of picking on them. They won't do that again. They leave Chuck and Roberto strictly alone.

"Like tonight, Raoul and Freddie, I noticed a couple of cowboys looking at you two. That I-don't-like-foreigners look. But it's clear you are under the protection of Chuck and Roberto tonight. So, unless you are just looking for trouble, you guys are just fine."

"We are grateful, Chuck and Roberto," said Raoul. "We certainly don't want to get into any kind of trouble during our brief stay in your country. No matter who started it, I'm sure PEMEX would fire us on the spot."

"Don't mention it," said Chuck.

After some talk about places in Vietnam where they might have almost run into each other, a lot of beer and watching a couple of fights, the evening was over. The five men parted friends and all were looking forward to the fiesta.

CHAPTER TWENTY

Might wake up one morning, and get a big shock. See the name "Ted and Jane" on your neighbor's mailbox. But it ain't Ted and Jane's fault. It's the ones who sell out. Put the money in a bank vault, before they get the Hell out. Ride Rangeland Rebel. Ride to beat the devil.

—Michael Martin Murphey

On Friday night, Chuck, Lou and Roberto showed up at the appointed time at the Koch Ranch. None of them had been to the ranch for several years. Not since it ceased to be a working ranch.

The over 150-year-old Koch Ranch folded because of the increased costs of grazing cattle on nearby public lands, the attacks by the politically-correct crowd upon red meat and punitive estate taxes designed to break up large land holdings. While the Koch children wanted to stay on the land and continue a family tradition that ran back into the previous century, they could not.

In its glory days, the Koch Ranch was large enough to provide a living for old man Koch, his three sons and two daughters and their spouses, their children and a raft of grandchildren. All the land was held in the name of old man Koch who directed the overall operation with each head of household assigned specific duties. In all, six families lived on the ranch on separate homesteads.

But when old man Koch died, his children found they couldn't afford to pay the "Death Tax" to the federal government. Faced with being jailed by the IRS or selling the ranch, they took the path which so many ranch and farm families must follow: sell the ranch and move to town.

Real estate developers bought the land and chopped it up. The choice view sites were sold to the wealthy for large, second homes. The lesser sites were used for high-rise condos and sold to the less wealthy. Of course, the land was too valuable to be used for affordable housing for local workers.

The Koch children paid off the estate taxes with the proceeds of the sale to the real estate developers, took what little was left and moved to town. Unfortunately, all they knew was ranching. So, when they sank their money in various small business ventures, they all failed.

Ultimately, all of the Koch children ended up living the ranchers' nightmare: working for wages. And, for minimum wage at that. Virtually overnight, the Kochs went from respected ranchers to just more mountain folks working at a bunch of low-end jobs to make ends meet. Stripped of their self-esteem, some of the adults took to drink and some of the children took to drugs. But most of the younger Koch descendants went on to college, learned communications-age skills and moved to the big cities—never to return to their beloved land.

When Chuck, Lou and Roberto pulled into the yard, they could tell someone had gone to a lot of trouble to make them feel welcome.

The traditional archway over the gate bearing the name: Koch Ranch was decorated with festive Mexican bunting and a banner saying Bienvenudo Americanos! A large charcoal-fired barbecue pit took center stage in the yard beside the main house and was filling the air with the aroma of fajita-spiced beef and chicken being cooked over mesquite.

Raoul was waiting on the veranda. Seeing the approach of Chuck's pickup, he stepped down to greet them.

"Welcome, amigos," said Raoul. "Come, let's have a Corona and we'll meet mi amigos."

Taking Coronas with a wedge of lime stuck in the top of the bottles, the Americans were led by Raoul to where the PEMEX crew was lined up in an informal reception line.

First in line was Federico who shook their hands and then introduced them to Regina. None of them were quite prepared for Regina who was one of the most beautiful women any of them had ever seen. Shiny black hair. Flashing dark eyes. Light Latino skin. Cherry Red lips. All packaged in the costume of a Flamenco dancer.

"Raoul says we are indebted to you for tonight's meal," said Chuck, handing Regina a nice bouquet of flowers. "But you look more like a fashion model than the cook."

"You are very gallant, Senor Lee," said Regina, "I thank all of you for the lovely flowers and I shall wear one of them in my hair this evening. As for the food, I had a great deal of help from the gentlemen you are about to meet."

Federico, very much the executive officer, led the Americans along the line introducing them to each of Raoul's men.

"My friends, I do not expect you to be able to remember the names of everyone you have just met. After all, we have the advantage. There are 19 of us and only three of you. So now, let's all have another Corona and get to know each other better.

"Within the hour, we'll have the fiesta buffet line set up and we'll eat. After that, we'll give you a little tour of our facility followed by some Mexican music and, the highlight of the evening, a flamenco dance by Senorita Regina.

To set the mood, Jorge, one of the technicians, took a large, acoustical guitar, sat down on the ranch house steps and began to play. While Jorge's mission was obviously background music, he hadn't played eight bars before it was clear to everyone that Jorge was terribly homesick. His music was plaintive and full of yearning. But after everyone had paid enough attention to his playing to be polite, individual conversations began to start up.

Earlier, the PEMEX crew filled a horse-watering trough with ice and beer. Everyone was expected to help themselves and did. Sensing it was time to eat while everyone could still taste her food, Regina signaled to Raoul to ring the dinner triangle.

Chuck, Lou and Roberto were treated to a feast of almost every conceivable Mexican dish. Virtually everything on the table had come from Mexico. The one, and welcome, exception: chilies from Hatch, New Mexico. Finally, when they could eat no more, Raoul suggested they walk off their meal with a tour of the PEMEX facility.

"I see you've still got some of the military mind left in you," said Chuck.

"How's that, amigo?" asked Raoul.

"You've got all your trucks and your helicopter lined up at dress-right-dress."

"Oh yes. I see what you mean. But it does allow me to look out the window and know when every crew is back from the field or which ones have yet to return."

"I bet you and Federico run a pretty tight ship," said Lou.

"A lot is riding on our success. If we can find significant reserves of natural gas it will mean a great deal to both our countries, not only in terms of money but in terms of what it will mean for the environment."

"You don't strike me," said Chuck, "as one of those wacky environmentalists."

"Oh, I'm not," said Raoul. "But we can only burn so much fossil fuel before we create a brown cloud around the earth. I notice quite a few pickups around here running on propane."

"I'll agree with you on that," said Chuck, "and if that's what your crew is all about, then I'm all for you."

After they had trooped the line of seismic vehicles and pickups and the helicopter, Raoul led Chuck, and Roberto over to the barn, now converted to a warehouse. Of course, Lou dropped out when they reached the helicopter and was lost for the evening in conversation with Jose.

Raoul opened the large doors to reveal a barn in an almost immaculate state. Obviously, his men had put in long hours cleaning out almost 100 years of the Koch's ranching detritus. But one section, in particular, caught their eyes.

Posted in several languages were warnings about an explosive hazard. Stepping closer Chuck and Roberto saw rack upon rack of high explosives. Dynamite sticks, blocks of TNT, long, square tubes of C-4 plastique, Det cord, blasting caps, timers—both mechanical and electronic.

"Holy shit," said Chuck. "You've got enough stuff here to destroy Grand County many times over."

"It's our stock and trade, Senor Chuck," said Raoul. "If we are to get the earth to tell us its secrets, we have to rough it up a bit."

At that point, Lou caught up with them and was standing there with his mouth open. "Jesus Christ, Raoul, have you got a permit for all this?"

"Certainly," said Raoul. "We have a permit for each type of explosive. But, I must admit, we were able to assemble quite a bit more inventory than the authorities think."

"You mean you've got more goodies than you're supposed to have?" asked Chuck.

"Well, you know how it is," said Raoul. "we couldn't get a permit for all of our needs, so we have done what your tax lawyers call: creative accounting."

"I've got some stumps on my place I need to remove," said Roberto, "you don't suppose I could come over and buy a little dynamite do you?"

"Roberto, you can't buy anything here; however, I would consider it an honor to give you whatever you want. Provided you know how to use it."

"Chuck and Roberto were in the Special Forces together," said Lou. "Chuck was an explosives expert among other things and Roberto was a medical specialist. But Roberto knows a few things about explosives."

"Then, you just come and get what you want, Roberto. Just check in with Federico or Regina. Well, that's the end our tour gentlemen. Let's go back to the fiesta and enjoy Regina's dancing."

For those who live in Grand County, there are many magical moments. They come at any season. But, for many, the best time of all is when the ice leaves the lakes and the mountains are still capped with snow.

In the late evening, the phenomenon of alpenglow coats the hillsides and anyone who still doesn't believe in God is obviously a fool or blind. The fiesta evening was one of those evenings.

Mellowed by beer and shots of tequila and more than satisfied with fajitas and all the Mexican trimmings, a bunch of rough men sat on bales of hay in a semi-circle facing the ranch house. Jorge had his guitar, Manuel produced an accordion, Salvador a trumpet, Miguel a violin and Jose another trumpet. They began with a spirited mariachi number that captured everyone's attention. Then, they deftly changed the mood by slipping to some hauntingly lovely Mexican tunes.

Lulled by the food, drink, the music, the alpenglow and the breath-taking scenery, the Americans, like the beer Ad, thought it couldn't get any better than this. But it did.

On an unseen signal from Raoul, the band struck a flamenco fanfare. Suddenly, Regina appeared on the veranda at the door to the ranch house. Everyone jumped to their feet clapping their hands. Chuck noticed the planking on the veranda was covered over with plywood giving Regina a smooth surface on which to dance.

After acknowledging the applause of the crowd, Regina motioned for everyone to sit back down.

The band began to play a slow flamenco song and Regina started to move her body in a sensuous tribute to the composer's genius.

From her waist down to her buttocks, her red dress was so tight it left nothing to the imagination. Below that, it flared out into a broom skirt of colored pleats and ruffles.

Her shiny black hair was plain. Just pulled back in a bun and tied with a scarlet ribbon. Over her left ear was a single, perfect red rose from the bouquet she accepted from Chuck Lee. Her stomach was flat and firm.

Lou was smitten and Regina sensed it immediately. Each time she would spin around, her eyes would focus upon Lou and Lou would blush. During portions of her dance, Regina would come down off the veranda and weave in and out among the men on their bales of hay. Of all the men in the semi-circle in front of the veranda, Regina came closer to Lou than any. So close her musky perfume seemed to invade his soul.

As the music began to build toward a grand finish, Regina's flashing feet took her back up onto the veranda to a position in front of the ranch house door. As the music ended, her fan was across her face as she disappeared inside the ranch house.

All of the men jumped to their feet pounding their hands together in wild applause and cheering themselves almost hoarse.

For a few moments, there was the kind of silence that follows the witnessing of something so special one feels they will never see nor hear such a thing again.

"Gentlemen," said Raoul, breaking the spell, "the campfire is still strong. Let us sit together and enjoy it."

Regina, after refreshing herself inside, came outside and took a seat on Lou's bale of hay.

While some of Raoul's men passed out more Tequila, Raoul said: "Amigos, you have been most kind to enjoy a taste of our Latino culture. But let us know more of your country. Could you honor us with a song or a story or even a poem from the American West?"

Chuck, Roberto and Lou each shifted a bit on their bales of hay as they tried to think of what they might do in response to Raoul's request. They felt heavily in debt.

After a moment, Chuck Lee said, "Well, I suppose I could recite a little poem I wrote. It's kinda sad but it's a true story. It's about my great-grandmother and how she came to be killed up there on The Grand Ditch."

"Sadness is part of life, my friend," said Raoul. "The best songs in our Latino culture are sad. So, please, Senor Chuck, favor us with your poem."

All around the campfire were still. Regina put her hand on Lou's knee and Lou felt he had died and gone to Heaven. Even if Chuck embarrassed them, Lou was far from caring.

With the flickering campfire reflecting on his weathered face, Chuck stood and faced the group.

Roberto and Lou had never seen Chuck like this. In Vietnam, it was not uncommon for soldiers to memorize and recite the poems of Rudyard Kipling or Robert Service and Chuck Lee was no exception. Chuck knew "Gunga Din" by heart and "The Cremation of Sam McGee," as well. During long night watches, Chuck used to entertain the members of his "A Team" by reciting complete passages from Kipling and Service.

But Chuck Lee as a poet? To cover what might be an embarrassment, Roberto took a small stick and made some idle circles in the dirt at his feet. Lou squeezed Regina's hand, but put on his hard face.

Chuck cleared his throat. "I call this poem: "The Tale of the Wandering Witch of the Great, Grand Ditch."

"But when I use the world 'witch' I mean no disrespect to my late, great-grandmother. But the fact is, if there can be facts with regard to the supernatural, some old-timers here in Grand County claim they have heard and seen a witch-like figure wandering The Grand Ditch. So, that's how this little poem got its name."

Taking another swig of beer, Chuck cleared his throat and recited:

"The tale of the wandering witch of the great, Grand Ditch is a story of water lust.

It is a tale of men with a water yen who were tired of eating dust.

To water find, over Poudre Pass they climbed, thinking only of their own parched sod.

They didn't give a shit whose land they split because they were bent on playing God.

They cut every water branch above Never Summer Ranch and drained the mountain's bowels.

And now, on moonlight nights on the shimmering heights, they say a banshee howls.

The sound she makes causes men to shake because they know that she's long dead.

A China gal taken up there with her body laid bare to lie in the coolies' beds.

To earn a crust she slaked the workers' lust, and that was all that she could do.

But when a baby came without a name, the headman told her she was through.

To save her a hike, someone drove a spike and killed her on the spot.

They called her a bitch as she fell from the ditch and quickly was forgot.

But on moonlight nights when the light is right, she walks the Ditch with her dead daughter.

She curses the sod of the men who played God and stole Grand County's water."

Finished, Chuck bowed his head and sat back down. At first, no one knew how to react until Raoul and his men broke into applause. "Bravo! Senor Chuck, Bravo!"

"Of course," explained Chuck, "she didn't really die up there. She and her baby made it down to Denver. Otherwise, I wouldn't be here. I just made up the dying part to make the poem seem more interesting."

Regina jumped up, ran over to Chuck and gave him a great, big kiss on the mouth. "Magnifico!" she cried.

Each one of the PEMEX team came over to Chuck and pumped his hand. Finally, Roberto and Lou walked over.

"That was really great," said Lou.

"Yeah," said Roberto, "that was terrific." But Chuck could tell his friends were somewhat embarrassed.

Regina drew Lou aside and they talked out of earshot of the others for a few moments. Neither Raoul nor Federico took any notice as Regina and Lou walked away. Raoul and Federico escorted Chuck and

Roberto toward Chuck's pickup. As Chuck expressed the thanks of all for such a wonderful fiesta, Lou rejoined them and expressed his thanks as well.

When the Americanos were gone, Raoul turned to Regina and said: "Well, what about Lou Leclerc?"

"I may have to fuck his brains out, but he'll do whatever I want."

"Just don't enjoy it too much," said Raoul.

CHAPTER TWENTY-ONE

Team Adams

Each spring, the Northern Colorado Water Conservancy District conducts a tour of the Colorado-Big Thompson Project for the public. It is such a nice outing some people sign up for the trip year-after-year.

The tour begins on the east side of the Continental Divide at Estes Park with a complementary continental breakfast. During the breakfast, the participants are given a briefing on the concept, design and operation of the Colorado-Big Thompson trans-mountain water-diversion project.

Most of the people who go on this annual tour live on the east side of the Continental Divide. Because they are the beneficiaries of this diversion of water from Grand County onto their side of the Divide, most of them think the Colorado-Big Thompson Project is splendid.

During their initial briefing, the tour participants are told that they will board waiting buses which will take them through Rocky Mountain National Park over Trail Ridge Road and the Continental Divide and then down to Grand Lake where they will be shown the West Portal of the Alva B. Adams Tunnel.

When the tour buses stopped near the tunnel entrance to dismount their passengers, Francisco and Miguel simply fell in with the official tour participants.

"You may notice," said the tour guide, "that the parking lot at the entrance to this tunnel is much larger than you might expect. That is because it is much more than a parking lot on which you are standing.

"Underneath your feet is a fan-shaped system of inlet pipes that take water here from the east end of Grand Lake and put it into the Adams Tunnel. If you will please follow me to the water's edge and look down, you will see the grates protecting these inlets.

"The number of inlets, the diameter of the pipes and the way they are arrayed underneath the parking area is designed to deliver a precise amount of water into the entrance of the tunnel.

"If you have no questions, please follow me into the entrance of the Adams Tunnel," said the guide.

The two half-inch steel doors supposedly securing the entrance to the Adams Tunnel made Francisco and Miguel smile. Each door was hinged to the doorframe with three hinges. Where the door halves came together, a simple hasp and padlock kept the doors shut. Francisco and Miguel looked briefly at the lock as the guide inserted his key. A needle-nosed bolt-cutter would make quick work of the lock. (See: www.the-grandconspiracy.com)

The guide stepped inside the entrance. "It's pretty crowded in here folks, so only about ten of you at a time can step in."

Francisco and Miguel were in the first group of ten to enter. Once inside the entrance, they found themselves standing in a small, dark foyer with a concrete floor. On the left side of the foyer was a large recess in the floor covered with steel grates. Looking down and through the grates they could see the collected waters of Grand County rushing below their feet and into the nine-foot, nine-inch diameter pipe that conducts the water under the Continental Divide to Estes Park.

A gentleman sporting the golf cap of his local country club asked: "Do you ever get inside this big pipe and inspect it for leaks?"

"Good question, Sir," replied the guide. "Yes. We inspect the entire length of the Adams Tunnel pipe in early spring.

"The way we do it is to shut off the flow of water from here at the West Portal making sure there is no water left in the tunnel. Then, we start down at the Estes Park end of the tunnel where we have a hatch large enough to allow us to insert a standard, World War II Jeep into the pipe. There's just enough room for the Jeep to fit.

"We take along food, water and some very strong spotlights which we use to inspect the welded joints between the pipe sections," said the guide.

"What if you find something wrong?" asked the gentleman in the country-club cap.

"We take careful notes so, if we see any thing suspicious, we can send in repair crews to do some spot-welding or whatever it takes to make sure the pipe does not leak anywhere along the 13.1-mile length of the system. Only rarely do we find anything wrong with the pipe.

"If any of you have teenagers, they might like to know that sometimes our repair crews use skateboards instead of the Jeep to move through the tunnel."

"How long does it take the water to go from the West Portal to the East Portal?" asked the golfer.

"It takes between two and three hours for the water to transit the 13.1 miles. So, figure two and one-half hours on average."

"What else is in the tunnel?" asked a lady with two cameras hanging from her neck.

"It is filled with communications cables linking the eastern United States with the western United States. That's another item we inspect each year. If anything happened to those cables not only business and personal communications would be severed but also some vital defense communications links which, of course, I am not at liberty to discuss.

"I can tell you, however, that there is a five-inch diameter steel pipe protecting these vital cables. The pipe is filled with nitrogen which serves to insulate and keep the electrical wiring dry."

"Does the tunnel carry anything else?" asked the golfer.

"Yes. It carries electricity. You see the water we send rushing downhill toward Estes Park drops 109 feet in elevation from the West Portal to the East Portal. Then, it drops another 2,800 feet before it reaches the Great Plains. That total drop of almost 3,000 feet provides the pressure needed to drive five hydroelectric plants.

"Some of the electricity we generate is then sent back up the tunnel and used to run the electric motors, pumps and turbines we use to lift the water from Willow Creek Reservoir and from Lake Granby into Shadow Mountain Lake and Grand Lake. So, to power the Lake Granby Pump Plant, the Willow Creek Pump Plant and the Lake Granby High Dam, for example, we use only the electricity we generate as the water rushes down to our hydroelectric plants. We don't use any electricity from generating plants located on the west of the Continental Divide. We are very proud to be totally self-reliant. We like to think we have come pretty close to the ideal of perpetual motion."

"Do the people who live up here in Grand County get to use any of the electricity their water produces?" asked an older gentleman wearing an old fishing vest.

"Actually, we don't have much left over to sell. But if we do have some, we just charge everyone the same price."

"Seems like since you took their water," said another man who looked old enough to have been around back during World War II when the tunnel was built, "I'd think you'd sell it to those poor folks at a reduced price."

"Ah, well. Like I say, it turns out we don't have much electricity to sell anyway. Again, we use up almost all of it to operate the pump plants and the Lake Granby High Dam. And besides, those kinds of questions are above my pay grade. So, let's have the next group to come in. You folks watch your step now going back out into the bright light."

Once outside, Francisco and Miguel took the opportunity as the other small groups were going into the West Portal to examine the area surrounding the parking lot and the tunnel entrance. One very nice home with its own boat dock was only 100 yards away on the north shore of Grand Lake. On the south shore was a large home hidden well back in the forest. Earlier, some locals told them that was the mansion owned by a wealthy Kansas City family who made greeting cards. Apparently, no vehicular road led to the big mansion. Guests had to either hike a narrow foot trail from the tunnel's parking lot or take a boat to the mansion. No trespassing signs discouraged uninvited guests.

Neither of the two nearby homes are occupied year round. For sure, not in winter. Like most of the homes around Grand Lake itself, these were summer homes. Even so, Francisco and Miguel reckoned no one would be out and about during the early hours of Labor Day.

With a last call of 'all aboard,' the tour buses left to go to the Lake Granby Pump Plant, eat a picnic lunch on the south shore of Lake Granby, tour the Windy Gap Reservoir and return over Trail Ridge Road back to Estes Park. A full day for a bunch of well-fed, happy day-trippers. Francisco and Miguel stayed behind to watch them leave. Then, they got into their pickup and went back to the PEMEX compound.

The following day, Team Adams met with Raoul and Federico in the main house. After they had gone over what they had learned, Raoul asked Francisco and Miguel if they had any recommendations.

"It's real simple," said Miguel. "We get our pet gringo to go out fishing and drinking with us on Grand Lake on the night before Labor Day. We'll fish down by the West Portal and keep drinking with our gringo for as long as we can. But, at some point, he'll want to leave. So, we'll put some knockout drops in his drink and tie him up in the back of our pickup. About 0430 hours, we move the pickup over to the door to the tunnel.

"We use bolt cutters on that pathetic little lock and drag our gringo and our waterproof bags of explosives inside. After we pry up the steel grates and gain access to the rushing waters down below, we tie one of the gringo's hands to the bags of explosives, set the waterproof timers and drop the gringo and the explosives into the water.

"We know it takes, on average, about two and one-half hours for the water to transit the entire pipe. Let's figure it takes an hour and thirty minutes for it to reach the mid-point of the tunnel. So, if H-Hour is 0700, we set the timers and drop the bags of explosives into the tunnel at 0530 hours.

"The explosives go off at 0700 hours, the tunnel collapses about 3,800 feet below the Continental Divide and, if and when they ever dig it out, they find the remains of the Americano who, most likely, will be blamed for the sabotage. How's that?"

"Not bad," said Federico. "But let me suggest one change, if I may."

"What's that?" asked Miguel.

"Sending the gringo down the tunnel does us no good in terms of the gringos being blamed right away. The problem is that they may never find his body."

"Good point, Federico," said Raoul. "What do you suggest?"

"I have an aerosol device that causes respiratory arrest in humans and then vanishes without a trace. We are going to use another can of it to kill the night watchman over at the Pump Plant, anyway. It is a combination of two chemicals. One chemical is used as a carrier because it penetrates the human skin instantly. That one's not all that toxic. But the other chemical is actually a highly-toxic paint solvent. On the street, it is called various names. Some gringo kids use it to get high because they are too stupid to understand that it destroys their brain cells. In the correct amount, it stops humans from breathing; especially, if the victim has been drinking. All Francisco and Miguel have to do is spray the aerosol in their gringo's face and he is out, forever. Then, they leave the gringo's body on top of the open grate where they insert the explosives.

When the sheriff finds the dead gringo, the obvious conclusion will be that the gringo put the explosives into the tunnel and then, in his drunken excitement, dropped dead of a heart attack."

"How does that sound to you?" Raoul asked Francisco and Miguel.

"No problem, Jefe," they both responded.

"Good. Then it's done," said Raoul. "That's the plan for Team Adams. We have the pickup. We have the lethal aerosol. We have the explosives; we have the timer and we'll procure some waterproof bags. Now all you need is a pet gringo who wants to go out drinking and fishing with you amigos on the eve of Labor Day."

"Por favor, Jefe," said Miguel. "I do have a question that I hope you do not think is stupid. But it has been bothering me."

"Go ahead, amigo."

"I can understand how the local gringos would want to blow up the water-diversion projects. But won't someone wonder if they blow up the Lake Granby High Dam? It holds water. It doesn't divert it."

"Excellent question. Not a stupid question, amigo. We are hoping the authorities will conclude that some of the local war veterans could not resist the opportunity to destroy a president they detest and could not resist the chance to kill the president of a country that some of the old Cold Warriors feel is just the Soviet Union lying dormant until it regains the strength to direct a fatal blow at the United States.

"In the minds of some of the rangeland rebels, this would be a rational decision. Timothy McVeigh and Terry Nichols thought they were doing the right thing when they blew up the federal building in Oklahoma City. They are not alone. There are other militia types across America who supported McVeigh and Nichols and some may still do so. To their twisted minds, those two are heroes who were just striking back for the slaughter at Waco, the atrocities at Ruby Ridge and other places where the federal government used excessive force.

"The FBI sniper at Ruby Ridge got off with a slap on the wrist despite several attempts by local people to have him tried and convicted. There are plenty of people out here in the West who see McVeigh and Nichols as merely applying vigilante justice to a government that abused its powers in so many places they've probably lost count.

"Americanos will put up with a lot. But when they perceive something to be unfair, they rebel. Out here in the West, and in the Deep

South, millions of Americans feel their voices are unheard by the power barons who live back in the East.

"So, amigo, I think the American mainstream media will jump at the chance to blame the destruction of the Granby Dam on what they will call the militia movement.

"Satisfied?"

"Si, Jefe."

"Well then, I congratulate the two of you on an excellent reconnaissance and a fine plan.

"By the way, I, too, have completed my reconnaissance of the Lake Granby High Dam. As it stands now, I will be able to destroy the dam without assistance although, after I set the timers, I will need Jose and the helicopter to come pick me up at the west end of the dam at a place called Sunset Point.

"Federico and I will be going over more targets tomorrow. But I must leave now. I've been invited by Chuck Lee and Lou Leclerc to have a drink with him over in Grand Lake. I think they feel indebted to us for the fiesta," said Raoul.

CHAPTER TWENTY-TWO

As the time drew near for the arrival of President Trimmer and his entourage, the pace of activity at Ouray Ranch, now Camp Hope, increased every day. Jonathan Winslow was so busy that his almost daily contacts with Buck and Dolly Madison became less frequent. Then, out of the blue, Jonathan called for help.

"Buck, I need some advice," said Jonathan.

"Buy low, sell high. How's that?"

"I'll write that down. Seriously, Buck, my men and I need to conduct our quarterly weapons training and we need a place to do it," said Jonathan.

"I was afraid you were going to ask me something difficult. This is easy. Grand County maintains a set of first-class firing ranges just west of the town of Parshall."

"Where's that?"

"Drive south on US 34 from where you are and take US 40 west through Hot Sulphur Springs, through Byers Canyon and before you know it the firing ranges are on the right-hand side of the highway."

"Do I need to reserve them?"

"Not really, but it would be a good idea to let your buddy, Sheriff Rob Cobble, know in advance. If you go tearing up his wooden target frames with UZIs, he might get a little upset."

"You're right about the UZIs. They do turn wood into toothpicks. Maybe, we'll just take our shotguns."

"Man, if your agents need to practice with shotguns, we are in trouble."

"We want to go to Parshall tomorrow. Can you go with us?"

"No, I have to fly up to Laramie to make a luncheon speech at the university. Even worse, I have to stay for the faculty tea."

"Who's playing for the faculty tea, Willy Nelson?"

"Ah, Jonathan, the eastern seaboard snob. Anyway, Dolly is here and she's signaling that she'll go with you and your agents to Parshall. She's was your old college marksmanship flame anyway."

"I hate to admit this, Buck, but she was always a better shot than I am."

"Aren't we all. Your platoon couldn't hit the jungle with a flame-thrower."

"We weren't that bad, Buck. So, what about tomorrow?"

"Dolly says she'll meet you at Ouray Ranch, sorry, Camp Hope, at 0800. She'll probably bring her .357 Magnum lever-action carbine. She needs to zero her new telescopic sight anyway. I bought her a 3-9X power scope for Christmas," said Buck.

"Is that to go with the push lawn mower you bought her the Christmas before that?" asked Jonathan.

"We don't have a lawn, smart-ass," said Buck.

"Well, tell Dolly I'll even let her drive one of our armored Suburbans and she can even bring Scooby along if she likes."

"Scooby hates noise, so she'll stay home. But I'll bet Dolly will want to drive your Suburban."

The next morning Dolly parked her Expedition in the newly-established visitor's parking lot just outside Camp Hope, walked over to the temporary sentry box and asked the uniformed guard to call Special Agent Winslow.

In a few moments a caravan of three black Suburbans left the main lodge and drove down to the gate and stopped.

"Do you really want to drive?" asked Jonathan Winslow as he stepped out of the lead Suburban."

"Yes, I do," said Dolly. Handing Jonathan her carbine and shooting bag, she walked around to the driver's side and waited for the driver to dismount.

"Agent McKay," directed Jonathan, "please hop in the next vehicle. Dr. Madison and I will lead the way."

Dolly adjusted the seat, looked over the controls and deftly drove off.

"Nice wheels," said Dolly. "But I can tell you've given up some acceleration in favor of armor."

"Well, we can't have everything."

The rest of the trip over to the firing ranges near Parshall was taken up with Dolly pointing out the Windy Gap Pumping Station, the wildlife viewing area and the beauties of the Colorado River as it accompanied them all the way to Parshall.

When they were down inside the confines of Byers Canyon, Jonathan said, "You know, this place seems familiar. Like I've seen it before."

"Ever see that Steven Segal movie 'Under Siege II?' a lot of it was filmed in this canyon."

"I knew it. I knew I'd seen this place before. But, you know, I think the real thing is scarier than the movie. I'd hate to drive through here in the winter."

"Everyone feels that way."

When the caravan of Suburbans arrived at the firing range, Dolly got out and assumed the role of officer-in-charge. She told the agents to leave their weapons and gear in the vehicles and to sit down while she gave them a range-safety orientation. Jonathan just shook his head in wonder as he thought how Melissa, now Dolly, had changed over the years from the shy, missionary's daughter to a take-charge woman able to order a bunch of Secret Service agents around. But in a very nice way.

The range-safety briefing over, the agents went to the vehicles to get their weapons, earmuffs and yellow shooting glasses. Dolly and Jonathan got their weapons and shooting gear out of the Suburban as well.

Jonathan explained to Dolly what weapons he wanted his agents to fire and in what order. As officer-in-charge, Dolly saw to it that Jonathan and all of the agents stayed on line and that no one went forward of the firing line until all weapons were cleared.

After Jonathan and his agents finished reducing not only the targets but also some of the target frames to toothpicks with their UZIs, Dolly took her place on the line.

"The County's going to send the White House a bill for those seven target frames," she told Jonathan.

"I knew that would happen. But I didn't mention it to Sheriff Cobble in advance because he might have balked at letting us use this nice range," said Jonathan.

"Of course, Rod would let you use the range. This county's so strapped for money they'd let you big spenders from Washington do most anything. Having all your agents, the White House staff, those pilots and aircraft up at the airport plus the national publicity is a gold mine. With the exception of blowing up Lake Granby, you guys could do virtually anything up here and the county commissioners would love it."

"No danger of that. Now, let's see what you can do with that carbine. I'll be your safety officer. Meanwhile, I'm going to send the other agents back to Camp Hope."

After the other agents departed and they were alone. Jonathan said, "This is great. We do some shooting and also catch up on days gone by. Just like old times under the football stadium at Harvard."

"Jonathan, we'll let days gone by be days gone by. We may have been serious about each other in college, but that was long ago and before Buck."

"Does Buck ever ask about you and me? You know, about the depth of our involvement?" asked Jonathan.

"No. I've never told him one way or the other and he never has asked."

"We could have made a go of it you know."

"Yes, except a little event known as Vietnam came along and you went off to war and got married."

"Dolly, Vietnam changed a lot of lives. It broke up love affairs, broke up marriages, upset the lives of so many children who couldn't understand what was happening to their parents."

"I see the damage the war did to a number of people we know right here in Middle Park. For example, Chuck, Lou and Roberto, although Roberto seems pretty stable," said Dolly.

"Funny how our paths keep crossing. Buck, Chuck, Roberto and I all in the same battalion in Vietnam. Lou, who crashed his Helio-courier at Ducco and we took him in and had him fight along with us as infantry. And now, I've picked a presidential retreat right in the middle of what seems to be their private playground. What did you call it? Middle Park?"

"Well, Lou Leclerc spells it Middle Parc. He claims his French ancestors were here before anyone and, if it weren't for the Louisiana Purchase, he'd own the place. And, because Chuck's great-grandmother 'worked' up on the Grand Ditch, he thinks he and Lou are co-owners."

"But if it hadn't been for the war, what do you think would have happened to us?"

"Who knows? You never forget your first love, Jonathan. So, I'll always care for you in a special way. But that's a part of me I keep in the past. Buck is here, now, tomorrow and forever. Let's change the subject."

"Okay," said Jonathan. "Let's see what you can do with that little lever-action carbine."

"You may think it's little. But these .357 Magnum hollow-point slugs can stop a bear in its tracks at 300 yards."

With an ease that could have only come with lots of practice, Dolly put on her earmuffs and yellow shooting glasses, took up the prone position and wrapped the sling around her arm to help her attain a rock-solid firing position. She adjusted the focus on her 3-9X scope and fired three rounds at the target.

She paused to look at the target through her binoculars, shifted her position just slightly and fired another three rounds.

After she showed Jonathan her weapon was empty, she secured it with a sandbag and they walked down range to inspect her target.

The first three rounds were in a tiny shot group you could cover with a half-dollar. But the shot group was up and to the left of the bull's eye by three inches. The next three rounds, were to the right by three inches. Dolly went back to her weapon, adjusted her scope and fired three more rounds down range.

Her carbine on safe and sandbagged, she walked down range again. The last three rounds were dead center on the bull's eye. The dime-size shot pattern was so tight the center of the target was completely shot away.

"You know I think you are a better shot today than when you were at Wellesley. How'd this happen?"

"Buck became my coach. You know at one time or another Buck fired Expert with every individual and crew-served weapon in the Infantry inventory."

"I knew Buck was a fine shot but he never told me that."

"Typical Buck. Actually, Buck made it quite simple. Make the front sight be in sharp focus, the rear sight fuzzy and then breathe, aim, slack and squeeze."

"Breathe, aim, slack and squeeze. The Army taught it as BASS. Been awhile since I've thought about that kind of BASS."

"When using the iron sights I remember to do that with each round and I also remember the eye can't focus on two objects at the same time. So, I just get the rear sight and the front sight lined up with the front sight post resting at the base of the target. Just as I get to the squeeze part, I make sure the front sight is in sharp focus while the rear sight gets fuzzy."

"Do you hunt big game around here, Dolly?"

"Heavens no. Jonathan really. Do you think I would shoot Bambi's father?"

"Okay, so you don't shoot up Bambi's family. But what do you think about people who do?"

"I try to think about the fact that a certain number of animals have to be harvested for the overall health of the deer or elk population. But I don't like it. Yet I think we would lose something very fine and precious about this country if we didn't have the Second Amendment."

"How so?"

"Buck and I lived along the *Zonengrenze* in Germany during part of the Cold War. Later, we traveled into the USSR before the Berlin Wall came down and communism collapsed. I saw what it was like for entire populations to have no weapons and to be totally at the mercy of their government. And, frankly at this point, I'm more afraid of runaway, big government than I am of Saddam Hussein or Sergei Popov or Fidel Castro for that matter.

"So, I defend our right to keep and bear arms and the hunter's right to go out and harvest some venison. Otherwise, every time I buy meat at the Fraser Safeway, I'd feel like such a hypocrite. Someone had to kill the steer or cow that provides the steak Buck and I like to enjoy, either with a gun or a sledgehammer.

"But I do object to hunters who come out here looking for trophy heads and then leave the rest of the carcass out in the forest because they are too lazy to pack it out and give it to the local food bank."

"And, I get livid with these so-called hunters who can't tell the difference between an elk and a moose or a deer and a moose."

"You've got to be kidding."

"I wish. Last season, 17 moose were killed in Grand County by hunters who we figure mistook them for elk or deer."

"How can anyone be that stupid."

"It takes work, but they do it. Of course, the Department of Wildlife is almost as much at fault."

"How's that?"

"They decided to have an either sex season on elk. Elk and moose cows can be mistaken for each other if you are not paying attention. But, even then, it takes a fairly stupid or drunk hunter to make that mistake."

"So, are they going to do away with either sex hunting?"

"Better yet, let's hope they do away with the Department of Wildlife. First, they infest our trout with Whirling Disease, thanks to one of their stupid experiments. Then, they create a situation that, statewide, cost us 35 moose in all last season. They should break the DOW up into regional commissions and give the locals more say in what's going on."

"Would you shoot a deer or elk if you were starving?"

"Starving? Of course, I would do whatever is necessary to survive and to protect those I love."

"I bet you would, Dolly. I guess all of us face difficult decisions in our lives. Times when we have to destroy one thing to save another. Oscar Wilde said, 'Everyman kills the thing he loves. The brave man with a sword, the coward with a kiss.'"

"Oscar Wilde was weird."

"Even so, I think there was something to what he said."

"Hey. We forgot to have that last batch of UZI shooters police up their brass."

"You're right. I'll send a detail back over here first thing in the morning."

On the ride back from the firing range, Dolly felt Jonathan was more reserved than when the day began. When Buck was with them, Jonathan seemed more relaxed. But when Dolly and Jonathan were alone, she always felt a slight bit of tension, an awkwardness. Probably some guilt on the part of Jonathan because he broke off their relationship without telling her. He just left her hanging. Or, maybe Jonathan was still in love with her. To break the silence, Dolly decided to talk about Buck.

"Do you think Buck has changed since you knew him in Vietnam?" asked Dolly.

"He looks fine to me," said Jonathan. "He's fit, he seems rested and relaxed. I guess I don't see anything wrong with Buck."

"But don't you find it a bit strange that Buck would give up the amenities of city life to move out to the end of the power line, the phone line and the snow plow route. We are about as isolated up here as you can get and still not be hermits. You don't find it a bit odd?"

"Well, whatever it is, a lot of people would like to trade places with the two of you. You live like God in France up here. For outdoors people like you, this is paradise."

"I know. I know. And, I'm not complaining. I love it up here. But we seem so removed from what is going on in the world."

"Removed? I don't know. Buck's still considered an authority in his field. He writes. He still goes out on the lecture circuit now and then, like today. I can't see how you say Buck has removed himself from society."

"Yes, he does all that. But don't you see how he's not a part of what the world is doing. Buck's become an observer, not a participant. It's like he goes around wearing a Teflon shield. The way he deals with the world is to just ride by and wave."

"That part I agree with," said Jonathan. "But you and he seem to relate."

"Oh yes, we are just as warm and loving and caring as ever. But our circle really only includes the two of us. Buck reminds me of Mark Twain's story about the cat that sat on the hot stove lid. It won't ever sit on another hot stove lid, but it won't sit on a cold one either."

"So, what burned Buck?"

"Vietnam and then the way the Army fell apart after Vietnam. The way combat leaders like Buck were cast aside in favor of the so-called managers."

"Dolly, let's face it. That happens after every war. The leadership traits it takes to be successful in combat the way Buck was, are anathema to the kind of wimps and REMFs the military wants to be in power in peacetime."

"REMFs? I haven't heard that term in a long time. But that's a perfect description for people not fit to tie Buck's shoe lace, or yours."

"Hey, I was just one of Buck's platoon leaders. Everything I know about valor and leadership I learned from Buck and one other guy."

"Who's the other guy?"

"The guy Buck credits with saving his life, Chuck Lee. Buck had Delta Company and Chuck had Charlie Company. They were soul mates. Buck says everything useful about small-unit tactics against the VC and the NVA he learned from Chuck."

"Buck is not one to talk much about Vietnam, but he told me how he and Chuck used to figure out ways to maneuver their companies together—hammer and anvil. That sort of thing."

"Oh, it went far beyond something simple like hammer and anvil. Chuck Lee could think up the most diabolical ways to get the enemy to come out and fight."

"Buck always said the NVA was so afraid of the 1st Air Cav that they would only hit and run from Cambodia."

"Before Vietnam, Chuck spent a lot of time with the Special Forces down in Central America. At least one dictator tried to get him to resign his commission and become head of his armed forces.

"Anyway, Chuck had all this actual, anti-guerrilla experience when he came to the 1st Air Cavalry Division. How he got command of a regular rifle company is a mystery because the line units have this prejudice against the sneaky forces types."

"Buck said your battalion commander, Lt. Colonel Robards, didn't like Chuck at first."

"He didn't at first," said Jonathan. "Robards had the typical large-unit commander's disdain for Chuck because he came up through the Special Forces. But Colonel Robards came to love Chuck like a brother.

"In fact, we didn't care about much except each other. Paradoxically, we were lean, mean, highly trained, highly disciplined, highly professional and highly effective in the jungle. But, at the same time, we didn't give a rat about Saigon or Washington. We saw them for what they were: REMFs.

"Fortunately, in the early days of the American troop build-up, we didn't see too many REMFs. It was just too wild and woolly for them. If we broke a machine gun beyond field repair, we just taped a hand grenade to it and blew it to bits. No paperwork. With a radio call on the admin-log net, a chopper would come out and lower another machine gun down to us.

"But, as the war dragged on, the REMFs, bean counters and nitpickers took over. It took two feet of paperwork to get a new machine gun.

"Fortunately, in the early part of the war, we were blessed with great battalion commanders. The kind of commanders who always march toward the sound of the guns. Colonel Robards was a genius at giving us support. He always said: 'Never plan to succeed. Plan so you do not fail.'"

"Sounds rather negative to me."

"Not really. Robards just wanted us to think ahead and be prepared when things go wrong as they so often do in combat. And, all those extra radios really helped with that because when Buck or Chuck heard those first contact reports, they immediately started calling up more gunships or more aerial-rocket artillery or even Air Force fighter-bombers. On top of that, both Chuck and Buck knew field artillery cold. They were much better at calling for and adjusting artillery fire than the regular artillery forward observers. Had to be because FOs were in short supply. After awhile, they quit requesting FO replacements and just did it themselves. Buck was so good at it that he could call in defensive concentrations so close to us that the shrapnel would cut the jungle right over our heads. It was also a good way to get us to dig in fast and deep."

"You make Vietnam almost sound like fun."

"It was fun in a strange way. When you're young, physically fit, have good equipment, have good support and have the kind of leadership we had from Colonel Robards, Major Sword, Chuck and Buck, actual combat can be very satisfying. Of course, it scares the crap out of you when those AK-47s start chugging at you. But, we kicked their butts so badly most of the time that, after it was over, we got this big rush. A big high."

"I guess that war was like the nine blind men and the elephant. It depends on which part of the elephant you were touching," said Dolly.

"Well, in our company and our battalion, we sure didn't have hold of the elephant's ass end. We had it by the trunk and we led it around," said Jonathan.

"Too bad it wasn't that way all over Vietnam."

"You know, Dolly, we could have won that war so easily. If we had been free to maneuver as need be in Cambodia and Laos, if the majority of the bombs had been dropped in the north instead of in the country we were trying to save, it would have been over by late 1967. Instead, Johnson and McNamara screwed around and let the war drag on too long. By the time we destroyed the Viet Cong during Tet of '68, the power elites back home and their wimpy draft-dodger off-spring had had enough and they pulled the plug on us and on the South Vietnamese," said Jonathan.

"What do think would have happened if you guys had been allowed to win that war?"

"Actually, we and the South Vietnamese had the war won by 1973. All we had to do was abide by the promises we made to the South Vietnamese when we left them alone to continue to defend their borders."

"Such as?"

"To get the South Vietnamese to sign the Paris Accords, we promised to come back in force if the South Vietnamese were invaded by the North again, we promised to replace their losses in artillery, tanks and personnel carriers and we promised major financial help. We broke all three of those promises and the NVA was allowed to invade all the way to Saigon."

"But what if we had not broken all those promises to the South Vietnamese?"

"The Cold War would have ended sooner than it did. At the outset, the situation would have been a lot like it is on the Korean peninsula. Commies starving in the north, a U.S.-backed ally in the south making electronic gizmos for American corporations and getting rich."

"What about the Red Chinese and the Soviets?"

"The Soviets might have gone into Afghanistan even sooner in an attempt to regain face over the loss in southeast Asia. Or, if not Afghanistan, they would have done something stupid along one of their non-European borders just to show they still had some muscle. But the internal rot in the Soviet Union was already so great their house of cards was in the process of crumbling. The proof of that is even though they got us to defeat ourselves in southeast Asia and should have gotten a huge lift from their victory, they did not. Instead, when Ronald Reagan came along with his massive military build-up, he convinced Gorbachev to throw in the towel.

"I told you I was in on those Reagan-Gorbachev summit trips. The Left can hate Reagan all they want and demean him as 'just an actor,' but if the way he twisted Gorbachev around his finger was acting, then I say let's recruit more presidents out of Hollywood. Somehow, Reagan was able to communicate to Gorbachev the basic goodness and the good intentions of the American people. In those private fireside chats we set up so carefully, President Reagan negotiated the surrender of the Soviet Union to the United States. Not to any other nation, but to the good old U.S. of A. Gorbachev surrendered because Reagan showed him how we had the economic means to keep raising the military stakes indefinitely. He surrendered because Reagan convinced him that America would not take military advantage of the situation and, in fact, would help rebuild the Soviet economy. That was personal diplomacy at it highest. If they ever add another face to Mount Rushmore, it should be that of Ronald Reagan.

"The pity is they will never give Reagan credit while he's alive. But, mark my words, Ronald Wilson Reagan will go down in history as the greatest President-Diplomat in U.S. History," said Jonathan.

"Did you know, Jonathan, I've never heard you call President Trimmer anything but POTUS?"

"Come to think about it, I guess you're right. Maybe it's just easier to fall into agent slang and say POTUS or FLOTUS or FDOTUS."

"Fuh-doe-tus, who's that?"

"First daughter of the United States. I know, it's an awkward acronym, but we all understand it."

"These acronyms and those radio call signs you use to refer to the first family, they all seem so cold and impersonal."

"This is a cold and impersonal business. We agents have a job to do and we do it."

"But you just spoke with such warmth and passion about President Reagan."

"Some protectees you like better than others. Anyway, we don't take sides. Besides, I thought we were talking about Buck and his being withdrawn from the world."

"We were before I started pumping you for the inside scoop on your job. But anyway, I know you can retire soon. Why don't you move out here?"

"I don't have any plans for the future," said Jonathan. "Besides, I thought we were talking about Buck."

"Buck's had several hard knocks since he left the Army," said Dolly. "But he always seems to get back up."

"Buck used to tell me: Victory is simply getting up one more time than you are knocked down," said Jonathan. "Doesn't he believe that anymore?"

"I'm not sure."

"So, why did Buck leave academe?" asked Jonathan.

"We had this wonderful opportunity to go to New York with a large investment banking firm where Buck would be in position to have a little bit of input on the restoration of our crumbling physical infrastructure. But just as we were about to arrive, the company was bought up in one of those big mergers. Our patron, whom Buck loves like a brother, got squeezed out and we had to cancel the move. Unfortunately, Buck had already resigned his teaching position at the university. So, we kinda had egg on our faces for a while."

"But, you bounced back."

"In a way. We went back to political consulting and public relations. We helped elect the first female governor our state ever had. We're proud of that. Against my better judgment we took over a failing newspaper. It should have been a success, but every time we would line up one of the major grocery stores to give us their advertising, the monster paper in our town would lure them back with prices way under their cost of production."

"That's illegal. It's a violation of the anti-trust laws," said Jonathan.

"You're correct. But we didn't have the money to take them to court and they knew it. That's when we got out of that business and moved up here in the mountains."

"So, you're saying all the stuff you did after Buck retired from the Army causes Buck to be withdrawn?"

"Let's put it this way. He just doesn't get involved in things the way he used to. He used to be a man who lived the *vita activa*. Now, he's living more the *vita contemplativa*. He's become an observer. In fact, in his commentaries on foreign and domestic affairs, he refers to himself as 'this observer'," said Dolly.

"But he's so active physically, Dolly. He skis, he hikes, fishes, sails, all that Rocky Mountain stuff and still flies his own plane. I'd say that's the *vita activa*."

"Yes, but mentally and emotionally, it's not the *vita activa*. He just observes life and, more as an academic exercise than anything else, he writes articles about his observations."

"This all makes perfect sense to me, and I don't see that it's a big problem," said Jonathan.

"The problem is that if something came up that would have compelled him to action in the old days, I don't think Buck would do anything but observe."

"Give me an example."

"Chuck Lee. As you know, Chuck lives up by Grand Lake. Chuck's a border-line alcoholic and the ring leader of a handful of disaffected vets who are so anti-government I sometimes worry about them."

"You mean the rangeland rebels?"

"Oh, they've gone way beyond the rangeland rebel stage. Mind you, they're not like the environmental kooks who burned down the Two Elks Lodge and some chair lifts over at Vail. These guys care for the environment too, but they just don't like to have their traditional way of making a living foreclosed. They even have a lot of sympathy for the plight of the American Indians because they see the federal government breaking promises made to them as veterans, particularly on health care. One of these days or nights, I fear they'll take the law in their own hands out of frustration. Ever since the drought of 1989, they've been talking about doing something to stop what they call the theft of the county's water by Denver and the Front Range."

"Dolly, let's keep this between you and me and Buck. But we've got Chuck and his friends in our computer. We know they get drunked up over at Happy Jacques most every night and talk rebellion. But, so far, it's just talk."

"Let's hope you're right. But I think Buck ought to try to get Chuck to sober up. They were so close in Vietnam, and now, they just sort of co-exist up here. Now and then they go fishing. After a few beers, Chuck starts in on how badly they were screwed in Vietnam and his anti-government diatribes go down hill from there," said Dolly.

"But other than talk, do you think Chuck and his rangeland rebels would go beyond that?" asked Jonathan.

"I didn't think so until those kooks blew up the federal building in Oklahoma City. Jonathan, you know as well as anyone that Chuck is some kind of genius when it comes to explosives and booby-traps."

"McGyver. When that TV show was running, I never saw it that I didn't think of Chuck Lee. When Chuck's company would ambush the NVA or the VC, it was SOP for Chuck to move his men back just far enough so he could register an artillery concentration near the enemy dead. Then, he would personally go back to booby trap the bodies with hand grenades. That done, he would pull his troops back again and they would just listen for the enemy to come and try to retrieve their dead. When NVA or VC moved one of the bodies the booby-trap would go off and Chuck would call for a battalion of 105 mm howitzers to deliver about 18 rounds of high explosive rounds on the ambush site. Usually, that would net him another half-dozen NVA dead," said Jonathan.

"I know. Buck told me about the times he and Chuck talked Colonel Robards and Major Sword into letting them pull off one of their diabolical maneuver schemes."

"My favorite of the Buck and Chuck show was the false ammo pallet drop."

"How'd that work?"

"Both the VC and the NVA loved to get their nicotine-stained fingers on unexploded U.S. artillery shells so they could mine the roads with them. We had these Ch-47 Chinooks, you know the choppers with the blades at both ends. They would carry pallets of artillery ammunition from our supply dumps up to the airmobile artillery batteries we sometimes had perched on the mountaintops in the Central Highlands.

"Every now and then, one of those pallets would get loose and fall. Either rigged wrong or the chopper started to lose power and the crew jettisoned the pallet to save the chopper. Anyway, this happened just often enough for Chuck's plan to be plausible.

"Chuck would get battalion to arrange for a Chinook to pick up a pallet that looked like it held artillery ammo only the ammo boxes were actually filled with sand. Chuck would maneuver his rifle company into position along the flight route of the chopper resupplying one of those mountaintop artillery batteries. Buck would maneuver our company down there too only we would be about five clicks away from Chuck. Just before dark, the chopper would be flying along toward the mountaintop and its load would fall loose.

"After dark, Chuck would quietly set his company up in a blocking position and dig in. Our company would be set to move in where the ammo pallet landed. The ammo pallet was booby-trapped with a flare and, usually about midnight, when the enemy reached the ammo pallet, they would set off the flare. Our company would come charging toward the flare firing like crazy and further lighting up the sky by calling for the Air Force to drop even more flares. All of this prearranged by Chuck, of course.

"The enemy would take off running, but they would run right into the ambush set up by Chuck. Chuck's men cut them down in droves. Chuck and Buck pulled this off several times. They'd take turns being hammer and anvil.

"After awhile the enemy caught on to this trick and we stopped doing it. But we gained a lasting benefit. They weren't so quick to go after dropped ammo pallets and we were able to recover more of the pallets before they did," said Jonathan.

"I notice you always refer to the VC and the NVA as the enemy, never gooks or slopes or dinks like Chuck does. Is that because of Jasmine?" asked Dolly.

"Yes, when you marry an Oriental you suddenly get sensitized to those kind of racial slurs," said Jonathan. "Before Jasmine, I used to sound just like Chuck and all the rest."

"Did Buck ever call them those names?"

"Not that I recall. But, if he did, he stopped when General Westmoreland issued an edict to stop the practice."

"Your kidding. Westmoreland actually sent out that order."

"Oh yes. Westy discovered it was offensive to our South Vietnamese allies for us to refer to their North Vietnamese brothers as gooks, slopes and dinks. So out came the order to cease and desist."

"How was it received?"

"Basically, with gales of laughter. Except for Colonel Robards who had this wry sense of humor. Robards augmented Westy's order by saying we were to refer to the South Vietnamese as 'our noble allies.'"

"Did you?"

"Of course. Actually, we shortened 'noble ally' to 'November Alpha'. The NVA had somewhat of a radio intercept capability so it took them awhile to figure out that 'November Alpha' meant we were doing something involving the South Vietnamese. But, in the 1st Cav we had another name for our noble allies Westy didn't know about."

"What was that?"

"We called them the *local* VC."

"Oh, Jonathan you guys were terrible."

"Of course, Jasmine wasn't Vietnamese. She was Chinese."

"How'd you meet?"

"Halfway through my first tour, the one where I was a platoon leader for Buck, I went to Hong Kong on R&R.

"I went over to the U.S. Consulate because my brother was a junior Foreign Service Officer and I wanted to see him. Jasmine was working there in the passport section. He introduced us and we fell in love."

"So you were like Lieutenant B.F. Pinkerton and promised to return when 'robins nest again'?"

"Better than that, I did return at the end of my tour and we got married."

"So then what happened?"

"It was time for me to go to the Infantry Career Course at Ft. Benning, Georgia."

"Did any of the rednecks give you a hard time about having a slant-eyed bride."

"Not really. There were so many Asian war brides around by that time I don't think anyone really cared. When you're a student they have small apartments set aside, so we didn't get out into redneck country very much."

"Buck showed me her picture. She was very beautiful and you must have loved her very much."

"She was my world. She was gentle and sweet and one of the smartest people I've ever known. In a way, I killed her."

"Jonathan, how can you say that?"

"I was so much in love with Jasmine I couldn't bear to leave her behind when they sent me back to 'Nam for another tour. With help from my brother, we arranged for her to get a job at the U.S. Embassy in Saigon.

"Because I already had one tour with a U.S. unit, the flesh peddlers at Infantry Branch said I had to be an advisor to a South Vietnamese Army unit. Being a paratrooper, I was lucky enough to be assigned to an ARVN airborne unit. They kept most of the airborne troops near Saigon as kind of a palace guard, so Jasmine and I were together a lot."

"Where did you live?"

"Jasmine and three other female embassy staffers rented a small villa not far from the embassy. They had an extra room and we stayed there when I could get away from my unit. We had just learned that Jasmine was going to have our first child. We were thrilled and everything was set for Jasmine to go home in two weeks to my parents on Cape Cod to have our baby.

"One night, when I was out in the field, a squad of NVA sappers got into the villa. They slaughtered Jasmine, our unborn child and the three women from the embassy and left, undetected.

When I came back a day later, I thought the villa was awfully quiet. I went inside and called her name, but there was no answer. Then, I found out why. The NVA had tied their hands behind their backs and slit their throats."

"My God, that must have been terrible."

"It was. I never knew what grief was until Jasmine was killed, no murdered."

"What did you do then?"

"I had her body cremated and the ashes placed in an urn. I took the ashes over to the embassy for safe keeping and returned to my unit."

"Having nothing to live for, I didn't care what happened to me. So, when that tour was over, I agreed to extend for another tour provided I could go back to the 1st Air Cav."

"So that's how you and Buck got back together."

"Right. As you know, Buck was detailed to the Company for two years in Europe. But when the KGB put a price on his head, he pulled a deal to get back to the 1st Air Cav. So, we both ended up back in our old battalion. Only this time, Buck was our battalion operations officer and I was one of the company commanders. Right after Buck finished that tour was when I stepped on a landmine and ended up in Walter Reed."

"But while we were together, Buck told me that you and he had met at CIA headquarters and that he intended to go back there and marry you."

"Buck said that, did he? Well, he was certainly sure of himself. Did you ever think about coming back to look for me?"

"Frankly, I was so broken up over the death of Jasmine that I wasn't looking for you or anyone else. I guess I'm still not."

"With the passage of time, you may think about looking around again," said Dolly.

"We'll see. But, you know Dolly, I think I've kinda come to the end of the trail. Retirement is just over the horizon. The North Vietnamese killed the woman I loved so deeply. They killed my unborn child. Also, my family back east never really accepted Jasmine to begin with. That hurts because I really can't talk about her with my folks or even my brother. My agents are about the only family I have now and I'll be saying goodbye to them soon.

"Oddly enough, I guess I feel closer to you and Buck and this strange collection of rangeland rebels, as you call them, than I do to anyone. You might say I'm at loose ends and hoping to find something meaningful to do with my life, or what there is left of it," said Jonathan.

Shifting the subject, Dolly asked, "Besides Buck, which of the rangeland rebels is closest to you?"

"That would have to be Chuck Lee. Did you know that Chuck never actually left southeast Asia for almost the entire time of the American involvement? Of course, he went on R&R lots of times. But he felt like he couldn't leave as long as his buddies were fighting and dying over there.

"After he left the 1st Cavalry, he went back into Special Forces running some kind of spooky cross-border operation with the Delta Force. He did that for about a year and extended for yet another tour."

"Why on earth for? You'd think even Chuck would have had enough fighting for awhile."

"They offered Chuck command of an airborne brigade of Hmongs."

"Hmongs. You mean those mysterious mountain people who live in Laos?"

"Yes. Read Jane Hamilton-Merritt's marvelous book, *Tragic Mountains,* and you'll really come to admire the Hmongs. But the CIA didn't tell Chuck up front that he had to go into Laos and recruit his brigade from scratch, give them basic training and then put them through airborne training."

"Chuck did all that?"

"He loved it. And, he loved the Hmongs. After he raised this small army of Hmongs, Chuck had the personal staff of a generalissimo. He had aides, cooks, mistresses like you couldn't believe. Of course, the CIA was footing the bill so Chuck wasn't worried if Lou Leclerc was going to bring him another load of prime rib or lobster or not."

"But were they effective?"

"Highly. The NVA had to divert huge resources away from South Vietnam to try to hunt down the Hmongs. But Chuck was a big student of Sun Zsu. When the enemy attacked, he retreated. When the enemy retreated, he advanced. He showed the Hmong's all his booby-trap techniques and they made life a living hell for the NVA."

"So, how did Chuck get out of there?"

"After awhile, the CIA got orders to terminate operations with the Hmongs. And, that's one of Chuck's big problems to this day. The CIA promised him they would evacuate the Hmongs, if need be. But when Congress pulled the plug on buying ammo for the South Vietnamese Army, it also cut off the funds to evacuate all of Chuck's Hmongs.

"After the collapse in 1975, the NVA hunted many of them down and they were slaughtered."

"How did Chuck get out?"

"He refused to come home, so the CIA sent in an agent who drugged Chuck's food and threw him on a black chopper. Ironically, it was Lou Leclerc who flew him out. Chuck woke up mad as hell in a naval hospital in Pearl Harbor. He was even mad at Lou for awhile. Chuck had so many tropical diseases they gave him an early medical retirement and he came back home here to the mountains."

"How do you know so much about Chuck?"

"Some of it comes from Buck. But also because Chuck has become such an anti-government figure that we keep an active file on him."

"You're having him watched?"

"Not really. But the FBI and the BATF try to keep tabs on some of these extremist groups. Chuck's name comes up now and then. But mostly he's carded as a loudmouth drunk who is more talk than walk. Take off a few years and a lot less booze and Chuck would be a real problem. We suspect he won't drink up that many more disability checks before his liver packs it in. It's really tragic. I never knew a more gifted military combat leader. I never knew anyone, maybe with the exception of Buck, who cared more about his men or cared more about accomplishing his mission.

"But that's what happens when you let amateurs like Johnson, McNamara and all those Harvard egg-heads get their hands on real soldiers and start to play games with them."

"Funny you should mention Harvard, Jonathan. I recall one summer when Buck went to Harvard to do some post-doctoral work. It made him so angry. I'd never seen him that way."

"What happened?"

"One evening he went jogging over where so many of the Harvard faculty live in those Ann Hathaway looking cottages. Tree-shaded lanes, snug as bugs in a rug.

"He called me on the phone that evening and I've never heard him so pissed. He said, 'I've just found the place where the real enemy lives. I found the homes of the so-called 'best and brightest' who turned out to be the 'worst and stupidest.' They got us into the Vietnam War and then, when things started to go badly, they retreated to their ivy-walled classrooms and their comfy Tudor cottages to critique those of us who were doing the actual fighting and dying'.

"Lordy, was he angry. But then, when the summer was over, he came home and never mentioned it again," said Dolly.

"We all have our Vietnam scars, Dolly. Buck's have to do with the folly of it all. Mine have to do with Jasmine. Chuck's are the betrayal of his beloved Hmongs. Chuck Lee's friend Lou Leclerc is hung up on being tortured in the Hanoi Hilton while Hanoi Jane was standing just a few feet away."

Dolly turned off Highway 34 into Camp Hope, stopped the Suburban by her Expedition and got out. Jonathan put her carbine and shooting gear in the Expedition.

"I can't thank you enough for making today's shoot run so smoothly," said Jonathan.

"And, I can't thank you enough for listening to my concerns about Buck. And, for that matter, about Chuck and Lou as well," said Dolly.

"When Buck gets back, give me call and we'll do something together."

"You bet. Try not to catch all the trout in the upper Colorado River."

"We're leaving them for POTUS to catch."

"If he catches anything more than VD, I'll be surprised."

"Now, Dr. Madison, you're being judgmental. Bye."

"Oh, there's no free lunch, Jonathan. I want an invitation to the big Labor Day cookout with President Popov. Can you arrange it?"

"It's as good as done. I'll see you are included in the group that gets to fish with POTUS. Wear your western duds. POTUS thinks it's macho," said Jonathan.

Dolly arrived back home just as Buck was returning from the airport. After Dolly cleaned and oiled her carbine, she put it under their bed where she always kept it for the times when Buck was away. Then, they had a glass of wine on the deck. Buck said the aircraft ran fine and his speech was well received. And, contrary to Jonathan's prediction, a string quartet, not Willy Nelson, played for the faculty tea. All in all, it was a very good day.

CHAPTER TWENTY-THREE

Team Pump

The team designated to determine how best to destroy the Pump Plant on the north shore of Lake Granby was composed of Antonio and Felipe. Typical of the PEMEX attack teams, Antonio, a graduate civil engineer, was the brains and Felipe, a former Golden Gloves boxer in Havana, was the brawn.

The official name of their target was the Farr Pump Plant, named after a prominent family of water-diverters from the Front Range. But Antonio and Felipe thought the name was too long and awkward. They wanted to be known simply as Team Pump and that was fine with Raoul.

Antonio and Felipe were eager to begin their physical reconnaissance of the Pump Plant; however, the regularly-scheduled tours of the Pump Plant do not begin until just prior to Memorial Day. When Memorial Day came, Antonio and Felipe slipped in among the many tourists who came to marvel at the central feature of the Colorado-Big Thompson trans-mountain, water-diversion project.

Prior to their physical reconnaissance, however, Antonio and Felipe worked long hours with Regina researching the Pump Plant via the Internet. They knew that construction of the Pump Plant was begun in 1948 and it was dedicated in 1951. The purpose of the Pump Plant was to take in the waters collected in Lake Granby and raise them up 90 feet into the 1.8 mile long Lake Granby Pump Canal and push them on their way through Shadow Mountain Lake and on to the east end of Grand Lake and then down the Adams Tunnel. They knew that, without the Pump Plant, it would be impossible to divert the waters collected in the Windy Gap, Willow Creek and Lake Granby reservoirs from Grand County to the eastern side of the Continental Divide.

With the Pump Plant destroyed, the Alva Adams Tunnel, a 13.1-mile bore underneath the Continental Divide, would be useless. Useless as well would be the five hydroelectric plants that would be deprived of the 310,000-acre feet of water they use each year to spin their electricity generating turbines.

Antonio knew it already but Felipe soon learned that one acre-foot of water is 326,000 gallons of water—the amount of water an American family of five or six consumes in one year.

If the Pump Plant sat on ground level, it would extend 16 stories into the air. Indeed, it would be the tallest building between west Denver and Salt Lake City. But only four stories meet the eye. The other twelve stories are underground.

Twelve stories or 137 feet below the lake's surface is where the water to feed the trans-mountain, water diversion is let into the Pump Plant. Three giant pipes, each seven-foot in diameter, run outward from the bottom of the Pump Plant and along the bottom of the lake for a distance of 440 feet to an inlet house.

While Antonio handled a rental boat, Felipe, an accomplished scuba diver, donned a wet suit and scuba-gear and dove on the inlet house. When Felipe returned to the surface, he reported that the entrances to the three pipes were well guarded with steel grates providing little or no opportunity for penetration.

They took their findings to Federico who retired to his room with all the notes made by Antonio during their guided tour of the Pump Plant and with all the literature gathered by Regina from the Internet. Three days later, Federico called Antonio and Felipe to the main house for a planning conference. Regina attended as well.

When they were assembled, Federico invited them all into the bathroom. "I have something interesting to show you, amigos," Federico began. "Here you see this bath tub full of water. Imagine that water is Lake Granby. In my hand, I have a half-gallon milk carton with the top removed. Imagine the milk carton is the Pump Plant.

"Also, please notice I have cut a round hole in the bottom of the milk carton. I have placed a cork in that hole to keep water from entering the milk carton. Now, I am going to force the milk carton down into the water until the water almost comes over the top of the carton. See how I have to use both hands and push very hard to force the carton down into the water?

"Now, I will ask Regina to reach down into the water underneath the milk carton and pull out the cork. Observe what happens."

Regina slipped her hands down along the side of the milk carton, found the cork and pulled it free. In an instant, water shot up through the hole filling the milk carton. In fact, the water rushed up from the bottom of the milk carton with such force that it splashed on Antonio and Felipe.

"Gentlemen," said Federico, "you have just seen the Achilles Heel of the Pump Plant. If one or more of those inlets pipes were allowed to vent its water unimpeded into the bottom of the Pump Plant, the Pump Plant would be flooded clear up to the level of the lake in minutes."

"Federico," said Antonio, "this little demonstration is very impressive and you have truly found the Achilles Heel; however, will just flooding the Pump Plant do enough permanent damage?"

"No, Antonio, it will not. Based on the research done by your team and by Regina, I have discovered some very interesting things about the structure of the Pump Plant. While their fancy literature claims the Pump Plant to be a 16-story building, it is unlike any 16-story building I have ever seen."

"What do you mean?" asked Felipe. "I've been in it. It has four stories above ground and 12 stories below ground."

"Si, however, most 16-story buildings have 16 floors. How many floors does the Pump Plant have?"

"I never thought about that," said Antonio.

"According to the drawings you brought back, this so-called 16-story building only has three floors between the bottom of the structure and the floor located at ground level. Gentlemen, this building is, essentially, a hollow shell."

"So, how does that fact translate to our being able to do more than just flood the Pump Plant?" asked Felipe.

"I think it is possible to use the force of the water rising upward to remove, or at least severely damage, the three floors that lie between the bottom of the plant and the ground floor. I am especially interested in the floor holding the three 6,000-horsepower electric motors. As you know, those motors rest on the floor immediately above the bottom of the Pump Plant."

"In short," said Antonio, "you want the electric motors to fall down on top of the impellers."

"Precisely," said Federico.

"Let us say the force of the water is strong enough to remove these three floors, would that mean the entire building would then fall in upon itself, implode?" asked Felipe.

"No," said Antonio. "The column of water rising inside the building will exert pressure outward and that will prevent the concrete walls from falling inward. Right? Federico."

"You are correct, Antonio. The structure goes from a hollow shell to a shell filled with water."

"So, how do we use the upward force of the water to damage the floors above?" asked Felipe.

"When the butterfly valves between the water inlet pipes and the impellers are open, the head pressure inside the impeller housings is tremendous. Just think about it. The lake with its 7,200 surface acres is huge. Then, you have these three seven-foot diameter pipes taking in water 137 feet below the surface of the lake."

"What keeps all that water pressure from bursting out of the impeller housings?" asked Regina.

"Good question, my dear. As long as the butterfly valves on the pump canal side of the impeller housings are closed, the water can't flow upward to seek its own level. Therefore, all of the water pressure is exerted against the tops of the impeller housings," said Federico.

"What keeps the impeller housings from coming apart?" asked Regina.

"I've been studying the photos taken by Antonio and Felipe. I see the top half of each impeller housing is bolted to its bottom half. These bolts stick up from the bottom and are topped with large nuts. Conveniently, there are huge open-end wrenches or spanners hanging on the wall next to each impeller. Obviously, these wrenches are there to service the impeller housings when they are off-line. It would be a simple matter to remove these nuts," said Federico.

"So, would that do it? Just removing the nuts?" asked Felipe.

"No, Felipe. One more thing has to happen. You see, the impellers are also held down by the stainless-steel drive shafts that come down from the heavy electric motors on the floor above. The last step to allowing the lake water to flood the building is to snap those three drive shafts."

"One at a time or all at the same time?" asked Felipe.

"All three at once," said Federico.

"How do we do that?" asked Antonio.

"Although each impeller has its own bay, there is an open passageway between each bay. According to my calculations, we need 20 wraps of Det cord around each stainless-steel drive shaft. We tie the three shafts together with one continuous piece of Det cord. Add a blasting cap and a timing device and everything would be in readiness. At the designated time, the Det cord explodes cutting each of the three drive shafts in half.

"Federico, all this sounds good in theory, but how would such a plan be carried out?" asked Felipe.

"You and Antonio will join the last tour group to go through the Pump Plant on the eve of Labor Day. Because of the Labor Day weekend, the Pump Plant will be operating a Special Sunday tour schedule.

"You will be dressed as typical, young tourists wearing shorts, sandals and carrying backpacks. When the tour group is down on the bottom floor where the impellers are and the guide has explained everything and is ready to put the tour group back on the elevator, Felipe cries out in pain saying he has been bitten by a wasp. This will be true because we are going to have a wasp bite Felipe before he leaves here for the Pump Plant. Sorry about that, Felipe.

"During this commotion, Antonio will hide himself in one of the many storage areas on the bottom floor. Antonio will remain hidden until the early hours of Labor Day. At that time there is never more than one person on duty in the entire building and that person stays in the control room up on the street level. There is, however, a shift change at midnight. The new person works from midnight to 0800 hours.

"At 0300 hours, Antonio comes out of hiding and begins the process of removing the nuts from the bolts on the impeller housings. There are 75 nuts in all and that will take some time."

"What if they start pumping?" asked Antonio.

"It is their policy only to pump during the daytime, when they have a full staff on duty," said Federico. "After you have removed all of the nuts, Antonio, you remove the Det cord from your pack and begin to wrap each shaft."

"Are you sure my pack can carry enough Det cord?" asked Antonio.

"You will also have Felipe's pack which he will hand to you before he moves to the elevator door and pretends to be stung. When you have wrapped all three shafts and tied them together with Det cord, you attach the blasting cap to the end of the Det cord and you attach the timing device to the blasting cap."

"How much time do I place on the timing device?"

"H-Hour is at 0700 hours. At 0630 hours, you set the timer to go off at 0700.

"That will allow time for several necessary events to transpire."

"Such as?" asked Antonio.

"The elevator is the only means of getting from the bottom floor up to the ground level and the control room. If you push the button to call for the elevator, the person on duty will be instantly on guard and might call the sheriff's office.

"So, at 0630 hours, Felipe arrives at the front door and rings the bell. When the night watchman comes to the door, Felipe claims he has been hurt in an accident and shows him a phony, but realistic-looking, wound on his arm.

"When the watchman opens the door, Felipe sprays him in the face with an aerosol of DSMO and GHB, the combination causes almost instantaneous respiratory arrest and then vanishes without a trace. Felipe drags the dying night watchman into the control room.

"Then, Felipe, because the work of Team Pump must be closely coordinated with what our Jefe is doing over at the Lake Granby High Dam, you must give Raoul a call on his cell phone and tell him that you have neutralized the night watchman at the Pump Plant. Is that clear?

"Okay. Meanwhile, Antonio must make sure the butterfly valves on the pump canal side of the impellers are closed. He must make sure the butterfly valves to the water inlet valves are open and he must make sure the timer for the Det cord is set to go off at 0700 hours.

"Felipe, you drag the now-dead night watchman down one floor and leave him there. When he is found by the authorities, it will appear that he drowned. But before you leave the watchman, you will place a drawing in his pocket. This drawing will show the wiring diagram for the Det cord around the shafts of the three turbines. The authorities will assume this poor wretch was in on the plot to destroy the Pump Plant and made a mistake.

Finally, you exit the building and the two of you return immediately here to the compound prepared to board the helicopter."

"What will happen then when the Det cord severs the three drive shafts at 0700 hours?" asked Antonio.

"If my calculations are correct," said Federico, "the force of the water will drive the three impellers up out of their housings and up through the floor above. The impact of those huge impellers will be sufficient to weaken the floor so that the three electric motors will come crashing down to the bottom of the structure. Perhaps, another floor will collapse as well. For certain, the lake will fill the Pump Plant up to the level of the lake surface," said Federico.

"This is very exciting and you are very clever," said Regina, giving Federico a hug.

"Thank you, my dear," said Federico, giving her an intimate, but surreptitious, pat on the behind. "But the real credit goes to the three of you for providing me with all the intelligence I needed to create this plan."

CHAPTER TWENTY-FOUR

The Lake Granby High Dam

Raoul picked a time when all of the seismic crews where out in the field. Calling Federico and Regina to the bedroom he used as his private office, Raoul briefed the two of them on the results of his reconnaissance of the Lake Granby High Dam.

Displayed on a small writing desk were the instant photos taken by Raoul at the bottom of the elevator shaft. In addition there were photos he had taken of what he felt were the key pages of the elevator operations Manuel he found on a shelf inside the entrance to the elevator shaft during a subsequent clandestine visit to the top floor of the elevator building.

"Jefe, how on earth did you obtain these wonderful photographs?" asked Federico.

"The photographs are a product of time and patience," Raoul responded. "It took several days of fishing near the spillway of the dam until I made contact with someone who could help me."

"Who was that?" asked Regina.

"One day, a gringo from the Northern Colorado Water Conservancy District stopped his pickup in front of the door to the elevator building. I quit fishing and walked over to where he was opening the lock on the door. After he got the padlock open, he hung the lock with the key still in it on the hasp and went inside.

"I looked inside the elevator house and saw him checking the fuses on a big electrical panel. He wasn't paying any attention to me, so I slipped the padlock key into the wax impression kit I had in my pocket and made a nice, clean impression. I put the key back in the lock.

"I shuffled my feet in the gravel outside the door so he would know someone was there and he turned and looked at me. He was real laid back and just asked me about the fishing. So, we talked about how the big Lake Trout eat up all the smaller fish and so on. I had a couple of nice trout that I caught that morning. So, I went over and pulled the stringer up and gave him two really beautiful trout. He really warmed up after that.

"Then, I started asking him about his work and he told me he had to come over from the pump plant every few days to check on the dam and adjust the amount of water being allowed to flow underneath the dam and into the Colorado River.

"I asked him how he did that and he said if I wasn't afraid of riding down in the elevator that he'd show me. Obviously, he was very grateful for the fish. Of course, I immediately agreed to go. But before we started down, he took the padlock and locked the door from the inside. He said it was company policy to do that because it would not be good for him to be down at the bottom of the elevator shaft and have somebody come into the elevator house and start screwing around with the elevator controls.

"The elevator is rather primitive. It reminded me of one of those elevators in an old apartment building in Paris. The sides are open, so you can see the concrete shaft and steel framework that guides the elevator up and down. On the surface of the concrete walls, you can see the knots, the grain marks and the seam lines left by the sheets of plywood that they used as forming when they poured the concrete.

"When you get to the bottom of the elevator shaft, the door opens out into a vault-like steel chamber. It's like stepping out of the elevator into the inside of a huge boiler. When you step out onto the floor of the chamber, the first thing you notice is how the steel deck plates of the chamber are vibrating. It makes your feet tingle." Said Raoul.

"So, you are saying that the big pipe isn't directly under the elevator shaft," said Federico.

"No, the pipe is apparently centered underneath the steel-clad chamber," said Raoul. "So it is below and at a slight angle away from the elevator shaft.

"The guy showed me a peep hole where you can actually look in and see the water rushing out through the pipe. It must be some kind of periscope only instead of being pointed up, it's pointed down into the pipe.

"Anyway, the gringo looks at some big analog gauges that told him how much water was flowing through the pipe. He pulled a scrap of paper out of his pocket and looked at it. Evidently, it was a note on how much water he was supposed to be letting out into the river.

"According to Regina's fine research on the Internet, the outlet pipe is 11.5 feet in diameter. But if they opened the outlet pipe fully, the flow would be so great that it would wash out footbridges and roads downstream. So, they have a 30-inch valve and a 12-inch valve to control the downstream flow. Each valve is controlled by a wheel that sticks up out of the outlet pipe. I watched as the gringo went over to the smaller of the two wheels and gave it a few turns. Then, he went back over to the gauges and checked them again. He must have been satisfied because he didn't go back to the small wheel and change it," said Raoul.

"Did you ask him any questions down there?" asked Federico.

"Oh no. The noise of the water rushing through that big pipe is so loud you can't even hear yourself think. I had to shout like hell to ask him if I could take some photos of the chamber. He just nodded, so I took the photos you see here on the desk.

"Anyway, after awhile, he pointed to the elevator and we got in and went back up to the top. I thanked him for a most interesting experience and he thanked me again for the fish. He unlocked the padlock so I could leave and he hung the lock and key back outside so he could lock up again when he left.

"I had Jose make me a key from the wax impression. That night, I went back over to the elevator house. I figured they had some way of monitoring the elevator from over at the pump plant, so I didn't fool around with the elevator. But I did find a copy of the operator's manual for the spillway gates and some very old and water-stained plans that must have been used during the construction of the dam and I took flash photos of the things I think we need to study," said Raoul.

"Jefe, it looks like so far, so good," said Regina.

"Actually, Regina, the destruction of the Lake Granby High Dam is going to be easier than I thought," announced Raoul with just a hint of smugness. "It is very thoughtful of the Americanos to provide us such an easy way of placing high explosives at the very bottom of the dam and at its most vulnerable point. Its Achilles Heel."

As he picked through the photographs, Federico asked: "Why do you think the bottom of the elevator shaft is the dam's most vulnerable point?"

"Because of the way they went about building the dam," said Raoul. "They built the elevator shaft first and then filled in around it with earth and rock."

"You mean they built the entire 298-foot shaft from bottom to top and then filled in around it?"

"No, they built the shaft in 20-foot sections. I could see the section seams from the elevator car as we went down and back up. I think they poured a section of concrete and then filled in around it with rock. Then, they would form another section on top of that and so on all the way up. By the way, on the way back up, I timed the duration of the ride. It took six minutes."

"So, you think," asked Regina, "that if you blow out the bottom of the elevator shaft that the entire dam will collapse?"

"Si. I noticed the steel framework inside the concrete shaft isn't very strong. The steel frame does not add much to the integrity of the shaft itself. It is really only there to guide the elevator car up and down," said Raoul.

"Then, all you have to do," said Federico, "is load the elevator with high explosives, set a timer to make it detonate when you wish, send the elevator to the bottom of the shaft and you depart the area."

"No, not quite. But you are close, Federico. We will need electricity to run the timer and set off the explosives, so when the elevator car full of explosives goes down the shaft, I must pay out 300 feet of electric wire and then connect the wire to the timer and connect the timer to the electrical buss. I can do all that without having to go down the shaft myself.

"So, the electrical hook-up is all pretty routine. My real concern is that if we rely on gravity alone to pull the concrete walls of the elevator shaft down upon itself, then I think the shaft would just fill up with debris. We need to create a continuous void at the bottom of the shaft so the falling debris has some place to go. I think we need to harness the power of the water rushing underneath the dam from the lake so the rushing water keeps cleaning out the debris as it falls and flushes it out the pipe into the Colorado River."

"Ah," said Federico, "you will be like the great Hercules who diverted a river to flush out the Augean Stables."

"Si, I will be like Hercules," said Raoul, "but instead of flushing out centuries of manure, the lake water will be flushing out decades of concrete and rock."

"So, how do you propose to create this flushing action?" asked Regina.

"Well, you are correct about filling the elevator car with high explosives. But I think inside those two drums of explosives we need to have shaped charges aimed at an angle so the water pipe is penetrated. In other words, I want to make sure that the bottom of the elevator shaft and the water pipe become one void."

"I see," said Federico. "As the elevator shaft collapses downward upon itself, you want the first debris to fall to be swept out of the way to make room for the debris to come."

"Precisely," said Raoul. "I want you to make some precise calculations Federico, but I think two 55-gallon drums of high explosives each with a shaped charge locked inside the drums at the correct angles will do the job. As you can see, the elevator shaft does not terminate directly on top of the water pipe underneath the floor of the chamber. Ideally, the drums would be taken out of the elevator car and placed exactly over the water pipe. I would like to avoid that labor.

"So, the reason for the angles is that I won't have to roll the drums out into the chamber and place them directly over the water pipe underneath the floor of the chamber. If you figure the proper angle for each of the shaped charges, the charges will be pointing directly at the under-floor water pipe from where they sit inside the elevator car. Just like armor-piercing tank shells, the shaped charges will penetrate the floor and rupture the water pipe. Let me suggest we mark the drums on the outside to show exactly how they should be oriented inside the elevator car so the shaped charges are pointing right at the water pipe when the elevator car reaches the bottom of the shaft.

"On D-Day, my pickup will look like one of the pickups belonging to the Northern Colorado Water Conservancy District and it shouldn't attract any attention at that early hour. I will be able to roll the drums from the bed of my pick-up using a sturdy plank. With a dolly, I can quickly roll the drums into the elevator house and into the elevator car."

"What if one of the workers comes to the elevator shaft?" asked Regina.

"On the morning of a big holiday like Labor Day, that shouldn't be a problem" said Raoul. "We know H-Hour for the Lake Granby High

Dam will be just after I receive the confirmation calls from Teams Adams and Moffat at 0700 hours or so.

"Bear in mind that by 0630 hours, Antonio and Felipe will have incapacitated the night watchman at the Pump Plant. After he is dead, I am then free to send the elevator down the shaft. Felipe will call me on his cell phone to let me know when he and Antonio have control of the Pump Plant.

"So far, I cannot find any flaws in your plan, Raoul," said Federico. "But how much time will you set on the timing device before you leave the elevator house?"

"Raoul had me do some research on the internet on that particular brand of elevator," said Regina. "For that old model to descend 298 feet requires five minutes. But Raoul's actual experience with that particular elevator says it takes six minutes for it to ascend. So, to play it safe, let's use the six-minute figure," concluded Regina.

"What about Team Ditch and Team Pump?" asked Regina. "How will you know if they have done their work?"

"I can see both the Pump Plant and The Grand Ditch from the road that runs across the top of the spillway," said Raoul.

"Are you sure about The Grand Ditch?" asked Federico. "I'm not sure you'll be able to tell if our gringo amigos have actually carried out their assignment."

"Who really cares about The Grand Ditch?" said Raoul. "It is not of the same strategic importance as the other targets. Actually, we only included it on the list of targets because it was the one target where we were sure we could get the gringos to take action. I think we can count on Senor Chuck to take revenge for the treatment of his Chinese great-grandmother. And, for his friends, the Hmongs, for that matter.

"As for the destruction of the Pump Plant, at 0700 hours, I'll be looking right at it across the lake. When I see smoke billowing out the windows of the Pump Plant, I will know we have succeeded."

"The timing device will give me enough time to jog over to a clearing beyond the northwest end of the dam where Jose will be waiting with the helicopter. Jose and I will return here to the Koch Ranch.

"Because the Huey cannot lift all of us, on D minus 1, we will send all the non-attack personnel on ahead to Montana by vehicle. From there, they go into British Columbia and to a Cuban freighter waiting for them in Vancouver Harbor.

"When all targets have been attacked, the members of Team Adams, Team Moffat and Team Pump and myself assemble back here."

"What about Team Ditch?" asked Regina.

"Our amigos Senor Chuck and Senor Roberto will meet with an unfortunate accident in the parking area near the Never Summer Ranch. It will appear that they made a mistake with some of the explosives they 'stole' from our shed," said Raoul.

"Then what happens?" asked Regina.

"As I said at the initial team briefing, when we are all assembled here at Koch Ranch, we fly the Huey to a secret spot in the New Mexican desert where a fuel bladder will be hidden for us by some communist comrades who work at Los Alamos. We refuel the Huey, then we fly low to stay below radar coverage and make it across the border into Mexico."

"How do we know we can find this fuel bladder out in the desert?" asked Regina.

"Those in charge of placing the bladder in the desert will use a GPS to establish its exact latitude and longitude. That information will be in our possession before we depart. Using our own GPS, we will be able to fly to within 30 meters of the fuel bladder's location. We will find it within minutes.

"Meanwhile, the Americanos will be looking for the bodies of Presidents Trimmer and Popov somewhere down river between Camp Hope and Kremmling. Cable communications between the eastern and western United States will virtually cease to exist," said Raoul.

"What if something goes wrong and our teams fail to destroy their targets?" asked Regina.

"That is the beauty of my plan for the Lake Granby High Dam," Raoul replied. "If your worst-case scenario takes place, I roll the drums of explosives back onto the pick-up and leave. In all probability, Senor Chuck and Senor Roberto will destroy The Grand Ditch and be killed for their trouble. Again, The Grand Ditch is of no great consequence and that is why we entrusted it to the gringos."

"At this point," said Federico,"I can't fault your logic. But I will do some careful calculations on which kind of high explosive will be needed to cause the Lake Granby High Dam to collapse from within."

"While we are working on worst-case scenarios," said Regina, "what if something goes wrong during our exfiltration, we get split up or something like that?"

"Ah, you have raised a very good point," said Raoul. "And, it is time to address the entire issue.

"Fidel saw to it that our comrades from China, Iraq and Iran provided a total of $30 million for this enterprise. Much of that money went to get our infrastructure in place and to provide for our equipment and operating expenses; however, Fidel, in his generosity, wants every member of our team to have $250,000 in U.S. currency for their services. Of course, the three of us will receive much more than that directly from Fidel upon our return to Havana. But I have the funds for our team members here in a chest hidden under the floorboards in this room. You two need to know that in case something should happen to me. Enough money is in there to carry out Fidel's wishes for our team members plus some emergency operating cash. When we pull out on D-Day we'll be taking those funds with us and distributing them to our team members once we are safely inside Mexico. Those who exfiltrated early by vehicle will be paid on board the freighter."

"This is very generous of Fidel," said Federico. "When we accepted this mission, I never knew it would be so lucrative."

"This is my retirement mission," said Raoul. "I plan to buy a nice Finca for Regina and me, put my feet up on the railing, light up a cigar and drink rum for the rest of our days. Federico, if you are smart, you will salt your portion away and be prepared to do Fidel's bidding. I have already recommended to Fidel that you become my replacement."

"You are most kind, Raoul," said Federico. "I know Regina and I will do everything we can to make sure you attain the rewards you so richly deserve."

CHAPTER TWENTY-FIVE

Buck Madison knew he ought to be working on his book. But it was one of those almost Indian Summer days when the urge to hike or sail or fish was nagging at him. So, when the phone rang, Buck was hoping it was one of his buddies proposing some kind of outdoor adventure.

"Buck, this is Jonathan."

"Every time you call up here, I know you need something. What is it this time?" asked Buck.

"POTUS wants to go boating."

"Doesn't he ever do any work down there? For $200,000 a year, free government housing, several aircraft and all those other perks, one would think he could find time to do the work he says the people elected him to do."

"Buck, I don't have time for your sermons. I need to know where I can get a boat and where it is safe to take POTUS for a ride."

"We have a sailboat, but you can't use it."

"Why not?"

"One reason is because I only own half of it and I'd have to ask permission of my partner and his wife to see if they would approve."

"What's the other reason or reasons?"

"The other reason is that I'd rather have a root canal performed with a post-hole digger than spend one minute cooped up on a 21-foot sailboat with Jim Bob Trimmer."

"But he's the President of the United States."

"Only for a few more months. Call me back when Maggie Thatcher or someone I admire wants to go sailing," said Buck, starting to hang up.

"Buck," Jonathan pleaded.

"Oh, okay. Here's what you can do. Call over to Highland Marina. That's where we moor our boat. Get them to rent you one of those party barges. You can give POTUS a ride on that. Also, the U.S. Coast Guard Auxiliary has a big Boston Whaler they use to patrol the lake. They keep that boat at the Lake Granby Marina. Call over there as well. You can commandeer the Boston Whaler and its crew as an escort boat for your agents. Does that solve your problem?"

"Yes, it does. But I need to know a lot more about this lake before we take POTUS out on it. Can you help me with that?"

"Yes. I should be writing today; however, Dolly and I'll take you for a sail and we'll show you the best places to go and some areas, for security reasons, you ought to avoid."

"Buck, I knew you wouldn't let me down. At least not completely."

"Be happy for small favors, Jonathan. I really should be writing because my editor is going to kill me if I miss my deadline. But, once again, I must save my former lieutenant from another screw up.

"Be at Highland Marina at 12 noon. Dolly and I will get there prior to that so we can be taken out to the mooring, get the boat ready to sail and bring it back to the courtesy dock to pick you up."

"There are hundreds of boats on Lake Granby. How will I know which one is yours?"

"It'll be the one with the beautiful blond standing on the bow with a line in her hand. Catch it when she throws it to you," said Buck hanging up."

Typical of a day in late summer, clouds were beginning to build up on the Continental Divide signaling the morning calm would soon be over and that some pretty stiff winds would whip across the lake until about sundown. A five-knot breeze was already blowing across the dock.

Precisely at 12 noon, the bow of *Windfall* came to a stop one inch from the courtesy dock at Highland Marina. Dolly handed Jonathan the bowline and stepped down onto the dock.

"How'd Buck do that without using a motor?"

"Do what?" asked Dolly.

"Tack back and forth through all those other boats and stop dead still at the dock."

"Buck was a sailing instructor at one time in his checkered past," said Dolly, making sure the bow line was secure.

Buck, who had just secured a stern line to the dock, stepped from the boat and gave Jonathan a handshake.

"Welcome aboard the *Windfall*, Jonathan. I assume you brought some champagne, caviar and lox from the presidential larder?"

"Would you settle for some leftover grits, red-eye gravy and a ham hock?"

"Actually, that sounds pretty good. But Dolly packed us German wine, cold poached Salmon, Greek olives, Feta and French bread."

"Seriously?"

"Yes, Jonathan," said Dolly. "Captain Ahab here not only insists that I perform as first mate but as his galley-slave as well."

"Captain Ahab should have been so lucky," said Jonathan.

"I must confess we won't be able to sail away from the dock without putting a lot of other craft in peril or taking all afternoon," said Buck. "So, as much as I hate to do it, we are going to crank up the little kicker motor and back out of here."

After a brief water-safety briefing for Jonathan and insisting that their guest don a life vest, Dolly cast off and *Windfall* proceeded away from the confines of the marina and out onto Lake Granby.

Buck operated the tiller and the mainsheet. Dolly dropped the centerboard and took care of the jib sheets. Soon, *Windfall* was moving smartly on a starboard tack and headed in the general direction of the Lake Granby High Dam at the south end of the lake.

"Why did you name this boat *Windfall?*" asked Jonathan.

"We bought it from distressed sellers," said Dolly. "The couple that owned it were divorcing. He tried to teach her to sail and that caused the divorce. So, it was our windfall."

"Dolly, didn't Buck teach you to sail?"

"Yes," said Dolly. "We also have wall-papered together and even built a house together. Obviously, we have a strong marriage. Otherwise, I'd have killed him."

Getting down to business, Jonathan asked: "What should we do with POTUS once we get the party barge and the Boston Whaler out on the lake?"

"You don't want an answer to such a dumb question," said Buck.

"No, we are not going to push him overboard," said Jonathan. "Seriously, what should we do?"

"The scenery is so drop-dead gorgeous anywhere you look, I don't think you have to 'do' anything. I'd just get out here in the middle of the lake and look around for awhile and go back in."

"Oh, Buck," said Dolly. "How about going up into Arapaho Bay? Or, up the old channel of the Colorado?"

"Okay. Let's sail up into Arapaho Bay. But I wouldn't recommend taking POTUS up the old river channel." (See: *www.thegrandconspiracy.com*)

"Why's that?" asked Jonathan.

"Well, it is beautiful up in there. But the banks are steep and, after a couple of miles, they begin to close in as the channel narrows. I don't think you have enough agents to post over three miles of river bank to guard against snipers."

"That's right, I don't."

"Even though the lake is over 7,200 acres in all," said Buck, "because of its irregular shape and its dozens of islands it's pretty hard to get very far away from the shore and places where people can hide."

"Maybe we could secure one of these islands. What are those islands over there?"

"That's Deer Island," said Buck.

"Is it one island or two?" asked Jonathan. "It looks like two separate islands and we could sail between them."

"We could try, but we'd run aground." (See: *www.thegrandconspiracy.com*)

"Why's that?"

"Because it only appears to be two islands. Deer Island is actually one island with a land bridge that disappears under water when the water is this high. Wait until later in the year when the people and the developers down on the Front Range suck more water out of the lake. Then you could walk between the two halves of Deer Island and not get wet. But the issue is moot because you can't go ashore there anyway."

"Why not?" asked Jonathan.

"Because of the Osprey nests," said Dolly. "Look up in that tall tree on the north side of Deer Island. Here, take the binoculars. See that big clump of brush in the top of tree? Look for a big bird with a white head feeding fish to her young. Also, you should be able to make out a sign that says: stay at least 100 feet off shore."

"I see the nest. I see the Osprey. I see the sign. So much for that idea," conceded Jonathan. "Now, what?"

"Well, if you look at the long, loaf-shaped hill to the south of the dam, you might be able to see our house peeking through the trees," said Dolly.

"I didn't realize your house is so close to the dam," said Jonathan.

"The dam's at one end of the loaf and our place is at the other end," said Dolly. "In fact, there's a footpath from our house to a cliff overlooking the dam. I like to take people up there to pick pinecones for Christmas decorations. But I don't take Scooby."

"Why's that? asked Jonathan. "I thought you took Scooby everywhere."

"We usually do. But as the trail gets near the dam, the ground falls off steeply on each side. In fact, at the trail's end, you're looking off a cliff, straight down onto the spillway. I'm afraid Scooby might slip and fall."

By now, *Windfall* was well up into Arapaho Bay and, up ahead, the lake was beginning to narrow.

"Gosh, it's beautiful in here," said Jonathan. "But is this it?"

"Jonathan," said Buck. "This is not Disney World. We don't have any water slides or rides out here. It's just Mediterranean blue water, surrounded by snow-capped mountain peaks. For heaven's sake, what more do you want for POTUS?"

"Maybe some history? Some stories we can tell him?"

"Well, you could take POTUS over to Grand Lake. That's where Sir Thomas Lipton issued a charter for their yacht club."

"You mean *the* Sir Thomas Lipton of Lipton Tea fame?"

"The very one. In fact good old Sir Thomas provided a silver cup for the Grand Lake Yacht Club and they hold a regatta each year so sailors from all over the world can come and compete for it."

"Okay, we might take him over and show him around Grand Lake. What else? Is there some other history around here?"

"You want history? I've got some history for you. Right now, we happen to be sailing over an airfield constructed for the use of Charles and Anne Morrow Lindbergh," said Buck.

"You're kidding."

"No, I'm not. See that ridge that forms the southeast shore of Arapaho Bay? That's called Knight Ridge and it gets its name from Charles Knight, a St. Louis banker who put together the financial syndicate that bankrolled the construction of 'The Spirit of St. Louis.' Prior to the flooding of all this land to make Lake Granby, the Knight family owned a large ranch that is under our boat right now.

"After Charles Lindbergh made his historic flight to Paris, Lindy and his wife were often guests at the Knight Ranch. Charles and Anne had a nifty little biplane they used for making personal appearance tours. From Denver, they would hop that little biplane over Corona Pass and land on a dirt strip provided for them right underneath us at Knight Ranch. I have newspaper clippings from back before World War II showing the Lindberghs and the Knights having a great time at the Knight Ranch."

"Right down below us," said Jonathan. "It makes me feel kinda creepy that we're in this boat and less than 200 feet below us must be the rotting remains of the ranch house and at least the trace of what once was another 'Lindbergh Field.'"

"Dolly and I feel the same way. But the ranch house was taken apart, moved to high ground and put back together. A friend of ours lives in it. We can take you there."

"I'll pass. But this is a terrific story to tell POTUS if he gets bored out here," said Jonathan.

By now, *Windfall* was almost to the National Forest Service campgrounds where Arapaho Creek comes down off the Continental Divide and enters Arapaho Bay. They dropped anchor in shallow water so they could enjoy a quiet lunch. But four jet-skis suddenly engulfed their quiet with ear-splitting noise and created four boat-rocking wakes.

"Lordy, I hate those things," said Buck. "They not only make noise and pollute the atmosphere, their wakes almost spilled my wine."

"Have you ever jet-skied?" asked Jonathan.

"Yeah, twice," said Buck. "First time and last time. Dolly and I rented a couple jet skis over on Lake Powell just to see what they were like. They're quick and agile. But give me the peace and quiet of a sailboat every time.

"Now that we've given you the grand tour, and you've sampled the cook's culinary efforts, we're going to have you sail us around Lake Granby."

"Hey, I may have spent a lot of summers on Cape Cod, but that was decades ago. I don't remember anything about sailboats."

"Come back here and take the tiller, Jonathan. Dolly and I'll be your crew. Lucky for you, we have a following breeze, so you might get us back to the marina before sundown. There's no free lunch, Mr. Winslow."

CHAPTER TWENTY-SIX

Chuck Lee was changing the spark plugs in his old pickup when Raoul Aredondo-Garza drove up in one of the PEMEX pickups and got out.

"Raoul, mi amigo," said Chuck, "what brings you to this neck of the woods?"

"Senor Chuck," said Raoul. "There is something I would like to discuss with you."

Whenever Raoul called him "Senor Chuck," Chuck knew Raoul wanted a favor.

"You need a favor?"

"Well, it might be one of those what you Americanos like to call a win-win situation."

"So, what is it?

"Well, and this is somewhat embarrassing so I trust you will keep this matter between just you and me," said Raoul, looking around to make sure they would not be overheard.

"Raoul, stop beating around the bush. Tell me your problem."

"Okay, it is this. We are in the process of making up our inventory sheets for the equipment and supplies we will be taking back to Mexico."

"So, you're short something and you want Robert and me to make a 'midnight requisition'?"

"No. No. It is not being short. It is being long that's the problem."

"Long on what?"

"Explosives."

"Long on explosives? Like some cases of dynamite?"

"No, my friend. I'm afraid it's more than that. Remember the evening of our little fiesta at the Koch Ranch? We took a little tour of our facility. Well, I'm afraid we are long on virtually every item you saw in our explosives inventory."

"How come?"

"First of all, we didn't do as many seismic shots as we thought we would. Secondly, you may recall I told you we thought we would need more than our permits allowed and we had done a little 'creative accounting'? All of that is coming back to haunt me. We can't leave this country or go back into Mexico with more explosives than we should."

"How do you know what 'should' is?"

"For every seismic location, we have to log everything. How many pods we put out. How much explosive we used. Everything. Those logs have already gone back to PEMEX headquarters in Mexico City. They know how much explosives we said we used. I still have on hand a lot more than we used."

"Okay, so you want me to take this stuff off your hands? Is that the favor you want?"

"Well yes."

"Fine. Box it up and truck it over to my place. Roberto and I'll store it. Roberto's always blasting stumps at that miserable little 'ranch' of his. If nothing else, when the fish won't bite, I'll do like we did in 'Nam in the central highlands. Blast the little bastards to the surface."

"Senor Chuck, this is very kind of you. However, there is still a problem."

"For Christsake, Raoul, now what?"

"We can't deliver these materials to you."

"Why not?"

"If my superiors learned I gave away this much explosive, it would mean my job."

"So, how am I to help you then?"

"Well, tomorrow we are working south of Kremmling. After work, I was thinking of taking the entire crew on down to the Frisco-Dillon area for a treat. There's an excellent Mexican restaurant down there. And, after dinner, we would just spend the night in a motel."

"So, while you cats are at play, someone relieves you of your excess inventory?"

"Precisely."

"How would these people know the difference between your excess inventory and your regular inventory?"

"The excess inventory will be clearly set aside from the rest. In fact, it will be marked 'excess'."

"You don't suppose there would be enough high explosives there to screw up The Grand Ditch?"

"Senor Chuck, there is enough there to do whatever you wish, my friend."

"Then, we'll clean out the bed of one of our pickups and make a little midnight requisition."

"Better bring two pickups," said Raoul, as he started to drive away.

"Holy shit, Raoul," said Chuck.

The next evening Chuck, Roberto and Lou arrived at the Koch Ranch about midnight in two pickups. The gate to the ranch house yard was closed but not locked. They drove straight to the barn which, like the front gate, was closed but not locked.

Lou took his flashlight and moved its beam about until it illuminated the explosives section of the barn. A huge mound of explosives were marked 'excess.'

"Jesus H. Christ," said Lou. "Would you look at that! Lord, we may need another pickup if that's the shit they want hauled out of here."

"Chuck, did you know there would be this much stuff?" asked Roberto.

"Hell no. I knew it would be a fair amount. But this is ridiculous." said Chuck.

"Look at this," said Lou. "There's not only dynamite, TNT, blasting caps, the usual shit, but there's C-4, Det cord and all kinds of timers. We could go into the arms business and make a fortune."

"No, Lou. We're not selling any of it. It's going to my place. So, let's start loading up."

"To your place? So, who will own this stuff.?" asked Lou.

"Well, it belongs to all of us. If you need something, just come over and ask for it."

"Oh, so you're suddenly in charge of the world. Who appointed you God?" asked Lou.

"Cool it, Lou," said Roberto. "Chuck's not the one who gets arrested for DUI. He's always been the responsible one and this stuff should be stored at Chuck's."

"Okay," said Lou. "But only because Chuck says I can come get some stuff if I need it."

"Like I said, Lou," said Chuck. "All you gotta do is ask. But, meanwhile, we're keeping it in my barn."

An hour later, the pickups were loaded and drove off into the night. But, tucked away in Raoul's office was a list of things-to-do prior to the departure of Team PEMEX. One of the last items on the list was to be done after the post office closed just prior to Labor Day. The item read: Mail letter to Sheriff Rod Cobble, reporting the theft of hundreds of pounds of C-4 plastique, Det cord and timers.

CHAPTER TWENTY-SEVEN

One afternoon, Jonathan stopped by to see Buck. But Buck had gone to the airport to change their airplane's oil filter and oil.

While Jonathan and Dolly were waiting for Buck to return, Dolly asked:

"I'm curious about President Trimmer? What's he like?"

"I've never met anyone who is more sincere about what he says and does at the moment he is saying it or doing it," said Jonathan."

"The problem is, the very next moment, with a different person or a difference audience, he can say or do just the opposite and be equally sincere."

"Then, he's always got his political finger wet and stuck up in the wind?"

"No. It's not so much political as it is personal. He has this over-whelming urge to be loved and admired by those he meets. So, he tells them whatever he thinks they want to hear, all the while, thinking he is telling them about his core beliefs. It's the most amazing exercise in self-deception I've ever seen."

"But he comes across, at least on TV, as really caring about people. Like he truly does 'feel their pain.'"

"Oh, he feels their pain all right. He's very empathetic and always has some government scheme on the tip of his tongue that is supposed to ease their pain.

"This probably sounds like psycho-babble, but what he thinks is his genuine desire to ease their pain, is just the traditional liberal impulse to exercise power over others.

"In a sense, he's like a physician who wanders around with this black medical bag. Only instead of a stethoscope or a blood pressure cuff and other medical stuff inside, he's got this hodge-podge of government programs that he's either tried or some other governor has tried and he prescribes them as if they were prescription drugs."

"No private sector prescriptions?"

"Nah. He doesn't think that way. To him, there's a governmental fix for everything. And, that's the liberal way. If there are problems afflicting humankind, you collect taxes to pay for the governmental program needed to fix the problem. Assuming the program works, he then gets the same kind of God-like feeling a physician gets when what he prescribes actually does relieve pain and suffering.

"But whether or not the afflicted obtain relief their money is taken in taxes that are used to increase the size of government which, in turn, gives more power to those who are in charge of the government. Either way, he can't lose.

"Once you understand the liberal's true motivation is power over others, the rest is easy to understand."

"That's a pretty cynical view of liberals," said Dolly. "What about the conservatives? Can't you say they are hard-hearted misers who don't care what happens to others?"

"I believe that people who actually get involved in trying to change the human condition are either motivated by love of the oppressed or hatred of the oppressor.

"I call that my crap detector. When I meet someone, the first thing I try to determine is where they're coming from. Are they doing what they are doing to help the down-trodden or are they doing what they are doing to punish those afflicting the down-trodden?"

"My Gosh, Jonathan, now you're beginning to sound like a dewy-eyed sociologist."

"I admit it, Dolly. In fact, that's why I stayed in the Army as long as I did. I saw the Cold War as a fight-to-the-death between the forces of good and evil. I had a dual mission. I wanted to protect and defend the United States and western civilization from the Evil Empire and I wanted to punish those rotten, communist sons-of-bitches. To this day I still can't understand how we can have so-called "normal" relations with Russia, not after the deaths of so many of my loved ones and friends at the hands of the Soviets and the CHICOMs. The death of Jasmine is just one example. Soon, we'll have President Popov, the former head of the KGB to protect as well.

"Oops. Dolly, forget I said that. The White House and the Kremlin will make that announcement together. But only shortly before it happens."

"Can I tell Buck?"

"Yeah. I suppose so. But make it clear it's hush-hush until it's officially announced. Okay?"

"No problem. Unless I think Buck has a need-to-know, I won't even burden him with that tidbit.

"Okay, Jonathan, getting back to you. I can understand how you feel in terms of geo-politics because Buck and I feel much the same way; however, how do your core beliefs fit into your view of domestic problems and politics?"

"Well, if you are asking how do I think we should deal with each other as human beings, then I'll say this: I think it's a wonderful thing to see someone helping others out of genuine love for those who need a helping hand. But it's a terrible thing to see the venom coursing in the veins of those who really don't give a rat about the afflicted but just want to punish those whom they think are responsible.

"This administration is full of people who, while serving in high office and drawing some pretty decent salaries, actually hate the United States of America because we operate as a democratic republic instead of a socialist state. The people under my protective service and virtually everyone else we see on a daily basis around the White House are products of the radical movements of the 1960s.

"They hate business, they hate the military, they hate our intelligence services—especially the CIA—they hate the police, they hate the DEA. They hate any aspect of government which might call upon them to serve their country in any way that might be uncomfortable, such as the military. They hate any aspect of government that might have occasion to tell them what to do such as stop smoking dope or snorting coke. Ironically, they push 'hate-crime' legislation.

"We had a FBI agent in the White House who got so disgusted with what he saw that he retired from the FBI and wrote a tell-all book about what he saw. Of course, the liberal media panned his book because he exposed them for the frauds they are as well.

"So, in some ways, they are no different than those kooks who blew up the federal building in Oklahoma City or the Unabomber or those so-called Freemen out in Montana."

"You mean they are motivated by hatred of the oppressor more than they are motivated by love of the oppressed?"

"Exactly. But there's one huge exception."

"What's that?"

"They love government when it gives them power over the lives of others. They love the idea of government handouts. I swear they would like to be there when some poor Bubba comes up to get his government check so they could see him touch his hand to his forelock in thanks. That's the satisfaction they crave. Not fixing that poor bastard's problem. But the rush they get from having power over that poor son-of-a-bitch. Of course, they are not all that bad. But, look at it this way. Let's say your government agency was created for the purpose of solving the problems of a particular constituency. If you solve all their problems, there is no need for your government agency. Ergo: the last thing you want to do is solve all their problems," said Jonathan.

"So, the bureaucrats just solve a few problems now and then," said Dolly.

"Right, but not all of them," said Jonathan. "That way, they get to keep their jobs forever."

"Jonathan, I've never seen you this worked up before."

"That's why this is my last assignment. I'm supposed to be cool and level-headed at all times. But I tell you Dolly, POTUS, FLOTUS and that bunch of clowns they have around them are driving me crazy."

"Then, how can you give them the protection the law requires and the public expects?"

"Truthfully, I can't. Again, that's why I'm bowing out soon. I've seen and heard more bullshit and betrayal of our country and traditional American values than I can stand."

"But aren't there times within President Trimmer's inner sanctum when he and FLOTUS, as you call her, and their politicos talk realistically about what official policies they should adopt?"

"Oh yes. They take their polling data very seriously. Every issue that comes up gets tested by polling and, if it's a major issue, they have their pollsters do focus groups."

"Frankly, Jonathan, I don't know how you stand working around those people and I can see why you want out. For someone who bought into the concept of Duty-Honor-Country so deeply, it must hurt."

"Dolly, it hurts more than you'll ever know."

CHAPTER TWENTY-EIGHT

In a high-rise in Denver, there's a C.E.O. Can't wait for the winter. Take your water for snow.
They'll charge you for water. They'll charge you for air. Cheat his own son and daughter, for his insider's share. Ride Rangeland Rebel. Ride to beat the devil.

—Michael Martin Murphey

Buck and Dolly were just finishing breakfast out on their deck when Dolly said: "Buck, you're not going to believe this, but I don't have anything to wear."

"To wear, where?"

"To the presidential Labor Day chuck-wagon breakfast, silly."

"The invitation said: western attire. You've got plenty of that."

"I know, but everyone has seen the broomskirts I have and they've all seen my only western jacket."

"But Presidents Trimmer and Popov haven't seen them."

"Yes, but most of the other guests have. I just want something new to wear."

"So, what are you suggesting?"

"Let's fly down to Denver early tomorrow. It's Saturday and we can get Bob and Carolyn to meet us at Centennial Airport. We'll all go shopping and we'll buy lunch for Bob and Carolyn at the European Café and, after some more shopping, they'll take us back to the plane and we'll come home."

"Would there be time for Bob and me to go to that sailboat place? The mainsail has a broken batten and we need to pick one up. Also, R.E.I. is having a sale on Swiss seats and pitons. I have always wanted to have some store-bought Swiss seats instead of having to make them out of rope. That way, the next time we take rappelling practice with the Grand County Search and Rescue Team we'll at least look like we know what we're doing."

"I don't see why not. We can leave Scooby here with plenty of food and water. She has her pet door so she can go in and out. She will be just fine for the day."

"Are you sure it's okay to leave Scooby behind? It breaks her heart whenever we leave her too long," said Buck.

"We won't be gone that long. We just hop down to Denver and back. Besides, it's too hot down in Denver this time of year. We can't leave her cooped up in a car while we shop."

"Okay. How about 0800 hours tomorrow morning? We take off for Denver Centennial Airport. You fly down and I'll fly back. According to the aviation weather on my computer, it's supposed to be fair weather all over Colorado for the Labor Day weekend. You call Carolyn and Bob. Hopefully, you gals can find something for you to wear," said Buck.

"I'll give her a call. Also, I'm having lunch with Donna today in Grand Lake. Maybe she'll have some ideas as well," said Dolly, picking up the telephone.

Doc Lee's Saloon in Grand Lake is a nice place for a quiet drink in the afternoon. The bartender must split his or her time between the bar and serving in the dining room making the bar a good place for private conversation.

Chuck Lee and Lou Leclerc were waiting in the bar for Raoul.

"Thank you for coming, Raoul," said Chuck. "We're just trying to repay you in some small measure for treating us to such a wonderful fiesta."

"It was nothing, amigos," said Raoul. "The pleasure was all ours."

Arriving a few minutes early for her luncheon date with her friend, Dolly Madison poked her head into the bar and was surprised to see Chuck Lee and Lou Leclerc in the back of Doc Lee's Saloon and sitting with Raoul Aredondo-Garza. Chuck gave her a dismissive wave and Dolly retreated back into the dining area.

"Was that Senora Madison?" asked Raoul.

"Yes, I'm afraid it was," said Chuck. "You know she has a background in psychology and I always feel like she's reading my mind. But she's been a big help to my kid sister and her son. She's given both of them a lot of free counseling."

"Do you think she will be upset because the three of us are sitting together?" asked Raoul.

"I hope the fuck not," said Lou. "Right now, her old college beau, Special Agent Jonathan Winslow, is up tight because, over the Labor Day weekend our so-called president is going to be playing kissy-ass with the Russian president over at Camp Hope, or whatever the hell they call it these days."

"Oh, how exciting for you," said Raoul. "I had not heard about this big event. But both of you seem troubled by the appearance of this Dr. Madison."

"I happen to know how Jonathan Winslow and those secret service toads work," said Lou. "Anyone who is on their shit list, and that probably includes me and Chuck, could be detained for 'questioning' while Trimmer and Popov are in the area."

"How terrible. This reminds me of the actions taken by the KGB or the Red Chinese against dissident elements," said Raoul.

"Oh no," countered Chuck. "The U.S. Secret Service is much more genteel in such circumstances than the KGB or the Red Chinese. First of all, they don't run you over with a tank. They just politely take you to a nice motel room and give you cokes and cookies while you play poker or cribbage with a couple of their agents until the person under their protection is back on Air Force One or whatever and headed for home."

"Should you and Mr. Leclerc be subjected to such treatment, when do you think that would happen?" asked Raoul.

"Hmmn. Labor Day will be celebrated on Monday. Trimmer's already here. Popov will probably arrive at Camp Hope on Saturday so they can begin their little talks designed to polish Trimmer's so-called legacy. A buddy of mine works at one of the local grocery stores and he told me they are supplying food for a chuck-wagon breakfast down on the banks of the Colorado River just after dawn on Labor Day."

"Damn," said Lou. "I didn't get an invitation."

"Somehow my engraved invitation must have gotten lost in the mail," said Chuck. "Anyway, I'll bet they'll all clear out for Washington and Moscow on Tuesday. So, unless we lay low pretty soon, I expect Lou and I will be playing games with some of Jonathan's agents from Friday to Tuesday. That could sure mess up the plans Roberto and I have for this weekend."

"Same here," said Lou.

"Well," said Raoul, "let us hope that Dr. Dolly Madison doesn't say anything to Special Agent, ah, Winslow, did you say?"

"Yeah, Jonathan Winslow," said Chuck.

Chuck told the bartender to bring a bottle of Tequila, six Coronas, some glasses, ice, salt and limes and put them on the table. After they had their drinks in hand and the bartender was back in the dining room, Raoul asked: "Tell me, Senor Chuck, about your business as a fishing and hunting guide? It is good, no?"

"It is good, yes, sometimes. Especially, when we have enough water in Lake Granby."

"Enough water. I looked at Lake Granby driving up here and it looks full to me and Shadow Mountain Lake as well."

"Listen, Raoul," said Lou, "there are times of drought when Lake Granby gets pulled down so low by water demands from the Front Range that it starts to look like the inside of an iron mine. Just a big pit."

"What does that do to your fishing business, Senor Chuck?"

"Kills it, Raoul. It just kills it. No one wants to come up here and look at all these huge banks surrounding so little water. It's flat ugly. But the marina operators have it the worst. Almost every week they have to pull up their docks and move them another few yards downhill. And the boaters hate it because sometimes they have to carry their supplies a half mile on their backs just to get down to the water."

"Chuck, coming from a very poor country such as mine, I find it hard to cry big tears over boaters having to carry their beer and sandwiches a half mile to their boats."

"I take your point, Raoul; however, we're talking about the U.S. of A. where a good tourism season or not is the difference between these marina operators making their bank payments, being able to send their kids to school, getting their teeth fixed, you name it."

"Of course, you are correct. It's all relative. But why can the authorities pull the level of Lake Granby down so low? Don't they have to take the needs of the people who live up here into consideration?"

"No, they do not. The people who run the Colorado-Big Thompson project have only two concerns: providing water to the Front Range cities and farms and sending just enough water on the Colorado so the trout don't die. Basically, nobody gives a shit if we starve up here or not.

"In fact, Raoul, the bastards even established a secondary market using our water." Said Chuck.

"Excuse me, Senor Chuck," said Raoul, "I am afraid I do not understand this term 'secondary market.'"

"Okay, I'll try to explain it," said Chuck. "Our water is so valuable, the bastards package it in what they call: water units. A water unit is about seven-tenths of an acre-foot. In other words, about 70 percent of the amount of water needed to cover one acre of ground one foot deep with water.

"Some allottees of the Colorado-Big Thompson Project have more water units than they actually need for their farming, golf courses, fancy landscaping or whatever. So, they sell those water units on what they call a secondary market."

"I see," said Raoul. "The primary market was when they bought the water units from this thing you call the Colorado-Big Thompson Water Project, Si?"

"Si, Raoul," said Chuck. "So, when they sell the water they don't need to some other dude, that's the secondary market. Last year, a water unit sold for between $4,000 and $4,500 on the secondary market. This year water units were being offered for as high as $20,000 and I know some of them sold for $15,000. Down in Weld County, some joker sold 135 water units for more than $1.9 million or almost $14,500 each."

"This is terrible, Senor Chuck. First, they steal your water and then they trade it like shares of General Motors and make a fortune on the water God intended for the people living west of the Continental Divide. Surely, there is something you can do?"

"Raoul, the less you know the better," said Chuck.

"Well, mi amigos," said Raoul, "let us hope the waters of Lake Granby never fall so low again as they did a few years ago. By the way, what about Shadow Mountain Lake and Grand Lake? Do they get low as well?"

"Hell no," said Chuck. "The water barons down on the Front Range got a law passed that says the levels of Grand Lake and Shadow Mountain cannot vary more than a foot. They didn't do that for our benefit. They did it to guarantee that there is water to pipe down the Adams Tunnel for their use."

"Why not move your business to Shadow Mountain or Grand Lake?" asked Raoul.

"Because the big Lake Trout, the real trophy fish, are in Lake Granby," said Chuck. "At 7,200 acres, Lake Granby is the second largest lake in Colorado. Shadow Mountain is only about the size of Lake Dillon, a relatively small 1,800 acres. And Grand Lake is really small, about 900 acres. But don't get me wrong. Shadow Mountain and Grand Lake are wonderful lakes. Still, I work Lake Granby because of its size and because my clients only want to go after the big, trophy fish."

"But if there's no water, then those other two lakes look like the only alternatives," said Raoul.

"I suppose they are," said Chuck. "But why in Christ's name do we always have to get the smelly end of the stick?"

"I see your point, Senor Chuck. I have a feeling that you will rise up as we have had to do so many times in Mexico to resist the hated dictator." surmised Raoul, as he poured more Tequila for Chuck and Lou.

"Yeah, but you just seem to replace one dictator with another dictator," said Lou.

"True, but maybe someday we will get it right. And, maybe someday, you and your people up here will be free of those who steal your precious water."

"Yeah, maybe someday," said Chuck. "By the way, that mining engineer of yours, Freddie, he really knows his explosives. He gave me and Roberto some good ideas on how to fuck up The Grand Ditch."

"Chuck, we are always glad to share our meager expertise with you and your friends," said Raoul.

"Are you and Roberto really goin' to pull off that trick?" asked Lou.

"Lou, if I told you the truth, I'd have to kill ya," said Chuck, with a wink toward Raoul.

Because the drink was causing Chuck and Lou to raise their voices to a level that increased Raoul's fear of their being overheard, Raoul decided it was time to move the conversation to some other subject. "Do you gentlemen follow major league baseball?" he asked.

"No," said Chuck, with a sad smile, "we are Colorado Rockies fans."

The sarcasm escaped Raoul who, otherwise, knew a great deal about baseball and was able to discuss the Arizona Diamondbacks, his favorite American team, at some length.

As the afternoon wore on, Chuck and Lou were getting very drunk. Raoul, who pleaded the need to keep a clear head, nursed his drink and kept them company. Later, when Lou started an argument with the bartender, Raoul suggested it was time to go. Chuck and Lou insisted on picking up the tab and Raoul insisted on driving them both to their quarters. After that, Raoul drove back to the Koch Ranch. On his return, he summoned Federico and Regina to his office.

"The Doctors Madison may become an obstacle to our plans," announced Raoul.

"How so?" asked Regina.

"According to Senors Lee and Leclerc," said Raoul; "the Madisons are close friends with the head of President Trimmer's protective detail. Both Lee and Leclerc think they may be on a watch list kept by the Secret Service. If that is so, and the Secret Service decides to place Lee and Leclerc in detention for a few days, we will have lost two of our key gringos.

"Regina, you have worked hard to convince Lou Leclerc to blow a hole in the water bore inside the Moffat Tunnel. By the way, I could tell this afternoon that Senor Lou has not told Senor Chuck about his plans. But Senor Chuck let it be known that he and Senor Roberto might do something to The Grand Ditch. Both of them drank enough this afternoon to loosen their tongues, but Senor Lou did not reveal the plan that he and Regina have for the Moffat Tunnel. So far, so good."

"Well, I wouldn't say what I've been doing with Lou Leclerc is actually 'work,'" said Regina.

"Regina, please do not remind me of that," said Raoul. "I say it is work because you are just doing your duty.

"Anyway, Senora Madison came into the bar this afternoon where I was meeting with Senor Lee and Senor Leclerc and she saw the three of us drinking together," said Raoul.

"Did she look at you as if she thought you were doing something wrong?"

"I couldn't tell. But Senor Chuck and Senor Lou looked very guilty when she appeared unexpectedly. They say she is an expert at reading body language and peoples' expressions. I'm sure she saw our gringos' guilty-looking reaction. We cannot have Dr. Madison or her husband telling Special Agent, Jonathan Winslow, that they think something suspicious is going on. Both of them have intelligence backgrounds. If anyone in Grand County might figure out what we are doing, I think it would be the Madisons," said Raoul.

"So, what can we do about the Madisons?" asked Federico.

"We put them under surveillance. Jose will not be doing anything with the helicopter in the time leading up to D-Day. Have Jose keep an eye on them. The Madisons spend a lot of time at the local airport fussing with their airplane. All pilots like to talk with each other. The Americanos call it: hangar flying. Jose can 'hangar fly' with the Madisons to see if Jose detects any animosity or suspicion on their part with regard to Senor Chuck and Senor Lou being so close to Team PEMEX. If it appears the Madisons are going to do something that might result in the detention of Senors Lee and Leclerc, then we must stop them. We have worked too hard to get Lee and Leclerc in the frame of mind to do something helpful for us than to allow the Madisons to fuck it up. Do I make myself clear?" asked Raoul.

"Si, Jefe," said Federico. "But what if the Madisons go off somewhere in their aircraft. What then?"

"Jose, follows them in the helicopter. Discretely, of course. In fact, that might be a good thing. We might arrange for them to have a little accident in their aircraft. That would put an end to the Madisons once and for all.

"It was a mistake for me to meet with Senor Chuck and Senor Lou in a place nice enough for Senora Madison. But I was their guest and they picked the place. Still, I am afraid I am responsible for what might be our first lapse in security."

"Jefe, it's not your fault," said Regina. "It was simply bad luck this afternoon. Your plan to keep them under surveillance is sound. We can count on Jose to keep us informed and, if need be, he can eliminate the Madisons before they can do us any harm."

"I hope you are right," said Raoul. "I hope you are right."

Chapter Twenty-Nine

Friday evenings were a special time for Dolly and Buck. When they were first married and Buck was a battalion commander, they always stopped by the officers' club after the Friday retreat parade. Happy Hour was a good time to visit with the other officers and their wives or dates. The habit of pausing for an hour on Friday evenings for a drink lingered on. Only now, they drank their wine alone on their deck in summer or before the fireplace in winter.

As they were sipping their Merlot out on the deck, Dolly said: "Buck, I know how you like to avoid unpleasant subjects when its time to eat or time for drinks, but I think this merits an exception."

"Okay, let's have it," said Buck.

"Chuck and Lou seem to be acting strangely now that El Presidente and his entourage have taken over Ouray Ranch and turned it into Camp Hope."

"They're always acting strangely. Do you mean they are acting more strangely?"

"On the strangeness scale, I think they are somewhere between eight and ten. It's nothing I can put my finger on exactly; however, I ran into Chuck Lee and Lou Leclerc over in Grand Lake at lunch today. Actually, I only caught a glimpse of them. I usually poke my head into Doc Lee's Saloon just to see if there is anyone I know. I did and I saw Chuck and that Raoul person from Team PEMEX huddled over in one corner of the bar. I could tell Chuck and Lou weren't thrilled to see me. In fact, they both looked guilty as hell about something. So, I backed off and stayed in the dining room.

"I suppose they thought they couldn't be overheard from where they were sitting, but there's a Dutch door between the saloon and the dining room and the upper half was open. Plus, a fan was moving the air toward where Donna and I were sitting and, while I couldn't hear every word, I could get the drift of what they were talking about."

"So, what were they saying?"

"First of all, they were downing Tequila and Coronas like they were going out of style and it was the middle of the day."

"Oh, that's nothing new for Chuck. When Chuck starts thinking about how the government screwed over the Hmongs, he sometimes does dumb stuff like that. But I'm surprised to hear about Raoul hitting the hard stuff so early in the day. He's earned a reputation around here for being pretty business-like."

"Well, anyway, Chuck and Raoul were talking about the injustice of how all the water is stolen out of eastern Grand County and diverted down to the Front Range cities and farms. Chuck even mentioned some of the water-diversion projects he'd like to blow up."

"I've heard Chuck and Lou, and even Roberto, discuss that subject before. But I think it's just talk. Anyway, before Jonathan would want to do anything about them, I think Jonathan would say that those guys would have to have: motive, the opportunity to do harm and the means to do harm. Right now, all I can see is motive."

"Well, to hear Chuck tell it, they have more than enough motive. As for opportunity, you know as well as I do that the water-diversion facilities are not well protected. Plus, I don't know how anyone could safeguard The Grand Ditch. And, as for the means, that Team PEMEX is always making the earth shake around here. Those Mexicans must have enough high explosives to blow up Hoover Dam."

"Dolly, I've told you a hundred million times not to exaggerate," said Buck, with a grin. "But I'll grant you that if those explosives ever got into the wrong hands, we could be in big trouble around here.

"Were any of Jonathan's agents around? Jonathan told me that, starting about now, he was going to stake out all the local watering holes so he can monitor the reaction of the would-be rebels to the visit of Trimmer and Popov."

"Well, I don't think Jonathan would be pleased with what Chuck and Raoul had to say about blowing up the water-diversion projects. Do you suppose that would be enough to get Chuck and Lou in trouble with Jonathan's troops?"

"Yes, it is. And, if you'll recall when we were involved in some presidential and vice presidential political events, the Secret Service usually rounds up the big mouth types and detains them until the person or persons they are protecting leaves town. Then, they turn 'em loose. Jonathan has already had to warn Lou about making threats against Trimmer. When Jonathan first came out last November and we guys skied across part of The Grand Ditch, Lou made some nasty cracks about President Trimmer that upset Jonathan. I had to step in and calm everyone down," said Buck.

"Evidently, all those special mission aircraft buzzing in and out of the Granby Airport and all the guards posted at the entrance to Camp Hope are making the situation worse."

"Well, Chuck and Lou needn't worry about getting an invitation to the presidential Labor Day brunch," said Buck. "They are obviously *persona non grata.*"

"Buck, if you really don't want to go to the big brunch, we could make some excuse."

"Dolly, the only reason we are going is because it would be an embarrassment to Jonathan if we don't show up. Truth be known, if it weren't for the chance to see a Russian president, I suspect only the county's handful of yellow-dog Democrats would show up. Remember, Jonathan picked this place for the presidential retreat. If we locals stiff the invitation to gather down on the banks of the Colorado and break bread with Trimmer and Popov, Jonathan's going to hear about it from Trimmer and Briccone."

"Buck, despite what you say, I think a lot of the prominent locals will show up," said Dolly.

"Why do you think they think that?"

"Because Jonathan says the event is divided into two sittings or, in this case, you might say: standings."

"So, which group are we in?"

"The first group is to be at Camp Hope at 0700 hours. The second group is to be there at 1100 hours and we're in the second group."

"Did Jonathan say why we're in the second group?"

"Yes. The second group is smaller and gets to fly fish with Trimmer and Popov. So, we're supposed to bring our fishing gear."

"Surely, they don't expect to catch much at eleven o'clock."

"Catching trout isn't the objective. I think the time has to do with the amount of light available for the photo op of Trimmer and Popov fishing along side of the common folk. Albeit, selected common folk."

"From the PR perspective, I suppose that makes sense," said Buck. "But, I'll sure be glad when all this phony stuff is over and we can get back to reality up here. The extra security at the airport and the police roadblocks when Trimmer decides to go somewhere by motorcade are a bloody nuisance."

"Well, at least the creation of Camp Hope has boosted the local economy. None of the stores for miles around have any western wear left. The White House staff and the media stripped their shelves," said Dolly.

"I'll grant you that, but I'll a lot happier when we can go down on that stretch of the Colorado and fish in peace again. I think I'll give Jonathan a call just to see if there's anything else we can do to ease his load."

"Okay, you do that."

Setting his wineglass aside, Buck picked up the portable telephone and dialed.

One of the duty agents answered Jonathan's special number then patched Buck through to Jonathan's condo.

"Jonathan, Dolly and I are going to do some shopping in Denver tomorrow. Is there anything I can pick up for you?"

"Do they sell aspirin by the car load?" asked Jonathan. "We've had our share of incidents along the outer perimeter. Mostly just gawkers who don't mean any harm. But a few of them gave my agents some modified victory signs."

"You mean the kind where they only use one finger?"

"You got it."

"Have you made any arrests?"

"Not yet."

Buck was on the verge of suggesting that Jonathan detain Chuck and Lou over the weekend, but he thought better of it. Instead, Buck made a polite inquiry about President Trimmer.

"Oh, Buck. POTUS is having a great time. He even quit chasing that newsie long enough to go down and take a good look at the river today. Briccone and some fly-fishing expert they hired showed him what to do when we let the media have their big photo op on Labor Day."

"Yeah. Dolly told me that we are to be there at 11:00 a.m. sharp and with fishing gear. But I'd rather be down on the river at 7:00 a.m. when the fishing would be better."

"Listen Buck, you and Dolly come at 1100 hours, or not at all. When I use military time, you know I mean it."

"Okay. Have it your way, then. Anyway, we're flying down to Denver early tomorrow morning and coming back before dark. You're invited over for Sunday dinner. You may need a good, home-cooked meal before Monday's big breakfast and photo op."

"Thanks, Buck. But with President Popov coming in on Saturday, I'm afraid to leave this place. By the way, if the weather turns bad while you are down in Denver, please don't get 'get-there-itis' thinking you have to get back here in time for Labor Day. We have plenty of RSVPs for both events. Remember what you always say: 'There's nothing you need to do tomorrow that's worth dying for today.'"

"I'll try to remember that," said Buck. "Right now, the forecast calls for severe clear all through the Labor Day weekend. So, I'll bet you will see our smiling faces at 1100 hours on Monday."

"Maybe so. By the way, give Melissa, I mean Dolly, a big hug. You both mean a lot to me," said Jonathan hanging up.

CHAPTER THIRTY

Edward T. Briccone ambled over to the luxurious chalet lodge occupied by President Trimmer. He checked in with the uniformed guard at the sentry box who took a cursory glance at Briccone's credentials, picked up a telephone and cleared Briccone with the agent standing inside the entrance to the chalet.

The agent slid open the front door just as Briccone was about to knock.

"Good morning, Mr. Briccone," said the agent. "The President is expecting you."

The living room of the President's lodge at Camp Hope had a rustic, but sophisticated, flavor somewhat like Aspen Lodge at Camp David. Here, the construction method was post and beam. The mortise and tenon joints were held together with timber pegs. According to the owners, no nails or screws were used to assemble the posts and beams. Clearly, it was Old World craftsmanship in a New World setting. The décor was a blend of Bavaria and Sante Fe. A large Navajo rug spread out in front of a cozy fire burning in a large fireplace faced with Colorado moss rock.

President James Robert Trimmer was having coffee by the fireplace while scanning his usual morning ration of six newspapers flown in each morning to the Granby Airport from Denver by a U.S. Air Force special-mission aircraft. He motioned for Eddie Briccone to help himself to some coffee and pastries.

"Jesus, Eddie, we don't seem to be generating much press from out here in this godforsaken wilderness. My wife's trip to Puerto Rico is getting more inches above the fold than I am."

"On Labor Day, that will change, Mr. President," said Briccone as he eased his huge bulk onto the couch opposite the President and downed his second Danish. "We've set up a deal with all the networks for an major photo op with you and President Popov down on the river."

"That's good, Eddie, but can't we do something special for TNN. Sheila, their stand-up gal, is awful nice to me. Maybe, we could be nice to TNN?"

"Ah yes, TNN. What our enemies like to call: the Trimmer News Network. Yes, Mr. President, I will arrange for Sheila to have a little more inside scoop than the others," said Briccone.

"Thank you, Eddie. Now, pray tell, my trusted counselor, what are the Russian President and I going to be doing on the river? At some decent hour, I trust."

"Let's back up a minute to the beginning of the Labor Day agenda, Mr. President. At 7:00 a.m., you and President Popov will be hosting a chuck-wagon breakfast down on the riverbank for some of the local nabobs. That session will last until 9:00 a.m. Then, the two of you get to come back up here to rest for a couple of hours.

"At 11:00 a.m., you both go back down to the river to host a second chuck-wagon brunch for a second group of local nabobs."

"What's the difference between a chuck-wagon breakfast and a chuck-wagon brunch?" asked Trimmer.

"One is at 7:00 a.m. and the other is at 11:00 a.m."

"I was afraid you'd say that, Eddie."

"Anyway, the 11:00 a.m. group is smaller in size and they are the ones who get in the water with you and Popov and fish."

"I hear Popov likes to fish. What if he catches one and I don't?"

"You'll catch one. I guarantee it. Just don't ask me how it happens."

"But wouldn't there be more chance of actually catching a trout at the 7:00 a.m. event?"

"Yes, but the lighting for the TV camera is better at noon. Earlier in the day, it's too dark down in that canyon."

"So, who besides Popov will be fishing with me?"

"The Secretary of the Interior and his son."

"Good move, Eddie, the environmentalists will love that. Especially, if that little twit gets to catch a trout and releases it on TV. Who else of note?"

"Those friends of Mr. Winslow, the Drs. Buck and Dolly Madison, although some of his old Army buddies, still call him Colonel."

"So, at last I get to meet the people who suggested this fucking fish camp to Winslow."

"Jim Bob, you have to admit this is a pretty nice fish camp."

"Yeah, it reminds me of Camp David. By the way, Eddie, I hope you've given strict instructions to Winslow to keep his fucking agents away from that little tumbledown cabin just below here."

"Yes, Mr. President. I've spoken to Winslow and he says his agents will continue their surveillance from up on the banks. They won't come any lower than before."

"Good. I don't want them to get the idea they can come roaming around down there when I'm 'busy' at the cabin."

"They won't, I assure you, Mr. President."

"So, what's the rest of my Labor Day like?"

"There is nothing more on your official schedule after the fishing photo opportunity except that you and Popov are supposed to hold talks in the afternoon about reducing the number of nuclear weapons in the arsenals of both countries."

"How much do they want this time?" asked Trimmer.

"For about $30 billion, they will probably agree to take down their nuclear forces by about ten percent; provided, we do the same."

"Nobody pays us to take down our nuclear forces another ten percent. How in the hell did we get ourselves in this position?"

"Beats the hell out of me, Jim Bob. I'll leave that to the revisionist historians. They'll blame it on the Republicans."

"Okay, so Popov and I play with the cookie pushers from State all afternoon. Then what?"

"We're having a strategy meeting with Vice President Holzhalter's campaign staff."

"Surely, that nitwit Holzhalter isn't coming out here."

"No, Jim Bob. We're meeting with his top aides to tie up some lose ends on how I want them to handle the election in Florida."

"Is it gonna be close in Florida, Eddie?"

"So close, Jim Bob, that if we don't win when the machine count of the votes is over, we gotta be prepared to undermine public confidence in how the election was conducted."

"Let's hear your plan," said Trimmer.

"Well, we figure when the overseas military send in their absentee ballots that those ballots will break at least 70-30 against Holzhalter, even though its you that the military is pissed off at. So, I've got a guy who has worked out a plan to keep the military absentee ballots from being counted."

"How the hell is he gonna do that?"

"Jim Bob, you've got our armed forces scattered over hell's half acre. They are hunkered down in places where there is no postal system except the military postal system, if even that. Depending on how far they are out in the outback, some GIs aren't required to put stamps on their letters home to mom or, in this case, their absentee ballots. On top of that a lot of military mail never gets a postmark because it gets handed up the chain-of-command from foxhole-to-foxhole or ship-to-ship and it's a wonder that the mothers of America ever hear from their sons and daughters overseas."

"Get to the point, Jim Bob. What does the lack of a stamp or postage have the fuck to do with absentee ballots?"

"There is a conflict between federal law that does not require military mail to have postmarks and Florida law that requires all mail carrying absentee ballots to be postmarked."

"I get it. You make sure that we have our party workers object to all absentee ballots from overseas that arrive without stamps or postmarks or both. Brilliant."

"Yes, that takes care of the overseas military absentee ballots. But we also have the problem of a large number of active-duty military being based in Florida. We don't want those gomers to vote either."

"So, how do you screw them out of their votes?"

"Simple. The day before the election we order a bunch of readiness alerts for military units in Florida. The Army and Air Force types will have to deploy to their alert areas out in the boonies. The Navy will have to put out to sea. We'll keep them in their alert areas or sea stations until the polls close the next day."

"That's terrific, Eddie. I wish I'd thought of that one."

"Wait, there's more. We think we can get about 5,000 Haitian votes for Holzhalter."

"See, I knew some of my foreign policy maneuvers would pay off. But are these voodoo-lovers U.S. citizens?"

"Makes no difference. We have some tame election officials in the Miami area who will look the other way. Once the Haitians punch their machine ballots, no one can tell if they were cast by Haitians or Martians."

"Don't tell me you have a plan to get the Martian vote."

"No, but we're gonna try for the felon vote."

"You've got to be kidding," said Trimmer.

"Holzhalter's opponent is big on law and order. As governor, he fried a bunch of murderers and rapists and he's not the felon's poster boy. The felons will go overwhelmingly for Holzhalter. So, we slip absentee ballots to the prison population and get 'em mailed in."

"But felons have lost their civil rights and aren't supposed to vote."

"Jim Bob, just like the Haitian vote, the fix is in. As the Nazis used to say: "Ve half our vays."

"Okay, Eddie, I understand how we are gonna exclude the military absentees, the active-duty military based in Florida and get the felon vote. But you said you were gonna cast doubt on the election process itself. How are you gonna do that?" asked Trimmer.

"Along the east coast of Florida, there's a ton of elderly Jews who have come down from New York to retire. Most of them will vote for Holzhalter. But the last person they would vote for is a splinter party candidate whom they perceive to be just short of a neo-Nazi. Just as the polls close, we are going to target about 5,000 elderly Jews via a phone bank and read a script to them that suggests that they might have misread their ballots and voted for the neo-Nazi. They'll go absolutely bonkers."

"Wait a minute. The targets you are talking about are pretty smart. Surely, they'd know how to punch a ballot correctly in a New York minute."

"Yes, but there's this one county where the ballot, although approved by our party workers, requires a little thought to complete. Even so, I'll bet 99 percent of the old folks we'll try to panic completed their ballots just the way they intended. But our phone bankers will place the suggestion that they might have gotten confused and punched the wrong place on the ballot and voted for the wrong person for president. We'll make sure our friends in the media are on hand to capture the wailing and nashing of teeth for the TV news shows."

"Eddie, your name ought to be Goebbels. Looks to me like you have thought of everything."

"Jim Bob, there's one last trick. Most of Florida is in the Eastern Time Zone. But part of the Florida panhandle is in the Central Time Zone, so the polls in the panhandle close one hour later than rest of Florida. There are a lot of military bases and retired military and other conservatives in the panhandle and we don't want them to vote. So, we get our little buddies in the media to fiddle with the exit poll data coming out of eastern Florida and announce that the entire state is going to give its 25 votes in the Electoral College to Holzhalter. I figure a lot of Holzhalter's opponents will hear that and be too discouraged to go to the polls and vote. The impact of calling Florida for Holzhalter early multiples in the Mountain and Pacific Time Zones where the polls close much later. We may discourage hundreds of thousands of people who were going to vote against us from going to the polls. When Jimmy Carter conceded too early in 1980, many Californians who were waiting in line to vote for him got that word and went home," said Briccone.

"Holy shit, Eddie, this is fucking tremendous. But I'm not attending your meeting. If the other side found out that we're doing this shit we could end up in jail. Forget you told me this stuff."

"So, how are you going to spend the time while I'm meeting with Holzhalter's staff weenies?"

"I think I need a little more media exposure, so I'm gonna give Sheila another 'interview' while you are doing your bit for Holzhalter. By the way, does Holzhalter know all this shit?"

"Most of it. But he's so fucking dumb that it may not register. But, if it works, he'll claim he thought it up. Hopefully, in private."

"Enough about Holzhalter. What's happening with Popov after we finish our little talk on nuclear arms reduction?"

"He wants to stay here for a few days and fish."

"Well, he's welcome to my share of the fish and more. But, I have to tell you, Eddie, this little adventure of yours hasn't been as bad as I thought it would be. This Camp Hope, or whatever it is, is really pretty nice."

"Thank you, Jim Bob. I'm glad it worked out."

"Tell me more about Mr. Winslow's friends. I hear the wife is quite a looker."

"Yes, she is. A tall, willowy, blue-eyed blond with brains. But making a move on Dolly Madison would not be advisable. Colonel Madison would kill you."

"That's an interesting thought. Would Mr. Duty-Honor-Country Jonathan Winslow shoot his best friend and mentor to keep Colonel Madison from killing the President of the United States? A choice between best friend and duty."

"Knowing Winslow, I'm sure he'd find some way to finesse it."

"I'll try not to put him to the test and ruin his Labor Day," said President Trimmer.

CHAPTER THIRTY-ONE

The shopping expedition and the lunch all went as planned. Dolly bought a new outfit for the President's chuck-wagon brunch. Buck bought the Swiss seats he had always wanted. After their friends dropped them off at the Denver Jet Center, Buck and Dolly began their preparation for the brief flight back to the Granby Airport. While Buck walked across the parking ramp to their aircraft, Dolly went inside the Jet Center to check the aviation weather and to file their flight plan.

Reaching into the cabin, Buck extracted the two war surplus U.S. Special Forces rucksacks containing their survival gear. The contents of each rucksack were almost exactly the same: fire starters, emergency rations, space blankets, ponchos, poncho liners, flashlights, first-aid supplies, maps, carabiners and the like. Neatly coiled and strapped to the outside of each rucksack was a coil of olive drab, U.S. Army rappelling rope. Buck opened each rucksack and inserted the newly-acquired Swiss seats.

Each spring, as soon as the snow was off the rock face adjacent to the Lake Granby High Dam, Buck insisted that he and Dolly take refresher rappelling training with the Grand County Search and Rescue Team. Although both were experienced pilots, neither liked heights and the annual rappelling refresher was akin to taking caster oil. Something you only took if you had to.

Buck put the rucksacks back into the aircraft and strapped into the rear passenger seats with seat belts. Weighing about 40 pounds each, the rucksacks could do a lot of damage if the plane came to a sudden stop. Strapped to the floor of the cabin under the passenger seats and hidden from view was a .30 caliber lever-action carbine, complete with carrying sling.

Buck was in the process of making sure the rucksacks were properly re-secured when he sensed someone was walking up behind him. Shortly after they had landed at Centennial Airport that morning, Buck noticed the PEMEX helicopter land and hover over to a tie-down spot. So Buck was not surprised when Jose Cruz approached.

"Hello, Dr. Madison," said Jose.

"Hola, Jose," answered Buck.? Como esta Usted?

"Muy bien, gracias," said Jose.

"What brings you down to Centennial, Jose?"

"Oh, Manuel and I flew down here because our helicopter over there needed some maintenance, actually only a routine inspection. Fortunately, she is in good condition so Manuel and I can leave now."

"Where's Manuel?"

"Oh, he is sleeping in the back of the helicopter. Is your airplane okay?"

"Well, she may be up in years; however, some airplanes are like wine and Dolly. They improve with age."

"Tell me, Dr. Madison, how do you like the radios in this airplane?" asked Jose as he peered inside the cockpit to see the instrument panel.

"They work just fine. But please, just call me Buck. That's what all my friends call me. To answer your question more fully, both radios are pretty strong. But the number two radio gets squirrelly sometimes."

"Squirrelly? I must confess I do not know the meaning of squirrelly."

"That's just American slang, Jose, for acting strangely."

"Squirrelly, I must remember that one and try it out on my teammates."

"By the way, Jose, how is the work of your team going? I understand you are packing up to move out soon."

"Si, we are taking advantage of the American Labor Day weekend to finish packing and we will fly back to Mexico on the morning of Labor Day."

"Can you get all of your crew on your Huey?"

"No, Senor Buck. Many of the crewmembers will leave over the weekend by ground vehicles. I don't envy them the long drive; however, they will see some beautiful scenery on their trip through New Mexico."

"The other day my wife, Dolly, saw two old Army buddies of mine having drinks with your boss. Jefe, I think you call him."

"Si, he is our Jefe. Our chief."

"Anyway, I'm somewhat worried about my friends, Chuck Lee and Lou Leclerc. They seem somewhat upset of late. What we Americanos call: uptight. Are they connected with Team PEMEX in some way? Or, maybe they are unhappy about the fact that you and your teammates are leaving?"

"That could be. We have all become good friends with Senor Chuck and Senor Lou. We have had many fine evenings together over at Happy Jacques. But I know of no business arrangements with them. It is purely friendship."

"Well, I was just wondering because Chuck mentioned to me the other day that he was helping your team get rid of some of its excess supplies and equipment."

"Supplies and equipment? Did he say what kind?"

"Not exactly. But he hinted it was something one just couldn't walk into a store and buy. What do you suppose that was?"

"I would have no idea, Senor Buck. That would be between Senor Chuck and my Jefe, Raoul."

"Well, it must be something special because Chuck Lee was grinning from ear to ear like a Cheshire Cat."

"El Gato? Cheshire El Gato?"

"Forgive me again, Jose. Another English expression. There was this cat in a children's story and it always grinned from ear-to-ear."

"Oh, I see. It is nice to know that Senor Chuck is so happy."

"Well, I didn't say he was happy. In fact, he was been rather morose lately. I think he is very worried about something."

"Such as?"

"I think the visit of President Trimmer has him upset. And also, there has never been any love lost between Chuck Lee and the Russians. You know, Chuck spent most of his life fighting against the communists in South America and southeast Asia."

"There are Russians in Grand County? And, they are upsetting Senor Chuck? I am afraid I do not understand."

"Oh, it's been in all the newspapers. President Popov is coming from Russia to be the guest of President Trimmer at the Ouray Ranch, only they call it Camp Hope while he is there."

"I am afraid my English is not so well that I can read your newspapers. But this President Popov, is he someone Senor Chuck does not like?"

"Senor Chuck, as you call him, is pretty set in his ways. The Cold War was a big part of his life and it is difficult for him to think of the Russians as anything other than enemies."

"Do you think Senor Chuck would do anything to make the stay of the Russian president unpleasant?" asked Jose.

"That is exactly what I'm worried about, Jose. In fact, when we get back to Granby, I think I'll call someone I know and ask him to give Senor Chuck some special attention this weekend. I'd hate for my friend to get in trouble."

"Si, that might be wise, Senor Buck. Please excuse me now. I must go check the weather and file a flight plan."

"Are you headed back to Granby this morning?" asked Buck.

"I'm going in that general direction; however, I'll be landing at our helipad at the Koch Ranch."

"That's right. You have your own helipad."

"Si, I only come over to the Granby Airport to purchase jet fuel for our Huey."

With that, Jose took his leave and walked into the Jet Center. He went straight to a pay telephone to call Raoul. He reported that Chuck Lee told Dr. Madison about some special supplies and equipment given to him by Team PEMEX. He reported Dr. Madison's concerns about the emotional status of Chuck Lee and that Dr. Madison said he might call "someone he knows" and get him to pay special attention to Senor Chuck.

Raoul's response was what he expected. Jose listened intently for several minutes. Hanging up the phone, Jose went immediately to his helicopter where he awakened Manuel and told him to make sure his AK-47 was fully loaded and working.

CHAPTER THIRTY-TWO

Fifty miles west of Denver. Altitude: 16,000 feet

The brief, 65-mile flight from Denver Centennial Airport to the Granby/Grand County Airport was proceeding on schedule. Dolly and Buck Madison leveled off at 16,000 feet and engaged the autopilot on their single-engine, Cessna Turbo Centurion.

The Madisons were about to relax and enjoy the breathtaking view of the rugged, snow-capped peaks along the Continental Divide when a burst of automatic weapons fire ripped through the roof of the cabin and shredded their instrument panel. A second stream of green tracers stitched across the engine compartment. A wave of black engine oil swept back out of the engine compartment and across what was left of the windshield.

Amazingly, the engine continued to run. But, without oil, it would seize up at any moment. As the windstream began to clear the oil from the partially shattered windshield, the now oil-starved propeller governor automatically adjusted the propeller blades into high-pitch mode. Buck Madison muttered a prayer of thanks to the designer of the propeller for making the blades change pitch automatically. That feature gave the aircraft some increased gliding distance.

A rush of freezing air shot into the cabin through the gaping hole in the roof and through the cracked windshield. Looking up through the rip in the roof, Dolly Madison caught a glimpse of a helicopter, a Bell "Huey." It displayed the logo of PEMEX, the Mexican National Oil Company.

"Those crazy Mexicans are trying to kill us!" yelled Dolly.

Buck banked the high-wing Cessna hard right to get the left wing up so he, too, could get a better view. "That's Jose and Manuel all right," called Buck. "They're circling above us."

Leveling the wings, Buck glanced at what was left of the instrument panel. The oil pressure gauge was gone. But the turbine inlet temperature gauge that monitored the operation of their turbo-charger was still working. Normally, at cruising altitude, it read 1650 degrees Fahrenheit. But now it was rising over 2000 degrees and climbing. Unless he took action fast, the engine compartment would burst into flames.

Quickly, Buck Madison shut down the engine. Taking her cue from Buck, Dolly reached down between the seats, found the fuel-tank selector lever and turned it to the "off" position.

Circling a few hundred feet above the crippled Cessna, Jose Cruz watched to see if the crippled aircraft would burst into flames. Jose turned up the volume on his number-two radio and listened carefully on 121.5, the international emergency frequency. He heard nothing.

Switching to his number-one radio, Jose checked the air traffic control frequency for Denver Center. Again, he heard nothing. Jose assumed, correctly, that the Madisons now had no way to communicate with anyone.

For his part, Jose had been careful not to talk on the radio or give his call sign to Denver Center, something he could legally refrain from doing at that altitude and in that particular sector of airspace.

But his transponder was another matter. To be legal, his transponder was supposed to be on and squawking Code 1200. But Jose wasn't about to give away any information through his transponder. It was turned off. Because Jose's helicopter was virtually on top of the Madison's airplane, all the air traffic controllers in Denver Center would see on their radarscope was a single blip.

Jose knew the Madisons always filed an instrument flight plan with Denver Flight Service even on the short trip from Denver Centennial Airport to the Granby Airport. Only a fool would venture into the Rocky Mountains without filing a flight plan and the Madisons were certainly no fools.

Up until the moment Manuel shot out their radios, Jose knew the Madisons were transmitting a transponder code assigned to them by Denver Center. Figuring the Madisons now had no way of overhearing him transmit to Denver Center, and couldn't do anything about it if they did, Jose called Denver Center giving the Madison's call sign instead of his own:

"Denver Center, this is Centurion November three-two-two-whiskey-papa. I have the Granby Airport in sight. I want to cancel my IFR flight plan from Denver Centennial to Granby."

"Roger, Centurion three-two-two-whiskey-papa," replied the sector controller at Denver Center. "We'll cancel your IFR flight plan. Frequency change approved."

At that point, Denver Center would expect November three-two-two-whiskey-papa to switch its transponder automatically to Code 1200 and proceed directly to its destination airport.

Quickly, Jose set his transponder to Code 1200 and turned it on. With the Madison's transponder no longer working, the controller would mistake Jose's Code 1200 radar return for the Madison's. To keep that false impression intact, Jose kept his helicopter about 50 feet above the Madison's airplane as it descended toward the St. Vrain Glaciers.

Tuning to a private, unauthorized frequency Jose radioed to the PEMEX compound just west of Lake Granby. "Mission accomplished," said Jose. He was answered by one of his fellow terrorists who simply pressed his push-to-talk button twice. Those two audible "clicks" told Jose his message was received.

In moments, the Madison's aircraft would crash just below him. It was time for Jose to break off contact with his prey and head for the Koch Ranch. As he and Manuel left Buck and Dolly Madison to crash and die somewhere among the jagged, snow-capped peaks of the Continental Divide, Jose wondered why Raoul ordered him to have Manuel kill the Madisons. Just because Senor Madison wanted to have someone look after his friend, Senor Chuck Lee, did not seem like a justification for killing him. *For gringos, they seemed like such nice people,* thought Jose.

In fact, Jose liked the tall, blond, blue-eyed Senora Madison very much. That spring, when the PEMEX team first arrived in Grand County to begin its natural-gas explorations, Dr. Dolly Madison was one of the few locals to welcome them. She had gone out of her way to bring them a big basket of chocolate-chip cookies and a card that said: "Welcome to Grand County!"

Of course, Senora Madison was probably twice his age. At 25, Jose felt lucky to be entrusted with an expensive, twin-turbine helicopter. Raoul kept telling how crucial his flying of the Bell "Huey" was to the real mission of Team PEMEX.

Senora Madison was not only beautiful but she was very athletic as well. Jose could easily fall in love with a tall, lanky woman like Dolly Madison. He loved her ash-blond hair and her skier's tan. She reminded him a bit of the American film star, Lauren Hutton. But back home in Cuba, a woman like that would probably weigh more than he did by now.

On the two occasions when Jose encountered Professor Madison at the Granby airport, they talked easily together about flying. Jose wasn't used to being treated as an equal by Anglos, much less by someone with such a distinguished war record and so many academic degrees. When he wasn't flying, Jose liked to read the dossiers on the local people that the Cuban Intelligence Directorate had so carefully prepared.

The dossier on Professor Madison told Jose that Dr. James Buckley Madison was ten years older than Senora Madison, But Jose figured a former paratrooper like Buck Madison could probably still handle himself in tough situations. In a way, Jose hoped the Madisons would survive the crash. But, if they lived, the only thing that would keep Raoul from having him shot was the fact that, of all the PEMEX crew, only Jose knew how to fly the helicopter. A troubled Jose flew back to the PEMEX compound to tell Raoul and the others that his mission was accomplished.

Engine out, radios blown away, and a crash landing imminent, James Buckley Madison wondered if he had survived two years in Vietnam only to be shot down over Colorado.

The flight controls still worked. The windstream removed most of the oil from the windshield, so he could see forward again. *The words of his first flight instructor came to mind: Land at the slowest possible airspeed and hit the softest possible object.*

"We'll try to land on the nearest snowfield!" Buck yelled.

Desperate for every inch of altitude and each knot of airspeed they could retain, Dolly helped to streamline the aircraft by reaching down and closing the cowl flaps. With the fuel shut off, there was no danger of the engine overheating now.

"What about the landing gear?" Dolly yelled.

"Leave the gear up. We want to land on the glacier with a slick belly. Besides, I've already shut off the master switch."

Due to the gaping hole in the cabin roof, the cabin cleared of smoke. But the acrid smell of burned plastic, electrical wiring and rubber tubing hung in their nostrils.

Making a shallow left bank, Buck pointed the Cessna's nose toward the nearest of the glaciers. Buck adjusted the elevator trim for a maximum power-off glide. Below and all around them were sharp, snow-crested peaks ranging in altitude between 10,000 and 14,000 feet. The tree line began below 10,000 feet and, from that level down; the mountains bristled with 80-foot-tall Lodge Pole Pines.

For a moment, Buck considered a descent into the treetops in the hope the aircraft might hang up in the trees and not fall down onto the unforgiving, rocky slopes. But his fear of fire nixed that idea. Buck had seen helicopters burn in Vietnam. Flying helmets with visors and flame-retardant flying suits saved many of those crews. But, other than their fireproof flying gloves, Buck and Dolly were unprotected. *So, what good would it do to hang in the trees if you were only to burn to death?*, he wondered. Ahead, the relative openness of the St. Vrain Glacier looked more promising.

The St. Vrain Glacier is the headwaters of St. Vrain Creek which, eventually, flows down toward Longmont, Colorado. Actually, it is a group of glaciers consisting of five large glaciers and dozens of smaller ones all nestled side-by-side in half-mile-wide cirques lodged on the east side of the ridge that forms the Continental Divide.

When Buck and Dolly were due east of the southern-most, and closest, glacier, Buck made another slight bank to the left turning the aircraft straight west toward the Continental Divide.

During the previous summer, Buck and Dolly hiked across portions of the St. Vrain Glacier. Buck recalled the lower lip of the glacier stood about 11,000 above sea level. From that elevation, a huge field of snow-covered glacial ice ran upward on a shallow angle toward the saw-toothed crest of the Continental Divide.

Buck glanced at the altimeter. They were descending through 13,000 feet. If they fell below 11,000 feet before they reached the glacier's snow-fields, they would crash head-on into the rock face marking the glacier's eastern edge.

If there were time and opportunity, Dolly would have thrown overboard everything that wasn't bolted down. But there was no time to do anything except stare straight ahead as the whiteness of the glacier loomed in front of their shattered windshield.

"Buck, we're too low! We won't make the lip!"

"Okay, let's try this."

Reaching to the left of the control yoke, Buck flipped on the master switch.

"Give me ten degrees of flaps!" he ordered.

Dolly pushed down on the flap control lever until it stopped on the ten-degree detent. After four seemingly eternal seconds, the electric wing flaps deflected ten degrees downward. In response, the Cessna seemed to rise slightly upward as if it had just crossed a thermal of hot air.

In truth, the Cessna wasn't gaining altitude. The use of wing flaps was just helping the aircraft hold altitude for a few moments. But then, as they were about half the length of a football field from the lip of the glacier, they could feel the aircraft sinking again.

From somewhere in the recesses of Buck's mind, came one of those Chuck Yeager flashes of flying brilliance. Buck reached forward, grabbed the prop controller and pulled it to him so hard that the knob almost came out of the control panel.

Just enough oil remained in the prop governor to change the propeller blades from high rpm to low rpm. With the still whirling propeller now using its last-remaining reserves of energy to bite more deeply into the air, the Cessna's sink rate was arrested just long enough for the Cessna to clear the lip of the glacier.

As they crossed onto the glacier, the inside of the cabin turned an eye-watering white as reflected, bluish-white glacier light flooded the cabin. Buck pulled the control yoke all the way into his leather-flying jacket to get the aircraft's angle of attack to match the upward slope of the glacier. The smooth belly of the Cessna slid lightly onto the surface of the glacier with a welcome, and reassuring, thump. The sound of the stall-warning horn was joined by a hissing sound as the Cessna slid across the ice and snow.

"Nice landing, Buck," said a trembling Dolly.

"It's only nice if we can walk away from it," said an equally shaken Buck.

Weighing almost as much as a luxury car, the Turbo Centurion was slowing very little as it bounced across the snow. Unfortunately, even with the landing gear retracted, the three-bladed propeller was too short to dig into the snow and ice.

Buck and Dolly shot upward across dozens of glacial crevasses, some of which seemed almost large enough to consume the entire aircraft.

If the aircraft didn't stop soon, it would slide up and over the crest of the Continental Divide and tumble thousands of feet down on the other side.

With the gear up, the slick under-belly of the airplane was not their friend. Both Buck and Dolly, in a natural car driver's reflex, pressed on the brake pedals forgetting, in their panic, that the wheels were still tucked up inside the belly of the aircraft. As the crest of the Continental Divide drew near, they could see the Never Summer Mountain Range beginning to loom up in the distance. In a few more seconds, they would be looking down into Lake Granby. After that, they would tumble end-over-end to their deaths.

But some time ago, some unknown, public-spirited volunteers working to improve the Continental Divide Trail, must have decided another rock cairn was needed to mark the trail. If they had chosen the spot for that particular cairn a few feet to the left or right of where they decided to pile all those rocks on top of each other, the aircraft would have fallen over the ridge line. Instead, the nose of the Cessna hit the rock cairn with a jolt. Momentum carried the Cessna up to the top of the cairn where it stopped and balanced precisely on its center of gravity, leaving the nose of the aircraft sticking out over the crest of the Divide.

"Lean back!" Push your seat back!" shouted Buck. As the pair forced their weight rearward, the tail tipped down and the Cessna slid back off the cairn onto a bit of rock rubble and seemed, at last, to be at rest.

Buck gave Dolly a big hug. Then, as they were offering a silent thanks to God for sparing them, they felt something move. At first, the movement was subtle, just a slight swaying in the wind.

Then, the movement was no longer subtle. The aircraft broke completely loose from the rock rubble surrounding the cairn and started back down the face of the glacier, tail-first.

"Oh my God," cried Dolly, "we're sliding backwards!"

Instinctively, Buck twisted the control yoke in a futile effort to get the aircraft to turn sideways. Sliding sideways might allow a downhill wingtip to catch in a crevasse. But the aircraft was no longer a creature of the air capable of responding to normal control inputs. It was just an aerodynamically shaped hunk of aluminum with a very slick bottom.

Faster and faster, the Cessna slid backward down the same snow track it had cut coming upslope. Unless something happened to stop its descent, when it came to the eastern lip of the glacier the Cessna would launch itself backward into space and fall, this time, onto the rocks west of Longmont.

Frantically, Buck and Dolly tried to open the cabin doors. But the impact of the forced landing and the punishing ride up the rugged snowfield had twisted the airframe to the point neither cabin door would open.

When the backward speed of the aircraft reached about 25 miles-per-hour, a simple law of physics took effect. The vast majority of the aircraft's weight was in the nose, in the engine compartment. Just like an arrow in flight, the aircraft spun around in order for the heavy end to be in front.

Now, the nose of the aircraft pointed downslope. But the Cessna was gathering speed at an alarming rate. While the slide up the snowfield had been rough, the ride down the snowfield was made rougher due to the aircraft's acceleration. Every few yards the Cessna hit a mound of ice and became, momentarily, airborne.

The airspeed indicator needle flickered in a feeble attempt to show some airspeed down the glacier. But Buck could tell they would never slide fast enough to attain flying speed and be able to fly off the glacier. They would simply tumble nose-over-tail.

If Buck and Dolly could figure out a way to slow down the aircraft it might stop shooting over the crevasses and fall into one. The solution occurred first to Dolly.

"The gear, the gear! cried Dolly.

The master switch was still on so all Buck had to do was push the landing gear control lever into the down position. Like all later model Centurions, the aircraft had no gear doors to get in the way of the main wheels as they strained to move down into position. But nothing happened.

"It's not working," called Buck, as he began to resign himself to tumbling over the lip of the glacier.

Dolly glanced at the circuit breaker panel and saw the breaker button for the landing gear was sticking out. Quickly, she pushed it back in and was rewarded with the sound of the landing gear motor interacting with the hydraulic power pack as it tried to expel the gear from the underside of the fuselage. But the landing gear motor was overmatched by the weight of the aircraft bearing down on the ice. The circuit breaker popped again and Dolly pushed it back in again.

Obviously, the landing gear wasn't going to be of help. Dolly, now resigned to their fate, crossed her hands over her face and prayed. She was just into the 23d Psalm when the aircraft hit a mound of ice and bounced into the air just high enough for the wheels to begin to come out of their wells.

But the aircraft wasn't airborne the six seconds needed for the main gear to extend. There was, however, just enough time in the air for the nose gear to pop forward and lock in place.

When the aircraft returned to the snowfield, the nose gear took a terrific beating as it bounced over ridge after ridge of boilerplate ice mixed with furrows of snow. With each jolt, the aircraft lost a bit of ground speed but still wasn't stopping.

At some level of consciousness, the two pilots knew that a nose wheel has no brakes. But they stood on the brake pedals anyway. In another 50 feet, they would tumble, end-over-end over the lip.

Giving up on the brakes, they pushed frantically once again against the jammed cockpit doors, Then, the nose wheel fell into the only remaining crevasse between the aircraft and the lip of the glacier.

The battered aircraft stood on its nose as the nose gear dug down into the crevasse. Only their seat belts and shoulder harnesses saved them from being thrown through what was left of the windshield and out into space.

When he could get his breath, Buck asked, "Are you okay?"

"Barely, are you?"

"Nothing's broken. Let's get out of here. Fuel's dripping down from above," said Buck.

Now, the cabin doors were no longer a problem. They popped wide open when the wrenching, sudden stop stood the aircraft on its nose. Buck and Dolly were now free to leave their mangled aircraft.

"Get your rucksack and let's go," ordered Buck. "I've got mine, and the GPS and the rifle. This gal's about to blow!"

"What about the emergency transmitter?" asked Dolly, as she dropped onto the edge of the crevasse.

"I don't think we stopped hard enough to make the ELT go off. If the plane doesn't burn, I'll come back and turn it on."

The pair crawled on all fours around the edge of the crevasse and were headed up the glacier when they heard frying sounds. Fuel was dripping down from the ruptured wing tanks and running into the still-hot engine compartment.

Dragging their rucksacks behind them, Buck and Dolly scrambled up the snowfield following the track of the Cessna. When they came to the mound of ice that propelled their aircraft into the air and freed the nose gear, they took refuge behind it. Just as they were catching their breath, the Cessna exploded. The heat from the ball of flame was so intense it sucked their breath away for a moment as what little oxygen was available at that altitude was consumed by the fire.

Lying behind the ice mound and too exhausted to get back up, Buck and Dolly did not see the remains of their Cessna melt into the crevasse. When they regained enough strength to stand up, Buck and Dolly looked out over the top of the mound for their aircraft. It was gone as if it had never existed. Only the blackened edges of the crevasse could be seen.

As Colorado old-timers say: Above 10,000 feet, every night is winter in the Rockies. Sometime after dark, even in late summer, it would begin to snow. And, even if the Civil Air Patrol learned of the crash, by dawn, the nightly snows would cover the fire-blackened edges of the crevasse and there would be no trace of the airplane.

Other than a few wisps of smoke and the sound of the aircraft burning, the St. Vrain Glacier was as it had been for millions of years except a husband and wife were now stranded on its icy slopes. Buck and Dolly watched in awed silence as the last of the day's sunlight left the Great Plains and the last wisps of smoke rose from the crevasse.

But they had their survival rucksacks. They had a rifle. They had a hand-held GPS. More importantly, they had each other.

Despite their aching lungs and legs, the pair climbed farther up from the abyss. Too fatigued to think clearly now, they only knew their survival depended upon making a shelter and starting a fire. Then they would have to find the energy to think about who wanted them dead and why?

To Buck and Dolly Madison, the day was September 2d.

But at the headquarters of Team PEMEX where Raoul Aredondo-Garza was waiting on the helipad for Jose to return, it was D minus 2.

"Are they dead, Jose?" asked Raoul, as Jose stepped down from the Huey's cockpit.

"Si, Raoul, Manuel hit the engine compartment for sure and he shot out their radios," said Jose. "Anyway, they did not use their radios on the way down. I monitored the Denver Center frequency and they did not transmit anything. Nada."

"So, you saw them crash into the ground and burn?"

"No, Jefe, but they were trailing black smoke and headed down into the mountains. There is no possibility that they could survive. I needed to get away from the area before I was seen."

"You idiots! I told you to kill them. What if they survive? What if they find a way to contact the Secret Service?"

Jose shifted his feet and hung his head.

"I do not care what it takes!" shouted Raoul. "You and Manuel go back up there and find the wreckage. If they are still alive I want you to kill them. If necessary, land and kill them with pistols, with AK-47s, with knives, with your bare hands. I do not care how you do it, but the Madisons must be silenced!"

CHAPTER THIRTY-THREE

After catching their breath, Buck and Dolly helped each other adjust their survival packs. Then, they began the trek up the glacier in search of a place to spend the night. If they could reach the Continental Divide Trail, they would be on somewhat more familiar terrain. After all, they had hiked across the top of the St. Vrain Glacier the previous summer, albeit under much more favorable circumstances.

Their upward progress was slowed by the need to circumnavigate the deep crevasses lying between them and the Continental Divide. Now and then, they would pause for rest taking the occasion to look down into some of the crevasses. They marveled at the contrast between the whiteness of the glacier's surface and the blue interior of each crevasse.

Taking a piece of loose ice, Buck tossed it into a crevasse and they could hear the ice bounce from wall-to-wall and until finally the sound was heard no more.

"Sounds like these crevasses average about at least 30-feet deep," said Buck. "Just in case we need to take cover, let's look for some that aren't so deep or maybe we can find one with some ledges near the surface."

Buck's comment was still reverberating down the walls of the nearest crevasse when they heard the unmistakable sounds of a helicopter about to come across the Continental Divide.

"Buck! Over here!" cried Dolly as she pointed to a crevasse opening that was much smaller than the rest.

Without hesitation, the pair converged on the small crevasse. They were checking to see how deep it might be when the PEMEX helicopter crested the Divide and headed directly toward them.

"There they are, Jose," said Manuel over the intercom. "Turn so I can use my AK-47!"

Jose banked the helicopter to the left so Manuel could have a clear shot out the chopper's right door.

A stream of green tracers ripped the ice just behind Buck and Dolly and ended their indecision about jumping into the crevasse in front of them. They fell five feet onto a ledge of ice. If the ledge gave way, they would fall another 15 feet.

After making sure Dolly was unhurt, Buck unslung his rifle and stood up on the ledge hoping to get a shot at the helicopter. The PEMEX chopper was already downhill from their crevasse but beginning a wide turn to the left. Buck figured the chopper would complete its turn so the co-pilot or whoever was in the right seat could bring his AK-47 to bear on them once again.

Buck rested his rifle on the edge of the crevasse to make it steady. As the chopper was completing its turn, Buck could see the AK-47 protruding from the side of the cockpit. A moment later, he could make out the head and shoulders of the gunner.

Breath, aim, slack, squeeze, thought Buck as he fired.

The round hit the gunner right in the larynx and the AK-47 tumbled to the ground. Immediately, the helicopter made a sharp turn away from Buck and headed at flank speed back up toward the Continental Divide. Then, the helicopter was gone as if it had never been over the St. Vrain Glacier and the flopping sounds of its rotor blades were no more.

"I got a hit!" cried Buck. "Here, let me help you up, Dolly. I think we got us another weapon to boot."

Buck pulled Dolly up out of the crevasse and they hiked along the contour line toward the point where Buck thought he saw the weapon hit the glacier.

"With luck, that AK-47 will be on the surface instead of down in some crevasse," said Buck.

In five minutes, they found the weapon intact. It hit the glacier barrel first and the warm barrel was stuck about 12 inches deep into the snow. Buck pulled it free and checked it over.

"It looks okay so far," said Buck. Deftly, he detached the banana-shaped magazine. He retracted the operating handle ejecting the unspent round that was in the chamber. Buck performed a quick inspection of the weapon.

"Thanks to PEMEX," said Buck, as he put the unspent cartridge back into the banana clip, "we've got ourselves a nice AK-47 and a magazine that's almost full."

"Buck, look over here," said Dolly, pointing to the ice. "There are little, red drops of something on the snow. Like a red spray. Looks like blood."

"That's what it is," said Buck, rubbing one of the drops of red between his fingers. "Scratch one Mexican."

"Now, they'll be back for sure," said Dolly.

"Oh, they'll be back all right."

"When?"

"It's almost dark now. Too late for that chopper to be fooling around up here anymore. But the chopper will be back at first light and if they can't shoot us from the chopper, you can bet they'll be sending ground troops up the Buchanan Trail to find us," said Buck.

"What now? Buck."

"We continue on up to the lee side of the divide and try to find a hole in the rocks or some snow we can dig into for a cave," said Buck.

Out of fear of being overheard and also out of embarrassment, Jose did not radio the grim message that Manuel was dead and his weapon lost. It was almost dark as he approached the Koch Ranch and he was relieved to see the security guards had already lighted the helipad.

As he hovered down to a landing on the white "H," Jose saw Raoul, Federico and Regina waiting for him on the steps of the ranch house. As soon as the rotor blades had wound down and it was safe to dismount the helicopter, Jose ran to the ranch house to report.

Raoul started to ask why Manuel did not come with Jose when he saw the right side of Jose's flying suit was streaked with blood.

"I take it that Manuel is dead," said Raoul.

"Si, Jefe, we had the Madisons pinned down inside a trough in the ice. Manuel was going to shoot them. We were trying to turn around so Manuel would have an easy shot. But they shot first. They got him right in the throat and he dropped his weapon overboard."

"Madre de Dios!" exclaimed Raoul. "Now, the Madisons have killed one of my men and captured one of our automatic weapons! You fool! Take Pancho with you and get back up there and kill them!"

"Wait, Raoul," said Federico. "If we send Jose and Pancho up on that glacier at night, we'll lose the helicopter and both of them. We've already lost Manuel. I'm afraid we must wait until dawn."

"Federico, Jefe, we must not lose the helicopter," offered Regina, without mentioning Jose and Pancho.

"And, I would shoot this worthless Jose right now," said Raoul. "But he's the only one who can fly the Huey."

"Jose, go get cleaned up. Burn that bloody flight suit. Organize a detail to bury Manuel. Make sure the grave is deep. We don't want any coyotes or dogs to dig him up. Pick a new gunner and then get some rest. I want you up on that crash site at dawn!" ordered Raoul.

"Jefe," said Federico. "Let me organize a ground party to start up the trail from Monarch Lake. Just in case Jose is not successful from the air, we may be able to ambush the Madisons on the ground."

"May be able? We must be able!" said Raoul. "Okay, as usual, you have a sound plan. But we can only spare six men. And, they must come from the security detail, not from our target teams."

"Si, Jefe," said Federico. "According to this topographical map, the Buchanan Trail is the only logical way down from the St. Vrain Glacier to the nearest telephone or help. My guess is that the Madisons will head for the nearest telephone or try to find someone with a cellular telephone.

"The first regular telephone they could find is at the ranger station at Monarch Lake. There are also some pay telephones at the campgrounds below the lake and there is a telephone at the souvenir shop. After that, the next available telephone is ten miles away at the Madison's house near the Lake Granby High Dam. I'll instruct our men on how to disable the phones at the ranger station, the campgrounds and the souvenir shop.

"At first light, let me send two of our men up the Buchanan Trail to ambush the Madisons and hide their bodies in one of those alpine lakes or set off an avalanche to bury them. The Buchanan Trail runs down to Monarch Lake. So, as a backup, I want two men to stay at the lake. Those same men can check out the telephones at the campgrounds and the souvenir shop and be prepared to disable them. Then, let's stake out the Madison's house with the remaining two men. That way, we'll have all our bases covered," said Federico.

"As you wish, Federico," muttered Raoul, as he turned and stomped back into the ranch house.

Buck and Dolly searched along the east side of the ridge for a place to dig a snow cave. Just as darkness descended, they found the walls of a natural cirque that the upslope winds from the east had packed with snow. Using their GI entrenching tools, they took turns digging a tunnel underneath the overhang of the cirque. After an hour of labor, they created a tunnel about six-feet-long and about four-feet in diameter. They made the bottom of the tunnel as flat as possible and lined it with one of their ponchos. Buck drove a piton into the ice on each side of the tunnel entrance and rigged a piece of parachute cord between the pitons to form a clothesline. He took their other poncho and hung it over the makeshift clothesline to create a way to close off the opening. That done, they crawled inside and lit a candle.

From his rucksack, Buck drew a metal coffee can that was packed with an entire roll of toilet paper. From Dolly's rucksack, Buck pulled a metal flask full of denatured alcohol. Dolly opened the flask and slowly poured the alcohol onto the exposed end of the roll of toilet paper until the paper could absorb no more alcohol.

Buck placed the coffee can full of toilet paper and alcohol near the entrance to the tunnel and set fire to the alcohol. The result was a clean, blue flame that gave off hardly any fumes. After a few minutes, the chill inside the snow cave began to give way to something bordering on warmth.

"According to our survival manual" said Buck, "our little heater will last until about dawn. It doesn't produce enough fumes to make us sick and we can just let it burn."

"Buck, we are so exhausted, I'm afraid we'll oversleep and they'll come up here and murder us in our poncho liners," said Dolly.

"Fortunately, I've been keeping my old Vulcan Cricket in my rucksack," said Buck. "It's a relic of the Vietnam War, but it still works. I'll set its vibrator alarm to go off at 0400 hours."

"Buck, that's only five hours sleep."

"Okay, I'll set it for 0430 hours. But we must get moving downhill until we can get below the tree line and find some concealment and maybe even some cover."

"Since I don't have to worry about make-up or my hair curlers, I can be on the trail in ten minutes. Honest."

Lying wrapped in their poncho liners and back-to-back for warmth, they watched the faint light from their make-shift alcohol heater play on the roof of their snow cave for all of about two minutes before they both fell sound asleep.

CHAPTER THIRTY-FOUR

"Did you sweep the 'working' cabin?'" asked Mr. Cannady, the agent-in-charge of what his fellow agents jokingly called: the POTUS 'working' cabin.

"Sure did. It only takes a few minutes to look underneath and all around. We ought to get the park or forest service down there to fix it up," said Jennings, one of the newest agents on the presidential protective detail.

"Nice thought," Mr. Jennings, "but POTUS likes that dump just the way it is. It serves his purpose."

"Speaking of his purpose, where is God's gift to the media?"

"She's resting, I suppose. It must be tiring as hell to have to hike down to the cabin so she can 'interview' POTUS on the state of the nation," said Cannady.

"I thought she had the international beat."

"Whatever. Okay, she 'interviews' him on the state of the world. Satisfied?"

"You know. I just like to be accurate. Speaking of accurate, how come we don't log her visits to the 'working' cabin like we do POTUS?"

"Because the story POTUS wants to come out of this fishing adventure is that he goes down to the banks of the Colorado all alone to meditate and to fish. I overheard Mr. Briccone saying POTUS should try to capture some of the aura of President Eisenhower's fishing trips."

"Then, why doesn't he go over to St. Louis Creek where President Eisenhower really liked to fish?'

"Because he doesn't have a secluded cabin on St. Louis Creek where he can be 'interviewed' and not be seen, you nitwit."

"You think FLOTUS knows about this one?"

"Probably. But I don't think she gives a rat."

"What does she care about?"

"Power. She's got the power; he's got the pussy. Simple as that."

"What's the time?"

"About time for Mr. Winslow to call down here to make sure you swept the cabin before dark and to tell me to remind the next watch to sweep it again before dawn. Even so, you know Mr. Winslow will be out there making sure the cabin is secure and that his snipers are awake."

"Don't you think we should have some agents closer to that cabin?"

"Yes, we should. But POTUS told Mr. Winslow he doesn't want anyone closer than 100 yards. Mr. Winslow wanted agents in fishing gear 100 yards upstream and 100 yards downstream but POTUS wouldn't hear of it. So, we've got agents fishing 101 yards upstream and 101 yards downstream. Plus, we've got the snipers perched up above the river on both sides. They keep the cabin under surveillance with night scopes all night and then switch to binoculars at first light. Pretty shitty duty. Even this time of year, it's colder than the Klondike down in that canyon."

"So, do the snipers observe Miss Media slipping down to 'interview' POTUS?"

"They'd better. They see, but don't record. But they do report by landline. Mr. Winslow forbids radio reports on the comings and goings of Miss Media because he's afraid some local yokel or county Mountie with a scanner will hear them."

"How come her media rivals don't blow the whistle?"

"Hey. They love this guy more than they hate her. They like his agenda or they hate the other party, I'm not sure which they do more. Anyway, when it serves their purpose, they actually can keep a secret."

"I just wish Mr. Winslow would let us go down there for some of that early-morning trout fishing. Can you imagine, getting paid to fly-fish the headwaters of the Colorado?"

"Yeah, but if you're doing your job, you would be concentrating on what's going on around you instead of some dumb trout."

"Okay. But I do see those agents down there fishing now and then. How can I get on that detail?"

"When you're more senior, Jennings, come back and talk to me. Just be glad you are not on the sniper detail. Meanwhile, go over to the main lodge and see if Mr. Winslow's back from visiting up at the Madisons," said Cannady.

"That's assuming they're back from Denver."

"How do you know the Madisons went to Denver?"

"Because they flew out in their plane yesterday morning. I was at the Granby Airport when they left and spoke with the professor himself. It seems his wife didn't have anything to wear to the Labor Day brunch. They flew down to Denver so she could shop. He said R.E.I. is having a sale and he needed some new survival gear."

"What the hell is R.E.I.?"

"Some kind of Disney World for outdoor types."

"Professor Madison is an outdoor type all right. A regular Mark Trail. You know who Madison reminds me of?"

"No, who?"

"There was this movie with Gary Cooper where Cooper was a professor at some college but he was also a crack shot with a rifle. This was set back right before World War II. Anyway, some spooks in Washington or London, or maybe both places, they want this professor to parachute into the Obersalzberg near Hitler's mountain retreat and nail the bastard with a big-game rifle."

"What happened?"

"The professor jumps in okay and he even gets Hitler in the cross-hairs of his scope. But, at the last second, he can't bring himself to pull the trigger."

"Dumb shit. If he'd killed Hitler just think of all the lives that would have been saved."

"Hey, it was just a movie."

"So what happened to the professor?"

"He went back to college."

"So, how does this Gary Cooper movie remind you of Professor Madison?"

"Oh, I just think Madison was a real action type in his youth. But now, he's mellowed out to the point that he's more philosopher than doer."

"You got all this from visiting with him up at the airport?"

"Partly. But I've heard Mr. Winslow talk about him a lot.

I guess they were really close in Vietnam."

"Yeah, and I guess Mrs. Madison and Mr. Winslow were pretty chummy in college. You think there's any 'interviewing' going on there?"

"No. I doubt it. But you never know."

CHAPTER THIRTY-FIVE

Even though Buck knew that Beginning Morning Nautical Twilight or BMNT began about 0500 hours, by mutual agreement, they both slept until Buck's Vulcan Cricket alarm buzzed at 0430 hours. At BMNT, a soldier is supposed to be able to see just well enough to identify and shoot at an enemy soldier standing at a distance of 100 meters. At 0430, they had just enough light to get their breakfast and prepare to get moving. According to their GPS, the sun would rise at 0634 hours and would set that evening at 1931 hours or 7:31 p.m., civilian time. That, plus the End of Evening Nautical Twilight or EENT would give them almost 16 hours of light in which to see and, hopefully, not be seen.

Quickly, Buck and Dolly took turns going outside the snow cave to relieve themselves. Then, Buck took some water from a canteen, put it into a GI canteen cup and set it on top of a folding stove. A commercial version of the GI heat tablet was set under the canteen cup and lighted with a waterproof match. In moments, Buck had some boiling water to which he added three bouillon cubes. That, plus some trail mix was their breakfast. By 0500 hours, Buck and Dolly began to climb the rest of the way to the upper edge of the glacier at the Continental Divide.

"As Robert Frost said, 'We've got miles to go before we sleep,'" Buck observed.

"More than the 12.5 miles shown on your GPS," said Dolly.

At 0634 hours, the sun peaked over the horizon to their east and began to bathe the snowfields around them with a warming, golden glow. By the time they climbed up to the rim of the Continental Divide and looked over and down into the valley of the Colorado River and Lake Granby, their backs were warm but their faces felt the dark chill of the western slope which would not feel the sun until much later in the day.

During the night, a westerly wind blew the crest of the Continental Divide free of snow revealing a footpath only about two-feet wide. According to their GPS, they were hiking along at 12,277 feet above mean sea level. Judging from the contour lines on his map, Buck estimated a slip and a fall to the western side meant a plunge of about 2,000 feet before the first bounce. A fall down the east side of the ridge would probably land them inside a deep crevasse. Even so, foot speed was everything. First, they had an urgent need to get down off the skyline and down into whatever cover or concealment the Buchanan Trail could afford. The PEMEX helicopter was sure to return soon and with guns blazing. Second, they had to make contact with Jonathan Winslow or reach anyone in law enforcement.

After an hour of creeping along the slippery ridgeline, Dolly asked, "How far to the trailhead now?"

Buck stopped and took out the GPS. After the unit acquired sufficient satellites to provide a position solution, Buck replied: "Looks like about 1.5 miles."

"Buck, at this rate, we'll be exposed up here on this ridgeline for at least another two hours," said Dolly.

"I don't know if you're game to do this Dolly," offered Buck, "but we could rappel down from here and intercept the trail much earlier."

"I suppose I'd rather risk rappelling than being ripped apart by an AK-47 out here in the open. Let's take a look."

Lying down on their stomachs for stability, they looked down. "Oh my gosh Buck," said Dolly. "It's almost straight down. I don't know if I can handle this."

"I know it's scary, but I figure by now that we are directly above the headwaters of Buchanan Creek. If we can rappel down to where the creek starts, we can follow it until it intercepts the Buchanan Pass Trail."

"How far is that?"

Consulting the map, Buck said: "If we follow the creek down about a mile, we'd hit the Buchanan Trail."

"So, when do we get to a place where there are some trees to hide under?"

"Not 'till we're about a quarter of a mile above the Buchanan Trail."

"Buck, you know I'm not a tree-hugging environmentalist, but if we make it down to a tree, I'm definitely going to hug it."

"I'm counting the contour lines from here on the Divide down to where the creek starts. I count ten, maybe more; they're packed so close together at the top it's hard to tell. The contour interval on this map is 40 feet. So, that means we've got to go about 400 feet almost straight down."

"Buck, we don't have that much rope."

"No, we don't have enough rope to reach the head of the creek in one rappel. But it looks like there's a series of ledges down there. If we could make it from ledge-to-ledge, we'd be okay."

"How much rope do we have?"

"Courtesy of an Army surplus store, we each have 50 meters of 11mm, flex-dry climbing rope. So, that's about 165 feet each or, all together, 330 feet.

"That's not enough to make a 400-foot descent."

"I'm not sure we'll have to rappel the entire face. We may be able to just mountaineer a good part of it."

"What if we have to do three or more rappels, yet we only have the two ropes?"

"Good point. But Chuck Lee showed me a special knot one time. It will hold your weight on rappel and then when you land and take the strain off the rope, you are supposed to be able to shake the rope and get it to release from up above.

"Chuck claims the Special Forces invented this knot; however, I looked it up in one of our sailing books. It's called a Blackwall Hitch or a Half-Becket Hitch. The book says it will hold as long as you maintain constant downward pressure on it. If you ever let up the pressure, you're toast."

"Have you ever rappelled off a Blackwall Hitch yourself?"

"No. Chuck just showed me how to tie it one time."

"One time. Are you sure you know how to do this?"

"No. And that's why we'll only resort to Chuck's knot if we have to. Also, he only showed it to me applied to a hook piton. I don't think I'd want to try a Blackwall Hitch applied to a rock," said Buck.

"How many pitons do we have?"

"More than enough to get down this face. Plus, I've got two hook pitons, the best kind to use with a Blackwall Hitch."

"You'd better save those hook-pitons for when we have no other choice but to use Chuck's knot."

"That's for sure. We'll tie off the rope for the first rappel using the standard knot. Which means we say goodbye to that rope forever."

"That will leave us with only one rope."

"Right. From that point on down, I'll have to tie the Blackwall Hitch each time and pray that it works. Let me have your pack."

Rummaging through their rucksacks, Buck pulled out leather rappelling gloves and a pre-made, padded Swiss seat for each of them.

"We've used those gloves before, but those Swiss seats are new," observed Dolly.

"Brand new. I just bought them yesterday when Bob and I were shopping. These are a big advance over just making a Swiss seat out of rope. They are made out of a special nylon. They're even padded. You just step in like putting on a pair of shorts, adjust the waist band to your waist size, hook your carabiner to the loop provided at the front of the Swiss Seat and you're in business."

Buck pulled a carabiner from each pack. When Dolly donned her Swiss Seat and pulled it tight, Buck snapped her carabiner in place.

"How do we know these carabiners won't break?"

"Supposedly, they are magna-fluxed to make sure they don't have any internal defects we can't see with the naked eye."

"These aren't government-issue are they?"

"You mean the result of the lowest competitive bid? No, way."

"I'll take your word for it." said Dolly.

They moved a few more yards along the Continental Divide until Buck spotted a boulder he felt would provide a secure tie-off. He looped the end of one of their two rappelling ropes around the rock tying it securely with a bowline knot.

"Who goes first?" asked Dolly.

"Another good question. If I go first and something goes wrong, you can always follow the Continental Divide down to Buchanan Pass and eventually make it down to where you can find help."

"Assuming the PEMEX door gunner doesn't cut me to pieces," said Dolly.

"But if you go first and something goes wrong, I'll be able to rappel down to where you are and help."

Swallowing hard, Dolly said, "I don't want to be left up here all alone. So, I'll go first."

Quickly, Buck gave Dolly a rappelling refresher course showing her how to hold the rope in front of her with her left hand and how to pay it out behind her back with her right hand.

"Remember, it's the hand behind your back and the friction of the loops of rope as it pays out through the carabiner that acts as the brake. The key is to push away from the mountain so your feet are bouncing down the mountain and not your face," said Buck.

After double-checking to make sure the rope actually could reach the first rock ledge down below, Buck made a double loop in the rope, opened the gate on Dolly's carabiner and inserted the rope.

"Aren't you glad we went out with the Grand County Rescue Team to practice this stuff?" asked Buck.

"Frankly, no. If I didn't know how to do it, I wouldn't be doing it now. But I'll try to think about being machine-gunned. Maybe that will improve my attitude."

"Okay, Dolly, do this face in ten-foot increments. Push out, let the rope slip, brake behind your back, hit the rock face with your feet and rest. Then do it again and again until you reach that first ledge below."

"Buck, have I told you lately that I love you?"

"You know, Dolly, you could be a country-western song writer. I love you, too."

With that, Dolly leaned back out over the abyss and began to walk down the sheer face. After several feet she felt a bit more confident and she tried a push-out drop. But, with so little real experience, she made the novice mistake of not catching the mountain with her feet when her body swung back in. She hit the mountain with her whole body, scratching her face. Fortunately, she didn't knock herself out and fall to her death.

"Push out with your feet, Dolly. Get some space between you and the mountain," called Buck.

Without a word, because she was fighting for breath, Dolly managed to pull up her feet and force her body away from the mountain. Grimly, she pushed away again letting out some rope. This time, she caught herself properly with her feet and Buck breathed a sigh of relief. After nine more drops, Dolly was standing on the rock ledge about 100 feet below.

"I'm okay, Buck," said Dolly. "Just some scratches on my face."

Dolly unhooked herself from the rope and gave the rope two jerks to signal she was free of it.

Buck disappeared from view to work with the rope. Pulling a hook-piton from his pack, he found a good place in a natural cleft in the rock. A few firm taps with his ice ax and the hook-piton was secure.

Taking the rope in hand, Buck experimented with making a Blackwall Hitch. The first two attempts slipped through the piton like butter. But, during the third try, he managed to recall how Chuck Lee had done it. The Blackwall Hitch was simplicity itself once he remembered the concept. The running end of the rope crosses on top of the standing of the rope. The weight of the object or body hanging down on the running end is supposed to be so great that it presses against the standing end so tightly that the standing end cannot move. Just to give himself an extra margin of safety, he left about six feet of excess rope at the standing end.

Well, he thought, *if it starts to slip, I'll have six feet of rope during which to pray.*

Buck attached himself to the rope with his carabiner, pulled hard against the hook-piton and the Blackwall Hitch, ran the rope around to his back hand and pushed off. With rappelling experience dating back to his years with the 1st Air Cavalry Division, Buck managed the face well. In moments, he was standing beside a very relieved Dolly. Quickly, he untied the rope from his carabiner. Taking a regular piton from his rucksack, Buck drove it into the rock face, then tied Dolly and himself to the piton.

"What are you doing, Buck? We can't rappel this way."

"No, we can't. But, I'm going to pull my rope down from above and I don't want the weight of 165 feet of rope rushing by and pulling both of us off this ledge."

"I thought you weren't going to use the Blackwall Hitch on the first rappel." said Dolly.

"I changed my mind once I saw how well you did on the first rappel."

"And, they talk about women changing their minds."

"Look out," said Buck as he gave the rope an upward flip. Almost immediately, the rope came tumbling down from above. The rope missed the ledge and cascaded on down below where it would have disappeared from sight except for being tied off to the piton.

The next drop was only 80 feet. Buck figured out the best place to drive his last hook-piton. Once again, Dolly went first. And, once again, Buck used the Blackwall Hitch successfully to join Dolly down below. Now, they could go back to the standard method of securing the end of the rope to the mountain because they could afford to begin leaving sections of rope behind.

The terrain became less steep. Dolly looked down and saw trickles of water, which had to be the beginnings of Buchanan Creek. "I think we can stop rappelling after we make this last pitch," said Dolly as Buck touched down beside her.

"I agree. We don't need to be carrying the weight of both ropes, so I'll just tie them both off with the standard knot. We'll rappel side-by-side for this last pitch. When we hit terra firma, we'll just abandon the ropes and start hiking. If we need to tie something or somebody, I still have some parachute cord."

CHAPTER THIRTY-SIX

Prior to first light on the day before Labor Day, Chuck drove his pickup to within a mile of the entrance to Rocky Mountain National Park, turned off his headlights and drove off the west side of the road at a certain spot. Years ago, Chuck found an abandoned trail that went around the entrance gate to the park. If he were ever too broke to buy a gate pass, Chuck thought he might use that hidden trail someday. The last thing Chuck and Roberto needed was for the park rangers to be making a record of their comings and going over the Labor Day weekend.

After parking in the lot for the Never Summer Ranch, they crossed over the Kawuneechee River bridge. The water flow was about a quarter of what nature had intended. *We'll soon fix that,* thought Chuck. Rather than run the risk of encountering the park rangers living in the former Never Summer Ranch guesthouses, Chuck and Roberto got off the well-marked trail and skirted the log cabins.

Then, Chuck and Roberto, their packs laden with C-4 plastique explosive made available to them by Team PEMEX, began the long trek up the trail toward the upper end of The Grand Ditch. When they served together in Vietnam, the two comrades thought nothing of humping rucksacks weighing 80 pounds plus their M-16 rifles and web gear laden with hand grenades, smokes grenades and clips of M-16 ammunition. By comparison, with each of them carrying rucksacks packed with only 50 pounds of C-4, their climb seemed like a nature walk.

Inside their rucksacks, the C-4 was already neatly divided into 25-pound units. Attached to each unit was the receiver module from a remote-control automobile starter.

Chuck had a neighbor whose second home bordered on Chuck's property. The wealthy Denverite insisted on installing a huge street light at the entrance to his road which he left on day and night, winter and summer. The neighbor never used the place in winter, but the bright light stayed on just the same. *The bastard has more money than brains,* Chuck thought. The light spooked the deer, the elk and moose, so game watching, one of Chuck's chief enjoyments, was diminished. Chuck had the remote-controlled car starters shipped to the ugly neighbor at a time when Chuck knew the neighbor would be yachting in the Caribbean. It was customary for any of the overnight package shippers to leave packages on doorsteps. Chuck simply checked the neighbor's house periodically until the package arrived and retrieved it. In the event the car starters were traced back to his neighbor, that would the neighbor's problem.

The instructions that came with the remote car starters showed a way that more than one receiver could be programmed to respond to the same transmitter. But Chuck decided the risk of messing something up wasn't worth it, so he decided to use all four transmitters and all four receivers. Besides the transmitters only weighed a few ounces each and were going to ride in Chuck's pickup anyway. Each man also carried two coils of 165-foot climbing rope. Their plan was to climb up above the largest scree field that looks down on The Grand Ditch. When they were over that part of the ditch, they would lower the C-4 clusters on the ropes until the clusters were resting about 150 feet down into the scree field. They would tie off the ropes using Blackwall Hitches which meant the ropes would hold securely as long as they were weighted down by the explosives. But once the explosions took place and the weigh of the explosives evaporated, what was left of the ropes would come tumbling down and be lost in the debris.

With the massiveness of the scree field as a background, the chances that the camouflaged bags of C-4 would be detected by other hikers or seen from the highway were between slim and none. The two men wore rubber gloves when they prepared the bags of explosives or handled anything that was to be taken on their trek up above The Grand Ditch. Once the four bags of explosives were lowered down and in place, and pressure applied to the Blackwall Hitches, the bags would remain in place until the remote receivers were triggered. That done, the two men retraced their steps down the trail, avoided the log cabins once again and returned to the Never Summer Ranch parking lot. (See: *www.thegrandconspiracy.com*)

Once again in the parking lot, they scanned the face of the scree field with binoculars to see if they could detect the presence of any of the bags of explosives. Even they, who knew exactly where to look, could see nothing out of the ordinary up above The Grand Ditch. They would return to the parking lot at 0630 hours the next morning, Labor Day. At precisely 0700 hours, they would press the transmit buttons on the four transmitters and watch about a mile of The Grand Ditch come sliding down into the Kawuneechee Valley. After that, they would make the short drive to where their fishing boat would be hidden on the north shore of Lake Granby and spend a good part of the Labor Day fishing and drinking beer. Piece of cake.

CHAPTER THIRTY-SEVEN

Buck and Dolly were rappelling side-by-side on their last pitch when they heard the unmistakable sound of a helicopter coming up the valley of the Buchanan Trail. Fortunately, at that moment neither of them were in motion.

"Stay perfectly still," called Buck. "There's a chance they won't see us and will just keep searching on up toward the Divide."

"What if they see us?"

"Then get down as fast as you can and look for a rock to hide behind."

Two climbers on a 400-foot rock face amidst hundreds of square acres of rock face don't stand out very much. Still early morning, they were roped to the shady side of the mountain's face. Their ropes were camouflaged and the only shiny objects were the two carabiners and they were hidden between their bodies and the mountain.

Twisting around very slowly in his Swiss seat, Buck could see the helicopter was following the Buchanan Pass Trail where the trail and the creek ran along together. Shortly, the helicopter pilot would have to make a choice where the trail and the creek began to take different paths. If he broke off the trail and followed the creek bed northward, he would see them hanging on the mountain. If he continued his eastward flight and stuck with the trail leading up to the Continental Divide, they would not be seen.

As the sound of the helicopter grew louder and louder, Buck and Dolly stopped breathing as if that would make the pilot decide to go the other way. Then, they heard the distinctive flap-flap sound made by a helicopter's rotor blades when it makes a sharp turn and the overall sound of the helicopter began to fade.

"Thank God he turned and thank God we decided to rappel," said Dolly. "If we had chosen to hike down the Continental Divide, that chopper would be finding us up there in a few minutes."

When the chopper disappeared over the Divide, Buck and Dolly quickly completed their last rappel, unhooked from their ropes and packed away their Swiss seats and gloves.

Yet, they were not to the trail itself. They needed to follow the ever-widening creek without the benefit of any kind of concealment for at least another half-mile. Preoccupied with finding secure footing and not looking very far downslope, they were startled when they almost ran into a herd of Rocky Mountain Bighorn Sheep sporting some dangerous looking curled horns. (See: www.thegrandconspiracy.com)."Be still," whispered Buck, "let's see what they do."

The sheep stared at the two human intruders for a few moments, evidently found them uninteresting and bolted up the canyon wall almost as if the wall were horizontal.

"I'd give anything to be that nimble," said Dolly.

"For a few moments, those sheep made me forget the fix we're in. I'm grateful to them for that," said Buck.

Buchanan Creek was gathering force now as the waters which were merely seeping into the creek from the rocks began to join the creek in rivulets. Initially, they had been able to walk in the creek bed itself without getting their boots wet. But now, the creek was so deep they had to hike along the side of the waters. Still, they made decent time. By 0900 hours, they were moving among the partial concealment of Alpine Willows. Fir trees greeted them as they got lower down, giving them good concealment at last. An hour later, they and the creek intercepted the Buchanan Trail at a place marked on the map as Fox Park. Dolly could see that Fox Park was flooded with larkspur, snowlilly, lupine, monkshood and Indian paintbrush and bunches of other flowers she couldn't name. But the firs receded away from the trail at Fox Park leaving them somewhat exposed again. They were in between Fox Park and the junction of Buchanan and Thunderbolt Creeks when they heard the helicopter searching for them.

Yet, luck was still with them because just ahead was the beginning of a rugged set of tree-shrouded switchbacks. Aside from the sheer face they had rappelled just after dawn, the trail down to the junction of Thunderbolt and Buchanan Creeks was the steepest yet.

Having already lost one of his security team members to the Madisons, Raoul ordered the installation of a 7.62 mm mini-gun on the left skid of the Huey. There wasn't time or a place to zero the mini-gun, so Jose would just have to use the tracers to adjust his fire.

Because Regina felt she could handle the attack on the Moffat Tunnel by manipulating Lou Leclerc, she loaned her teammate, Pancho, to the effort to kill the Madisons. Hopefully, Pancho would come back from flying with Jose in one piece and be available just in case Lou Leclerc came out from under her sexual spell. It was a risk she, Raoul and Federico felt they had to take.

"Look, Jose!" called Pancho, "there they are down in that ravine. Turn around! Go back! Go back!"

"I'm trying," said Jose. "But the ravine is too narrow right here. We'll hit our rotor blades on the side. I'll gain some altitude. You keep your eyes on where they are."

Hearing the helicopter climbing, Buck said: "The terrain's too tight and there's too much vegetation for them to do anything in here. Let's move down as quickly as we can. The switchbacks are so close together, if we come to any open spots, we'll back up to where there are trees and take a shortcut down to the next switchback. I know. I know. We tell other hikers not to shortcut the switchbacks. But, the Great Ranger would forgive us this time."

"Do you still see them?" asked Jose.

"No, I can't see anything down there but tall trees and bushes," said Pancho. "Wait, Jose. See if you can drift down more to where two trails and two creeks are coming together. I think I see something."

"See what? Do you see people?

"No. What I see is a part of a log bridge over a creek bed. Maybe, we'll see them cross the bridge."

Just then, Buck and Dolly were approaching the upper end of the bridge. "Can you see the helicopter," asked Dolly.

"I hope not, but I sure hear it. It sounds as if it's hovering 300 or 400 feet above us."

"Now, what do we do?"

"I see dapples of sunlight on the logs. That means they can probably see at least a portion of the bridge."

"Can't we just hide here 'till it goes away. It can't hover up there forever."

"True, but we don't have forever either. We've got to reach Jonathan or somebody. We've stayed pretty dry so far, but I'm afraid here is where we get our feet wet."

"You don't mean we're going to ford Buchanan Creek underneath the bridge do you?"

"Precisely. Take off your boots and socks. Put your socks in a water-proof bag. Tie your laces so you can hang your boots around your neck."

When they were ready, Buck held Dolly's hand and helped her down and under the logs where they were met by an icy tide of rushing water that took their breath away. The force of the water was so great Buck decided they couldn't cross without a rope or some kind of lateral support.

After they slung the two weapons around their necks, Buck said, "Dolly, I'm going to reach up and grab the log on the upstream side of the bridge and walk us hand-by-hand across. You grab my belt and hang on 'till we reach the other side. It's only about 12 feet. Let's go."

Jose and Pancho were just in the process of losing some altitude to get a closer look at the log bridge when Pancho saw movement along the upstream edge of the bridge. He saw a pair of white hands on a brown log moving sideways like a crab.

"Shoot the bridge!" cried Pancho. "They are trying to cross underneath the bridge!"

Jose tipped the nose of the helicopter down so it pointed directly at the bridge and squeezed the red trigger on his control stick. A shower of wood chips flew into the air as the mini-gun began to reduce the log bridge into a pile of toothpicks.

The shock of hundreds of machine gun rounds hitting the bridge made Buck lose his grip and he and Dolly were swept downstream. So much for dry boots.

"Hold on, Dolly! Kick for the other side." Dolly had both arms around Buck's neck and the pair kicked furiously with their legs in an attempt to steer themselves toward the bank. But, they weren't successful. Then, a large rock loomed ahead in the middle of the stream. When they came to it, Buck pushed off the rock and that gave them the steer they needed for the waters to deposit them scratched and bleeding on the opposite bank.

As they gasped for breath, they watched pieces of the log bridge float by them. Jose was in the process of cutting the log bridge into tiny pieces. But seeing no blood in the water, Jose began to walk his fire downstream, hosing down each side of the creek bed in turn.

But the Gods of geology were with them. Ions ago, the receding glaciers left behind large boulders and one of them was nearby and large enough to provide shelter from the chopper's mini-gun.

"Under here, quick!" said Buck, as they scrambled into a large indentation.

"Is this Shelter Rock?" asked Dolly.

"No, the Shelter Rock you're thinking of is farther down when we join with the Cascade Creek Trail."

"Well, if we survive all this, I'm going to name this one Shelter Rock II."

The helicopter continued to strafe the area for another few minutes and then, inexplicably, it flew off downhill and its rotor blades were heard no more.

"What do you suppose they're up to now?" asked Dolly.

"I suspect they are low on ammunition or fuel or both," said Buck. "A Huey's only good for about four hours on a load of fuel and they've been searching around up here a long time. But they'll be back. So, let's shake the water out of our boots, put on dry socks and press on."

"What about the weapons?" asked Dolly.

"Oh yes. Good point. The AK-47 won't need cleaning. That was its only advantage over the M-16. But I'll have to field strip the carbine, give it a few shots of WD-40 and put it back together. Five minutes at most. While I do that, please put two iodine tablets in each of our canteens and fill them from the creek."

"Buck, I know we have to treat the water against giardia, but the iodine will make the water taste funny."

"Actually, I think the iodine makes it taste like scotch."

"Then, you need to start buying a better brand."

"I'll take that as approval to move up to single malt."

"Darling, if we get out of this mess alive, I'll buy you a case of single malt."

CHAPTER THIRTY-EIGHT

Under the cover of darkness, Ruiz and Julio slipped by the ranger station at Monarch Lake and started up the Buchanan Trail. The mission given to them by Raoul was clear. They were to continue up the Buchanan Trail until they intercepted the Madisons and kill them. If possible, the murders were to be made to look as if the Madisons were victims of an avalanche.

Federico gave them a topographic map on which he marked the locations of several scree fields upslope from the Buchanan Trail that might be caused to avalanche. But if an avalanche could not be triggered to cover the bodies, then Ruiz and Julio were to dig graves away from the trail and then cover them with rocks.

In addition to AK-47s and several banana clips of ammunition, Ruiz and Julio were given U.S. Army surplus entrenching tools. Even though cellular phone coverage was known to be spotty in the Indian Peaks Wilderness, Raoul insisted they take a cell phone along. At the earliest opportunity, Raoul wanted Ruiz and Julio to report the termination of the Madisons.

The Buchanan Trail begins its upward course toward the Continental Divide along the north shore of Monarch Lake. Trees and bushes closely flank the trail and numerous small streams cross the trail. In the darkness, even those who know the trail well can't help but get their feet wet or avoid being scratched by the bushes along the trail. Eventually, the atmosphere gets too thin to support trees and the trail is much more open. In places, the trail is just a narrow ledge either just below or just above a scree field.

Buck and Dolly were feeling their way across a narrow ledge that ran across the top of a scree field when Buck gave Dolly a hand signal to halt.

"Look down there," Buck whispered. "It looks like two people carrying flashlights or lanterns are coming up the trail." *Apparently, they never learn,* Buck thought to himself.

In South Vietnam, the North Vietnamese Army and the Viet Cong often used lanterns as they moved along the trails at night. It was a poor practice that made them easy to ambush. But the diet of the NVA and the VC was so poor, in general, and in Vitamin A, in particular, that the NVA and VC were virtually night blind and the lanterns were almost a necessity for them to be able to move at night. In fact, the enemy sometimes resorted to capturing fire flies in thin, screen-wire cages and trying to navigate by the intermittent light provided by dozens of fire flies.

Both Chuck Lee and Buck knew that smoking seriously degraded night vision and, for that reason, neither company commander allowed their troops to smoke after mid-day. In fact, out on patrol, smoking was forbidden lest the enemy pick up the aroma of American cigarettes. By the same token, the NVA and VC were heavy smokers of an extremely poor grade of tobacco that gave off a pungent and distinct odor that frequently gave their presence or positions away. Some GIs developed an uncanny ability to smell the enemy long before they could be sighted. More than once, artillery concentrations were called in on areas from which the smell of enemy cigarette smoke was detected, and sometimes, with devastating effect.

Unlike Raoul, neither Ruiz nor Julio served with the NVA in Vietnam. But both men were heavy smokers and had almost no night vision. Even though Raoul warned them to only use their flashlights for checking their map and then only under the cover of their jackets, Ruiz and Julio got tired of tripping over rocks and being scratched by branches alongside the trail and just said the hell with light discipline.

"I wonder if those two are just innocent hikers or Mexicans sent up here to kill us?" whispered Buck.

"Oh Buck," whispered Dolly, "it would be awful if we brought harm to some innocent people. Isn't there some way we can find out who it is?"

As they watched the lights bobbing up and down on the trail below, Buck got an idea. "While we still have this scree field between us and them, how about I fire a shot that will go over their heads and fall into the valley below. If they shoot back, then we can figure they are from Team PEMEX. If they don't shoot back, we'll have to think of some other way to check them out."

"It's worth a shot," said Dolly. "Buck, I didn't mean that as a pun."

"I know, we're both too tired for puns," said Buck, as he unslung his rifle and rested it on a large boulder. "Here goes."

In the stillness of the night, the shot sounded like a cannon as it echoed from rock face to rock face all along the Indian Peaks. But the silence was totally shredded when a burst of green tracers came up toward them followed by the signature chug-chug sound of an AK-47.

"Most innocent hikers aren't armed with AK-47s shooting CHICOM green tracers," observed Buck. "Let's see if we can get this scree field to help us out."

Recalling a stout log that had fallen across the trail about 100 yards behind them, Buck retreated to find the log. In a few moments, he returned to the large boulder. Placing the log under the boulder, he motioned for Dolly to help him pry the boulder out of its resting-place. It took their combined weight applied to almost the very end of the log, but the boulder began to move. Slowly, as if an object being filmed in slow-motion, the boulder toppled over, left its perch and fell ten feet before it hit the scree field.

Scree splattered in all directions like what happens when a rock is thrown into a pond of water. But then, all the scree surrounding the boulder began to move along with it. Slowly, like a gathering flood, the scree field began to move en masse. At first, the sound was that of a distant freight train. But in seconds the sound of the scree field in motion equaled that of a jet engine being run flat out on a test bed.

Buck and Dolly threw themselves on the ground and held on for dear life. They prayed the thundering collapse below would not set the scree field above them in motion as well. Then, almost as soon as it began, the only sound was the tinkling of smaller rocks finding their way into yet unfilled voids. Finally, there was an eerie total silence and a wall of dust rising up from below that was so thick that it blotted out the stars above them. Buck and Dolly had to take their bandanas and place them over their noses to try to keep the fine particles of dust from entering their lungs.

After half an hour, they could see the trail once again. But just barely. Carefully, they started down the trail and followed it until it disappeared in a ridge of scree. Gingerly, they made their way across just guessing where the trail had been.

Dolly saw it first. "Look Buck," she said, "there's a gun barrel sticking up over there."

Buck saw it and climbed over to it. He touched it with his fingers. The barrel was still warm. Somewhere, underneath the scree, was the person who fired it. They listened intently for the sound of breathing or a cry for help. Nothing.

Careful not to get directly in front of the barrel, Buck gave it a tug. It wouldn't move. Buck surmised, correctly, that the banana clip was under a lot of weight and the AK-47 wasn't going to come out of the scree without bending the banana clip. As much as they would have like to have that AK-47, Buck knew it was not to be without a lot of digging and spending a lot of time they did not have. The AK-47 would serve as a grave marker for at least one, probably two, of Raoul's henchmen. While Dolly held his poncho over his head to block the light, Buck marked the location of the AK-47 on his map. If and when they got in contact with Jonathan Winslow or anyone in authority, they would report the site and just hope no one hurts themselves with the AK-47 before it could be reported and recovered by people who knew something about weapons.

"Buck, what do you think they'll do next?" asked Dolly.

"They won't give up. That's for sure. I suspect their next ambush site will be down at Monarch Lake. They've already missed their best chances of nailing us because, once we get near the lake, the trail splits giving us two ways around the lake. I fear for the couple at the ranger station. And, you can bet they either have the telephone at the ranger station covered or destroyed. So, I think our best bet is to try for the phones farther down hill at the campgrounds or somehow get home and call Jonathan from there."

"Tomorrow is Labor Day," said Dolly. "Jonathan told me that President Trimmer leaves the day after. If they are after Trimmer, then it stands to reason that whatever they are planning will take place on Labor Day."

"That means, my dear Dolly, that we must push on downhill tonight and through the wee hours of Labor Day morning if we are to help resolve this crisis or whatever the hell mess we've literally stumbled into."

"Buck, my feet and my back are killing me. Do you think we can actually keep going that long?"

"Gravity, Dolly. We have gravity and the Lord on our side. It's all downhill from here."

"The Lord? Do you think the Lord wants us to save Jim Bob Trimmer?"

"That's not for we mortals to say, Dolly. But He sure as hell wants us to save Jonathan and a lot of innocent folks who may just be standing around when whatever the bad guys have planned happens."

They drank some water from their canteens, adjusted their packs and warily worked their way down the Buchanan Trail toward the shallow end of Monarch Lake.

In a few hours, it would be the beginning of Labor Day.

CHAPTER THIRTY-NINE

Raoul announced the final briefing would be held in the ranch house beginning at 0001 hours on Labor Day. Everyone who wasn't looking for the Madisons or already positioned at their target locations was present.

Their numbers were fewer now. The lower-ranking team members were sent out the day before to make their way to Canada to board a Cuban ship in Vancouver Harbor. Raoul and Federico, of course, remained. But Regina and Pancho were not present for the final briefing. Regina and Lou Leclerc were shacked up in a motel in Winter Park. Pancho was sleeping outside the motel in a pickup fitted with retractable railroad wheels.

Francisco and Miguel of Team Adams were not present because they were in a fishing boat at the east end of Grand Lake with a gringo who liked to drink and fish. By now, the gringo was probably dead from a combination of alcohol and a shot in the face with the DSMO/GHB aerosol spray. Later, the gringo's body and incriminating drawings would be found inside the entrance of the Adams Tunnel.

Felipe of Team Pump was present; however, his partner, Antonio, was already hidden on the bottom floor of the Lake Granby Pump Plant. That left only Salvador to secure the entrance to the PEMEX compound.

Jose sat next to the door while he fiddled with his calculator. Because he would have to lift himself and his remaining teammates and their baggage at 0800 hours the next day, Jose was worried. If the morning were typically cool, density-altitude would not be a problem. But, if the departure were to be delayed into the heat of the day, the flight must be cancelled or someone would have to be left behind. He considered off-loading some fuel, but then he would not have the range to reach the refueling bladder hidden in the New Mexican desert.

For his part, Raoul felt badly about the loss of so many of his men. Manuel, Jose's former door gunner was dead and buried deep down in the far recesses of the Koch Ranch. As for Ruiz and Julio, Raoul assumed they were killed by the Madisons. If so, Raoul hoped those two security men were buried somewhere under a huge avalanche and never found. Other than wish that Ruiz and Julio were alive and would make it back in time for the exfiltration, there was nothing he could do about them.

As far as Raoul could tell, the Madison were armed with some kind of survival rifle they must have been carrying in their aircraft and with the AK-47 that once belonged to Manuel. Just how much ammunition they had was unknown. But Raoul suspected they didn't have a lot of ammunition.

But, in a way, Raoul was hoping the Madisons were able to recover all of the AK-47s and take them with them. That way, if the bodies of Ruiz and Julio were ever found they would appear to be innocent, unfortu-nate hikers who were caught in a landslide. Once the Madisons were caught, his men would take their weapons and make the Madisons and all the weapons and ammunition disappear for good.

Raoul felt confident the Madisons would be caught. After all, they must have suffered a great deal of hardship in the preceding 48 hours. She was 50 and he was at least 60. Living exposed in the wilderness must be taking its toll on them both physically and mentally.

Ramon and Sancho were much younger and in fighting trim. Plus, his men had the advantage of knowing the Madisons must come through a narrow corridor to reach help. If his men had not killed them already, the odds were in his favor that sometime between the final briefing and H Hour that the Madisons would be dead, weighted down and dropped into the deep, cold depths of Lake Granby.

The driver of a D-7 bulldozer would dig a deep pit into which the survey vehicles would be dumped and then covered over with dirt. Every piece of equipment, to include the expensive seismic instruments had been removed from the vehicles, placed on a rented fishing boat and dumped into the Sea of Cortez. If and when All of the PEMEX survey vehicles were back in Mexico in a remote coastal region far from prying eyes. the vehicles were uncovered, there would be nothing to connect them with Team PEMEX. Other than the attack personnel themselves, the only vehicles left at the Koch Ranch, were the rent-a-wreck pickups which, by pre-arrangement with the rental company, would be left at the Koch Ranch for retrieval after Labor Day.

Raoul and his crew made no secret of their impending departure. On the 1st of September the team members starting saying goodbye to the people who had been kind to them during their stay. They handed out their bogus Mexican home addresses, urged their American friends to write and to come see them sometime in Mexico. A number of Grand County residents were making plans to visit their newly-acquired Mexican friends when the ice and snow of winter became too much to bear. The compound was combed time and time again to make sure no compromising documents or evidence were left behind. All of the explosives were either expended on the job or had been hauled away by Chuck Lee. The detailed maps and charts in which Federico and Regina took such pride were gone. For his final briefing, Raoul was reduced to using a grammar-school chalkboard. A bottle of strong solvent and some rags sat on a nearby table for Federico to use to clean the final briefing notes from the chalkboard. After the briefing, the chalkboard would be burned.

At the first minute of Labor Day, everyone but Raoul and those who were either excused or unaccounted for were assembled in the living room of the ranch house. Raoul was outside making sure the lone security guard understood his duties. Satisfied, Raoul entered the ranch house.

"Well, amigos, this is it," Raoul began. "Soon our mission will be accomplished and we will be on our way home. I will begin this briefing with an overview and then I will ask each team leader to give us a back-briefing on how each target is to be attacked. "I shall begin with our exfiltration plan and work backward. H-Hour is set for 0700 hours this morning. Precisely, at H-Hour, I expect Teams Adams, Moffat, Pump and our gringo friends at The Grand Ditch to have done their work. I will be able to see and hear the work of Teams Pump and Ditch. From teams Adams and Moffat, I will require a cellular phone call confirming their successes.

"When I am assured the other attacks have gone off as planned, I will set in motion a device to destroy the Lake Granby High Dam. On call, Jose will bring the helicopter over to Sunset Point to pick me up and bring me back here. I insist that all team members be back here at the Koch Ranch no later than 0745 so Jose can fly us out of here at 0800 hours to New Mexico and then to Mexico. Anyone not back here by 0800 hours will be left behind. This order applies to everyone, including myself.

"Now, Federico, let's review the plan for the destruction of The Grand Ditch," said Raoul.

"Thank you, Jefe. This will only take a few moments because I feel confident that Senor Chuck Lee and Senor Roberto Chavez have that mission well in hand. We monitored them yesterday as they climbed above The Grand Ditch to attach their bags of explosives to the scree field. Of course, they know nothing of the other attacks we plan. So far, we have no indication that Senor Lou Leclerc has told Senor Chuck about the 'little prank,' as he calls it, that he and Regina plan to play on the water pipe in the Moffat Tunnel.

Senor Chuck and Senor Roberto think that stopping the theft of the water from the Never Summer Range will be of great benefit to their friends and neighbors, not to mention the wildlife of the Kawuneechee Valley.

And, their vanity is such that they are eager to leave their indelible mark on a mountain range that they hope will be seen for dozens of kilometers.

"Regrettably, they won't live to see their handiwork because the same radio transmitters they will use to make The Grand Ditch of no further use, will also trigger the explosives I hid under Senor Chuck's pickup.

"I might add, amigos, that as we fly away from here, we will be able to look back to the north and see their handiwork. If my calculations are correct, the original scar The Grand Ditch made across the Never Summer Range will be expanded and extended so that it will appear to be the gray-white beard of a giant St. Nicholas hanging down so far that it almost touches the bottom of the Kawuneechee Valley.

"An excellent briefing so far, Federico," said Raoul. "Now, in the absence of Regina, please tell us about the attack on the Moffat Tunnel."

"With the exception of The Grand Ditch, the destruction of the Moffat Tunnel is the only other target where we are actually using the *active* help of a local gringo. I stress the word active because in the case of Team Adams, that gringo is probably already dead. But at the Moffat Tunnel we plan on having the active help of Louis Leclerc, the former Air America pilot.

"Senor Leclerc met Regina at Kings Crossing in Winter Park yesterday evening. They are, as the gringos say "shacked up" in a local motel. Regina has two pickups prepositioned at the condo. The pickup containing the explosives is fitted with retractable railroad wheels and will be used by Senor Leclerc to transport the explosives into the Moffat Tunnel. The other rental pickup will be used by Regina and Pancho for their return here for the helicopter flight to Mexico.

"Regina, who hacked into the railroad's scheduling system, assures me no trains are scheduled to be transiting the Moffat Tunnel for an hour prior to and for an hour subsequent to the time of the attack. This lack of train activity is due, in no small measure, to the fact that the

American labor movement takes Labor Day very seriously and train traffic, nation-wide, is severely curtailed.

"I will not belabor you with all the details of what we have planned for Senor Leclerc. Suffice it to say that Senor Leclerc thinks he will simply place his explosive charges next to the water bore inside the Moffat Tunnel, set the timer, exit the tunnel and rejoin Regina in their motel room. Reality will be far different from what he expects," said Federico.

"But what if Senor Leclerc gets cold feet at the last minute?" posed Raoul. "How will Regina and Pancho deal with that?"

"Regina will not let that happen. She assures me that she has Senor Leclerc completely under her spell. She and Pancho will have him driving into the Moffat Tunnel on schedule."

"We can't have any screw ups," insisted Raoul. "What if he changes his mind?"

"It is of no consequence," said Federico. "If that happens, Regina will spray him with the lethal aerosol." Regina and Pancho will place him in the pickup and drive him in the pickup up to Refuge 11. They know where to place the explosives. They will leave Senor Leclerc's body at Refuge 11, set the timer to allow time for them to back the pickup down to the West Portal where they will set off the explosives that will close the West Portal. That puts the entire plan back on track, if you don't mind a little pun. The explosions at Refuge 11 will go off on schedule and the water will do the rest.

"Again, Senor Leclerc's body will be the signature. With or without Senor Leclerc's active help, the end result is the same," concluded Federico.

"Excellent," said Raoul. "Because Francisco and Miguel of Team Adams are currently in place at the east end of Grand Lake, I will also ask Federico to tell us about the work of Team Adams".

"Thank you, Raoul," said Federico." "The work of Team Adams is almost as simple as that of Team Ditch.

At 0615 hours, they load the body of their gringo fishing companion into a rental pickup and drive up to the steel doors guarding the West

Portal of the Adams Tunnel. Although the lock on the door is protected by a metal guard designed to prevent the lock being cut by a bolt cutter, they have a needle-nosed bolt-cutter which can reach in and allow them to cut the lock.

"Once inside, they remove one of the metal grates over the channel where the water rushes in from Grand Lake into the water tunnel. They take the water-proof bag of explosives from the pickup, set the timer and drop the bag into the rushing waters at 0630 hours. It takes the water approximately two and one-half hours to make the journey from Grand Lake to Estes Park. We want to rupture the water pipe approximately halfway down its length. So, the timer will be set to go off in 75 minutes or at 0745 hours. By the time the explosives go off half-way down the Adams Tunnel, Franciso and Miguel will be here prepared to board the Huey for Mexico," said Federico.

"Now, it is time to hear about the attack on the Lake Granby Pump Plant," said Raoul. "Felipe tell us again what you have planned."

"At first," began Felipe, "we thought it would be possible to recruit locals to conduct this attack. In fact, we thought about trying to recruit Chuck Lee and his amigo, Roberto Chavez, to do the job. Although both men expressed enthusiasm for the destruction of the pump plant and, indeed, all the water-diversion projects, we decided Lee and Chavez would not, in the end, carry out such an attack. For that reason, Senor Chuck and Senor Roberto were not actually approached. We did, however, gain a great deal of information from Senor Lee about the internal staffing and operation of the Pump Plant, primarily because his former brother-in-law is the plant's night watchman.

"Indeed, we gained so much information from Chuck Lee and through our own personal reconnaissance of the plant, that we have formulated a plan that we can carry out without the help of Chuck Lee or Roberto Chavez or any of the gringos.

"Well, that is not exactly correct because Lloyd Garvey, Chuck Lee's former brother-in-law, will be killed and implicated in the attack which will be conducted as follows:

"My colleague, Antonio, is already inside the pump plant. He and I joined the last tour group on yesterday afternoon. Just as our tour group was about to board the elevator to leave the lowest floor of the pump plant, we staged a diversion that allowed Antonio to depart the tour group unseen and to hide himself for the night.

"At 0600 hours, I will appear at the front door of the pump plant and ring the bell. This will bring the night watchman, Senor Lloyd Garvey, to the door. I will be wearing a moulage kit that simulates a bloody wound and I'll be appealing for help. When he opens the door, I will spray him with just enough of the aerosol to render him unconscious. I will put Senor Garvey's body on the elevator, taking a moment to place incriminating documents inside his pockets.

"Next, I will take Senor Garvey's body down to the next level which is below the level of the lake. I push his body off the elevator and proceed all the way down to the bottom and pick up Antonio who will have completed his work with the drive shafts of the three electric motors," said Felipe.

"Go over what Antonio is doing, por favor," said Raoul.

"At 0300 hours this morning, Antonio will begin the process of wrapping Det cord around the drive shafts of each of the three electric motors. Having done that, Antonio will take the huge wrenches which are so conveniently placed adjacent to each of the impeller housings and remove their retaining nuts.

"He then sets the timer to explode the Det cord which will snap the three drive shafts at 0700 hours. When those drive shafts are gone, there will be insufficient pressure on the impeller housings to hold them in place. The enormous pressure of the lake water will force the impellers up out of their housings allowing water to flood the entire structure. On its way to reaching the lake level, the water will rise above the floor where I placed the Senor Lloyd Garvey. Hopefully, he will still be breathing when he is covered over by the rising waters and he will appear to have drowned.

"But before the explosion takes place, we return to the first floor and the control room where we make sure the butterfly valves on the uphill side of the impeller housings are closed. Then, we check to see that all the butterfly valves on the lake side of the impeller housings are open.

"All that remains is to exit the building and return here," said Felipe.

"From the elevator building at the dam," said Raoul, "I will be able to see the explosions at both the pump plant and on The Grand Ditch. With those indicators, plus confirming cellular phone calls from the Adams Tunnel and the Moffat Tunnel, they will be my signals to turn on the switch that starts the timer in motion. I will have five minutes to jog to the end of the dam where Jose will pick me up.

"Well, I think that finishes our final briefing. I wish each of you good luck and I remind you to be back here no later than 0745 this morning for the first leg of our trip home." concluded Raoul.

CHAPTER FORTY

In the wee hours of Labor Day morning, Roberto and Chuck, both dressed for a day of fishing, met at Chuck's place.

"Ready?" asked Roberto.

"Ready as I'll ever be," said Chuck. "But I had a thought. What if my old pickup craps out on us and we can't make our little, sneaky drive back out of the Park to get to our boat? We'd be FUBARed for sure. So, how 'bout we also take your pickup?"

"Okay by me," said Roberto, and they drove off toward the Never Summer Ranch parking lot in two vehicles. About a mile before the entrance gate to Rocky Mountain National Park, they turned off their headlights and took the hidden road around the entrance gate.

When they reached the parking lot, Chuck said: "Let's not park right beside each other. Let's spread out so we don't attract the attention of some park ranger looking to ticket a bunch of kids for having a party. We'll leave my truck down at this end of the lot and we'll drive your truck to the far end. I've got the transmitters in my fishing vest."

With that, Chuck got out of his pickup and got into Roberto's. They drove to the other end of the parking lot where they would have an unobstructed view of the Grand Ditch.

It was now 0630 and the sun was just up. They checked their Rolexes. Both men had Rolex watches from their days in Special Forces. Among the Special Forces there was a saying that you couldn't truly be in

Special Forces unless you had three things: a Randall knife, a Rolex watch and a divorce. Chuck had all three. But Roberto somehow managed to keep his Rolex, his Randall knife and his family.

Chuck pulled a pair of binoculars from his fishing vest and scanned The Grand Ditch just below the scree field. He wanted to make sure there were no hikers up on that section of The Grand Ditch. He couldn't see anyone. (See: *www.thegrandconspiracy.com*)

At 0655, Chuck handed Roberto two of the radio transmitter units and Chuck kept two. They stepped out of the pickup and aimed the transmitters up toward The Grand Ditch. At 0659 hours, Chuck began a countdown. When he came to the end of the countdown, Chuck quietly invoked the ritual: fire-in-the hole, fire-in-the-hole, fire-in-the-hole.

But before Chuck Lee gave the command to fire, added:

"Here's to you, Great-grandmother Lee." Then, he commanded: "Fire!"

The blast erupting from Chuck's pickup blew him sideways and up onto the hood of Roberto's truck. Roberto, who was standing on the driver's side, wasn't affected, other than a ringing in his ears.

"Chuck! Are you okay?" called Roberto, reaching for his friend.

"Yeah, I'm okay," said Chuck as he slid down off the hood and checked his body for shrapnel wounds.

"Some sonofabitch booby-trapped my pickup."

"Jesus, Chuck. Who'd do such a thing?"

"Raoul and Federico. They were the only ones I told about this dumb stunt."

At that moment, the sound of the explosions above The Grand Ditch reached the parking lot. The two men looked up to watch the avalanche that had been descending while they were talking about Raoul and Federico. They saw the falling rock sheer off a mile-long stretch of The Grand Ditch. When the dust settled, the result was just as Chuck predicted: the avalanche not only took off a portion of The Grand Ditch, it also denuded the slope below. (See: *www.thegrandconspiracy.com*)

Awed by what they had done, it took a few moments for Chuck to get his brain back in gear. Let's get the hell outta here," said Chuck.

"What about your truck?"

"Shit. There's nothing left of it."

"But I'll bet there's enough pieces that the FBI will figure out it was yours," said Roberto.

"Damn it. You're right. I'm in deep Kimchi," said Chuck.

"But just think. If we hadn't taken two trucks or even if we had taken two trucks and decided to sit in yours, we'd be dead," said Roberto.

"That's why if we can catch up with Raoul, I'm gonna kill him. And, Federico, too!" said Chuck.

"Is that where we're going next?"

"No. We're going to get in our fishing boat and motor across the lake to see Buck and Dolly."

"At this hour?"

"Hell, yes. We're in big trouble. Our little prank has gone fucking-awry and Buck's the only one I can trust to get us out of this mess."

CHAPTER FORTY-ONE

Killing the Madisons was proving to be more difficult than Raoul and Federico could ever have imagined. One of Jose's door gunners was dead and secretly buried on the Koch Ranch. Jose had to repair a bullet puncture in his main fuel tank. Ruiz and Julio were dispatched up the Buchanan Trail to intercept the Madisons and were never heard from again.

"If we have to commit any more men to killing the Madisons," said Federico, "I'm worried about being able to attack all our targets and still maintain security here at the compound."

"We've got Ramon and Sancho waiting in ambush at Monarch Lake," said Raoul. "And, we've got Jorge and Ernesto occupying the Madison's house. If, by some trick of the devil, the Madison's get by Ramon and

Sancho and get home, Jorge and Ernesto have orders to capture them and then call you for instructions.

Surely, the Madisons can't elude all four of them."

"But what if the Madisons aren't killed by our men? What if they go directly to the dam or, Dios forbid, somehow reach Camp Hope? Or, what if they have split up? What if he goes to one place and she goes another?" asked Federico.

"Federico, we must not let the Madisons cause us to lose our focus on our mission. We still have enough men to take out the two tunnels and the pump plant. We've made it possible for Chuck Lee and Roberto

Chavez to blow up the Grand Ditch and we still have Salvador left over to maintain security here at the compound. We'll be just fine."

"And, let's not forget Regina, Jefe. She and Pancho are responsible for getting Lou Leclerc to drive the explosives into the Moffat Tunnel."

"I guess I just don't like to think about what Regina has to do to control Lou Leclerc and so I've put her out of my mind."

"Regina has used her body in the service of our revolution before, Jefe. Surely, you know she puts her love for you and her devotion to our glorious cause before her personal desires?"

"Si, Federico. But I still don't like it. Anyway, let us get back to work," said Raoul.

"Jefe, I told Ramon and Sancho it is essential for them to gain control over all the telephones at the Monarch Lake ranger station, at the campground and at the little trading post. That way, if the Madisons do manage to escape, the closest telephone is back at the Madison's house and that's another ten miles away."

"But what if there are signal strength monitors on the telephone lines? asked Raoul.

"That's why I told them to just take the microphones out of the handsets. If they are careful, the line strength won't be affected."

"What if Ramon and Sancho have to kill some people at Monarch Lake? Won't that point the finger at us instead of the local rebels?"

"Hopefully, Jefe, it won't come to that; however, if anyone must die, I suspect it will have to be the old couple that sleeps in their recreational vehicle at the ranger station. According to the map here, that RV is located right where Ramon and Sancho need to set up if they are to ambush the Madisons."

"All right, Federico, but let's say Ramon and Sancho have to kill the old couple. How do they cover that?"

"I told them to make it look like a robbery. The Madisons, however, are another matter. If and when, they are caught and killed we cannot afford for their bodies to be found."

"How do they manage that?"

"The water at the bottom of Lake Granby stays so cold year-round that drowning victims almost never surface. When I dispatched Ramon and Sancho, I made them take several bags of heavy chain and some cinder blocks. If they follow my instructions, the Madisons will never be found.

"Jose knows where their aircraft crashed and even he can't find it. Obviously, it melted into the glacier and has been covered up by snow. If the aircraft happens to be found someday, the authorities will have to assume the Madisons wandered off and fell into a crevasse," said Federico.

"But what about the radio call Jose made to the FAA giving the Madison's call sign and saying that they had the Granby Airport in sight?" asked Raoul.

"The FAA only keeps those kinds of tapes for a few days. I wager they have already been erased. Given what is about to happen on Labor Day, I doubt that anyone will be thinking about the Madisons. It will be assumed that they were drowned along with Presidents Trimmer and Popov," said Federico.

"Federico, when I chose you to be my second-in-command, I chose well. I would trust my life to you."

"Gracias, Jefe. You are very kind. But you are the one who is leading us to a great victory over the Americanos. When this mission is over, I'm sure you will get your reward."

It was already dark when Ramon and Sancho stopped at the Arapaho Trading Post down below Monarch Lake. The proprietor was closing up for the day when Ramon and Sancho entered the old log building. They asked the proprietor where they could find a telephone. He told them that there were two pay telephones at the entrance to the campground across the road. He did not offer the use of his phone even though it was sitting on the counter in plain sight.

"I see you sell night crawlers here. Could we buy some?" asked Ramon.

When the proprietor shuffled off into the back room to get the night crawlers from his icebox, Ramon stood between the doorway and the counter while Sancho unscrewed the telephone mouth piece, removed the microphone and put the handset back together. Unless the man tried to call out or someone called in, he wouldn't notice. They asked if there as a phone up at the Monarch Lake ranger station. They learned the old couple staffing the ranger station had two telephones: one in the ranger station plus an extension phone in the large RV where they slept at night. "By the way, you fellas can't use them night crawlers in Monarch Lake. Can't use nothing but artificial lures up there."

"Yes, that's right," responded Ramon. "We're just using them in Lake Granby."

In addition to the night crawlers, Ramon bought a pack of Camels and the pair took leave of the trading post. Once back in their pickup, they discussed killing the proprietor but decided that was an option they could leave open for the moment. They drove across the road into the campground and found both pay phones. Quickly, the handset microphones were removed. If any campers tried to use the phones, they would find them dead and just give up for the night. Once the Madisons were caught, they planned to come back and replace the stolen microphones.

They drove up the narrow, dirt road to Monarch Lake. After leaving their pickup in the parking lot, they walked up the trail to the darkened, log cabin that served as the ranger station. The lock on the screen door was a joke. Ramon took out his multi-purpose tool and removed the screws that held the hasp. Sancho found the telephone, made sure he did not lift the handset off the cradle as he deftly removed the microphone. Ramon screwed the hasp back in place and they set off in search of the RV. They found it only 100 feet up the Buchanan Trail on the north shore of the lake. The lights were still on inside the RV indicating the ranger and his wife were still awake, probably reading.

This posed a problem for Ramon and Sancho. To proceed up the Buchanan Trail to set up their ambush, they would have to walk right by the RV. Even if they could slip by the old couple, a shootout or a fight with the Madisons would be sure to wake them. Just outside the RV, they found a telephone pedestal.

Lying exposed on the ground was a telephone cable running from the pedestal into a connector on the side of the RV. They considered simply disconnecting the cable. But concern about setting off a signal-strength monitor nixed that idea. The old couple would have to go. Thinking there was always the chance that either the ranger or his wife or both of them would step outside the RV and be easier to attack, Ramon and Sancho decided to wait just outside the RV for awhile before making their assault.

Hiding behind some Yew bushes just outside the RV, they listened to the night sounds of the forest and the lake while a hoard of mosquitoes assaulted their exposed faces, arms and hands—a fact that began to hasten the time when Ramon and Sancho would begin their own attack.

One would not expect to find a man-made lake sitting out in the Indian Peaks wilderness. But, in 1904, the Monarch Consolidated Gold and Copper Mining and Smelting Company placed an earthen dam across the narrow valley where Arapaho and Buchanan Creeks run together. The result was a mile-long lake they called: Monarch Lake.

The company never found much gold or copper but they did find plenty of logs up on the steep slopes flanking the lake. They brought in wood-fired donkey engines to turn huge drums of cables that pulled the logs down into the lake. A stern-wheeler steamboat then pushed the logs into neat log booms. The logs were then pflumed down Arapaho Creek to a factory that made wooden boxes for grocery stores. In the days before brown-paper bags and plastic bags, groceries were carried or delivered in wooden boxes. The demand for these boxes was so great the Rocky Mountain Railway Company was formed for the sole purpose of transporting the grocery boxes down to the railhead at Granby. At only 16 miles in length, it was one of the world's shortest rail lines.

But the advent of the brown-paper bag killed off the grocery box industry. For a time, the railroad was used to transport tourists between Granby and Monarch Lake. But when a road was build somewhat along the same route, the railroad was abandoned. Eventually, Monarch Lake and its environs became part of the Arapaho National Forest. Today, a hike along the banks of what is now a pristine mountain lake makes for a most enjoyable adventure. Hikers have a choice of two trails. Arapaho Pass Trail crosses the lake's earthen dam, then proceeds across a small bridge that arches above the dam's concrete spillway, skirts the south edge of the lake and begins its steep ascent toward the Continental Divide. The Buchanan Pass Trail runs from the ranger station along the north side of Monarch Lake. After leaving the lake, the Buchanan Trail turns sharply uphill and, eventually, leads to the Continental Divide at the Buchanan Pass.

Two hours before midnight, Ramon and Sancho could no longer endure the assault of what seemed like a million mosquitoes. Quietly, they threaded noise suppressors to the barrels of their .22 caliber, Browning semi-automatic pistols.

"Help! Help, I'm hurt!" called Ramon as he pounded on the screen door of the RV. When the ranger opened the inside door, Ramon shot right through the screen hitting the ranger between the eyes. Stepping inside and over the dying ranger, Ramon burst into the tiny bedroom and shot the ranger's wife through the heart as she was reaching for the telephone. To make sure no one could come along and use the phone, Ramon removed its microphone as well. As ordered by Federico, they ransacked the RV, took the dead ranger's wallet and filled their pockets with what few valuables they could find. The most valuable articles, to Ramon and Sancho anyway, were two cans of insect repellant which they immediately emptied on their exposed skin.

After closing up the RV, Ramon remained by the north end of the dam while he sent Sancho up the Buchanan Trail to act as a listening post. An hour later, Sancho returned.

"Why did you come back?" asked Ramon. "I sent you up there to listen for the Madisons."

"Si, but I found another way around the lake. There's a connecting trail between the Buchanan Trail and the Arapaho Creek Trail. When the Madisons come to the upper end of this lake, they could take the other trail and come down the south side of this lake. Or, they could split up. But I doubt they would ever do that."

"That means we will have to split up," said Ramon. "I'll stay here on the Buchanan Trail. I want you to cross over the dam and go up the Arapaho Creek Trail a short distances, find a good ambush site and set up."

"How will we communicate?"

"Let's try our cellular phones."

The attempt to communicate by cell phone failed because there is no cellular service reaching up into the steep valley that formed Monarch Lake.

"Now what?" asked Sancho.

"Then, we each stay in our ambush sites until first light. If they haven't fallen into our traps by then, you come back over here. Understand?"

"Si, Ramon."

"And, don't fall asleep, Sancho."

"No chance of that, amigo, the mosquitoes won't let us.

Every mile or so, Buck would use his GPS to check their position. Already they had passed the point where Buchanan Creek and Cascade Creek merge. When they came to where Hell's Canyon Creek intercepted the Buchanan Pass Trail, they took a break.

"Where do you figure they'll put the next ambush?" asked Dolly.

"That's all I've been thinking about," said Buck. "Seems to me they might be getting a bit short-handed. We know I hit one of them when the chopper came back and attacked us on the glacier and we have his AK-47 with us.

"We know at least one of their men is buried back up in that avalanche. Maybe two, because they seem to operate in pairs. I suppose I'd conserve my forces and concentrate them at the point where the enemy is likely to attack."

"Oh Buck, you sound like you're giving a lecture back at the Infantry School."

"Dolly, the Principles of War are always in effect. I'm betting those PEMEX troops apply the principles of Objective and Mass whether they learned them in school or not.

"To cut to the chase, and the pun is intended, they will be waiting for us at the ranger station and on the south side of the lake near the dam as well."

"So what do we do?" asked Dolly.

"Let's apply a little General George S. Patton strategy."

"What's that?"

"By-pass and haul ass."

"Buck, watch your mouth."

"Seriously, Dolly, we go where they ain't."

"And, just how do we do that?"

"The east end of the lake is a marshy bog. It's nothing but reeds and more reeds. Just like the mother of Moses, we will build rafts made of reeds. Only we don't ride on top of them. We use the reeds to hide us as we float right down the middle of the lake in the dark and let the current carry us right over the dam and down the stream leading into Lake Granby."

"Buck, do you realize just how cold the water will be?"

"Take your choice. A firefight against probably uneven odds or a cold trip across Monarch Lake wearing a reed bonnet?"

"I'll take the bonnet."

A half-hour later, they came to the marshy end of Monarch Lake. Using his hunting knife to cut the reeds, they bound dry reeds into bundles with the parachute cord. When they had enough bundles, Buck tied them together in rows until they resembled rafts. When the rafts were completed, they placed their rucksacks and weapons on top of the rafts and secured them with parachute cord.

Grimly, they led their rafts out into the cold waters of the lake. The rafts supplied just the buoyancy and concealment they needed. The current was strong enough to carry them slowly toward the dam at the far end of the lake, but they still kept their feet moving quietly underwater in an effort to keep warm.

After about an hour of body-numbing cold, Dolly whispered, "Buck, I hear water rushing."

"Good, that means we're coming to where the lake becomes Arapaho Creek again."

"Oh my gosh. We're going to be shot over the spillway."

"That's exactly what we want to happen. It's only a seven-foot drop. Try not to scream when you go over the spillway."

Just as they joined hands, they were caught in the powerful tow of the water rushing over the small spillway.

Over they went and down into the catch basin hollowed out by years and years of falling water. They held onto each other as the current carried them about 100 yards below the dam at which point the water became too shallow and they were beached on some very hard rocks. The drop over the spillway was too much for their flimsy reed rafts and both rafts broke apart dumping their rucksacks and their weapons into the catch basin below the dam.

"Now what?" asked Dolly. "Should we try to recover our weapons?"

"I wish we could," said Buck, "but I don't think either of us have the strength to dive that deep and find them. Let's just get out of here and find a telephone."

After a brief rest on a nearby log, they began to hike along the side of the creek that would lead them down to Lake Granby and to the road toward home and, maybe, to a telephone or someone who would help them.

It was almost Beginning Morning Nautical Twilight. Ramon was beginning to make out the outline of the south shoreline. So far, the Madisons must not of come down the south shore trail by the dam. Or, maybe they did already and, somehow, managed to silence Sancho. Between his imagination and growing impatience, Ramon decided he wanted Sancho back at his side. Walking to a position halfway between the ranger station and the dam, Ramon called out across the water to Sancho.

"Sancho, come back over here!"

For his part, Sancho welcomed the summons to leave his lonely post. Slinging his AK-47 over his shoulder, Sancho was jogging back over the dam when something in the water caused him to stop.

"Ramon, come here!" he called.

Ramon came out of the shadows of the ranger station and started jogging toward the dam. When he reached the dam, Sancho said: "Look. Those clumps of reeds. They don't look right."

Sancho fumbled around in the flotsam and jetsam piled up at the edges of the dam until he found a piece of Lodge Pole Pine about 12-feet long. Reaching out with the stick, Sancho was able to hook one of the clumps of reeds.

Ramon illuminated the reeds with his flashlight. The reeds were tied together with short pieces of nylon parachute suspension line.

"Madre de Dios!" cursed Ramon. "They've gotten by us. Run for the truck!"

Even though the sky was beginning to lighten just a bit in the east so they could see better, Buck and Dolly were having a hard time walking along the edge of Arapaho Creek. There really was no trail. Just bushes and brambles that cut their skin and hidden branches that tripped them every few paces. But the creek was getting wider and deeper. They knew it would not be long before they would reach the point where Arapaho Creek opens out into Lake Granby's Arapaho Bay.

The tree line was receding back from the watercourse and between the trees and the water a small sandy beach was beginning to open up. They ran along the sand desperate to get under the cover of the bridge that crosses Arapaho Creek at the point that it empties out into Arapaho Bay.

When they could begin to see the outline of the bridge downstream, they saw something even better. Two jet skis were sitting on the creek bank. A brightly-colored hex tent was pitched about fifty feet from the water's edge. Rather than take the chance that some of Raoul's men might be hiding in the tent, they decided to avoid the tent and go directly to the jet skis.

There was just enough light to search the jet skis for the required deadman keys. They found the key lanyards tucked neatly inside vinyl pouches on the side of the seats. Together, they quietly pulled each jet ski into the water. Then, putting the lanyards around their necks, they inserted the keys, turned them to the 'on' position, nodded to each other, and hit the starter buttons.

Instantly, the jet-ski engines sprang to life. Buck and Dolly did not dally. With both engines wide open, they bolted out into the channel and shot underneath the bridge into Arapaho Bay going flat-out for the Lake Granby High Dam. A half-naked man stuck his head out of the hex tent and cursed as the jet skis disappeared from sight.

Ramon and Sancho raced their pickup down the road from Monarch Lake toward the campgrounds at Arapaho Bay. Just as they were about to ask an early morning fisherman if he had seen a man and a woman hiking along the shore, two jet skis squirted out from under the bridge and into Arapaho Bay.

"There they are!" cried Sancho.

The fisherman turned to watch the jet skiers flash by. Picking an oar out of the fisherman's runabout, Ramon clubbed him over the head. Quickly, Ramon and Sancho picked up the fisherman and threw his body into the runabout. Then, they pushed the runabout out into the water, jumped in, hit the starter button and took off full-bore in pursuit of the two jet skiers.

Looking back, Buck saw a runabout throwing up a rooster tail of spray. A burst of AK-47 fire kicked up the water between the two jet skis.

"Spread apart," called Buck as he maneuvered his jet ski away from Dolly's. That drew two more bursts of fire, first at Buck, then at Dolly.

"Criss-cross," ordered Buck. Just like the expert skiers do on untracked powder in the Warren Miller ski movies, Buck and Dolly put together some figure 8s that frustrated Sancho's aim so much that he quit shooting.

But the runabout had a powerful engine and it was slowly beginning to narrow the gap between it and the two jet skis. Wisely, Sancho decided to hold his fire, to save his ammunition until he could get close enough for sure kills. Suddenly, Sancho remembered the fisherman.

"What about this hombre?" asked Sancho.

"Throw him overboard," said Ramon. "That way, we can go faster."

Buck looked backward in time to see a body being thrown from the runabout and then he saw Sancho preparing to bring his AK-47 to bear on them once again.

"We've gonna split up!" yelled Buck. "You head for the house. Call Jonathan! Call the Sheriff! Then, come to the Granby Dam!"

"But what about the boat? They'll catch us!"

"No, they won't. Head for the gap that splits Deer Island. Get in line and follow me through!"

The sight of the two jet skis moving into trail as they shot between what looked like two tiny islands was too great a temptation for Sancho. Long range or not, enfilade fire is the machine gunner's dream.

With his AK-47 on full automatic, Sancho stood up and leaned over the windshield. He was about to stitch Dolly and Buck right up their backs with his assault rifle when the runabout hit ground. Sancho went flying forward, tumbled onto the water's surface and broke his neck. The steering column drove itself into Ramon's chest. Its keel broken, the runabout rolled upside-down, spilling Ramon into the water. Only its foam flotation compartments kept the runabout from sinking completely into the chilly waters of Lake Granby.

As the two jet skis emerged on the west side of Deer Island, the casual observer would just think they were two carefree jet skiers having a ripping good time shredding the morning calm with their personal water craft. Dolly made a graceful arc in the water as she turned to the southeast and toward home. Buck headed directly toward the dam. But, after a moment, he decided it would be better to run the jet ski ashore where he could not be observed from the dam. Cutting the power, he let the jet ski's momentum carry him silently to a tiny bit of beach just southeast of the dam.

CHAPTER FORTY-TWO

In the wee hours of the morning on Labor Day, Regina awakened Lou Leclerc from a sleep that Chuck Lee, using the ultra-precise terminology of the Army barracks, would describe as "pussy-whipped." A combination of lovemaking and too much alcohol put Leclerc in bed about midnight. Since that time, Regina and Pancho had been loading the explosives on the pickup that Lou would drive, on railroad wheels, into the Moffat Tunnel. Regina rubbed Lou's face with a cold washcloth and handed him a steaming cup of black coffee.

"Get up, Lou, it's Labor Day. Time for you to labor," said Regina. (See: www.thegrandconspiracy.com).

"How am I supposed to blow a hole in that freaking water tunnel when I can't even see?" asked Lou.

"Drink your coffee and you'll see just fine. You're just hung over. After your little prank is over, you can come back here and we'll stay in bed all day," said Regina.

The prospect of more sleep, in general, and the thought of sleeping with Regina, in particular, improved Lou's mood. Pulling on his leather flying jacket against the September cold, Lou stumbled out the door of the motel and got into the pickup with the retractable railroad wheels.

Standing beside the cab, Regina repeated his instructions. "Okay, Lou, you drive up onto the railroad track at King's Crossing, get squarely over the tracks and drop your railroad wheels. Turn on the yellow strobe light that Pancho attached to the top of the pickup. When people see your strobe light blinking they will think you are on official business in the tunnel. I just checked my computer to confirm that there will be no trains approaching the tunnel for several hours. You'll have it all to yourself.

"Now, Lou, all you have to do is drive uphill beyond the Winter Park Ski Resort and into the Moffat Tunnel. You will see that each refuge leading from the train tunnel to the water bore is numbered with a 12-inch-square reflective sign. Keep driving until you come to Refuge 11. You can't miss it."

"Okay, okay, Regina," responded Lou. "I know the rest. Just get back in bed and wait for me to return," said Lou.

Regina planted a great big moist kiss on his mouth and Louis Leclerc drove off toward King's Crossing.

The pickup lurched a bit as Lou positioned it over the railroad tracks. But, after putting the railroad wheels in place, he switched on his yellow strobe light and moved the pickup steadily up the incline toward the Moffat Tunnel. After an almost three-mile drive into the tunnel, he eventually came to Refuge 11 and stopped.

He lowered the truck's tailgate, unloaded the dolly needed to move the 55-gallon drum of high explosives and put the portable ramp in place. Making sure that it did not get away, Lou carefully rolled the 55-gallon drum of high explosives down the ramp and wrestled it onto the dolly. Within five minutes, the drum was resting at the other end of Refuge 11 and just barely touching the side of the water tunnel.

That done, he checked his watch. It was 0650 hours. Time to set the timer for the explosives, stow the ramp and the dolly back in the pickup and back it down out of the tunnel. When he reached the first railroad crossing, he would retract the railroad wheels, turn off his strobe light and drive the pickup to the rented garage selected by Regina. After hiding the pickup, he would walk to the motel and the waiting embrace of the stunning brunette.

Making sure the timer spring was fully wound; Lou turned the timer on, rolled the dolly back to the pickup and made it ready to roll. Backing a pickup sitting on railroad wheels was almost as easy as driving it forward. The only difference was that you just had to look over your shoulder instead of straight ahead.

After almost three miles of driving backward, Lou could see the fabled light-at-the-end-of-the-tunnel. Lou was breathing a breath of relief when the light became a blinding explosion. Bits of flying rock and metal pelted the back of the pickup and broke a big hole in the back window. The obligatory high-country rifle rack fell into the cab. When the debris stopped flying, Lou set his parking brake and ran down toward the pile of rubble. He found the West Portal of the Moffat Tunnel closed.

Lou scrambled up the rubble hoping to find an opening at the top. But whoever placed the explosives knew what they were doing because there was no opening. *If I live to get my hands on Regina and Pancho, I'll give'em the same treatment I got in the Hanoi Hilton*, Lou swore.

The tunnel was completely blocked. That meant his only choice was to drive the pickup up over the apex and try to escape through the East Portal, which was over six miles away.

He looked at his watch. The time was 0700. Right on time, the tunnel acted like an echo chamber as the 55-gallon drum of explosives blew a hole in the side of the water tunnel up above at Refuge 11. *Maybe, the water cascading down this side of the apex will wash away enough debris that I can get out of here*, thought Lou.

A few minutes later, Lou got to test his speculation as a rush of water began to run down the railroad track from Refuge 11. He had to climb back up into the pickup to avoid being washed into the wall of debris. The water rose rapidly against the blockage; however, the rubble showed no signs of giving way. To keep the rising water level from entering the cab of his pickup, Lou had to keep driving uphill. His hope of seeing the blockage washed away glimmered and then died.

Driving the pickup uphill on railroad wheels against a steady torrent of descending water was like trying to drive across a downpour-flooded street. But, to his relief, he finally passed Refuge 11 and left its gushing torrent of water behind. The track on up to the apex was dry and the track stayed dry all the way down to the East Portal.

When he reached the East Portal, Lou dismounted and searched for an exit. He found two heavy steel doors along the south side of the tunnel. Each door had an L-shaped handle. But neither of them would budge. They were locked shut from the other side. He took a crowbar from the pickup's toolbox and tried to pry open the doors. He broke the end off the crowbar to no avail.

Remounting the pickup and fastening his seatbelt as tight as possible, Lou backed uphill over one hundred yards and then drove the pickup as fast as he dared against the huge door that sealed the East Portal. All he got for his effort was a bad gash on his forehead and a stomach pain from the seatbelt. He banged against the huge door again and again with the pickup, until the pickup's front end was so badly damaged that the radiator exploded and began to spout steam.

He made one last effort to ram the door open and he hit the door so hard that the pickup was knocked off the tracks. Now, it was useless.

Thinking he might find a way out at one of the upper refuges, he set off on foot back uphill toward the apex. His heart pounding from the effort of running uphill, he had to stop before he reached the first refuge. Looking down as he put his hands on his knees to catch his breath, he saw a stream of water beginning to come down from the tunnel above.

Oh my God, he realized, *the west end of the tunnel is full of water now and it will come over the apex and begin to rise up against the gate blocking the East Portal.*

With sinking hopes, Lou walked back downhill toward the East Portal. Sure enough, the water was now beginning to rise against the huge gate. He figured it would take several hours for the water level to rise so high that he would drown and maybe help would come. He climbed up on top of the battered pickup, lit a cigarette, and awaited his fate.

But Lou Leclerc did not have to wait long. As soon as the water level at the East Portal rose high enough to reach the explosives preposi-tioned near the tunnel's entrance by Salvador and Pancho, the water spanned the narrow gap between the two electrical contacts and Lou Leclerc was blown into small, but identifiable, pieces.

CHAPTER FORTY-THREE

Standing in the shadows just inside the door of the elevator building, Raoul looked at his watch. It was 0635 hours. Just then, his cell phone rang. It was Felipe calling from the Pump Plant to report the elimination of the night watchman.

Immediately, Raoul sent the elevator car containing the two 55-gallon drums of explosives to the bottom of the elevator shaft. As the elevator car descended, Raoul carefully played out wire from the spool of WD-1/TT military field wire at his feet.

He went over his checklist for a final time. The in-line rocker switch was now wired to the electrical buss. The timer was connected to the in-line switch. He checked again to make sure the rocker switch was in the OFF position. The switch was easy to check because the rocker switch emitted no light when it was OFF. But, when it was ON, it turned a bright red. The timer was set to cause a five-minute delay. Plenty of time for Raoul to jog to the west end of the dam and rendezvous with Jose and the helicopter.

All that remained was for Raoul to connect the two wires leading up from the elevator shaft to the timer. As soon as he received telephone confirmation of the attacks on the Moffat and Adams Tunnels and as soon as he saw and heard the explosions at the Pump Plant and up on the Grand Ditch, all he had to do was push the rocker on the on-line switch to the ON position and start jogging. The timer would do the rest. After checking the switch once again, Raoul wired the ends of the wires to the timer with wire nuts and then overwrapped them with electrician's tape.

Satisfied with the connections, Raoul stepped outside the elevator tower and looked across the lake at the Pump Plant. At precisely 0700 hours, he saw smoke billowing from the windows of the Pump Plant. A few moments later, he heard the sound of the explosion that was gutting the inside of the Pump Plant and causing it to fill with water.

Almost at the same time, he saw the grayish dust produced by an avalanche of scree falling onto the Grand Ditch. The sound would arrive later.

Thank you, Senor Chuck and Senor Roberto, you did well, thought Raoul.

At 0701, he received a call from Regina confirming the attack on the Moffat Tunnel and that she and Pancho were en route to the Koch Ranch. At 0703, Raoul received a similar call from Team Adams. Now, there was no going back. The attack on the dam must commence and must succeed.

Stepping back inside the elevator tower, Raoul calmly pushed the rocker switch to the ON position. The switch moved easily to the ON position, but there was no red light. Quickly, he stepped outside the building and looked up at the light fixture hanging over the entrance. That light was always on around-the-clock. Something was wrong.

He dialed his cell phone for Frederico at PEMEX headquarters. "Frederico, something's happened! I can't get a red light on my rocker switch and the light above the elevator entrance is out. Without power, I can't set off the charges down below!"

"Be calm, Jefe," replied Frederico. "Let me check the power distribution chart for Grand County."

"Hurry, Frederico, hurry!"

"Jefe," said Frederico, coming back on the phone, "was the Pump Plant destroyed?"

"Si. What's that got to do with my problem?"

"Everything. The power distribution chart shows the electric power for the Lake Granby High Dam comes from the Pump Plant and the Pump Plant gets its power through the Adams Tunnel. If either one of those have been destroyed, there's no power to the dam. That's why you don't have any electricity over there."

"Madre de Dios! We are imbeciles!"

"Wait, Jefe. There's still a way. There's a public power line that spans the Colorado River gorge and it runs to a transformer station right across from the elevator building. The chart shows it as a back-up power supply for the dam. Unfortunately, it is a manual system. Someone will have to come from Granby to the transformer station or to the elevator house and flip some switch somewhere. Do you see the transformer station?"

"Of course I see it. It's just across the dam road on a rocky peak that overlooks the spillway. It's only about 80 feet away. I can see three transformers up on a platform. One transformer has a wire running from it to over here. The transformers are up pretty high, but I've got a ladder in the pickup."

"Okay, but before you do that. See if you can find a switch either in the elevator building or at the transformer station that would let the public power into the elevator building.

"Federico, I'm looking here at the electrical buss. There are all kinds of wires leading in all directions, but I can't see anything marked emergency or back-up power. Wait a minute. Here's a placard that says: 'In case of power outage, call Middle Park Electric Company,' and gives a phone number."

"Okay, Jefe. There isn't time to call the electric company. Besides, you'd have to kill whomever they sent. Let's keep it simple, Jefe. Let's just run our own wires from one of the transformers into the elevator building and hook them to the rocker switch.

"Here's what you do. There is another spool of WD-1/TT military field wire in your pickup. Run a pair of wires from one of the trans-formers back to the elevator building.

"But be careful, Jefe! Those transformers are coming off a high-voltage transmission line. You touch the wrong terminal and you'll be killed."

"Si, Federico, but all this will take some time. The transformer station is guarded by a chain-link fence."

"Jefe, I put a pair of bolt-cutters in the pickup. Cut through the fence."

"Si, I will do that. Again, it will still take some time to run the wires and make the splices."

"What other choice do you have, Jefe?"

"Nada. I will do it Federico. Tell Jose to shut down the helicopter until I call."

"Si, as you wish, Jefe."

Raoul took the spool of military field wire from the pickup, carried it into the elevator building. Quickly, he spliced the new wire into the cir-cuit and led it across the dam road where he left the spool on the ground just outside the chain-link fence.

Raoul moved to the pickup, donned some heavy leather gloves and took the bolt-cutters to the fence surrounding the transformer station. After cutting through the fence, he pulled enough wire off the spool to reach the base of the transformer platform. With a GI lineman's tool, he cut the field wire off from the spool and stripped about eight inches of insulation from the ends of the pair of wires. He left the wire lying at the base of the platform and weighted it down with a rock.

Raoul estimated how much wire he would need to run back down from one of the transformers to the base of the platform. He cut off about 20 feet of wire and stuffed it in his jacket. The height of the plat-form was designed to discourage unauthorized visitors. He went back to the pickup and got the ladder.

Time was of the essence now and Raoul was beginning to sweat. Soon, news of the attacks on the other targets would reach the Secret

Service at Camp Hope and the two presidents would be sequestered in their quarters and out of harm's way.

Propping the ladder against one of the telephone poles supporting the transformer platform, he climbed up to the transformer that was connected to the elevator house. He carefully looped one of the bare wire ends around one of the output terminals and twisted the wire so it was snug around the terminal. Next, he took the other bare end and fixed it in similar manner to the other output anode. Taking care that the free end of the wire would not come in contact with the bare ends of the wire lying at the base of the platform, he climbed back down the ladder.

Raoul collected the ends of the wire running from the transformer. He led that wire over to within a foot of the wire running from the elevator building. But before he could connect the two wires, he would have to go back across the road to the elevator house and make double sure the rocker switch was in the OFF position. He was on his knees looking for a rock to weight down the transformer wire, when he heard footsteps behind him. Looking around, he saw a grimy and exhausted Buck Madison standing between himself and the elevator house.

With one motion, Raoul scooped a handful of dirt and hit Buck right in the face with it. Blinded, Buck could only flail away at the shape of Raoul in front of him. Raoul tackled Buck driving him backward down the slope toward the dry spillway. Locked in an embrace, the two men rolled over several times until they toppled down into the race of the spillway. Buck was on the bottom when they hit and the impact knocked him out cold.

After catching his breath, Raoul grabbed Buck by the feet and started dragging him toward the lip of the spillway. The floor of the spillway was littered with large rocks that had fallen down from the steep hill that flanked the south end of the dam. Some of the rocks were so large that Raoul had to drag Buck around them and that made the distance to the lip of the spillway even longer.

CHAPTER FORTY-FOUR

Reaching the shoreline, Dolly nimbly dismounted her jet ski as she let it run up onto the rocky beach. Without a weapon, she felt defenseless. But she had no choice but to climb up to the lake frontage road, cross it and start climbing toward her home. Fearful of Raoul's men, she took the more difficult route up through the trees.

Everything looked in order. No cars or pickups in the circle drive. The house looked just as they left it on what now seemed like weeks ago. She tried the front door. It was locked, just as it should be.

Bending down, she found the emergency key in its supposedly secret recess. Accidentally being locked out of one's house in the dead of winter could be fatal. So, like all prudent mountain-dwellers, the Madisons always kept a spare house key hidden somewhere around the front door.

Slipping inside, the only sound she heard was the hum of the refrigerator in the kitchen. *I wonder why Scooby isn't here to greet me? she thought.* Then, she discovered the answer.

When she reached the living room, Scooby was lying in a pool of her own blood. There was a bullet hole in her forehead. The blood was congealed meaning her dear Scooby had been dead for a day or more.

Dolly fell down on her knees and pulled Scooby's stiff body to her breast. Her eyes were so full of tears she did not see the movement behind her.

Someone threw a blanket over her head while someone else grabbed her wrists and pulled them painfully behind her back. She felt the sting of a rough rope being used to tie her hands. Dolly tried to scream, but it was useless. The blanket was suffocating her.

Suddenly, she was jerked to her feet and the blanket was removed. As she was gasping for breath, a Latino she had never seen before stuck a gag in her mouth and someone standing behind her tied it tightly behind her head. From behind, a pillowcase was slipped over her head and the two men drug her up the stairs to the master bedroom. Without a word, they picked her up and threw her facedown on the bed.

"Do as we say, Senora Madison, or we will kill you just like we did that cur of a dog downstairs," said one of the men. Then, he said: "Jorge, call Federico and tell him we have the woman. Find out what we are supposed to do with her." Then, they slammed the door, locked it, and stomped back down the stairs.

Dolly told herself to calm down, to put the shocking image of her beloved Scooby lying in a pool of blood out of her mind. *At least, the bastards shot her in the head and she didn't suffer, thought Dolly. But if I can get untied and find my revolver, they are going to suffer.*

Dolly squirmed around until she worked her head out of the pillow-case. Now, she could look around for something she could use to cut her bonds. Nothing caught her eye. Then, she remembered Buck kept a bow saw on the woodpile out on the deck off the master bedroom.

Quietly, she rolled over to the edge of the bed and slid her feet onto the carpet. She scuffled backwards until she came to the door to the deck. She aligned her hands with the doorknob and tried to figure out which way she needed to turn it. Lefty-loosey, righty-tighty was the rule Buck taught her. But this situation was backwards and she went against the rule. She felt the bolt retract and she pulled the knob toward her. The door eased open.

The bow saw was lying on top of the woodpile. Fortunately, it was not lying loose. Buck must have placed several logs on top of the saw to keep the wind from blowing it off the deck. Dolly backed into the woodpile and tried to position her bonds against the teeth of the bow saw. Her first attempt cut her wrists and she could feel warm blood running down her fingers. Adjusting her stance, she managed to get some of the rope between her wrists and the saw. By bobbing up and down, she got the saw to work against the rope. But the saw was biting into her wrists about as much as it was cutting into rope. Something had to give. She realized she was in a contest between her ability to accept pain and more bleeding and the rope's ability to resist the saw.

Dolly won. The pressure on her wrists began to loosen and she pulled the remaining strands of rope apart. She examined her wrists and was relieved to find she had not sawed them to the point of severing a vein. But first aid would have to come after she found Buck.

Getting down on her hands and knees, she looked under the bed. She found what she was looking for: her lever-action carbine and her six-shot .357 magnum revolver. The carbine was the one she recently zeroed on the range with Jonathan and his agents. The revolver was a present from Buck who wanted her to have a close-range self-defense weapon under the bed.

She liked the revolver, but she had been slightly resentful that Buck's gift came complete with a laser sight attached to the trigger guard. Given her proven marksmanship skills, she didn't think the laser sight was necessary. But Buck said there is a big difference between shooting paper targets on a range and shooting an intruder in a bedroom. Besides, Buck explained, the laser sight itself was a deterrent. Seeing the laser's red dot centered on one's chest not only told the intruder that the householder would not miss but also exactly where the bullet would enter his body. According to the laser-sight manual, the size of the red dot at a range of 75 feet was 1.75 inches. Of course, at bedroom range, the red dot would be smaller. But, in a darkened bedroom, even the smaller red dot would get the message across.

Dolly put the revolver in the pocket of her bush jacket, slung the carbine over her back and slipped back out onto the deck. Due to the danger of forest fires, Buck insisted on attaching a collapsible fire escape ladder to the outside of the deck railing where it rested inside a break-a-way container. Because the floor of the deck was 35 feet above the ground, the emergency ladder was an absolute necessity.

Taking the bottom rung of the escape ladder in hand, Dolly quietly paid out the ladder to its full length. After scrambling over the deck railing, she climbed down the ladder. It wasn't quite long enough to reach the ground. It looked like a fall of about five feet.

One time Buck showed her how to do a parachute landing fall or PLF. Turning loose of the ladder, Dolly remembered to relax her legs and not land stiff-legged. She also remember to roll to one side letting her body absorb the shock of landing over the length of her side instead of absorbing it all in one place. She did a perfect PLF and scrambled back to her feet. Now, she had to find Buck.

Instead of taking the road toward the top of Sheepdog Hill, she stayed inside the woods that paralleled the road. The road ends short of the ridgeline, but a footpath continues along the length of the loaf-shaped Sheepdog Hill and leads to a point that looks almost straight down on the dam and the spillway.

The trail along the top of Sheepdog Hill runs alternately through open areas where low-lying sage is the only vegetation and wooded patches of pine and fir. After she reached the ridgeline, Dolly stopped running to catch her breath inside the concealment afforded by one of the wooded areas. Despite the ringing in her ears from a splitting headache, she heard voices.

"Jorge, this way!" shouted Ernesto. "She must be running toward the dam."

In a moment, the person who must be Jorge joined the other man on the trail. The two men paused in the middle of a clearing to consult a map. After a moment of discussion accompanied by a lot of arm waving and pointing, they started to run toward her hiding place.

There was no question that she was going to kill both of them. Dolly's only concern was how. Using the carbine with the 3-9X power scope offered the advantage of dealing with them at a longer range than with the revolver. But she had never engaged two moving targets before at any range. She might miss. But if she waited until they were within 75 feet or less, the revolver's laser sight offered a definite advantage. It would be almost impossible to miss. Also, if she waited until they got close enough and if they stayed in trail, one .357 magnum round might kill or, at least wound, both of them.

Dolly rested the barrel of the revolver on a branch sticking out from a sturdy pine. Just to the right of the trail and about 30 feet away was a large rock about the size of a man crouched over while running forward. She turned on the laser beam and took a sight picture on the rock. Because she was so nervous, her hand trembled and the red dot on the rock trembled as well. Forcing herself to get control of her breathing, she got the red dot to stay within a three-inch circle. She would hold the red dot on the rock until her pursuers came abreast of it. Then, she would simply move the red dot from the rock and over onto the belly button of the first man to come even with the rock. (See: *www.thegrandconspiracy.com*)

From her discussions with Buck about close combat, she knew not to try for a headshot and to go for the larger torso area instead. Logic told her to aim for the heart. But emotion told her to aim for the belly. A heart shot would kill almost instantly. A gut-shot produces a lingering and agonizing death.

Now, the two men were almost even with the rock. The second man was running virtually on the heels of the man in front.

As the man in the lead reached the big rock, Dolly shifted the laser beam onto his stomach. In mid-stride, he saw the red dot on his belly just as a hollow-point .357 magnum round blew right through him. The second man never knew what hit him. One moment, he is running forward. The next moment, he is being hurled backward as his intestines were ripped to shreds by a bullet that was already tumbling as it erupted from his comrade's body.

Both men were on their knees trying to hold their guts in with their hands when Dolly came out from the copse of trees and walked over to them. Using her foot, she kicked their weapons far enough away that they could never reach them. With their eyes, they begged her to put them out of their misery. Instead, she pointed her finger at them and spoke. But they couldn't understand what she was saying because she was cursing them in Chinese. Before he passed out, Ernesto had the feeling she was saying something about a dog. Satisfied that the men would die in a few minutes, Dolly turned on her heel and disappeared up the trail toward the Lake Granby High Dam and, hopefully, to help Buck.

CHAPTER FORTY-FIVE

Chuck and Roberto recovered their fishing boat from where they left it in the shallows near the North Shore Marina. Together, they grabbed the bowline and pulled the boat down the slope and into the water. As soon as Chuck had the four-stroke, outboard motor purring like a kitten, Roberto took an oar and pushed them away from the bank.

Turning toward the open water, Chuck ran the motor at full throttle across the lake toward the home of Buck and Dolly. Soon, they were speeding by Deer Island where they were puzzled by the flotsam and jetsam of debris from what appeared to be the wreck of what must have been some kind of speedboat. They saw two bodies floating face down in the water. Chuck slowed down long enough to give the bodies a cursory look that confirmed that the victims, whoever they were, were quite dead. *We've got our own problems,* thought Chuck; *someone else will have to deal with those poor suckers.*

Chuck looked toward the south shore to see if he could see anyone he could hail and tell them about the bodies. His eyes caught movement at the southeast end of the Granby Dam. *There was that sonofabitch Raoul.*

Chuck pointed toward the dam and Roberto signaled with a thumbs up that he saw Raoul as well. Chuck gave the quiet sign by placing his index finger over his mouth and Roberto nodded. Chuck cut the throttle to idle and glided toward the steep bank of riprap that guarded the entrance to the left of the spillway. (See: *www.thegrandconspiracy.com*)

"It looks like you and me are the real suckers," whispered Chuck. "Raoul and his team aren't here to look for gas, they're here to assassinate Trimmer and Popov."

"So, what do we do?" asked Roberto.

"I don't give a shit about Popov and I can't stand Trimmer," said Chuck. "But we both swore an oath to defend this screwed-up country from all enemies, foreign and domestic. So, let's get up to that dam and kick some foreign ass!

"I'll put the bow up against the riprap. You jump ashore and wait for me while I put this baby on the little beach away from the dam. Just keep an eye on Raoul until I get there. Try not to let him see you."

Roberto did as he was told. He even made it ashore without getting his boots wet. But when he reached the top of the embankment, Roberto looked down into the spillway. He saw Raoul dragging the limp body of Buck Madison toward the lip.

There was no time to wait for the arrival of Chuck. Roberto crossed the road and started running toward Raoul and Buck. Raoul was about five feet from the end of the spillway and, even dragging the weight of Buck's body; Raoul would easily reach the lip and throw Buck to his death before Roberto could stop him.

"Stop!" yelled Roberto, as he continued to run toward Raoul and Buck.

Raoul stopped all right, but only long enough to draw his Markarov. Roberto didn't even have time to stop and put up his hands before Raoul shot him right through the heart. Roberto's body toppled off the roadway and fell down into the spillway race.

Now, Raoul had two bodies to get out of sight before someone came along the dam road and saw what was going on. He ran back up to the spillway gate to get Roberto's body and started dragging it to where he left Buck.

As Chuck was tying his fishing boat to a tree, he noticed a jet ski resting on the tiny beach. Apparently, it had been abandoned by its owner or renter. Starting up the steep slope to the road that ran across the dam, Chuck heard the sound of a shot being fired. Knowing Roberto was not carrying a weapon, Chuck assumed the worst.

Reaching the dam road, Chuck ran toward the elevator building. The door to the building was standing wide open. Wires ran from the building and across the road. Following the wires brought the spillway into view. At the far end, Chuck saw what looked like Buck Madison lying on the edge of the spillway lip. Then, looking almost straight down into the race of the spillway, he saw Raoul trying to drag a bleeding and unconscious Roberto down the spillway. (See: *www.thegrandconspiracy.com*)

Quickly, Chuck leapt over the railing that bordered the dam road and landed on Raoul's back. The blow from above staggered Raoul who tried to draw the Markarov, but Chuck knocked it out of his hand onto the concrete.

Breathing hard, the two men faced each other in a gray-walled arena. Hands held low and outward, they circled each other. Chuck knew time was on his side. All he had to do was keep Raoul from throwing Buck off the lip of the spillway. His friend, Roberto, was clearly dead and was beyond help.

Given enough time, someone would come to Chuck's assistance. Raoul realized this as well and knew he had to kill Chuck quickly, then get the bodies of all three of his victims out of sight. By now, the other attacks must have the entire county in an uproar. Soon, someone in authority was bound to come check on the Lake Granby High Dam.

Each time Raoul would lunge at Chuck, Chuck would give ground. In time, Chuck was pinned back against the huge metal gates that separated the waters of Lake Granby from the spillway. They traded Karate blows back and forth just as their Masters taught them to do. When Chuck parried a thrust, Raoul would spin and kick and then try to get in close to score a chop to one of Chuck's vital organs.

Chuck was more than holding his own when he backed onto one of the rocks lying on the spillway floor. Falling backward, he twisted his right ankle. As Chuck reached down to grab his ankle, Raoul picked up a rock the size of a grapefruit and hurled it at Chuck. Looking down at his ankle, Chuck didn't see the rock coming. The rock hit Chuck full on the forehead. Chuck fell forward and Raoul was on him instantly. With one blow from behind, he broke Chuck Lee's neck.

It took Raoul several moments to catch his breath and, as he panted, he realized he was running out of time. He abandoned his plan of throwing all the bodies over the lip. The explosion would dispose of the bodies, anyway. For now, all he could do was pull Chuck and Roberto over to the side of the spillway where they could not be easily seen from the road. He thought about going out and pushing Buck off the lip, but there wasn't time. (See: *www.thegrandconspiracy.com*)

Forgetting to check the rocker switch in the elevator house to see if it was ON or OFF, a rattled Raoul climbed out of the spillway race and up to the base of the transformer station. He was about to connect the two wires together when he heard the distinctive sound of a round being chambered in a lever-action carbine. He looked up the steep cliff that flanked the southeast side of the spillway just in time to see Dolly Madison pull the trigger on the round that burst his head like a melon.

Seeing Raoul go down, Dolly chambered another round and put her carbine on safe. She swung her 3-9X power telescopic sight over onto Buck. She could see he was still breathing. *Please, God, don't let him be badly hurt.*

She started to pick her way down through the trees that clung to the rock face when a black, U.S. Government sedan pulled up and stopped near the elevator house. Because she had just killed three men that morning, the government vehicle gave her pause. *What if they don't believe what I did was in self-defense?* Dolly stopped her descent and ducked behind a tree. As she looked down through the foliage, she saw the driver's door open and out stepped Jonathan Winslow. He was alone.

Dolly considered calling down to Jonathan, but thought, *I'd better stay hidden for now. If I can get down to Buck, he can help me sort things out.* To see better, she trained her powerful scope on Jonathan.

She tracked him quietly with her sight as Jonathan looked briefly inside the elevator building. Lying across the threshold of the building was an electrical switch of some kind. She watched as Jonathan bent down and started flipping the switch on and off, on and off and then stood up and gave the door to the elevator shaft an angry kick. Then, Jonathan stepped back out of the doorway and started following the wires from the elevator building across the dam road and through the hole in the fence surrounding the transformer station. The wires led him upward to the body of Raoul Aredondo-Garza. Raoul was still clutching a wire in each hand.

Whether Jonathan was aware that Buck was lying unconscious down at the lip of the spillway or not Dolly would never know. All she knew was that Jonathan reached down and jerked the two wires from Raoul's hands. Jonathan was about to touch them together when she shot him right through the heart.

Dolly half-skidded, half-fell down the rock face. Jumping the last few feet into the race of the spillway, she dropped her carbine and ran to Buck. She pressed her fingers on his carotid arteries. His pulse was strong. She didn't know if he had a spinal injury or not, but she felt Raoul's men must be everywhere and she couldn't allow Buck to remain so close to the spillway's edge. She grabbed Buck's feet and started pulling him away from the lip. The pulling brought Buck back to consciousness.

She stopped pulling and helped him into a sitting position.

"What happened?" Buck asked.

"Raoul was trying to blow up the dam and I shot him."

"Good work. Are you okay?"

"No, I'm not. I had to kill Jonathan, too."

"You what?"

"Jonathan must be in on whatever's going on around here or, at least, he wanted it to succeed. Jonathan was trying to connect the wires to blow up the dam and you and him with it. The wires were only an inch apart when I fired."

"Jonathan would try to kill me?"

"Buck, I don't think he knew you were down here. Jonathan was way up at the base of the transformer station when I saw him trying to connect the wires."

"Did you shoot him with your carbine?"

"Yes, I dropped it over there. Do you need it?"

"Later. Right now, I'll go take a look. Stay here."

Slowly, a bloodied and bone-tired Buck climbed out of the spillway and up to the base of the transformer station. Jonathan was lying face up with his eyes wide open. The look on his face was one of total disbelief. Buck took his hand and closed the lifeless eyes. Even though neither man was Catholic, Buck made the Sign of the Cross over the body of his former lieutenant. It was all he could think to do.

Then, Buck turned his attention to Raoul's body. Figuring Dolly must have been firing down at Raoul, he calculated the angle of fire. The rocky ground around the transformer station was barren of grass making it easy to find the spent .357 round from Dolly's carbine. Buck put it in his pocket.

Buck climbed back down to the edge of the spillway. He asked Dolly to wrap the pistol lying on the concrete with her bandana and hand it to him. It was a 7.62-millimeter Markarov, so Buck figured it belonged to Raoul. Buck checked its markings. There was the name "Ernst Thaelmann," the premier East German maker of the Soviet Markarov. *Whoever is behind these people, they can afford the best*, thought Buck.

"Dolly," said Buck, "you will hear two shots in a minute. Don't worry. I'm just going to alter reality somewhat."

Buck climbed back up to the base of the transformer station. He found the pair of heavy leather gloves and put them on. He located the entry wound in Jonathan's chest and fired a round from Raoul's Markarov right through it. He placed the Markarov right next to Raoul's right hand. Rolling Jonathan over on his face, Buck found Dolly's spent .357 Magnum round in the blood-soaked dirt. He picked that up with the bandana and put it in his pocket. He rolled Jonathan back over again so he was facing up. Then, he reached inside Jonathan's jacket and pulled Jonathan's Model 92 Beretta from its shoulder holster.

He put the pistol in Jonathan's hand and released the safety. Buck aimed the pistol at what was left of Raoul's head and pressed the trigger. He left the Beretta as if it had fallen from Jonathan's hand. The inevitable paraffin tests would show both men fired their weapons. Buck took off the leather gloves and dropped them on the blood-soaked ground next to Raoul.

"You don't want to look up there Dolly," said Buck as he helped Dolly up out of the spillway. Once they reached the road running over the spillway, Buck said, "Here, let me have your carbine. I'm going to throw it in the lake."

"Buck, I suppose you have to throw my carbine away. But, I must keep my revolver. I shot two of Raoul's men with it this morning. It was self-defense."

"You what?"

"When I went up to the house I ran inside and there was Scooby's body lying on the floor. She must have tried to defend the house and the bastards killed her. I knelt down to hold her and started crying. Two men came out of nowhere and grabbed me. They locked me upstairs in our bedroom while they called to ask someone for instructions.

"I got my carbine and the revolver out from under our bed and climbed down the escape ladder. I started running to find you here at the dam. But I could hear the two men shouting and running after me. So, I set up an ambush on Sheepdog Hill. When the two men got close enough, I stood up and gut-shot both of them. That was for Scooby. I really wanted to stay there and watch them die, but I had to come find you. You know the rest."

"Looks like we'll have to hang onto the revolver and show it to the Sheriff. You're right. Clearly, a case of self-defense. Too bad the credit for shooting Raoul will go to Jonathan. You know, Dolly, you stopped the plot to kill Trimmer and Popov and a lot of innocent people along with them," said Buck.

"Believe me, Buck, I never thought about that. I was just trying to keep that awful Raoul person and poor Jonathan from blowing you to kingdom come.

"Buck, let's go home and have a huge glass of Merlot. Then, we'll have to bury Scooby. Damn! Damn! How could they kill my poor, dear Scooby? She never harmed anyone in her life. Give me back my carbine! I'm going back up on Sheepdog Hill and shoot those bastards again."

"I can't do that," said Buck, as he wiped her carbine clean of fingerprints and threw it into 190 feet of water.

"I know how you feel," said Buck as they walked along the lakefront road toward home. "But, we can't spoil your case for self-defense. I'll call Sheriff Cobble and lay out the scenario of how Chuck and Roberto and Jonathan were killed trying to stop Raoul from assassinating Presidents Trimmer and Popov. Also, I'll have to tell him where to find the bodies of the other scum who have been trying to kill us for the last three days.

"And Dolly, about Jonathan. I want you to think about this: Apparently, Jonathan wanted the attack on the dam to succeed and he was willing to kill himself to make that happen. I know you must feel terrible about shooting him. But, always keep in mind that he was determined to die anyway. Your shot made no difference in his life, but it sure as hell made a big difference in mine and the lives of hundreds of other people down below.

"But how can we be sure Jonathan was in on the plot?"

"For one thing, Jonathan made it clear that he did not want us down on the river at 0700 hours. Jonathan was willing to drown along with Trimmer and Popov, but he did not want us down there with him. When the dam did not blow at 0700, Jonathan got in his sedan and came up here to see what went wrong," said Buck.

"Oh Buck, please keep telling me that Jonathan was going to die any-way. And, when I have nightmares, hold me in the night and tell me that again and again," said Dolly, as tears streamed down her scratched and bruised face.

"Dolly, next time you are in town and you see people who were included in that early morning soiree down on the river, remind your-self that they are alive and around to be loved by their children and grandchildren because you fired that shot. They will never know how you saved their lives. They will never know the personal pain you are suffering. But you and I and God knows you did the right thing given the circumstances you were facing," said Buck.

"But Buck, my only thought was saving your life. I didn't really think about anyone else."

"I know, Dolly. But isn't that was love is all about? When we base our actions on love, good things happen.

"One time, Jonathan and I had a long talk about the difference between basing one's actions on love of the oppressed or hatred of the oppressor," said Buck. "I think the death of Jasmine pushed Jonathan over the edge. Somehow, Trimmer and Popov became the focus of his hatred. And, I think there was some self-hatred in the mix as well. Jonathan and his brother pulled a lot of strings to get Jasmine stationed in Saigon."

"Buck, I'm supposed to be the psychologist in the family. But I think you are right on track," said Dolly.

As they turned up the gravel road leading to home, Buck wondered, "I wish I knew what Raoul thought we knew. I never thought someone would try to kill us for something we didn't really know. There must be a lesson in all of this."

"Yes, there is. Like Candide, we should just stay home and tend our garden," said Dolly.

"But, we don't have a garden."

"That's right. Okay, we'll raise another Sheepdog," said Dolly, as she burst into tears again at the thought of her dear Scooby.

CHAPTER FORTY-SIX

The scene at Koch Ranch was mixed with excitement, concern and dread. All of the men from the target teams were excited and pleased that their operations had gone off so well. Salvador, the remaining security man kept asking questions of the target teams because he wanted to feel like part of the successes as well. But there was dread because Raoul never called to have Jose come pick him up with the Huey. There was concern because Ramon, Sancho, Ruiz, Julio, Jorge and Ernesto were missing as well.

Other than those men and Raoul, every remaining member of Team PEMEX was packed and ready to board the helicopter for the flight to Mexico. *Well, thought Jose, if this is all the load I have to lift, then I won't have to worry about the density-altitude factor anymore.*

The men gathered around Federico and Regina listening with concern as Raoul's second-and third-in-command debated about what to do next.

"Raoul's instructions were quite clear," explained Federico. "If he did not return here by 0800 hours, we are to leave without him. Remember, he told us 'no exceptions' to include himself."

This brought an uneasy reaction from the men. Regina was outspoken. "Federico, we can't fly off and leave Raoul here. The authorities will question him and our plot will be exposed."

"But Federico" said Jose, "with so few of us here, we don't have to worry about the heat of the day affecting our helicopter so much. We could wait until noon for Raoul."

"Si, and what if all of our men do make it here to our rendezvous by noon, then what will you do?" asked Federico. "Order the temperature to drop? No, Raoul had sound reasons for ordering us to leave at 0800 hours, no matter what. The refueling bladder in New Mexico and all our arrangements depend on maintaining our schedule. We must get to Mexico and give everyone the bonus that Fidel wants them to have and meet the ship for Havana." Several of the men smiled at that.

"Very well," said Regina. "We'll send the men out at 0800. But you and I will stay and find Raoul. I refuse to leave him like this!"

"All right," said Federico. "Listen up men! You will fly out with Jose a few minutes from now at 0800. I've already loaded the chest with your bonus on board. When you get to Mexico, shoot off the lock. Your shares are all marked in packets with your names on them. Because there are fewer of you now, you may divide the shares of the comrades we have lost among you." That brought more smiles.

Still hoping Raoul and the others would arrive, Jose asked if he could delay his departure until 0810 hours. Federico granted the request. But, by 0810 hours, there was still no word from Raoul or anyone. A reluctant Jose brought his rotor blades up to speed and lifted off. Federico and Regina stood on the veranda of the soon-to-be-deserted ranch house and waved adios.

Turning south, the chopper headed across Berthoud Pass, intercepted Interstate 70 and flew west until it came to Frisco where it turned south over the Breckenridge Ski Resort and out over the vast, open expanse called: South Park. When the helicopter was almost directly over the Antero Reservoir, the chest that was supposed to hold their bonus money exploded. Of the burning helicopter and the men inside, only tiny fragments made it all the way to the water.

Federico checked his watch as he and Regina loaded a chest full of money into an old International Scout. "They should be over Antero Reservoir by now."

"You know," said Regina. "I feel badly about Jose. He was kind of cute."

CHAPTER FORTY-SEVEN

Epilogue

Grand County

Just as Fidel Castro hoped, the destruction inflicted by the late Raoul Aredondo-Garza and his team of terrorists was far-reaching. But not even Fidel Castro was immune to the operation of the Law of Unintended Consequences which, ironically, made life better for many of the residents of Grand County, Colorado.

As soon as he returned to the White House, President Trimmer signed a disaster-area declaration for eastern Grand County and for the counties east of the Continental Divide that had become dependent upon the waters of Grand County for irrigation, electricity and human consumption. The Federal Emergency Management Team (FEMA), the U.S. Army Corps of Engineers and the U.S. Bureau of Reclamation immediately sent teams into Grand County to determine which water-diversion facilities, if any, could be rebuilt.

At the Moffat Tunnel, they found no permanent damage. The rupture in the water tunnel could be easily repaired. The explosion that closed the West Portal of the train tunnel was quickly cleared. But the smoke evacuation blowers at the East Portal would, of course, have to be completely rebuilt. Other than that, the Adams Tunnel was relatively unharmed.

But, after careful study, it was decided that the water tunnel would not be rebuilt. Instead, it would be re-bored and enlarged and then converted for use as a tunnel for automobiles and small trucks. This would be done for three reasons: One, the Interstate 70 corridor leading from Denver to the ski resorts of Summit, Eagle and Pitkin Counties and on west to Grand Junction was choked with traffic virtually year-round. Two, converting the Moffat water tunnel into a tunnel for light vehicles would relieve some of the pressure on Interstate 70 West and provide a new means of vehicular access to the Berthoud Pass, Winter Park and Silver Creek Resorts. Three, skiers and other outdoor enthusiasts living from Denver to Ft. Collins and on east to Nebraska and Kansas would, at last, have an easy corridor through which to approach the scenic beauty and recreational opportunities of north-central Colorado.

Another irony was that the major beneficiaries of the closure of the Moffat Tunnel would be the Front Range communities. Now, the city planners in the Denver Metroplex were faced with a difficult choice. They would either have to find a replacement water source or accept what the loss of the water from the Moffat Tunnel meant in terms of reducing urban sprawl. Politicians who had hitherto been afraid to place limits on urban sprawl, could now take a stand against growth that did not involve the passage of draconian, and probably unconstitutional, regulatory restraints on growth. Now, the restraint would be what Nature had intended all along and would be easy for elected officials to defend.

Mining engineers from the Colorado School of Mines in Golden determined it would take years to rebore the Adams Tunnel under the Continental Divide between Grand Lake and Estes Park. Moreover, the reconstruction of the pump plant on Lake Granby would cost hundreds of millions of dollars. Therefore, the Adams Tunnel would be closed and the aboveground portions of the Lake Granby Pump Plant would be turned into a natural history museum. The farmers of the over-watered and over-fertilized farmlands from Ft. Collins to the east would have to convert to the environmentally more sound methods of low-till, dry-land farming. The unfettered growth that had been blighting the land from Boulder to Ft. Collins would have to slow down and might even become manageable.

With the closure of the Adams Tunnel, the Three Lakes area of eastern Grand County would be able to retain its waters at a constant level and become even more attractive to boaters, sailors, hikers and fishermen. Grand Lake, the largest natural lake in Colorado, would no longer be a pass-through lake for water headed for the Adams Tunnel. As a result, Grand Lake would return to the crystal-clear state that attracted the rich and well born to its shores since the late 19th Century. The man-made Shadow Mountain Lake would clear up as well.

No more would the water level of Lake Granby be pulled down by the water demands of the northern Front Range cities and by the truck farms on the Great Plains. Encouraged by the prospect of constant water levels, a number of existing businesses announced plans to improve the accommodations afforded to vacationers. By the same token, new capital was pledged by far-sighted investors back east who saw money to be made in the reclamation of northeastern Grand County.

A study of the damage done to The Grand Ditch determined that the rock structure needed to support over a mile of the ditch was completely blown away. The amount of water that was diverted by The Grand Ditch to Ft. Collins would not justify the enormous expense of trying to bore a through-mountain tunnel to reconnect the parts of the ditch that were not affected by the explosions.

Now, the waters from the eastern slopes of the Never Summer Mountain Range were flowing down into the Kawuneeche Valley as nature intended. Once again, the deer, elk, beaver, trout and other wildlife of western Rocky Mountain National Park and northeastern Grand County would have the water and foliage they need to prosper. What nature lovers had been forced to call: The River of No Return would return.

From a historical perspective, the suffering of the Orientals who built The Grand Ditch was forever monumented. The avalanche of scree shaved off over a mile-long stretch of The Grand Ditch that can be seen to this day.

With their natural water resources no longer being plundered by the big money interests along the Front Range, the Fraser and upper Colorado Valleys would be able to sustain some light industry and some modest growth. New jobs would be created that did not involve making beds, washing dishes and helping tourists onto ski lifts. Some of the children who left Grand County to earn college degrees would be able to come back home and find a growing number of college-level jobs. The boom and bust cycle of the tourism industry would be leveled out with the creation of more year-round jobs.

The cable communications links that ran through the Moffat and Adams Tunnels would be replaced by faster and less environmentally harmful satellite links.

None of these benefits to the people of Grand County were understood by Fidel Castro or he would have been even more upset about the failure of the assassination attempt on Presidents Trimmer and Popov. Moreover, the safe return of Frederico and Regina to Cuba was of small comfort compared with the loss of, Carlos, his favorite illegitimate son. Fidel did not bother to explain to the man's mother that someone known to the Americans as Raoul Aredondo-Garza was killed on the Lake Granby High Dam. Instead, Fidel sent a bouquet of flowers to Carmen Aredondo along with a note that simply told her that their son, Carlos, died as a Hero of the Revolution.

The engraved invitation bore the Presidential Seal and came from the White House. It was addressed to Lt. Colonel James Buckley Madison, USA Army, Retired, and to Dr. Melissa Rennie Madison. It invited Buck and Dolly to sit with James Robert Trimmer, the President of the United States, at the combined funerals of Lieutenant Colonel Charles Lee, United States Army, Retired and Major Roberto Chavez, United States

Army, Retired and Special Agent Jonathan Winslow of the United States Secret Service.

Buck and Dolly were heartbroken over the deaths of Chuck, Roberto, and Jonathan and even over the death of Lou. Buck grieved mainly for Chuck, the man who saved his life in Vietnam and, once again, on the Lake Granby High Dam. Dolly grieved for Jonathan. She would never forget that terrible moment she had to shoot Jonathan in order to save Buck. They both felt badly for Roberto's wife and their children. Fortunately, neither Chuck nor Jonathan nor Lou had dependent children.

To sit with President Trimmer was out of the question. So, Buck called the White House and declined. The staffer who handled the call took it well. But Buck could tell it wasn't the first time that invitees let principle stand in the way of accepting a White House invitation to appear in public with President Trimmer.

Buck and Dolly would, however, attend the funerals. They would stand at the back of crowd, listen to the ceremony and try to control their tears, their anger and their sorrow.

Arlington National Cemetery

Washington, D.C. can be pleasant in September, after the swampy heat and humidity of August are gone.

Buck and Dolly walked across the lush grass to where a large crowd was surrounding three, freshly-dug graves. A military band was supporting a Regimental Piper in the playing of *Amazing Grace.*

The Piper's tune took Buck's mind back to those formal dining-ins and dining-outs that Chuck, Jonathan, Roberto and he enjoyed so much. In Vietnam, "formal" meant clean jungle fatigues instead of their dress mess jackets and decorations. But the camaraderie and the boozy good times were the same.

We were all so different in our backgrounds, thought Buck, Chuck part Chinese, part Swedish, part Hispanic. Jonathan whose blood was so blue it could have been used for printer's ink. And, Roberto whose ancestors had been Mexican Braceros. But how we all loved it when the Regimental Piper played Scotland the Brave. The Piper made us forget our differences and made us one in the fraternity of brothers-in-arms. When the Piper played, we were transported back to the French paras at Dien Bien Phu. We imagined ourselves defending the Kyber Pass with the Bengal Lancers of India and we were side-by-side with the Royal Army of Great Britain that had twice laid down its life in Flanders Fields. But just as all Americans are Irish on Saint Patrick's day, when the Piper plays Amazing Grace, all soldiers and policemen are Scots.

"Buck," whispered Dolly as she offered him her already soggy handkerchief, "something must have gotten in your eye or maybe your allergies are acting up again."

Wiping his eyes, Buck turned at the sound of the approaching presidential motorcade. Standing at the back of the mourners, they couldn't actually see President Trimmer and Edward T. Briccone step out of the bulletproof limousine. But when they heard the band strike up Hail to the Chief, they knew President Trimmer was on his way to his seat in the center of the roped off enclosure where he joined the families of Jonathan and Roberto. Because Chuck Lee had no family, other than Buck and Dolly, there was no one there for him.

What a contrast, thought *Dolly. If Roberto's ancestors had come up from Santa Fe to New Plymouth in 1620, they could have welcomed Jonathan's family as they disembarked from The Mayflower.* Democratized in grief, the family members hugged each other.

Buck and Dolly moved around the edge of the crowd to better see who was in the center. Standing together were several officers and NCOs who served with Chuck, Jonathan, Roberto, Lou and Buck in Vietnam and Cambodia. Buck's heart swelled with the emotion of seeing them again. As much as he wanted to reach out to them at the end of the service, he knew he would not. He would stay inside his shell. *Maybe, in a month or so, he told himself, he would write to some of them. But then, probably not. The heart of the mythical 10th Colonial Parachute Regiment was being buried today. Better to let this be the end of it.*

A military chaplain said a few words of consolation to the families and those assembled. Dolly recognized the scripture from Thessalonians telling how Christ will resurrect those who have died and how those of us who live now will be raised when we die someday to meet Christ Who will make everything perfect and whole once again. Then, he turned the service over to the President of the United States. *From the sublime to the ridiculous*, thought Buck.

"My fellow Americans," President Trimmer began. "We are gathered here on this field where so many great American heroes of the past are buried to honor three new American heroes: Lieutenant Colonel Charles Lee, Major Roberto Chavez and Special Agent Jonathan Winslow.

"As I am sure you know from press accounts, these men gave their lives to save the life of the Russian President and myself. Moreover, they saved the lives of countless others living downstream from the Lake Granby High Dam. They gave their lives to prevent a band of foreign terrorists from changing the governments of two sovereign nations by unlawful means. They gave their lives to save the lives of their fellow countrymen.

"Who knows what ordinary men would be thinking in the final moments of their lives? But these were no ordinary men. I can assure you their final thoughts were not of themselves but of their country and the preservation of their country for the benefit of their loved ones and for generations of Americans yet to come. I must confess that these men were neither of my own political party nor of my own political point of view. But, when put to the test, they placed the Rule of Law and our Constitution above all other concerns and, in so doing, gave their lives in the service of our nation.

"Yet that fateful day was not the first time that these fine men served their country. All of them served more than one tour in Vietnam. All of them were wounded in Vietnam. Colonel Lee several times. Today, I am announcing the posthumous promotion of Lieutenant Colonel Lee to full Colonel and the promotion of Major Chavez to Lieutenant Colonel. Special Agent Jonathan Winslow is awarded the highest civilian award for valor our nation can bestow.

"But, if I may, I'd like to paraphrase an old saying by suggesting that service lies in the eye of the beholder. There are many different ways that one may serve his or her country. As you may know, I did not go to Vietnam because I thought I could be of better service to my country by…"

Before they both became nauseous, Buck signaled to Dolly that it was time to go. Buck and Dolly knew President Trimmer would not be able to resist the temptation to inject himself in some self-aggrandizing way into the burial services for the fallen warriors. That is why they declined the presidential invitation.

Hand in hand, they detached from the crowd of mourners and walked slowly back toward the parking lot. They could still hear President Trimmer trying to justify his yellow streak when they reached their rental car.

But over to the side of the national cemetery, they noticed a group of gray-faced men in dark suits standing around another freshly-dug grave. Buck knew a few of them. But Dolly recognized almost every one of them.

A civilian chaplain was leading a simple service. The Director of Central Intelligence and several of his senior staff stood by the grave. They were burying one who had served them well in many dangerous assignments.

Even though Buck led the FBI debriefers to believe that Lou Leclerc must have been trying to prevent the destruction of the Moffat Tunnel when he died, Buck suspected the DCI knew his former star aviator hadn't ended up on the right side of the law. But how decent of them to remember the unsung good he had done in Laos, Cambodia, Vietnam and Nicaragua.

They stopped to listen as the DCI quietly announced the posthumous award of the CIA's highest medal for valor. *Well at least,* thought Buck, *Lou only agreed to blow up a water tunnel. Tortured soul that he was, Buck knew not even Lou would have joined the plot to kill President Trimmer. Popov, well, that was another story. Jonathan, on the other hand, wanted the assassins to succeed and he gets a presidential funeral and a medal. Dolly gets no credit and our dog is dead.*

Buck recalled that Lou's parents served with the French Resistance and were executed by the Nazis. Buck and Dolly watched as the DCI handed a tri-folded American flag to a frail, gray-haired lady who must have been one of Lou's great-aunts. The DCI spoke to her in French. That ended the service. There was no band. No volleys were fired. No one played taps. Dolly knew what Buck was thinking: *How typical of a covert service. Its good deeds go unreported, its inevitable errors make headlines and its warriors are unheralded.* The small group of mourners broke up and headed for the nondescript sedans that would take them back to Langley.

President Trimmer was still holding forth over the public address system when Buck and Dolly drove away toward Ronald Reagan Washington National Airport and home.

The End

ABOUT THE AUTHOR

William Penn is the *nom de plume* of a husband and wife writing team. After retiring from military service that took them all over the world, both authors pursued careers in state government, academe, political consulting, public relations and journalism. Following that, they settled in Grand County, Colorado, to enjoy its myriad outdoor sports opportunities, its scenery and the wonderful people who live there or come to visit. When not downhill skiing, sailing, flying, hiking, fly-fishing, doing volunteer work and writing, the authors try to be good companions to an Old English Sheepdog.